BELOW THE HUNTER MOON

SILVER RAPIDS
BOOK TWO

A. KNIGHTLEY

For the prickly ones.

AUTHOR'S NOTE

This book contains descriptions of graphic violence and murder, brief descriptions of being trapped in a confined space as an adult, brief descriptions of kidnapping an adult, mentions of past childhood neglect and abuse, parent death (in the past, during childhood), mentions of past pet loss, mentions of parent alcoholism (in the past, during childhood), brief mention of mild alcohol use before a sexual encounter (not on page and not between MCs), and descriptions of struggling with anxiety, depression, and PTSD.

It also contains descriptions of consensual, sexually explicit content that is only appropriate for readers who are 18+ years of age.

If you have any questions regarding the content warnings, or you identify additional content warnings that should be included, please reach out to the author on Instagram (@author.aknightley), or via email (author.aknightley@gmail.com), and I would be happy to discuss.

PROLOGUE

SILAS

TWENTY-SEVEN YEARS AGO

Silas was six the first time he met the boy who smelled like toasted marshmallows.

"Where are we?" he asked, bouncing in place and trying to undo the seatbelt, eager to go explore.

His parents had parked outside of a huge building made of concrete and wood, right in the middle of a real-life city.

It was the biggest place Silas had ever seen. Well, the main gathering hall in the pack den was probably the same size, but there were always so many people packed inside that it felt smaller.

While driving into the city—*Anchorage*, his parents had called it—Silas had seen so many buildings of all different sizes; he'd pressed his face up against the glass to gape as they drove by. And there were houses everywhere!

Back home, only a handful of families lived in their own

houses, his included, but the rest of the pack lived in small private dwellings crammed into several large buildings surrounding the main den. There were a lot more people here in the big city, but it felt different—it didn't seem as crowded.

And there were so many cars. The whole lot in front of the building was full of them, coming and going as they pleased. And in those cars, were *humans*.

Real-life humans!

His mom and dad's hushed murmurs quieted, and they lifted their heads from where they were bent close. Turning to look from the front seat, his mom's face transformed into the smile she always gave him. "Your dad has some things to do for Alpha Cain, so you and I are going to wait in the library until he's finished. Doesn't that sound like fun?"

He beamed. *A library!* "Yes! Let's go, let's go!"

Maybe he could *talk* to a human in the library. Or, even better, maybe he could make a *friend* in the library!

All of the other pups back home looked at him funny, like they were scared of him, or trying to see whether they were as strong as him.

None of them actually wanted to be his friend.

But a human wouldn't know any of that. His dad said humans couldn't even smell each other. They wouldn't know he was meant to be an alpha someday, so there wouldn't be a reason he couldn't be their friend.

Silas hopped out of the car, his boots splashing in the dirty, salt-clogged slush.

His father shut the door and swooped him up into his arms. "You'll be good for your mother, yes? No running off?"

Silas nodded vigorously. "I'll be good, I promise!"

"Hmm..." his dad said, adjusting Silas' stocking cap down against the cold nipping at his soft human ears. "If you are, maybe we'll get hot chocolate after this. Would you like that?"

Silas couldn't keep his voice down. "Yes!" he exclaimed.

When his father pressed growly kisses all over his face, he giggled and squirmed until he was gently set back on his own two feet. Silas took his mother's hand and looked up to see his parents staring at each other for a long time.

"I'll be back soon," Dad said.

"Be safe," Mom replied, wiping at her face.

His father cupped the back of her head and gave her a firm kiss. "Just a little longer," he whispered.

She nodded and pulled Silas toward the library entrance.

"Why can't Daddy come with us?" Silas asked, watching his father wave and drive away.

She was smiling again even though her face was still wet and squeezed his hand. "He has important things to do, baby, but he'll be back soon. Now, what kinds of books should we look at?"

Silas ran ahead, tugging her along behind him. "Oh, firetrucks! No, volcanos! Wait, what about dinosaurs?"

She chuckled. "I bet we can find books about all of those things."

Twenty minutes later, Silas wandered up and down the aisles of the children's section, his arms full of books about anything and everything that caught his eye.

His mom was sitting at one of the tables near the

entrance, next to a woman trying to soothe a fussy toddler, but he wasn't worried about wandering off. He could hear people talking all the way on the other side of the library—she could certainly still hear him.

Humans were so loud! No one tried to keep their voice down or hide what they were saying.

Just as he rounded the corner of a shelf, adding a book about foxes to his stack because the one on the cover had pretty red fur, he caught a scent. It was warm and sweet—nothing like the fake flowers or fruit that some of the humans stank of.

He'd never smelled anything like this before—it crackled in his nose like an ember popping in the great den fire. It was so overwhelming he nearly sneezed.

But it was *good*.

Silas needed to know where it came from.

Curious, he followed, tracking the scent between the shelves as he wove further into the children's section, thinking he'd find the source to be someone handing out a sweet, hot treat.

Instead, he found a human boy.

Silas blinked.

He was small. Well, smaller than Silas, and the fur on his head was a shade lighter than the fox on the cover of the book he'd just picked up. But when Silas cautiously padded over, head angled to show he meant no harm, the boy looked up at him without any of the fear or submission he saw in the other pups' eyes back home.

It warmed him, just like that sticky-sweet smell.

Looking down at where the boy was sitting cross-legged on the carpet, Silas asked, "Why do you smell like that?"

The boy cocked his head. "Like what?"

Oh, right. Humans can't smell each other.

Scrunching his nose, Silas said, "Like marshmallows."

That wasn't quite right, but it was close enough.

The boy paused, thinking. "I had Lucky Charms for breakfast; maybe that's why?"

Silas smiled, remembering at the last second to hide his teeth. He wasn't good at putting them away, yet. "I love Lucky Charms!" His mom and dad brought them home anytime they bought groceries from the little town near the den. "Can I sit with you?"

The boy nodded, and Silas plopped down next to him, only just remembering he shouldn't lean in to get a better whiff of his new friend.

Even if he was the best thing Silas had ever smelled.

He stayed quiet, his own collection clutched to his chest, and watched the boy flick through the pages of his book. For having never met a human before, Silas thought he was doing pretty well. Maybe he had more in common with them than he thought, and he really could make a friend!

When they finished the first book, Silas sprawled his stack all over the rainbow-colored carpet. "What should we read next?"

The boy scanned the titles before pointing to one that had an eagle on the cover. "That one. Birds are so cool, I wish I could fly way up high to see everything!" he said.

His enthusiasm was contagious, so Silas nodded along.

"Yeah! My dad's friend can shift into a hawk, which is *awesome*."

His cheeks flamed at the outburst, remembering humans didn't know about shifter forms, and he wasn't supposed to tell them any pack secrets anyway.

But didn't friends tell each other secrets?

Were they friends?

Probably not, Silas thought glumly. He'd probably messed that up already, and the boy thought he was weird now, or some kind of freak.

Silas peeked over, expecting to find him gaping or pointing and laughing, but he just cocked his head at Silas again and shrugged, saying, "Huh, that's cool!"

Silas smiled and forgot to hide his teeth. "What's your name? Can we be friends?"

The boy smiled back. "Sure! I'm Sammy. What's yours?"

"Awesome! I'm—"

"Silas!" his mother called.

He looked up to see her and his father hurrying over, accompanied by another wolf he vaguely recognized from the pack. His mother's face was pinched, her voice tight. "Come on, baby, let's go," she said, taking his hand to pull him to his feet.

The unfamiliar wolf stared at Sammy in a way that raised Silas' hackles. Like he was a pest; one of the mice that made its way into the den during the cold months and chewed through their pantry stores.

"Sammy is my friend," Silas said to him, frowning.

When the other wolf raised an eyebrow and tilted his head in challenge, Silas didn't break eye contact.

The wolf smirked but turned away first. "I'll wait for you outside," he said to Silas' dad.

"Sammy?" The woman who'd been sitting near his mom came up to them, the fussing toddler on her hip. "Let's put those on the return cart and go home," she said, looking at his parents with wary eyes.

"But we just got here. I made a friend, Mom, look, this is Silas!"

Her eyes crinkled when she smiled. Silas' mom looked at him like that, too. It soothed his frayed nerves. "Hi there, sweetie. It's nice to meet you. I'm sorry, Sammy, but we've got to go home for your brother's nap."

Sammy huffed, pouting, but gathered his books and stood. "Bye," he said, waving at Silas.

"Bye," Silas whispered, waving back while he watched Sammy, his very first friend who smelled like toasted marshmallows and talked to him like he was normal, walk away.

He hoped they would see each other again soon.

SOMETHING WAS REALLY WRONG.

The car was silent for the whole drive home.

His dad held his mom's hand across the console, and his eyes kept darting up to check on Silas through the rear-view mirror, looking at him like he was going to disappear.

He didn't look mad, but still, Silas couldn't help but think this was all his fault.

Were they angry with him for making a human friend?

Or maybe they'd heard him tell Sammy about the hawk shifter? And why had the other wolf been there?

When they arrived back at the den, they parked outside Alpha Cain's house instead of home. His mom held his hand the whole way inside. He knew his uncle would disapprove, confirmed by the angry look on his face when they stepped into the foyer, but Silas didn't let go.

An alpha stands on his own, Silas. He isn't coddled by his mother.

He'd scolded Silas for hugging her goodbye after she'd dropped him off for alpha lessons a few weeks ago. She didn't drop his hand though, even when they all followed Alpha Cain into the study.

No, she held him tighter, and for some reason, Silas felt like he was going to cry.

Stop whining like some pathetic human. You are a wolf, Silas, and someday you will be alpha. Alpha's don't cry.

He blinked away his tears before anyone saw them so that his uncle wouldn't discipline him like he had the time he'd caught Silas crying at the end of *Homeward Bound*.

"Wait out here," Alpha Cain said to them both, his piercing yellow eyes drilling holes into Silas before he directed his dad into the study and shut the door.

Silas could feel his mother's trembling, but she never let go of his hand—not even when she lurched toward the door after they heard both men begin to shout, followed by a scuffle and the rip of sharp claws through flesh.

The study door flung open.

Silas nearly didn't recognize the man who stumbled out after Alpha Cain, and not only because of the jagged, bloody scratch marks down his cheek, already knitting themselves together.

No—it was the defeat and fear in his eyes.

He looked nothing like Silas' strong, confident dad; nothing like the warm, loving man who'd wink at his mother to make her laugh, and scoop Silas up after dinner to dance them around the living room before tucking him into bed, promising he'd always be there to protect him.

This man looked hollow, staring at his feet.

"We had an agreement, Meera," his uncle said. The jagged claw marks slashed across his face were deeper, taking longer to heal. "Silas is an alpha—my heir. He'll live with me from now on so I can raise him properly. You're far too soft on the boy. He needs to learn what it is to be strong and how to run this pack."

His father's gaze remained lowered, but when his mother recoiled, looking back and forth between him and Alpha Cain, he gave the smallest shake of his head. It was so tiny, that Silas wondered if he'd made it up.

She didn't seem to see it, though, because she shakily said, "He is ours, Cain. You cannot take our son."

Alpha Cain's snarl was vicious, and he reached out, gripping the back of his father's neck. "*Kneel,*" he commanded in that deep, scary alpha voice Silas hated so much.

Silas began to cry harder when his father dropped to his knees, helpless to disobey. Was this his fault? Had he gotten his father in trouble somehow?

"Daddy," he said, stepping forward and wiping the tears from his face. "I'll be better, I'm sorry I—"

"*Quiet!*" Alpha Cain growled, stealing the words right

out of Silas' mouth and preventing him from speaking. He wasn't strong enough yet to fight the order.

"Don't speak to him that way," his father hollered, trying and failing to stand, earning a backhanded slap from Uncle Cain.

Silas shoved a fist into his mouth and quickly shuffled behind his mother, afraid his tears would only make things worse.

"You made your choice," Alpha Cain said with deadly calm, looking back up at his mom. "Don't blame me for the consequences. I am your alpha, and you will do as I say or your mate will pay the price for your insubordination."

Confused and afraid, Silas remained quiet. He was frozen by the terror on both his parents' faces.

Alpha Cain nodded in the silence. "I'll give you the night to pack up his things. *You'll bring him to my home in the morning,*" he said, lacing his words with another command.

Once released, his father stumbled to his feet and stepped over to them, placing a hand on his mother's shoulder and Silas' back, quickly shuffling them out at the dismissal.

Just as they were almost to the door, Alpha Cain's voice cut through the heavy silence. "Cal? If you seek to break our bargain again, you know how it will end."

He pulled a handkerchief from his pocket, wiping the blood from his face and claws. "I always collect what's owed to me, one way or another."

PART ONE
WANING

CHAPTER I
SILAS

Silas was having a shitty day. Well, a shitty week, actually.

"You need to calm the fuck down. You're making me anxious," Sheppard said, his low drawl interrupting Silas' brooding.

"You've never been anxious a day in your life. And I'm fine," Silas replied before reflexively checking his phone for any missed texts or phone calls—not that he'd left it out of sight long enough to miss one.

The no reception icon mocked him.

Sheppard didn't call him out on the lie, but he shot a pointed look to where Silas' knee had been bouncing nonstop for the last three hours before turning his eyes back to the road.

Silas did the same, willing the long highway in front of them to shorten. He snipped and folded the miles in his mind until he could imagine Silver Rapids, the sleepy little town full of paranormals they called home, laying just over the next ridge, out of sight, rather than another hour's drive away.

Home isn't safe.

Pack is vulnerable.

He is vulnerable.

Run. Go. Go.

Fuck. Silas scrubbed at his face and reasoned with his wolf, for the thousandth time on their four-hour long drive, that at this distance, staying in the truck was faster than bursting from the confines of his human form and taking the four-legged route home.

He debated doing it anyway—if only to shut up the incessant growling and pacing in his mind.

He envisioned himself cutting over the fog-laden mountains on his giant wolf paws, already capped in snow, and loping through the forest thick with tangled brush and shocks of early October yellow and orange foliage.

Surely, sheer willpower alone could carry him faster than Sheppard was willing to drive their work truck on the old patched-up asphalt.

Obviously, Silas hadn't done a good enough job hiding the near-constant drone of anxiety prowling around his mind all week, because Sheppard softened his tone and said, "I'm sure everything's ok. Finn would have used the satphone if Cain or anyone else from Salt Creek showed up, or if he needed us to come back early. We'll be home soon."

Silas grumbled in answer. *Soon* wasn't soon enough. "Seriously, why were we out there anyway? All that guy wanted to do was play *Survivor Man*."

Chuckling, Sheppard replied, "If you can call pre-planned, brush-cleared hunting expeditions and sleeping in a warm bed every night *Survivor Man*, sure. Really fucking roughing it."

"Don't forget the private chef," Silas finished, shaking his head.

Fucking celebrities.

Meanwhile, he and Sheppard had slept in a camper van and ate microwaved food out of a bag for a week while they acted as additional security for some actor's vacation getaway deep in Alaska's interior.

Needless to say, five days of double shifts, shit sleep, and lack of cell reception had grated on Silas' nerves, and he ached to be back home in Silver Rapids; needed the incessant monologue in his head to go quiet, if only for a few hours.

Go.

Go.

Go.

"Really, though. You good? You don't seem good," Sheppard said, surprising Silas a little bit.

Usually, he left the feelings check-ins to Finn, Silas' best friend of twenty-seven years, and only offered a grunt in return if either of them asked anything deeper than whether or not he needed a Tums.

"I'm fine. It's just not usually like this."

"What's not?"

Silas huffed. "Leaving home. It never used to bother me this much. I feel like I'm going to pull my hair out if my wolf doesn't shut up about getting back to Silver Rapids and making sure Sa—uh, *everyone's* safe."

"Don't pull your hair out. You'll regret it later," Sheppard said, taking off his baseball cap and rubbing a hand over his buzz cut.

Silas gave him a flat stare.

Sheppard shook his head. "Do you really think Finn would have let five seconds go by without calling if something had happened? If Jaime, or *anyone else,* was even remotely in danger?"

Silas sighed, some of the tension leaving his shoulders. "No. No, he wouldn't."

Jaime, Finn's mate, had been their client last spring. He'd actually met Finn through a dating app a year and a half before, but a series of unfortunate circumstances prevented them from seeing each other face to face until Jaime's brother, Sam Lamont, had hired their security firm to look after him.

Jaime's identity and involvement as a witness in an internet-famous murder case had been leaked online, and upon showing up at Jaime's house for the first time Finn had thrown off a yard full of reporters swarming the poor man.

And then he'd promptly fallen in love.

Right before his eyes, Silas watched his usually taciturn friend turn into a giant lovesick puppy, swooning over every bashful flutter of the redhead's eyelashes. It was disgustingly adorable.

Silas' heart warmed thinking of the light in his best friend's eyes nowadays. He'd been so muted before, tucking himself away from the world in fear of being found wanting. It had taken Jaime's wide-eyed boldness and earnest love to pull Finn from that dim, gray place, and Silas would love him forever for being such a good mate to his best friend.

But Jaime wasn't the Lamont brother that Silas' wolf was chomping at the bit to get back home and check on.

Even if he wanted absolutely nothing to do with Silas.

Go. Find him. Go.

"You're usually itching for a traveling job. I thought you loved getting out of town for a few days," Sheppard said. There was a hint of guilt in his voice like he felt responsible for how terribly Silas had handled being away.

Fuck.

"I am," Silas quickly reassured. "Or, I was. I'm not sure what's changed."

Sheppard's brow raised. Silas had never been good at lying.

Usually, it was the thought of being trapped in one place that made him antsy. He'd always jumped at the opportunity to travel somewhere he'd never been before, to meet someone new. Up until last spring, Silas had been content to wander, searching for whatever it was that drove his wolf to *look*, to *see*, to *find*.

He hadn't even been conscious of what he was looking for, just that he knew he hadn't found it yet.

Occasionally, he'd have nightmares where all four of his paws were stuck in mud, glued down so his steps were heavy and slow even as he tried to run for the horizon. Growing up, he'd hear his uncle's voice drilling words into his head that made him feel small and alone.

Alphas don't hug their mothers, Silas, and they don't need anyone else to defend their territory for them.

Humans are weak and pathetic. They'll only take from you. They don't belong in a pack.

More recently, his dreams were filled with running toward someone; a man who had his back to Silas, walking away at a steady clip while Silas tried to keep up, thick muck clogging his steps so he'd never catch him.

Silas would wake feeling suffocated, yearning to shift into his wolf so he could run and run and run uninhibited until the memories of a bleak, lonely future were nothing more than wisps of smoke on the wind, easily forgotten.

While he padded through the trees, scenting the air and earth all around his home, Silas would remember his family —his mother and father who loved him so fiercely they'd risked everything so he'd have a future of his own making.

He'd remember Finn, his best friend whom he'd found a brother and confidant in.

And when the sights and sounds weren't of his home anymore, but of the forest surrounding a small, one-bedroom apartment on the outskirts of Monroe, a town halfway between Silver Rapids and Anchorage, Silas would remember the man from his dreams.

And then remember why he shouldn't remember; why he shouldn't be patrolling the perimeter of that small apartment at all.

Go.

Go.

Go.

Reeling his thoughts back in, Silas shook his head to clear

the near-constant rumbling. He glanced over and found Sheppard looking at him expectantly. Fuck, had he said something?

"Sorry, what?" he asked.

Sheppard smirked and flipped on his blinker to signal their turn off the highway toward home. "I said, we can't keep up with these jobs that take us away from home anymore. Not when there are only three of us. I have a buddy; he's in a bit of a tough spot right now and will be looking for some work. I'm thinking of hiring him to join the team."

Silas blinked, his surprise finally silencing the growling in his mind.

Sheppard had started their security firm right after the three of them were discharged from the military following the death of their teammate and friend, Joe Renner. He'd asked Silas and Finn to come work for him, and they'd been a trio ever since. Silas couldn't imagine their dynamic with an additional person involved. And a stranger, for that matter.

But Sheppard never voiced his thoughts or opinions half-baked. If he was sharing this with Silas, it meant he'd been thinking about it for a while, and had already made up his mind. He was just giving Silas a courtesy heads-up.

"Is he looking to move to Silver Rapids?" Silas asked.

Sheppard made a noncommittal hum. "He's looking to move *somewhere*."

He must have read the confusion on Silas' face because he continued, "He's being released from prison in a few days and needs to line up work and somewhere to live. I've turned away quite a few jobs outside Silver Rapids in the last few months, and he's willing to travel and live on the road most of the time to fill in those gaps. He wouldn't be a permanent resident here. Not yet, anyway. But I think he'd be a good fit."

Silas raised his eyebrows. "You have a friend getting out of prison, and you want him to come work *here*? Is he a paranormal?"

Sheppard nodded. "It's a long story, and not mine to tell. But yeah, he's a deer shifter. He's a decent guy, just a bit rough around the edges. We both know Finn has wanted out of the traveling gigs for years and even if you hadn't volunteered to take the double shifts this time, I seriously doubt he would have agreed to leave. So, I thought we could do a test run for a few weeks, and see how Buck does with the team."

Silas guffawed. "Buck? Your friend is a deer shifter, and his name is *Buck?*"

Sheppard smirked. "It suits him. When you meet him, you'll see. And I'd suggest not teasing him about it." He paused. "Actually, please do. Things have been too boring around here lately, I'd enjoy seeing that."

"Alright," Silas said, shrugging. "I mean, I'd have to meet the guy first before I invited him over for Christmas dinner, but it's your team. You hire whoever you want."

"It's my security firm, yes, but he'd be moving to Silver Rapids. I thought it would be best to run it by you."

Silas blanched. "Why would it matter what I think about him living in Silver Rapids?"

Sheppard let the question hang in the air for the rest of the drive home, the silence thick as they finally crossed back into cell phone range. Silas watched as a few brief texts from

Finn came through, updating him on the lack of activity during his nightly patrols.

That was the crux of what Silas had tried avoiding for the last five months, wasn't it?

He was the alpha, and now his best friend sent him updates like a sentry; like a *Second*. Now, his other friend, who had been his commander and boss for over ten years, was suddenly asking his permission to hire someone new.

All because of something Silas had never wanted and had done his best to ignore and suppress his entire life.

Silas tried not to be disappointed that he hadn't heard from anyone *else* in the week he'd been away, including a certain short, stocky, deliciously sturdy and grabbable green-eyed redhead. Who'd probably punch him in the teeth if he knew half of the filth Silas thought about him late at night.

Or in the morning. Or after he'd finished a run—sweaty and out of breath and raring to go, with only a hot shower and his hand for relief.

Find him.

Go. Go.

Silas sighed heavily, all at once exhausted as Sheppard pulled into town.

The gnawing edge of his wolf's anxiety waned the further they cruised into Silver Rapids; passed the pharmacy, Jared's bookshop, the Silver Dollar general store, and the handful of drinking and eating establishments surrounding the town center, already decorated for Halloween even though it was still a few weeks away.

Silas waved as they passed people he recognized, making note to check on some of the elderly residents in the coming days. Winters here weren't for the faint of heart, and it made him sleep easier knowing everyone had a good stockpile of wood to keep warm.

Silver Rapids was almost exclusively a haven for para-normals. Local lore varied on how the town was settled, but every version included some form of magic that explained why humans generally avoided the area unless brought in by a paranormal resident.

Jaime had lived just outside of town for a couple of years and never visited until he and Finn met. Silas theorized Jaime had been drawn to settle nearby *because* of Finn—the pull of the mate bond bringing them closer even then.

Most Silver Rapids residents maintained a modicum of subtlety and plausible deniability when out in public, but some were more comfortable walking around in their partial or full shifts. As they passed the bookstore, Silas watched Jared clear the recent dusting of snow off the hood of a vehicle with a single swipe of his giant polar bear paw before shifting it away to appear entirely human again.

A family of vampires bustled into the cafe across the street that served *specialty* beverages and pastries.

Finally, Sheppard pulled up to the home Silas used to share with Finn. There were no lights on to greet him, no tantalizing smells of his brother's cooking beckoning him inside. Just a cold, empty house.

He hated coming back here alone.

Yes, Silas missed his best friend. More than that though, he missed what he'd never actually had. He missed the opportunity for a future he'd seen, so briefly, before it was ripped away by a few short words and the sight of a man walking away from him.

I don't want you.

So yeah, maybe he hadn't just had a shitty week. Maybe it'd been more like a shitty few months.

"Take next week off, Silas," Sheppard said, shifting the truck into park. "Maybe go see your parents. We haven't had any new client requests come in, and you've earned it with the overtime from the last five days. I'll just be catching up on paperwork in the office, anyway."

Silas heaved a sigh. "Thanks, Shep. Give me a call if you need anything," he said, grabbing his bag from the backseat and heading inside.

Upon entering the house, Silas flicked on the lights and dumped his dirty clothes in the laundry to be tomorrow's problem. While he showered and fumbled his way through a stir fry that Finn had always made a million times better, he contemplated Sheppard's suggestion.

It had been too long since he'd visited his mom and dad. He'd give them a call tomorrow and ask if it was a good time to come stay for a few days.

After he finished dinner, he crashed onto the sofa. In the quiet stillness, with nothing left to distract him, the inner soundtrack of his wolf's delusional pining grew too loud to ignore.

It was a constant litany of *protect pack, gather pack, keep pack close, make sure pack is safe, keep watch over territory, call Finn, check in on Jaime, ask Sheppard if he needs someone to talk to.*

Find Sammy.

Go to Sammy.

Make sure Sammy is safe and warm and inside for the night. Does he have enough wood chopped for his stove to last the season? Has he been eating enough? Ask Finn to make him some meals to heat up. Does he have flannel sheets to keep extra warm at night?

What does Sammy's bedroom smell like?

Go ask Sammy if he's hungry. Make sure Sammy's warm. Make him smell like us.

Sammy.

Sammy.

Sammy.

Go. Go!

Go now!

It was unbearable.

He'd been trying to shut it up all week. Silas had thought being back in Silver Rapids, being closer, would soothe his aching need—make it more tolerable. Clearly, he'd been wrong.

It was just getting louder.

Go. Go. Go.

Sammy.

Sammy.

Sammy.

Silas huffed and pushed himself up off the couch to pace around the living room.

Shut up! Shut up! Shut up! Silas hollered back. *He doesn't want us, you stupid dog! No amount of whining will change that!*

Go!

Go!

Go!

"SHUT UP!" Silas roared, slapping his palms over his ears, desperate to drown out the howling, but the ringing of his phone cut him off.

He rushed to pull it out of his jean pocket, hoping and wishing and *praying* he'd somehow willed Sammy into calling him, but sighed heavily when he saw Finn's name on the caller ID.

"Hey," he answered, clearing his throat.

"Are you ok?" Finn asked, voice full of worry.

Silas' brow furrowed. "I'm fine, why?"

He should really stop telling people that.

"I'm—I can't explain it. Anxious? It felt like I should call you. My wolf was telling me to call you."

"Your wolf told you to call me?" Silas asked. Between the two of them, Finn was usually the one whose wolfy instincts were quieter, given he was only half shifter.

GO.

GO.

Finn blew out a breath. "Yeah. It felt the same as that night in the restaurant when I was waiting for Jaime but he never came. My wolf told me to find him. I didn't realize what was happening at the time, but... Are you sure you're ok? I can come over."

GOFINDSAMMYGOFINDSAMMYGOFIND-SAMMY.

GOGOGOGOGO.

Silas couldn't feel his face. He made for the front door,

stumbling and cursing as he tripped over the coffee table on his way across the room, blindly fumbling for his keys.

"Si? Please talk to me. It's getting louder." Finn's voice wobbled; he was scared now, too. Somewhere in the background, Jaime said he'd start their truck.

"I think something's wrong, Finny. Something's wrong with Sammy. I've got to go." Silas couldn't hide the way his voice shook, either.

He hung up, and as soon as he had the truck started and reversed out of the driveway, he began calling.

It rang. And rang.

Voicemail.

GOGOGOITWILLBETOOLATE!

Silas called again.

ITWILLBETOOLATEITWILLBE-TOOLATEITWILLBETOOLATE!

Voicemail.

TOOLATETOOLATETOOLATE!

With how fast he was driving he'd make the twenty-eight-minute trip to that little one-bedroom apartment in Monroe in fifteen, but Silas still felt like he'd been thrown into one of his nightmares.

Unable to catch up to the man walking away, his paws were stuck in mud and slowed down every step he took while he tried to sprint toward the horizon.

Toward Sammy.

He kept calling.

GOGOGO!

I'M GOING!

Sammy. The man who'd flipped Silas' world upside

down with one look; who'd shifted the magnetic poles of his heart, waking him up and shining a bright light on every instinct and desire he'd ever tried to ignore.

Sammy. The man who'd shown him *yes, this is what you've been waiting for. This is what it feels like to want a partner; an equal. Someone to build your life around. Someone to start a family with. Someone to make a pack with.*

Sammy. The man who'd made Silas believe he could be a good alpha someday, maybe, if he only had Sammy by his side, directing his inner compass away from an ephemeral, uncertain future, toward one thing, and one thing only.

Solid, and unwavering.

Pack.

And at the center of it—Sammy.

GOGOGO!

Sammy had become his lodestone.

His True North.

Silas had been chasing him his whole life without even knowing.

So what do you do when the one person you long to know most in this world says they want nothing to do with you?

Five months, thirteen days, and two hours later, Silas still didn't have an answer.

But if a world where Sammy didn't want him was excruciating, a world without Sammy in it at all was intolerable.

So, fuck staying away. Fuck protecting what remained of his shattered heart. Fuck ignoring what his wolf had been shouting at him all week to do.

All his life, really.

Silas would finally listen. He'd hunt Sammy. And when

he caught him, he'd probably get his heart broken all over again.

I don't want you.

But that was ok. Silas would beg Sammy to come and break his heart every day if it meant he picked up the goddamn phone.

Silas called again.

Finally. *Finally,* after the fifth or eleventh or thirty-sixth time he called, someone answered.

And Silas knew something was very, very wrong when Sammy, his mate, the man who smelled like crackling embers and toasted marshmallows, said, "Silas? I think I need help."

PART TWO
NEW

I'M FINE

FIVE MONTHS, THIRTEEN DAYS, AND TWO HOURS AGO

Standing before his Uncle Cain, alpha of the Salt Creek pack, Silas felt six years old again. His insides trembled beneath that cold, yellow gaze—the one that'd always made him feel so alone and unworthy.

It'd been twenty-seven years since he last saw his uncle, and frankly, another twenty-seven wouldn't be long enough for him to feel ready for this confrontation.

But then Finn shifted to his right, stepping close. Sheppard did the same on his left. Their movements were subtle—probably undetectable to anyone else, and more intended to block the three humans behind them from Cain's vicious gaze, but it focused Silas.

He wasn't that lonely, afraid little boy anymore. He had

friends that made him strong. He had Finn and Sheppard, and Sammy, Jaime, and DA Rivera, too.

Yes. He could be brave for them. He could be brave *because* of them.

"What are you doing here?" Silas growled, hoping his uncle couldn't hear the slight tremor in his voice.

His smirk told Silas he had. Instead of answering, Cain spewed some bullshit about not being aware one of his pack members had been trying to kill them. Honestly, Silas barely heard him. He was too focused on breathing steadily.

Then, Cain turned to the DA. "Prosecute Jeffrey Dugan and let that be the end of it, District Attorney Rivera. I would hate for the career that you've worked so hard for to be jeopardized over a few files you shouldn't be digging around in, anyway."

Sheppard didn't take that very well.

Looking back at Silas, Cain continued, "And the same goes for you, Nephew. Let's set the past aside. I would hate for something to happen if you go poking your nose where it doesn't belong."

Silas growled, hackles raised. But before he could tell the man who'd taken the instincts he'd been born with and tainted them, twisted them into something to fear to fuck right off, someone pushed their way in front of him.

Sammy. Stupidly fearless Sammy.

His Sammy.

"Is that a threat?" Sammy snarled, and Silas felt like he could fly. He could conquer the world; he could do anything as long as this recklessly bold, fierce man was at his side. Silas wanted to throttle Sammy for standing up to

Cain, and he wanted to howl for all to hear that this man was *his*.

Sammy's scent had been stuck in the back of Silas' throat for nearly his entire life. He had no way of knowing when they crossed paths that fateful day twenty-seven years ago who Sammy was—what he would mean to Silas when they were older.

He'd all but forgotten the encounter ever happened; with the upheaval of fleeing the pack and starting their lives over with Silas attending a human school, his memory of the fox-haired boy had faded, settling into the pockets of his subconscious, disappearing from view entirely.

But his scent lingered, like freshly made waffle cones over a roaring fire.

It was just strong enough for Silas to know he should chase it. To remind him, deep down, that even though he'd enjoyed a night or two with many beautiful men, he hadn't found what he was looking for.

It also explained why he'd popped an involuntary boner on a camping trip with Finn when they were fourteen, sitting in front of a campfire eating s'mores.

He'd never been able to properly explain that.

Cain's pallid yellow eyes, full of calculating awareness and open resentment, tracked Silas' movements as he banded an arm across Sammy's broad shoulders, pulling him back against him.

Sammy didn't cower beneath the gaze Silas himself struggled to maintain, and Cain's eyes narrowed. Could he sense the same thing Silas saw, staring back at him whenever he looked at Sammy Lamont?

He was human, yes. But also something else. Something more.

Alpha sang through Sammy's blood, calling to Silas, to his wolf; a beacon in the dark. A demand to rise and face his birthright head-on. A warm hand in his, fingers linked, as he stepped into the role he'd run from his entire life; the one he couldn't do alone.

An equal. A match.

Mate.

Matematematematemate, his wolf chanted.

Cain's eyes flicked up, and his slimy grin made Silas' stomach curdle.

He knows. He knows.

Protect. Protect. Protect.

"I would also hate for your growing pack to be held accountable for your meddling," Cain crooned.

Silas snarled, the sound rumbling up from deep in his chest, and he gripped Sammy tighter, pulling him flush against him. He may be more than a head shorter than Silas, but he was not a delicate man. The red stubble that had grown on his chin scratched along Silas' arms, giving him goosebumps.

"Get out of here, and do not threaten me or mine again, Cain," Silas growled, and his voice finally steadied with Sammy in his arms.

None of them breathed until the Salt Creek intruders were gone.

Finn clapped him on the back before throwing an arm across Jaime's shoulders, guiding him toward their truck. He looked back long enough to cock an eyebrow at

Silas' hold on Sammy, before nodding, ushering Jaime along.

DA Rivera and Sheppard disappeared back inside.

Sammy seemed to realize they were alone and still pressed together because he huffed and stepped out of Silas' space. "Don't manhandle me, you giant oaf."

Right. Back to Giant Oaf, were they?

"You shouldn't have done that. It was dangerous," Silas said, because it was easier than falling to his knees and asking Sammy to come home with him and never leave.

"I don't like bullies. Don't read into it," Sammy said, waving Silas off like it didn't matter; like he hadn't just challenged the alpha of the most violent pack in the whole state for threatening him.

Matematematemate.

Yes, I hear you. Shut the fuck up so I can do something about it.

"Still. I can handle Cain, Sammy. You don't need to do that again. I can protect you. Come on, let's go home and then we can talk about—"

Sammy cut him off. "Don't call me that. And yes, I am going home. *My* home. Now that Jaime's with Finn and not in immediate danger, he doesn't need the security detail anymore. Which means I don't need to be updated by you anymore, either."

He turned and began walking away from Silas toward the truck.

I don't need to be updated by you, anymore.

What did he mean by that?

Silas stumbled forward, nearly tripping over his feet

before he caught up, keeping pace beside Sammy. "What do you mean? Nothing's over. We're not—I mean, you just—we can't be done. And Jaime might not be in imminent danger, but you sure fucking are. I heard what you told him. I've seen the way you look over your shoulder whenever we're in public. You have a fucking *stalker*. Let me help—"

Sammy scowled, whirling on him. "You shouldn't have been listening in on that. Just because you have... *super hearing* doesn't give you the right to eavesdrop on my private conversations." He waved his hands in front of him as he spoke, like Silas' enhanced senses were some kind of magical spell.

Silas balked. He hadn't meant to hear it—Sammy had just been talking loudly. And ok, maybe he'd been curious and wanted to know what had kept Sammy away from Jaime this past year.

Because none of it made any sense. Sammy wouldn't have dropped thousands of dollars for an around-the-clock security detail on someone he didn't care for; he wouldn't have demanded twice-daily updates on Jaime's well-being if he wasn't invested in making sure he was ok.

Sammy's care for his brother poured out of him. His need to protect the people he loved was tangible; it called to Silas as fiercely as that song in his blood.

Matematematematemate.

"I wouldn't have to listen in on your conversations if you were more open with me," Silas said, his frustration bleeding through. He stepped forward, crowding the shorter man. "You should've told me about this, Sammy. I can help. It's literally what I do for a living. You don't have to do this alone."

Something flashed in Sammy's eyes. Fear? Pain? Regret? He looked like a cornered and wounded animal. Near-snarling, Sammy said, "*Stop* calling me that! And I don't want your help. I want to go home, and move on with my life."

Silas took a step back, feeling like he'd been slapped. The backs of his eyes burned. "You can't be fucking serious," he said, voice breaking. "Why won't you let me help? *Please.* Stay. I need—"

I need you, he'd been about to say. *I just found you, and I can't do this without you. I can't be an alpha alone.*

"I can figure out who the stalker is and track them down," he went with instead. "I can make sure they stop. I can make you safe. Please."

He reached for Sammy's—*Sam's*—hand. It had been so warm before; smaller, and soft, but strong. Was it really only a few hours ago that he'd held it the whole way to Finn and Jaime's safe house?

His hand was cold and clammy in Silas' grip, now. Sammy yanked it away.

His voice became detached and remote like he was speaking to Silas from the other side of an unscalable wall—infinitely worse than the snarl it'd been a few moments ago. "I don't know what misunderstanding there's been between us, but I don't want your help. I don't want you to track them down. I don't want *you*, Silas. I want to go home. Alone."

No, no no no no no.

"Sammy, *please*—"

But before Silas could beg him not to do this, to just give him a chance, to give *them* a chance, DA Rivera walked out of the security office. He glanced between them, clearly sensing he'd interrupted something, and said, "Sorry, I'm just on my way back to Monroe. I don't want to interrupt."

He walked around them but Sammy followed, voice horribly neutral. "Can I get a ride? I'm going that way, too."

NONONONO. *Go with mate. Stay with mate. Protect mate.*

He doesn't want us to go with him. He doesn't want us.

How was Sammy so calm and collected when Silas was fractured glass?

DA Rivera cast a weary glance toward Silas before he said, "Sure thing. No problem."

Sammy didn't even fully turn around to look at him. Over his shoulder, he said, "Thanks for... thanks. Bye, Silas."

He couldn't reply. It would only be his wolf's distraught wailing, anyway.

Silas watched Sammy get into the DA's car and buckle his seat belt. He watched them pull out of the parking lot and drive off. He continued to stand there until Sheppard exited the office minutes or hours or years later, startled at the sight of Silas still in the same spot Sammy had left him.

"Woah, I didn't think you were still here."

Silas turned. "Hmm? What?"

Sheppard cocked his head in question. "You good?"

Silas headed for his truck, hollow and alone, with the image of Sammy walking away from him playing over and over in his head.

I don't want you.
"I'm fine."

CHAPTER 2
SAM

"*Oh, fuck yes! I want your big cock inside of me. I want to feel you deep in my belly, feel your cum in my ass, keeping me warm and full. Please put it in me, Alpha. I need it, I need it, I need it—*"

"Fucking hell, tell them how you really feel..." Sam mumbled, scrunching his nose up as he hit pause in the audio editing software.

The sounds of his pleading were cut off, along with the wet slide of Sam riding a dildo like his life depended on it.

He sighed, rubbing at the ache in his temples. The balance was off between his moans and the lube-covered silicone cock, but last night's recording session had been fueled by a five-month-old itch he'd been frantic to scratch, rather than a script he'd carefully choreographed and set up.

He hadn't been in the mood to contemplate the appropriate microphone placement.

He slid the laptop onto the couch next to him, tipped his

head back, and closed his eyes, trying to fight off the eye-strain-induced headache. He'd been staring at his computer for way too long today.

Listening to the sound of his own voice never got easier, even now with years of experience creating and editing erotic audio content. Sometimes he still doubted whether what he made was any good. Did he talk too much? Or maybe not enough? Were his moans sexy or weird?

By now, he could reliably predict the comments.

A little over the top, but I'm into it.

It would be hotter if you stopped talking so much.

You should film yourself next time, I want to see you.

Yeeess more of this, please.

Once, on one of his earlier audios, someone had commented that he sounded like the squirrel from *Ice Age* when he came.

He'd stopped reading the comments for a long time after that.

Sam shook off the thoughts. He'd taught himself early on when he was brand new to the NSFW audio industry, equipped with only the built-in microphone on his iPhone 6, to ignore most of what people said.

For every person who told him to shut up and moan, three more would say they couldn't get off anymore without his voice in their ear.

Which would always be fucking weird.

It paid the bills though, and made it so that his younger brother Jaime had a relatively good college experience without worrying over where their next meal would come from. After a shitty childhood spent tip-toeing around a drunk and ambivalent father and fending for themselves, it was a goddamn blessing.

Plus Sam enjoyed having something of his own.

He'd kept the exact details of his work a secret from most of the people who knew him, including his brother, but not out of shame. It was just one of the only things that'd ever been his, and only his.

And really, he didn't want Jaime stumbling across his subscription account by accident. Neither of them would ever recover from the embarrassment.

Opening his eyes, Sam realized it had already gone dark outside, the sun no longer shining in through the curtains.

He'd been editing for longer than he thought.

Pulling his headphones down so they hung around his neck, he stretched his arms over his head, groaning at the stiffness that'd built up in his neck and shoulders.

"Right. That's dinner."

Sam talked to himself a lot. It helped with the loneliness.

Growing up, if Jaime wasn't around, he'd talk to his dog, Alfie. The habit stuck even after he'd passed. Sam couldn't bring himself to stop saying things out loud, wishing he still had his fluffy companion to pad around the house with.

Standing from the sofa, Sam made his way to the kitchen and pulled something vaguely burrito-shaped from the freezer. After popping it in the microwave, he stood and watched it spin in slow circles through the hazy glass, looking more and more like plastic the longer it cooked.

Yay, another simultaneously frozen and scaldingly hot cheese-filled bread pocket. How delightful.

At least he hadn't said that out loud. Small wins.

A *thump* and *swoosh* at his front door drew his attention away from the depressing meal, raising the hairs on the back of his neck. A quick scan showed both deadbolts were engaged. Good.

Not that deadbolts would keep out the monsters that stalked his nightmares, but still. Maybe it would slow them down.

Sam reached for his phone, the instinct to call someone—to call Silas—coming to him like a habit he couldn't kick. He stopped himself though, just like he had every other time he'd wanted to call for the last five months.

Those monsters were exactly why he *couldn't* call Silas.

Because nothing had changed. Silas was still *Silas*—still overwhelmingly everything, all warmth and goodness and eagerness to help, with hands that healed and eyes that saw too much.

You should have told me about this, Sammy. I can help. It's literally what I do for a living. You don't have to do this alone.

Sam had panicked at Silas' words.

It *was* his job to root out people's nefarious intentions—the stalkers, murderers, thieves, and liars of the world. And the more time Sam allowed himself to spend around Silas, drawn in like a moth to a flame, the more likely he was to realize Sam's stalker wasn't a stalker at all, and he was trapped in a web of lies so intricate, there was no escape.

So he'd made a choice standing in front of that piece of shit, Cain. Sam had seen the recognition on his twisted face.

He knows who I am. He knows what I've done. He knows.

"I would also hate for your growing pack to be held accountable for your meddling," Cain had said.

A threat flung at Silas, yes, but underneath it... a threat for Sam, too.

So Sam had shoved Silas away, hating himself a little more with each word out of his own mouth. He'd barely been able to look at Silas when he'd said he didn't want help, didn't want *him*.

Sam was a liar. He'd told many in the last year and a half, but what he'd said to Silas that day was among the worst of his offenses.

He startled at the sound of the microwave beeping, alerting him that dinner was ready. He set the lava-hot burrito-ish meal on the coffee table, cutting it into pieces in an attempt to cool it to an edible temperature before he died of old age.

While he waited, he pulled up the app connected to his doorbell camera. It was cheap—one of the ones that wouldn't even record and store video clips, only capturing a live feed. He couldn't afford anything more high-tech than that anymore.

He certainly couldn't afford an around-the-clock bodyguard.

Sam breathed a sigh of relief upon seeing his empty porch through the black-and-white night-shift camera feed. The only movement outside came from the crispy, dried-up remains of a lonesome potted plant swaying in the breeze.

He'd bought the cheerful flowering thing last spring on a trip to the garden center at Jaime's encouragement, knowing full well he'd probably end up forgetting to water it and kill it well before the cold would. Sam had said as much, but Jaime's enthusiasm was infectious as always, so he'd caved.

He'd been right, of course. It hadn't even made it through July, but Sam was still glad he'd bought it. He collected those bright, happy moments with his brother—tucked them close to his heart and hoarded them like he was afraid every new shiny memory would be the last Jaime wanted to make with him.

Sam hadn't been able to face him for most of last year.

He'd assumed he was the one hurt by staying away, and if he looked too closely at that he'd probably been punishing himself, but when he'd finally seen the wounded look in Jaime's eyes he'd realized how much pain his absence had caused.

He was terrified that he'd never be able to mend what he'd broken.

They were trying, though. Their phone calls and lunch conversations were stilted, but it was better than it had been. Sam told himself that was all he could hope for, because if Jaime ever found out their reconciliation had been founded on even more lies... no.

He wouldn't. He couldn't—Sam wouldn't allow it.

That was why it was better for everyone if Sam stayed away from Silas and kept Jaime at arm's length, only showing him what he wanted to see—the happy, carefree moments they could share together.

Not wanting to think about it anymore, he picked through bites of burrito, avoiding the large chunks of something that looked vaguely like chicken but chewed like rubber, and scrolled through social media.

A drop-down notification alerted him to a new text, and upon opening the message, he was startled by a very risqué photo of his closest friend and online mutual, Lana, featuring an alarming amount of cleavage.

LANA

Thoughts?

Engagement on last week's audio was shit, I need something eye-catching.

SAM

Wtf, warn a guy first. I could have been in public.

But, hot.

Please. You barely go outside.

Rude. True, but rude.

And hot like, "Hmm, hot," or hot like, "I'm gonna subscribe to see what else is going on there," hot?

Sam huffed a laugh.

Hot like if I were into boobs I'd be smashing that top tier button and grabbing the bedside lotion bottle.

Perfect. Thanks, sweetie. 🤍

Sam studied the picture again. She was splayed out on a bed, naked below the waist with her legs angled so you couldn't see what she was doing, but the look of pleasure on her face and the placement of her hand between her thighs was... suggestive. Across the top in bold letters she'd written, "*I need to come... want to listen in?*"

The whole thing was a celebration of her soft, full figure, and it was objectively gorgeous. Lana knew her angles and marketing well—she'd be reeling in new subscribers with that teaser.

If Sam ever decided he was comfortable sharing photos or videos of himself, he'd ask her for pointers. He'd done well enough without it, though, and found it was important for his well-being to maintain a level of privacy.

Lana was one of Sam's very first industry friends when he was new to NSFW voice acting. They'd both started accounts around the same time, and even though they'd never met in person they'd grown close as they navigated the murky waters of social media algorithms.

Her friendship had been a lifeline through many of Sam's darkest days.

After cleaning up his dishes Sam sat back on the couch, deciding he'd clip down the portion of audio he'd listened to earlier into a teaser. It was right when things were starting to get interesting, and would be sure to lure listeners in to "*Subscribe for over 200 full-length audio clips!*"

When the teaser was ready to post, Sam took a few minutes to scroll through some of his older titles before picking a new one.

Needy Brat Bounces on it Until He's Bred and Leaking | M4M NSFW Audio

It's Too Big! Feral Fucking From my Alpha | M4M NSFW Audio

He Makes Me Swallow All of It | M4M NSFW Audio

Come with Me... Please? I Need You | M4M NSFW Audio

Eventually, he decided to go with *Big Alpha Cock Fills up My Tight Hole and Makes Me Cry | M4M NSFW Audio*, and hit post. It was painfully on the nose, but it had all the buzzwords people clicked for and was certainly on theme with his last five months' worth of content.

His inspiration wasn't difficult to guess.

Just because he'd set a firm boundary that actually speaking with Silas was a terrible idea, he couldn't help but imagine what it would be like to lose himself beneath all that warm, brawny muscle. Last night Sam had stared at the ceiling for an hour, convincing himself for the thousandth time not to call Silas.

What he'd say, Sam had no idea. He'd just wanted to hear his voice.

Instead, he'd fumbled for the lube he kept in his bedside drawer, perfunctorily prepped himself with a few fingers, and rode the largest dildo he had through the fucking mattress.

He'd made sure to hit record on the audio app on his phone first, though, tossing it on the bed next to him, so that later he could tell himself it'd been for work.

In any other context, the name *Alpha* skeeved him out, but when he'd thought about Silas while saying it Sam came so hard he was left shaking, face down on the bed with tears running down his cheeks.

And then the post-nut clarity slammed into him.

Five months had passed. Whatever inkling of *something*

that'd been between them, Silas had surely forgotten about it. He'd stopped calling, at least.

It didn't matter, anyway. Sam would die before he offered up the broken pieces of his heart only to be dropped like a rag-doll the first time Silas caught a whiff of a stranger and realized they were his *mate*.

Jaime had explained the concept when Sam asked what the deal was between him and Finn. "It's like soulmates," he'd said, "except *more*."

"More as in, you can't leave the house without each other? That sounds suffocating," Sam had responded, wrinkling his nose.

Jaime had laughed. "No, not like that. You're still an independent person. More like, sometimes I can sense how Finn is feeling. I can tell when he's close. I'll always choose him, and he'll always choose me. Everything makes sense when I'm with him. He's my person."

Honestly, Sam would've said it sounded made up if he hadn't seen people turn into animals with his own eyes, or witnessed the way Finn and Jaime were with each other. Their connection was tangible—the wolf had imprinted on his brother like some kind of freaky *Twilight*-for-grownups mating ritual. Silas had never acted that way with Sam—in fact, he hadn't had any trouble staying away at all.

Magic was real, it just wasn't for him. Not after the things he'd done, and not with Silas.

So, Sam kept his fantasies and secrets to himself, and someday he'd pretend like it didn't make his skin crawl to see Silas happily mated in marital bliss to someone else.

Sam had just shut his laptop for the evening and made

his way back into the kitchen to refill his water bottle when he heard a second *thump* against his front door. A bolt of fear shot down his spine, and Sam held his breath while he listened for any subsequent shuffling from outside.

Pulling up the camera feed again, he still couldn't see anything out of place, except for a car idling a little ways down the lane.

Peering through the kitchen curtains out back, he only saw the meager pile of wood he used to keep the stove going in the winter. He'd have to remember to get more, soon.

It'd probably been one of the neighbors, or an animal scurrying around outside. Still, Sam couldn't shake the feeling he was being watched.

The buzz of his phone against the kitchen counter startled him, and as if he'd willed him into existence through some invisible thread of connection tying them together, Silas' name appeared on the caller ID.

Sam sucked in a breath. No. He couldn't answer. He'd just finished reminding himself why opening that door with Silas was a bad idea. He scooted the phone further back on the counter, as if physically shoving it away would help him maintain his emotional distance.

When the call ended, Sam told himself he was relieved.

The revving of an engine drew his attention back to the front door. What the hell was going on out there?

But just as he was halfway across the small apartment to peer out front through the living room window, his phone rang again.

What were the chances it was someone else, and not Silas calling a second time?

What if something had happened to Jaime?

What if something had happened to Silas?

Sam huffed and returned to the kitchen, hovering over the phone like it was a bomb ready to detonate if he breathed too deeply.

Just as he reached to answer, a beam of light shot through the cracks in his living room curtains, the way head-lights sometimes reflected from a passing car.

Sam turned and squinted against the glare. He didn't have time to think about why the angle of the headlights looked wrong, pointing directly into his windows, or why they were far too bright.

He didn't have time to answer Silas' phone call either—the only reason he stood in the kitchen right now, and not at his living room window.

He didn't have time to think about fate, chance, or how he'd never believed in coincidences before a car crashed through the front of his apartment, blowing his living room apart.

PART THREE
WAXING

CHAPTER 3
SILAS

"Silas? I think I need help," Sammy said through the phone, before he broke into a cough, breathing rapidly like he was on the verge of panicking.

"Sammy, oh thank God. I'm almost there, love. What do you need help with? Are you ok?" Silas white-knuckled the steering wheel while speeding down the winding tree-lined lane that led to Sammy's apartment, also on the verge of panicking.

"I'm ok, I think. I'm in my apartment. Something happened; everything's gone. I can't move," he said. There was a muffled shuffling noise in the background, and Sammy grunted like he was lifting something heavy.

Silas couldn't explain how he already knew where Sammy was, or that he was in danger. He'd just started driving. Finn's reminder that his wolf knew something had been wrong with Jaime before they'd even met had snapped Silas to attention.

His wolf knew. Somehow, his instincts knew that Sammy was in trouble, and where to find him.

Silas had spent all summer throwing up wall after wall between himself and those instincts, blocking out the mourning of Sammy's rejection because wallowing in it was too painful. Had he not listened now, though, had Finn not called...

Silas shuddered. He couldn't think about the other possibilities. Not until he knew for sure Sammy was safe.

"What do you mean everything's gone? Are you trapped somewhere?"

"I'm not sure," Sammy said. "It just happened so fast, and now I can't get up." His breaths grew more frantic, either in panic or because he was trying to lift something again, Silas couldn't tell.

GOGOGOGOGOGO.

Flashing red and blue lights appeared in Silas' rearview mirror, still a ways off. Someone must have already called the police.

That was good, right? If Sammy needed medical attention, help would only be moments behind him. But what the fuck had happened for someone to know they should call in the first place? Had there been a natural gas leak? Had a nearby meth house exploded?

"I'm almost there, love. Almost there. Try and relax, don't get yourself worked up. It'll be ok."

It was all Silas could say, over and over while Sammy huffed and struggled against something. It was all he could think, all his wolf could think as they drove those last few miles.

Almost there. He'll be ok. Almost there. He'll be ok. Almost there. He'll be ok.

"I can't stay like this, I'm going to try and get out," Sammy said before the line went dead. He'd either hung up or the call dropped.

"Fuck!" Silas yelled, slamming a hand into the steering wheel.

ALMOSTTHEREALMOSTTHERE!

The emergency vehicles had nearly caught up as he rounded the final bend, the handful of one-and-a-half-story duplex apartments scattered along the road just coming into view.

Sammy lived in number seven, the last door on the left of the first row. However, as Silas skidded to a halt in the gravel lot, slamming on his breaks, it was immediately clear he wouldn't have to direct the emergency personnel to the right apartment, after all.

"Oh my God..." Silas breathed.

A handful of people, probably neighbors, stood in a half circle around Sammy's apartment.

Or, what was left of Sammy's apartment.

The back end of a car jutted out where the windows and front door used to be, leaving a gaping hole of shredded building material and wires. Tire marks led from the road right up to his front door, the grass torn in muddy gashes.

Silas was out of the truck and pushing his way through the small crowd in a few large strides. He clawed at the gap between the wall and the vehicle, tearing his way inside, the absolute worst-case scenarios flashing through his mind.

What if Sammy was under the car? What if a beam had

fallen on him, pinning him? What if he'd hit his head, or cut himself on something?

GOGOGOGOGO!

Fuck what the onlookers thought when they saw a giant man Hulk smash his way through the wreckage—he just needed to hear Sammy's voice in person. See that he was ok. Feel his chest rise when he took a breath.

"Sammy? SAMMY?" Silas shouted, fear and adrenaline fueling his final shove through the last bit of resistance until he was standing inside what remained of the small apartment.

"Silas?" Sammy called, his voice muffled.

"Are you under the car?" Silas asked, praying the answer was no. It was difficult to make anything out of the wreckage, with dust coating everything and throwing off his sense of smell.

"No, I'm back here! In the kitchen!" Sammy said.

Silas rushed toward the sound of his voice, clearer now that he was further inside. Boards snapped and crushed beneath his giant strides while the first responders fired up some kind of power saw to cut their way in behind him.

The half wall separating the space from the living room had partially collapsed, and the cabinets and shelves had fallen, lying broken and scattered haphazardly all over the tile floor.

Sammy was in the middle of the debris, sitting with his back against the lower cupboards, completely covered in a fine layer of dust. He looked more like a ghost than Silas' heart could handle, but his eyes were bright and alert.

Silas rushed over and knelt before him, uncaring about

the sharp wood and broken tableware cutting into his knees. Cupping his face, Silas asked, "Sammy, love, are you ok?"

One of Sammy's hands came up to clutch at Silas' sleeveless hooded sweatshirt—he hadn't even thrown on a proper coat before he left the house.

Sammy was breathing heavily, near panting. "I'm—fine," he gasped. "I just can't free my legs. I've been trying to get out since—since the crash, I think my foot is caught. It's going numb."

Silas felt along the back of his head, cradling it away from the hard wood as he checked for bleeding or bumps. "Shh, it's alright. It's alright. We'll get you out, I promise. Deep, slow breaths, yeah? Were you thrown? Did you hit your head? Did you pass out?"

Sammy shook his head. "No," he said, words choked on emotion. "I'm just stuck. The phone kept ringing and I knew it was you, but I couldn't reach it. I can't get my foot free. I was able to lift far enough to finally grab the phone, but—"

He took a gasping breath, tears threatening to fall. "Fuck, I'm sorry. I don't know why I'm crying. I'm ok, I promise. Really. I just want to stand up—" His shoulders lifted in another big breath.

Silas placed his hand on Sammy's chest. "It's going to be ok. Let yourself cry, love. Or scream, if that would help. Or maybe calling me Giant Oaf would make you feel better? I've gotta say, I've missed it."

Sammy tried to scowl, but his wet laugh gave him away. "You're terrible at calming someone down in a crisis."

Silas gave Sammy the sly half-smirk that had always

gotten a rise out of him. "Ahh, are you gonna leave me a bad review? At least throw me a star for showing up early."

Sammy's scowl was a little more effective this time, but he placed his hand over Silas' on his chest, almost like he didn't realize he was doing it. "Fine. One star for timeliness. But I'm docking half of it because of the mud you've tracked all over the floor."

Silas laughed and felt like he was the one about to cry when Sammy's breaths evened out. By the sound of it, the first responders were nearly through the wall.

Satisfied that he wasn't going to pass out, Silas asked, "How about we get this cabinet off of you, yeah?"

Sammy took a deep breath, steadier than he'd been a minute ago. "Yeah. Ok."

Silas shuffled back, chucking the loose debris that lay nearby to the side so he'd have room to move. Reaching underneath, he felt for where Sammy was caught. He didn't want to lift the structure right away, for fear of hurting him.

Silas found Sammy's foot lodged in between the shell of the cabinet and an interior shelf that had snapped in the fall, pinning him down.

"Can you feel my hand?" Silas asked.

Sammy nodded quickly. "Yeah, I feel that. It doesn't feel like I'm cut, it just feels like I'm caught and I can't scoot far enough to twist my foot out."

Silas gingerly bent Sammy's foot to the side, careful not to twist his ankle, and slowly lifted the cupboard with one hand. "Am I hurting you?"

"No. Keep going. I can pull it out once you lift enough."

Silas let go of Sammy's foot and used both hands to lift

the cabinet further, until he bent his knee and retracted his foot, finally free of the structure.

In one swift movement, Silas heaved the broken cupboard away and knelt back down in front of Sammy right as the first responders cut through the wall, carefully making their way through the debris.

"Thank you. Thank you, Silas," Sammy said.

Silas blinked, unsure how to handle this softer version of him now that he wasn't stuck. But then a paramedic along with a couple of EMTs were there, ready to provide medical aid, so he stepped back to give them a chance to work. He never took his eyes off Sammy though, and listened intently while he answered their questions.

"Did you fall?"

"Yes."

"Did you hit your head?"

"I don't think so."

"Did you ever lose consciousness? Are there any periods that are missing or fuzzy since you fell?"

"No. I was awake for everything." Sammy's eyes flicked up at Silas, almost shyly. His phone was resting on the ground beside him.

They began palpating Sammy's chest and legs, presumably checking for breaks or other injuries, and asking him a handful of topical questions to check if he was cognitively sound.

"Can you stand on your own?" The paramedic asked.

"I think so..." Sammy said, and made to stand.

Silas rushed forward. "Let me help you," he said.

He didn't know whether to gnash his teeth or whoop in

thanks when Sammy snapped back, "I can stand on my own. I'm fine."

Silas followed behind while they walked Sammy out through the hole they'd cut next to the car. As they passed, another group of first responders pried the driver's side door off the vehicle.

"Could have been ejected..." Silas heard one of them say after peering inside.

He'd completely tuned them out while they were working, so focused on making sure Sammy was safe he'd entirely forgotten there would be someone driving the car.

"Are they alive?" Sammy asked quietly.

"Let's just focus on getting to the ambulance. They'll take care of the driver," an EMT said.

Something was wrong, though. Silas hadn't smelled or heard anyone else in the apartment—no blood to indicate a person lay injured among the rubble. It was possible he'd missed them in the dust and debris, but not likely.

It seemed that whoever they were, they were gone.

Silas wasn't sure what to make of that, still reeling and fresh off the relief that Sammy appeared to be ok.

They'd barely made it out of the makeshift door cut into the exterior wall when someone came running up to them. "Sammy!" Jaime's voice rang out. He threw his arms around Sammy. "Oh my God, are you ok? What happened?"

Finn had parked further back to allow the ambulance, fire trucks, and police cars closer access, and was hurrying over behind Jaime.

Sammy shook his head, gripping Jaime tightly before releasing him. "I'm fine. I was caught under a cabinet, but

Silas helped me out. I don't even think I need to go to the hospital."

"Yes, you do," Silas, Jaime, Finn, and the paramedic said at the same time.

And yet, Sammy only turned and scowled at Silas. How was that fair? "I'm fine," he repeated.

"You seem fine, love. But five minutes ago you had half the kitchen in your lap. Let's let a doctor take a look, yeah?"

When Sammy's eyes narrowed like he would argue again, the paramedic interjected, "How about you agree to go get checked out, and we won't make you lay down on the gurney while we wheel you over to the ambulance?"

Silas wanted to grumble about her being the one Sammy listened to, and thank her for reading his prickly nature well enough to understand they were never going to get him on that gurney to begin with.

When they reached the ambulance, the paramedic and EMTs helped Sammy step up inside the vehicle, and before anyone could argue, Silas crowded in behind him.

Sammy turned and did that thing with his eyebrows that meant he was going to argue.

"I'm coming," Silas said, with enough of the alpha in his voice to let Sammy know he meant it.

Sammy softened and nodded.

Fuck. He shouldn't have done that—he shouldn't have used the alpha that way. Cain used to do that all the time, and Silas had fucking hated it.

"Only if you want," Silas added, softer.

Sammy studied his face. Unafraid, like always. His brows pinched before they smoothed out.

Beneath that gaze, Silas felt like Sammy had pulled back the curtain he hid the alpha behind. "You don't scare me when you do that, and you can stay," he whispered, nodding as if the matter was settled.

Twice in the same night, Silas felt relief so tangible it brought tears to his eyes.

"I'll take your truck. We'll meet you there," Finn hollered out from where he and Jaime stood. Silas waved in thanks before the ambulance doors closed.

~

SILAS PACED UP and down the row of chairs in the emergency room waiting area.

They hadn't let him go back with Sammy when they arrived, and he was contemplating why he'd been cursed to turn into a giant wolf and not something small and easily overlooked—like a lemming, or a fly. Or maybe one of those tiny adorable owls.

Then he could slip past those annoying automatic double doors and find Sammy.

Thankfully, Jaime and Finn arrived a few minutes later. "They're only allowing *family* back there right now," Silas growled in greeting, trying and failing to put his teeth and claws away.

The nurses at the check-in station were eyeing him warily like he was some tweaked-out meth head.

The canines definitely didn't help.

"I think they may have just said that because you look unstable..." Jaime mumbled. "I'll go back and see what they're saying. Please try and stay calm, or they'll call security," he finished, giving Silas a look.

Silas nodded, and Jaime disappeared behind the double doors.

Finn crashed onto one of the bench seats with a heavy sigh. He scrubbed his hands through his golden-blonde hair while Silas continued to pace. "Please come sit down, Si. You're making me and those nurses anxious."

Silas huffed but conceded. Finn and Jaime were right, he needed to chill out. It wouldn't do anyone any good to seep his anxious thoughts all over the place through whatever connection they shared.

Silas sat on the padded bench next to Finn and let out a deep sigh. Immediately, his friend shuffled until they were tucked right up against each other, with their arms pressed together, the way they had when they were boys.

"Do you have any idea what's going on?" Finn asked.

Silas hated how small his voice sounded. "Do you mean about the car parked in Sammy's living room? Or your sudden ability to sense my emotions when we aren't anywhere near each other?"

Finn huffed. "Both, I suppose. But let's start with the shared emotions thing. I'm not gonna lie, that scared the shit out of me. I thought—" Finn shook his head. "If Jaime hadn't been there to calm me down, I think I would have driven myself mad. I just knew I had to find you. I knew something bad had happened, and I needed to find you."

The fear in Finn's eyes made Silas want to say everything would be ok, that it would all work out. Wasn't that what an alpha was supposed to do? Make everything better for their pack?

He wanted to take back whatever he'd done to trigger this shift in all of them. Clearly, he was fucking it up, and stressing everyone out even more than they were already.

As if to prove Silas' point, Sheppard strode through the revolving doors, pushing the one in front along so he could get through faster. His eyes locked in on where Silas and Finn sat, and he hurried over.

How did he know where to find us?

"I called him," Finn said, in answer to a question Silas hadn't asked out loud.

"Fucking hell, you two," Sheppard said, drawing the attention of the nurses all over again. "I haven't felt like this since—" Sheppard cut himself off, a slight hitch in his voice, then he yanked Silas and Finn out of their seats together and gave them each a fast, tight hug.

It was gruff in the way Sheppard always was, but he couldn't hide the moisture in his eyes before Silas noticed. "I haven't felt that panic since we lost Renner. What the hell happened? Is Sam alright? Where's Jaime?"

Silas and Finn gaped, stunned.

Sheppard never spoke about Renner. Silas could probably count the number of times he'd even alluded to him on one hand, let alone spoken his name. Sheppard had been closest to him and had taken it the hardest when he died.

"Sammy's fine, I think. Jaime's back with him now to get looked over. He was up and walking around just fine at the house. Some debris fell on him in the initial impact, but he was lucky. If he hadn't been in the kitchen..." Silas trailed off, shaking his head.

"What happened?"

Together, they sat back down on the bench. It wasn't large enough for three grown men of their size, but Finn and Sheppard squeezed in anyway flanking Silas and pressing their sides tight into his while they updated Sheppard on everything they knew so far.

It was comforting in a way that was deeply familiar and yet brand new, and Silas was so grateful for it—even if the nurses were now staring at them like they'd all grown antlers.

Pack is close. Pack is safe.

Check on Sammy.

SammySammySammySammy.

Great. That was back.

Finn rumbled, soothing Silas' frayed nerves. "Jaime's with him, and he's calm. I think Sam'll be ok."

Silas raked his claws through his hair, tying it away from his face in a messy half-bun. "Can you please not read my mind? There has to be a way to shut that off," Silas mumbled.

Finn chuffed. "It's not reading your mind, exactly. I can't hear words. Just... big feelings. And it seems clearer when we're closer."

Sheppard nodded in agreement, and Finn continued, "Before, I just knew I needed to get to you. Now, I can tell you're happy we're here. You're worried about Sam. You wish you'd paid better attention when I showed you how to make that stir fry."

Silas whipped his head around. "I was not thinking that. There's no way for you to know I was thinking that."

Finn shot him a fanged grin. "I can't, but I can smell it on your shirt. You used too much ginger and not enough oyster sauce."

Sheppard chuckled, and Finn joined in, so Silas did too. He'd never been able to stop himself from laughing when he heard theirs. Maybe there was a chance this wouldn't be such an unmitigated disaster, after all.

That is, once they figured out who drove a car into Sammy's apartment, and why.

"Speaking of..." Sheppard said.

The three of them turned at once as Gabriel Rivera, the District Attorney of Monroe County and the man responsible for indicting Jackson Bishop and then Jeffrey Dugan last spring for Vera Novikova-Dugan's murder, walked through the revolving doors.

He'd also learned of the existence of paranormal creatures last spring at Sheppard's insistence, to help them deal with the mess of Bishop's mysterious "disappearance" after he tried to kill Jaime and Finn.

Detective Sutton stood next to him. She was more of an enigma to Silas, but she'd never been outwardly hostile or accusatory. They flashed their credentials at the front station and made their way over to where the three of them sat.

Great. Now the nurses absolutely thought they were criminals.

"I called him when I was on the way. It sounded like they'd wind up being involved anyway," Sheppard said, almost defensively.

Finn and Silas looked at each other with raised eyebrows. Sheppard had found a lot of reasons to call the DA, lately.

"Finn, Silas, Cam. I wish I could say it's a pleasure," DA Rivera said. Detective Sutton only nodded.

"Gabe. Thanks for coming. We thought we'd get ahead of things this time and give you a call. What can you tell us about the crash? Did you track down the driver?" Sheppard asked. Silas had filled them in on their absence from the scene of the wreck.

Detective Sutton shot a weary glance toward the DA. "We're following up on several possible leads. Actually, we're here because we have a few questions for Sam Lamont. Is he able to talk to us?"

Silas' hackles raised. That sounded benign enough on the surface, but he knew how they'd treated Jaime before they accepted he wasn't involved with Vera's murder. Silas wouldn't allow them to treat Sammy that way, no matter what was going on between Sheppard and the DA.

Jaime's arrival through the double doors interrupted the dismissal poised on the tip of Silas' tongue. He hurried over, and before anyone could warn him of their company's intentions, he said, "Sam's fine. A few scrapes and bruises, but no broken bones or reason to suspect concussion or head trauma or anything like that. They're going to give him something for the stress and anxiety from being stuck. We're just waiting for that to be filled and then he'll be discharged. We can go back and see him now if you want."

Detective Sutton smiled, not unkindly. "Great, we have a few questions for him."

CHAPTER 4
SAM

The nurse had just handed Sam a cup of water and an Ativan when a crowd of people filed in past the curtain partially concealing his room, including Detective fucking Whatshername and the DA.

Great.

Sam threw back the anxiety medicine and took a big gulp of water before anyone could start talking. He was going to need it.

"Um, Detective Sutton and DA Rivera are here to ask about the accident," Jaime said, gesturing vaguely toward them.

"It wasn't an accident," Finn cut in gently.

All eyes turned to him, the Detective in particular zeroing in. "Why do you think that?" she asked.

He angled his head, his tone implying her question was rhetorical. "I saw the tire tracks, same as you. There were no skid marks on the road; they didn't swerve around something and crash. They drove right into his apartment without even trying to stop."

The whole room was quiet, contemplating what Finn had said, but Detective Sutton didn't reveal her feelings regarding his statement either way. She turned to Sam and asked, "Is there anyone who might want to hurt you? Have you had any recent threats? Anyone who's made you feel uncomfortable?"

A couple of names flashed through Sam's mind, none of which benefited from him being smashed under a car. "Hurt me? No, nothing like that," he said, picking at the blanket thrown across his lap.

The detective hummed. Silas was looking at him with that stare that stripped him naked, and not in a fun way.

He knows. He knows you're hiding things.

"So you *do* think it was targeted?" Jaime interjected. "You think it's someone who knows Sam?"

"We're just following leads, I'm afraid I can't disclose more than that at this time," Detective Sutton said.

He wanted to roll his eyes, but the anxiety medication was beginning to set in, making his eyelids heavy.

"If they fled on foot, they could be seriously injured, or even dying somewhere without medical assistance," she continued, still staring at Sam. She was trying to bait him into reacting—looking for some sign that Sam knew who'd done this and was upset at the thought of their death.

He wasn't—for once, Sam was telling the truth. He had no fucking idea who was in that car.

"How terrible," he responded flatly.

The silence in the room was deafening. Another tactic to

get him to talk, he imagined. If she was hoping he'd fill the silence, she'd be waiting a long time. He didn't give a fuck about awkward silence.

He was rapidly becoming sleepier and sleepier, though.

"That's enough questions. He needs rest," Silas said, motioning for the detective to leave and ending their silent stand-off.

Sam was too sleepy to rebuff the help.

DA Rivera smiled apologetically. "I'll give you a call when we know more," he said to Sam, before following the detective out, Sheppard close behind.

Jaime let out a heavy sigh when they were gone, his shoulders falling. "Sam. Seriously, what the fuck is going on? Could this be the stalker you talked about? I don't know why you won't tell them about that, or let Silas and Finn help you—"

"Jaime, I love you. But please not now," Sam interrupted. "I really don't know who would want to do this. I swear. And I didn't say anything about... the other thing, because it's not relevant."

Jaime and Silas looked ready to argue, so Sam continued, "I haven't heard anything from that... *situation* in months. It's totally blown over, I promise," he finished, yawning.

He hated that he'd lied to them. Some nights, it made him physically ill that he hadn't just come clean about every-thing. He was in too deep now, though, and doing his best to not add to his dishonesty was exhausting.

Jaime's face was grim, but he nodded. "As long as you know we're here for you. Us, in this room," he gestured to Finn and Silas, the latter of which was still staring holes through him. "And Sheppard too. You're safe with us. You can trust us."

Oh, Jaime. It had never been about trusting them.

"Thank you," Sam said, not knowing what else to say, tongue-tied beneath Silas' intense stare.

Jaime nodded. "We'll make up the guest room for you, Finn can bring the truck around."

"I'll be fine in a motel—"

"He's staying with me," Silas spoke over Sam, their words running together. He'd used that *tone* again—the one that made something inside Sam sit up straight, alert.

Not a challenge, but a call.

"I'll be fine in a motel," Sam said again, gaze fixed on Silas.

Never mind that I can't afford a fucking motel. Details.

"You'll stay with me," Silas repeated, enunciating every word while that underlying growl yanked on something tied to Sam's ribcage.

Maybe he needed an MRI after all.

He opened his mouth to decline again, but surprised himself and probably everyone else in the room when instead, he gritted out, "Fine," through clenched teeth.

Sam blamed his acquiescence on the anxiety medication.

Jaime and Finn's heads bobbed back and forth between them as if they were watching a sporting match, both wide-eyed and a little lost, like they hadn't quite grasped the rules of the game yet.

Sam hadn't either, really. He just knew he wasn't losing.

Finn cleared his throat. "Right. Well, I'm sure you're exhausted. We'll let you rest until they discharge you." He put an arm around Jaime's waist, pulling him close. Jaime wrapped an arm around his back in return.

Their easy intimacy was hard to watch.

"Call me, Sammy. I mean it. Please." Jaime's eyes were big and pleading, begging him not to disappear again like he had last year.

"I'll call. I promise."

He would. Sam would keep that promise this time. He just wasn't sure what there would be to say.

It's why he'd avoided Jaime—why Sam had sat in silence when he was woken late into the night by one of his phone calls, panicked after a nightmare.

Sam had been unable to voice words of comfort and companionship, choking on his guilt and shame. So he'd sat there, frozen, unable to speak while he listened to his little brother cry for so many nights, both of them broken in different ways.

Sam swallowed his explanations—they wouldn't want to hear them.

A nurse came in as Finn and Jaime left for one final check of Sam's vitals before discharging him.

Thirty minutes later, he batted Silas' hands away and heaved himself up into the passenger seat of the truck, plunking down heavily and fumbling with the seatbelt until it latched.

"I can get myself up here just fine, Oaf," Sam said, stifling another yawn.

Silas snorted but backed off, holding up his hands. "Alright, sleeping beauty. Three hours ago you were under a kitchen, and you nearly tripped over your own feet on the way out here. Forgive me for worrying."

Silas shut his door, and Sam rolled his eyes—or he tried to, anyway. Silas wasn't worried about him, he'd probably just caught on that there was more to the situation than Sam was sharing, and he wanted to keep tabs on him. Like a threat. He was the *alpha* after all.

Sam hated that take-charge voice Silas used, even if it made him want to climb him like a goddamn tree.

Why the hell had he agreed to stay with him, again?

Sam could get away if he needed to—if being so near each other became too overwhelming. His car hadn't been damaged; once they picked it up, he could leave Silas' whenever he wanted. It wouldn't be long before he had insurance called and everything sorted out.

He'd start when they got home.

Maybe in the morning, he thought sleepily, barely able to keep his eyes open now. He'd only be at Silas' for a few days, tops.

Sam would need his security deposit back first, though... and he'd need to sift through the wreckage to find his salvageable belongings. *Fuck,* his laptop had been in the living room when the crash happened. It was probably still under the car. There was no way he could afford a new one before an insurance payout...

So, he'd work from his phone. No problem. iPhone microphones were so much better now than when he'd first started recording NSFW audio content, and he'd made it work then. He could make it work now, too.

But that meant being out of Silas' house. Hell would

freeze over before Sam let Silas hear him getting off to thoughts *about him*. Which meant he'd also need to find another apartment he could afford in Monroe.

That might take a few more days, and there hadn't been many in his price range to begin with.

Thirteen years ago, the day Sam had turned eighteen, he'd packed Jaime, Alfie, and all of their worldly possessions up in his car and drove out of Anchorage, their father barely even acknowledging their departure. Sam had sworn he'd never be back. In the end, they hadn't gone far; Monroe was only twenty miles or so north.

But to Sam, it had felt like they were a million miles away from that awful man and that awful house.

Still, if he couldn't find what he was looking for in Monroe, he could make Anchorage work. It would be fine. He'd just have to make more of an effort to see Jaime with the extra distance—that's all. Maybe being further away from Silver Rapids, further away from *Silas* and his all-knowing gaze, would be for the best.

Sam hurt everywhere thinking through it all, and things were going a little bit fuzzy as he settled further into the seat. Silas' truck was very comfortable.

"You're flagging, love. Whatever you're thinking about so hard over there can wait for the morning," Silas said as he stepped up into the truck, far more easily than Sam had.

Damn him and his giant... giant-ness.

They were turning out of the hospital parking garage when Sam looked down at his dust-covered hands and clothing. He scratched at his beard—it would get itchy if he didn't wash up and keep it moisturized. "I need clean clothes. And a toothbrush. And face wash. And moisturizer. And beard oil," he said, his words dangerously close to slurring.

Silas turned to look at him, awe in his expression.

Sam narrowed his eyes in defense. "What? It's autumn in Alaska. My skin will dry out in the cold. I need those things," he huffed.

Silas blinked, then shook his head and smiled. In Sam's tired, medication-induced loopy state, he forgot to tell himself he hated it. "It's one o'clock in the morning, love. Let's get you home and rested, and we can worry about everything else tomorrow, yeah?"

Sam pouted. "I don't want to be itchy when I wake up, Silas."

Silas whined. He actually *whined*. How could such a cute noise come out of a man so big and burly?

Words began spilling out of Silas' mouth, some of them more growl than anything human. "I have a spare toothbrush at home. And moisturizer. And face wash. And shampoo, hot water, clothes, and a bed. It's a warm bed. I put flannel sheets on. You'll be cozy. Finn showed me how to make chocolate chip pancakes because I know you like them. I can make them for you in the morning. And I have wood ready for the winter; lots of it. In a pile outside. A big pile. Plenty for us, more than anyone else on the street has ready. Our house will be the warmest. I'll cut more for you tomorrow," Silas finished, looking out of breath and a bit dazed.

Something hot popped and crackled to life in Sam's chest, like an ember among the ashes. "You're not very goodatthiss," he said, smiling even though his words were definitely slurring now.

Silas looked like a kicked puppy. "I'm not?"

"No, that's not what I meant. I'm sure your wood is the biggest. Put your face away." Sam shook his head, waving his hands in front of Silas' face. That look was terrible; he'd do anything to never see it again.

"You're not very good at keeping me as your prisoner," he continued. "I know you're only taking me back to your house so you can watch me, make sure I'm not a lllliabil-ty—liabil-it-y—to you and your friends. You shouldn't offer such nice thingsssto your captives, Sssilas," Sam said, his words running together.

Silas perked up a little and preened, looking so smug and happy Sam wanted to kiss his face. A pulse of arousal shot down his cock at the image, even though there was no way he'd be able to get hard right now.

"Valiant effort," Sam said, nodding down at his own crotch.

"What?" Silas asked.

"Nothing, I wasn'ttalkingtoyou." Sam sighed and nestled further into the warm seat. When had he turned the heater on? He'd just rest his eyes for a minute, and then he'd be ready to call his landlord. Or whatever it was he had to do. Why did he have to do all of that, again?

"Go to sleep, Sammy. We'll be home soon," Silas whispered.

As Sam dozed off, lulled to sleep by the steady hum of the road and Silas' claws gently massaging along his scalp, he forgot to tell himself that he hated the way that nickname sounded in Silas' baritone voice.

When he felt the truck come to a stop and shut off, signaling their arrival back in Silver Rapids, Sam forgot to tell himself that he hated the warm strength of Silas' arms wrapped around him, carrying him inside and up the stairs to the on-suite bathroom.

He forgot to say he didn't need help when Silas drew him a bath and turned away while Sam undressed, resting his back against the tub just in case Sam slipped or fell asleep in the water while he washed off all the itchy dust.

He forgot to tell himself it was annoying when Silas held open a warm, soft towel with his head turned, and then ushered Sam into the bedroom where he dropped one of his own giant t-shirts over Sam's head.

He forgot to say he especially hated the way Silas tucked him in between the sheets, which were indeed flannel and soft from wear, smelling like Silas and safety.

Sam forgot to say he hated any of it because he never had in the first place. Quite the opposite, actually.

Silas flicked off the bedside lamp and quietly closed the door behind him, leaving Sam to press his cheek into the soft pillow that wasn't his, but felt like a home he'd never known.

He almost wished he could forget it all by morning.

Would it be worse to not remember the warm tenderness that Silas had shown him, or to have it burned in his memory forever, haunting him with a taste of what could never be his?

Both, he thought. Both would be worse.

A. KNIGHTLEY

Just as Sam drifted off to sleep, a text lit up his phone.

UNKNOWN NUMBER

Don't forget our deal. I'm calling in my favor soon. Be ready. And say hello to my nephew for me.

WILL THERE BE CHOCOLATE CHIP PANCAKES?

SAM

FIVE MONTHS, THIRTEEN DAYS, AND FOURTEEN HOURS AGO

Sam was still in bed when his phone rang, even though he'd been awake for a few hours. "I thought I told you to never fucking call me again," he answered, foregoing a greeting.

"Actually, you told me to walk off a cliff and make the world a better place," Derek responded, his voice like nails on a chalkboard to Sam's nerves.

Sam sighed heavily. "What do you want?" He was already exhausted, and it was only nine o'clock in the morning.

"Did you call the number I gave you?"

Sam massaged the ache in his temples. "That's none of your business."

"You did, didn't you? You can't fuck around with Cain. Whatever the terms of the loan were, he'll expect you to pay up when and how he demands. You can't get out of it. I know guys who've tried."

Sam's lip curled. "You're the reason I'm in this mess in the first place, and you have the fucking audacity to give me *advice?*"

Derek's laugh was grating. "You can't pin this all on me. Just do what he asks. I'd rather not be reporting on your murder, too."

"I'm blocking your number. Don't call me again."

Sam hung up and chucked his phone down the foot of the bed. "Fuck. Fuck, fuck, *fuck!*"

He blew out a huge breath and raked his fingers through his short hair, pulling at the ends. As much as Sam hated Derek for being the worst sort of spineless, slippery coward, he was right. This wasn't his fault.

It was Sam's.

One mistake. One slip-up on his worst day to the worst possible person, and Sam's whole world had come crashing down.

"It's going to be ok. It will be ok," Sam whispered to himself, pulling in deep breaths.

He forced himself out of bed and into the shower, getting ready for the day. All the while, he repeated his plan over and over.

Sam would make back all the money he'd borrowed from this Cain guy. He just wouldn't take a break from his audio work, like he'd planned. That was fine. After a few months, he'd have enough to repay him, and then he wouldn't owe him anything. No favors, no debts.

Whatever the terms of the loan were, he'll expect you to pay up when and how he demands. You can't get out of it.

Derek's words rang in Sam's ears. Cain hadn't seemed interested in his assurances that he'd have the money in a few months—all he'd asked for in return was a "favor", to be called in on his terms.

But how the fuck would a favor from Sam be of any value to a man like Cain? The dude was clearly involved in organized crime of some flavor. He certainly wasn't someone Sam, or anyone he knew, interacted with regularly.

Sam was a nobody, and he was certain Cain would take the money instead. He probably just hadn't believed Sam when he'd said he'd be able to pay him back.

After that, his life could go back to normal. He'd try repairing things with Jaime. He'd let himself think more about the way Silas' smile tugged at his ribs.

Everything would be fine.

Just as Sam finished dressing for the day, a truck rumbled to a stop outside his apartment. Peeking out the window, Sam saw Silas walking up the gravel path.

Sure enough, his stomach flip-flopped just like every other time Silas had come for his daily updates on Jaime's security. Sam had tried to tell him he didn't have to drive to Monroe every day, that a phone call would be fine, but for some reason, Silas had insisted.

Sam ran a hand through his quickly-drying hair, coaxing it to lay flat, and opened the front door. "Oaf," he greeted, tipping his chin up to distract from the fact that he never knew where to put his hands when Silas was nearby.

Silas grinned down at him, fangs flashing. His smile never failed to take Sam's breath away, twisting him up in knots. "Sammy, always good to see you staying away from the moose."

Sam rolled his eyes. "It's too early for your terrible jokes," he said, mostly to hide the way that nickname coming from Silas made him blush and feel a little off balance.

He wasn't sure why Silas had only ever called him Sammy—maybe he'd heard it from Jaime? It'd been what his mom called him before she died. Honestly, had anyone else used it, he'd make sure they knew to never do it again, but coming from Silas it almost felt... *familiar.*

For the past few days, Sam had made him stand on the porch while he gave the update, but Derek's phone call earlier had him feeling a bit raw, so Sam found himself saying, "Um, come inside," without really thinking it through.

He stood back to let Silas in, the butterflies in his stomach taking flight when he walked past. He smelled like damp, freshly split firewood.

The way Silas' gaze turned to drink up every detail in Sam's small living room made him suddenly self-conscious. It was simply furnished, decorated with mementos and pictures of him, Jaime, and Alfie, scattered around to make it feel like home.

Thankfully all of his recording equipment was shoved away in his bedroom—that was not something he was prepared to explain.

Finished with his perusal, Silas faced him. "We haven't heard anything new on Bishop in a few days, but—hey, are you alright?" he asked.

Sam blinked.

He'd thought he'd collected himself pretty well after speaking with Derek, but for some reason, the earnest way Silas was looking at him made him want to cry. Was he coming down with the flu?

"I'm fine. Why?" Sam asked, lifting his chin again.

Silas hummed and stepped toward him.

The small living room made him look even bigger than he already was; taking up all the space in Sam's world. Silas sucked up the air around them both, stealing every bit of his attention. "You look like you should eat something. Want to get breakfast with me? There's a place in Silver Rapids that has pancakes so good you'll dream about them forever."

Sam opened and closed his mouth.

He really shouldn't. After the unmitigated disaster of meeting Derek and everything that'd happened afterward, he'd sworn off spending any sort of quality time with, well, anyone.

"I have a lot I need to work on today..." he said, avoiding eye contact.

Silas tipped his head, trying to catch Sam's gaze. "Please? I'm starving. We can try calling Jaime and Finn again together, too, if you'd like."

Sam's eyes darted up to meet his. It's not like this was a social outing, right? Silas hadn't meant the invitation as a date; he was updating a client on work-related topics, that was all.

Surely their conversation wouldn't stray beyond that? There'd be no reason for Sam to have to explain that the money he'd used to pay for Jaime's security had been a loan from some creep or to talk about Derek at all.

Maybe it would be nice to take his mind off things and have a normal conversation with someone. Still...

Sam grimaced. "I don't think Jaime wants to hear from me."

Silas' face softened. "You love him very much. And he loves you. Give it time; you'll mend your fences."

That warm feeling inside Sam flared to life, and he had the sudden urge to apologize to this man who'd only ever offered him kind, healing words. "When I found Jaime and Finn together, what I said... I didn't mean that. I thought—" he sighed. "I thought Jaime was in trouble. I don't actually think Finn is a monster."

I don't think you're a monster.

Silas smiled like he'd heard Sam's unspoken words. "I know. I don't hold that against you, and I'm sure Finn doesn't either. I'd have done the same for him," he finished, shrugging. "Now, how about breakfast?"

Sam scuffed his foot on the carpet. "Do they have chocolate chip pancakes?"

Silas grinned again. "I'm sure Andi would throw a handful of them in the batter if you ask nicely."

Sam nodded. "Alright. But only because there will be chocolate chip pancakes. And you're calling Jaime."

Silas began making some sort of rumbling noise as he ushered Sam out the door.

"Do you need to use the bathroom before we go?" Sam

asked, because he'd almost gone an entire conversation without being an ass, and that wouldn't do.

Silas blushed and cleared his throat, patting his chest. "Sorry. No, I'm fine. Uhh, yeah, let's go."

Once they were in the truck and on their way to Silver Rapids, he finished updating Sam. "The search parties are back out looking for Bishop this morning, but I wouldn't count on them finding him. Finn texted late last night that there weren't any signs of him near the safe house."

Sam breathed a sigh of relief. "Would he be able to reach them on foot this quickly, even if he knew where they were? Aren't they out in the middle of nowhere?"

Silas nodded. "If he knows where to go, yes, he could get there in a couple of days in wolf form."

"So, you're like, fast?"

Silas' chest puffed out a bit, and he sat up straighter in his seat. "Yeah, we're fast. And strong. And big. Like, really big. I can show you, sometime."

Sam tried to hold back his smile and opened his mouth to say something he probably shouldn't about wanting to know just how *big* he was, but Silas' phone rang, and Finn's name flashed on the built-in display caller ID.

Silas swiped to answer. "Hey. I've just picked up Sammy, we're both—"

A rustling sound interrupted him, and an unfamiliar voice filtered through the truck speakers. It was muffled and cutting in and out like they were speaking through an underground tunnel.

"—He's not dead. Yet. Just tied up—will decide what to do with him—"

Silas' brow knit in confusion. "Finn? What's going on? Who's there with you?"

Jaime spoke then, sounding far away. "How did you find me?"

"Jaime?" Sam said, raising his voice. "Jaime, what's happening? Where are you?"

Silas shushed him and reached over to take his hand. In a whisper, he said, "Quiet, love. Please don't panic or shout. But I think Jaime is speaking to Jackson Bishop."

Dread filled Sam's chest, his bones suddenly heavy as lead. "Where's Finn? How could this happen?" he frantically whispered back.

Silas shook his head. "I don't know," he answered, the knuckles of his other hand white on the steering wheel as they continued to listen to Jaime's conversation.

Confused and devastatingly helpless, Sam didn't know what to do. He couldn't do anything from this far away, he just had to sit and listen. It was unbearable.

"I'm going to record this," he mumbled, scrambling to pull up the recording app on his phone and capture all of Bishop's incriminating words.

He had to do *something*. He could only make out bits and pieces of their conversation, but what he heard terrified him.

Silas drove right past the turn they'd normally take to head toward Silver Rapids, speeding up till they were flying down the highway. "The coordinates for the safe house are in my phone. Pull those up and plug them into the GPS, and then text Sheppard to let him know what's happening," Silas said, quietly calm.

Too calm, like it was forced.

Sam reached for Silas' phone with his free hand and did as he asked, all thoughts of chocolate chip pancakes gone.

His other hand shook in Silas' firm grip.

Sheppard texted back moments later, and Sam held the phone up so Silas could see his response.

SHEP

On my way.

Sam's heart stopped when Jackson Bishop snarled something at Jaime, and then Jaime spoke directly to Silas, his voice suddenly much clearer. "Silas, how much of that did you hear?"

Silas' answer rumbled in his chest. "All of it."

Jaime and Bishop exchanged a few more heated words before there was a great commotion, followed by a loud *BANG!*

"Jaime! JAIME!" Sam shouted as if he could will himself there to help, to stop whatever was happening, to trade places with Jaime.

Jaime didn't respond. "JAIME! What's happening?" Sam cried. Again, he didn't answer. All they could hear was snarling, and then the call disconnected.

"Silas, what the fuck is going on? What do we do? I don't know what to do, I don't know how to help—" he sobbed, confused and frantic and horrified, hitting the redial button over and over. Jaime never picked up.

He began shaking so hard he couldn't control his voice. This couldn't be real. This couldn't be happening. The last words he'd exchanged with Jaime had been full of anger and hurt.

Sam had so much he needed to say—so much he needed to apologize and atone for. He needed Jaime to know how much he loved him, how much he'd tried to be a good brother, and a good friend—how *sorry* he was that he'd failed at both.

Silas squeezed his hand, pulling it to his chest. "We're on our way there. I'm going as fast as I can, love. I can't—I don't know—" his voice trembled and then broke.

Sam kept trying to call Jaime back, even though the phone rang out every time. "Silas, I can't do this. This can't be real," he said thickly, voice choked with tears.

He was so helpless.

"I know, Sammy. It's ok. It'll be ok. I'll make sure it's ok."

Of course, Silas was just as worried about Finn as he was about Jaime, so he squeezed his hand tighter. "Finn's ok. Wherever he was, he found Jaime. They're both ok, Silas. They're ok."

Neither of them knew that for sure, but they passed words of comfort back and forth anyway, because the reality that the two people they loved most were too far away for them to help was unbearable.

They flew down the highway.

With Sam's hand clutched to his chest, Silas whispered reassuring words while they called over and over.

Just as Sam began to really lose it, Jaime finally answered the phone. "Silas. We're safe. We're fine, both of us. Finn got here in time."

Sam sobbed. "Jaime. Oh, thank God, Jaime. We thought —all we heard was... Oh my God."

All of his fear and regret rushed out through his tears, too much to hold inside any longer. He had no words right now, only overwhelming relief that they were alright.

Silas clutched at Sam's hand, tears tracking down his own cheeks. "Finny? Are you alright?"

"Si. I'm here, brother. I'm ok."

Silas pulled Sam's hand up and kissed the back of it. "Good."

"Um. So, not to put a damper on things, but there is a very large, very dead, decapitated wolf in the living room. Who is also a man. What are we going to do about that?" Jaime asked.

Sam let out an incredulous laugh, because really, what the fuck was he supposed to do with that?

Silas filled Finn and Jaime in on where they were, and they discussed how Sheppard would decide what to do about Bishop's body.

"What about all that stuff about Jeffrey Dugan wanting the three of you dead? And his real motive for killing Vera? And why would he want to kill you, anyway?" Jaime asked.

Sam quickly looked over at Silas. He hadn't processed what he was hearing through the muffled phone, too panicked to think clearly, but it seemed Silas had.

"I'm sure Sheppard is relaying the information we have about Jeffrey Dugan to DA Rivera as we speak so that he's arrested and can't hurt anyone else," Silas said carefully.

Sam narrowed his eyes at Silas' side-step.

Apparently, Finn caught it, too. "What does that mean, wanting to kill the three of us? Why target you? Us?"

Silas glanced over at Sam, eyes wary, and sighed. "Alpha Cain is my uncle. And he probably had his Second planning to kill me because none of his children inherited the alpha line. I did."

His words washed over Sam like a sneaker wave, unsuspecting and sudden, knocking him off his feet and pulling him out into the freezing depths.

Cain.

Alpha Cain.

Sam's breaths quickened.

Surely, Silas' uncle couldn't be the same Cain that Sam had borrowed the money from—the man they suspected had orchestrated Vera's murder and the attacks on Jaime and Finn?

Muscles bunched and tense, frozen in place, Sam stared out the windshield, vaguely aware of Silas coordinating their arrival with Finn and Jaime before hanging up the phone.

"Cain?" he croaked, unable to voice the rest of his question. He wasn't even sure what his question was—only that he desperately hoped Silas would say something that proved Sam's fears were mistaken.

Silas squeezed his hand. "I spent the first six years of my life in the Salt Creek pack. My parents fled after he threatened to take me away and kill my father if they intervened. Being around him as a child was... upsetting. They left everything behind to protect me."

Sam felt like he was standing still while the world sped

by, dizzy and nauseous. *It can't be the same Cain. Surely, it can't be.*

"I've never wanted to be anything like my uncle," Silas continued, almost pleading, as if he thought Sam would think less of him for the connection. "He manipulates and twists people into doing what he wants, through bribes and loans and favors. He's a terrible man. I won't let him hurt Jaime again. I won't let him hurt any of you, again. I'd do anything to keep him out of our lives, Sammy. I promise."

Through bribes and loans and favors.

It'd been clear Cain wasn't a good person, but if Sam had known who he was, what he'd done to Jaime and Silas and so many others, he would've found another way to pay for the security. He would've pushed Derek harder to give him his money back.

He would've never called that fucking phone number.

Instead, he'd allowed himself to be manipulated, just like Silas said. Had that been Cain's plan all along? Had Derek been a plant from the start? Someone to keep tabs on him and Jaime?

Or maybe Sam's plight had just been an opportunity Cain couldn't pass up; a pawn to move around the same way Jaime had been an accidental bystander in a larger scheme.

In the end, it didn't matter. Sam was indebted to him either way.

He couldn't feel his body.

No. No. He wouldn't do it. No matter what favor Cain asked of him—he'd refuse.

He'd work extra hard over the next few months and save up what he'd borrowed. He'd pay Cain back. With interest, if he had to. Then he'd cut ties and never tell Silas or Jaime any of it.

He'd never have to face the shame of what he'd done, or that he'd inadvertently been trapped in that awful man's web in the process.

He was going to be sick.

"Pull over," Sam choked out, already feeling the bile surge up his throat. He threw the door open when Silas came to a quick stop and spilled the meager contents of his stomach into the ditch.

Silas was out of the truck and bent over next to him in a flash, gently running his claws up and down Sam's back in soothing passes.

When Sam finished throwing up, Silas pulled him into his arms and held him close, his soft, dark hair tickling Sam's cheek. "Shh, it's alright, love. It's alright. Jaime and Finn are safe, and I'll do everything I can to make sure Cain can't hurt any of us again. I'm sorry. I'm so, so sorry, Sammy. It'll be ok," he crooned.

Sam began to cry harder.

Silas was apologizing to *him* when it should be the other way around. If Sam were a better man, a braver man, he would have. He'd confess everything and tell Silas that in trying to make it better, he'd accidentally fallen further into a pit of his own making and become indebted to his uncle.

But he couldn't face it. He couldn't expose his throat so freely, couldn't share his greatest shame with anyone, let alone Silas.

Good, caring, whole Silas, who deserved someone whole in return, and a life free of Cain.

Clearly, Sam could never give him that.

I'd do anything to keep him out of our lives.

It didn't matter that Silas' smile stole his breath away, or that his name in Silas' mouth felt warm and familiar. Sam had fucked up any chance they'd had before they'd even met, and now all he could do was try and minimize the damage.

He wouldn't allow himself to be Cain's pawn in manipulating Silas' life. In Jaime's life. In any of their lives.

Silas continued to hold him for long minutes, whispering gentle, calming words. Sam clung on, feeling the moments slipping away before he'd have to let go.

Forever.

CHAPTER 5
SILAS

Sweat dripped from Silas' brow, stinging his eyes with each heavy swing of the axe. His breaths puffed out in great white clouds in the misty, cold morning air.

Crack

Mate is here.

Crack

Mate is home.

Crack

Mate is in our bed.

Crack

Go check on him. Go scent him again, make sure he's warm and safe and watch him breathe and find moisturizer and feed him pancakes and—

Crack

The repetitive exercise helped soothe the anxious thoughts still bouncing around in his head.

Silas had tried to sleep.

He'd shoved the lumpy pile of weeks-old clean laundry up against the wall and lay in the guest room for hours, listening to the sound of Sammy's steady breathing across the hall.

But the itch to go stare—to watch those breaths move his mate's chest up and down had been too much. He wasn't ready to accept that he was that much of a creep.

Not yet, anyway.

So, after a few hours of fitful sleep, he'd shed his human clothes and shifted, donning the fur and teeth he'd been far more comfortable in for most of his life.

Setting an easy pace, he'd loped through the trees, planning on a quick perimeter run around Silver Rapids to ease his mind after everything that'd happened the night before.

Things were always simpler in his wolf form. He still felt emotions and understood that he wasn't entirely an animal, but in this body, fully in his wolf's mind, he could set aside the nagging anxiety over the future or fretting about the past, and focus on the *now*.

Usually, that was a relief. This morning, it'd been a constant stream of *mate is at home, go back. Mate is alone, go back. Mate isn't protected, go back.*

He'd recognized the difference between this need to be close to Sammy and his wolf's frantic warnings that something was wrong from the night before.

Still, the overwhelming sense of dread he felt when he thought about what could have happened was too fresh, too raw. So he'd circled back and decided to make the wood pile even bigger.

Just because.

Silas' awareness of Finn and Sheppard had faded quickly last night. Either by distance or because no one was in imminent danger, Silas wasn't sure, but he was relieved they weren't all subjected to each other's innermost thoughts all the time.

He'd never be able to look Jaime in the eye again if that were the case.

He added their newfound connection to the list of things he needed to ask someone who knew more about pack dynamics than him. Silas couldn't remember his uncle ever mentioning a connection like this in any of his alpha lessons, and he was certain Cain would have used it to his advantage had he been able.

He'd planned on using this week off work to visit his parents, anyway. Maybe they'd be able to help. Silas' insides warmed when he imagined bringing Sammy home to meet his family.

Yes, take him home.

Make him ours. Make him pack.

Silas wiped at his face with the bottom hem of his sleeveless hoodie and tied his hair in a half-up bun around his wolfy ears before he began stacking the split logs. He spent most of his time in his partial shift during the winter, unless he had to put his ears and canines away in town or around humans. It was easier to keep warm with the extra body mass and hair.

He really did have enough wood for the whole winter—more than enough, now. He'd have to take some around town for anyone who needed it.

As the pile grew larger and larger with each row he

stacked, Silas thought back on last night, and how his wolf had chosen to posture the size of his wood pile in the most cringe-worthy speech he'd ever given.

He'd panicked when Sammy asked for his help in a '*these things would make my life a little better right now,*' sort of way, and not a '*my life's in danger, please come save me,*' way.

Silas nearly wrecked the fucking vehicle when Sammy had *pouted*. God, he'd been so embarrassing after that.

It hadn't been all bad, though. He grinned thinking back on a loopy, sleep-addled Sammy. He'd practically purred in Silas' arms by the time he'd tucked him into bed, too sleepy to stop himself from nuzzling in close when Silas carried him up the stairs.

Once he was shown a little tenderness and affection, Silas' alley-cat put the claws away and transformed into a fluffy kitten. Who knew?

While he stacked the firewood, Silas pondered a few other ways he could temporarily tame his mate, all of which included fewer clothes and sounded infinitely better than taking an Ativan.

I'm sure your wood is the biggest.

Oh, Sammy had no clue.

By the time Silas was finished, his cock was hard and aching, laying thick down the leg of his jeans from images of him and Sammy together. Fuck. He needed to take care of that before Sammy woke up, or else he'd be uncomfortable all day.

Quietly, Silas shuffled up the stairs and headed for the empty bathroom attached to Finn's old room before he realized he'd need to grab the shampoo and body wash from his own shower first.

Moving so that his steps wouldn't creak against the hardwood floor, Silas crept up to his bedroom door, where Sammy still lay asleep, quiet as a mouse.

Except, the room wasn't entirely quiet. Just faintly, Silas could hear Sammy's voice... calling out. Pleading? Yelling?

"Please, it's too much. Oh, fuck, it's too big!"

What the fuck?

Mate needs you! Mate is yelling! Protect! Protect!

Before he realized what he was doing, Silas whipped open the bedroom door, eyes darting around the room, searching for a threat—ready to rip out the throat of whoever had dared sneak past him and enter his mate's room.

But he didn't find a stranger.

Instead, his gaze settled on the bed, where Sammy was sitting up and very much awake, with a pair of Silas' earbuds in.

He'd been listening to something on his phone.

Oh.

Oh.

Sammy reacted at the same time Silas realized he'd probably just walked in on his mate watching porn, which only made his hard-on worse.

"What the fuck are you doing? Do you not know how to knock? I thought you were outside!" Sammy yelled, taking out the earbuds and stomping right up to him.

"I heard you calling out. I thought you needed help, I didn't realize..." Silas trailed off as he tried to process everything that'd just happened.

That hadn't been porn. He'd heard Sammy's voice through the earbuds; Silas was sure of it. And if he'd been speaking out loud, Silas would have heard him long before he'd crept over to the door.

Just to be sure, Silas scented the air around Sammy—he hadn't been masturbating, either. There was a hint of fresh arousal, but nothing so strong as to suggest he'd just been interrupted.

"What were you listening to?" Silas asked.

Sammy clammed up, the tips of his ears turning delightfully pink. Silas would have to apologize for making fun of Finn's inability to keep his hands to himself whenever Jaime blushed.

"Nothing," Sammy said quickly. "I was... I was watching porn. Which is totally normal, by the way. What's not normal is storming into someone's bedroom!"

Silas cocked an eyebrow. He knew Sammy. Better than Sammy probably realized. He'd die before admitting he was doing something embarrassing. Which meant he was covering up for doing something else—something he thought was even *more* embarrassing.

Silas took a step closer. "You're right. I would have knocked, had I not heard you calling out, begging for someone..." One more step. His cock throbbed when he realized Sammy was still in the oversized t-shirt he'd dressed him in last night.

He hadn't let himself look, then. Hadn't even wanted to, really. What Sammy had needed was to be cared for. He'd needed to be shown that he could let go and be soft, and it wouldn't hurt.

And Silas had needed to be the one to give him that.

Nothing about sitting in the bathroom with his back to the tub while Sammy bathed, or even dressing him for bed had been sexual. Neither of them had been in the right frame of mind for it, and yet, it had been one of the most intimate moments of his life.

But this morning...

Yes. Sammy looked *very* good in Silas' old t-shirt this morning.

Sammy still hadn't spoken, so Silas leaned all the way down to whisper right into his ear. "That was your voice, love. I'd know it anywhere. What did you need help with so badly, hmm? I'd be happy to oblige if you'd repeat yourself."

Sammy gulped, his fingers finding the hem of Silas' sweatshirt. "It's not what it sounded like. It's... I wasn't... It's..."

He cut himself off, and Silas saw the shutdown coming. Saw the vulnerability leaving Sammy's eyes.

With the lightest touch, Silas tilted his chin up and quietly asked, "Please, Sammy? Tell me *something*."

Sammy's eyes darted back and forth between his. Deciding.

They were at a crossroads. Silas hadn't meant to bring them to one. Not now—not over this, when there were clearly far bigger secrets between them, but there they were, regardless.

Something shifted in Sammy's gaze, as subtle and delicate as the ember of trust they'd coaxed to life last night. It was faint, smoldering low, but alive all the same.

"It's for my job," he said. "I was editing an audio

recording for my job." His voice was low but steady, and his shoulders relaxed as he spoke, like finally opening up relieved him of a heavy weight.

"Your job?" Silas asked, not understanding.

Sammy took a step back, pulling his face from Silas' gentle grip, but he didn't drop eye contact. "I record erotic audio content and post it on the internet. Sometimes for free. A lot of people pay though, through a subscription platform. It's how I make money. I've never told Jaime, because... well, because. It's my thing. Something that's just for me. And it pays well."

He finished with a defiant tilt of his chin, almost daring Silas to shame or tease him. To call him all the terrible things people in the sex industry had been called before.

Silas would never do that. "Do you enjoy it?" he asked.

Sammy blinked, opening and closing his mouth like he'd expected a battle, only to be shown a white flag. "Yes. Or, I did. I still do, I think, if I wasn't..." he shook his head.

"If you weren't..." Silas prompted.

Sammy pursed his lips. "You know how it is with every job. People get burned out. I'm burned out. I have been for quite a while, but I can't stop, because... because. But yes, I do still enjoy it."

The heat of arousal that had been clawing up Silas' spine a few minutes ago was all mixed up now with the sheer joy of being trusted with something so dear to Sammy.

Silas nodded. "Ok."

"Ok?" Sam asked.

Silas took another tentative step forward, closing the distance between them again. "Yeah, ok. Thank you for telling me. I'll keep it to myself, but only because you haven't shared it with anyone else we know—not because I don't like it, or because I don't think it's hot."

He leaned down to whisper in Sammy's ear again; it had made him shiver and lean into Silas ever so slightly the first time. "Because I do think it's really fucking hot, love."

The second was just as rewarding.

Sammy's breath whooshed out of him, warm on Silas' neck through his sweat-soaked hoodie. His hands came up to press on Silas' chest, not shoving him away, but not pulling him closer, either. "You don't know that. You haven't even heard it."

Silas chuckled. For someone who was so cocksure most of the time, Sammy was clueless when it came to Silas' feelings about him. "I don't need to have heard it to know it's hot. But I'd like to if you'd ever let me. Maybe we could listen together." Silas' face split in a wide smirk. "Or even better, maybe I could help you next time. I'd love to be your *inspiration*."

Sammy's surprised gaze darted up to meet Silas', before flicking down to his mouth and lingering there. "You're teasing me," he said, breathless.

Silas danced the tip of a claw along Sammy's ear. "About this? Never," he replied, leaning into the magnetic pull between them.

Sammy's fingers dug harder into Silas' hoodie, pulling him close, and his mouth was just a breath away. He smelled like simmering coals and Silas' warm sheets. What would his lips taste like?

But then Sammy stepped away, releasing his hold on

Silas as if it burned. "I should get ready for the day. I want to go pick up my car and see if anything's salvageable from my apartment. Hopefully, I can find at least some clothes that'll fit," he said, so casually it gave Silas whiplash.

Fuck. It was always one step forward, ten steps back with them.

Every time Sammy opened up, Silas pushed too far, too soon. "Of course. I'm sorry if I've made you uncomfortable," he said, hoping the break in his voice wasn't noticeable.

Sammy didn't turn to look at him, but he surprised Silas for the second time that morning when he asked, "You said... last night, you said you could make pancakes?"

Silas had said a lot of things last night, but he took the olive branch for what it was. Rubbing the back of his neck, he answered, "Uh yeah, I did say that. And I can. Finn showed me how. He tried, anyway. He's the one who's good in the kitchen, not me."

Sammy did turn then and smiled. Silas could bask in the warmth of it forever. "I'm a shit cook, too. The microwave is pretty much the only kitchen appliance I know how to use."

Silas' shoulders dropped, and he returned Sammy's smile. "If I remember correctly, I still owe you breakfast. What do you say we get chocolate chip pancakes from someone who knows how to make them?"

That ember sparked in Sammy's eyes. "Alright. Let's go get chocolate chip pancakes."

~

THEY ACTUALLY MADE it to Andi's this time.

"Silas, good to see you!" she greeted from the kitchen pass, dropping off a few plates.

He waved. "Morning, Andi."

The surly teenage vampire she'd hired over the summer to help wait tables showed them to Silas' usual back booth.

Andi had already decorated for autumn, tastefully weaving in warm oranges and yellows to the usual string lights she kept up year-round. She'd probably put up her Halloween decorations soon, too, like some of the other establishments had.

"Do you already know what you want?" the teen asked Silas, her mop of dark curly hair covering half her face. It was a fair question, considering he ate here three times a week.

"Could you give us a minute?" Silas asked, unsure if Sammy wanted to look over the menu.

She nodded and slinked back into the kitchen.

Sammy stared for a beat before leaning toward Silas across the table. "Was she...?" he whispered, gesturing vaguely at his own blunt canines.

Silas chuckled. "She's a vampire, yeah. There's a coven here in Silver Rapids. It's small, but well-established. Depending on who you ask, they're the ones who founded the town."

Sammy cocked his head. "Really? How long ago? How does a place like this come to be? I mean, do you have like, underground advertisements or something? Is there a color spectrum all paranormals can see that humans can't? Do you have a wolfy bat signal?"

Silas laughed. Was Sammy a history buff?

"No underground advertisements or secret color spectrums. At least none that I know of. But the paranormal community is fairly small—word about places like Silver Rapids gets around. And if you ask the vampires, the town was established hundreds of years ago," Silas waved a hand, "before Alaska was even purchased by the U.S. from Russia."

"So the vampires established Silver Rapids first?" Sammy prompted, eyes bright.

Silas tilted his head in a yes or no gesture. "*Maybe*," he said. "They say they were the first permanent paranormal community in the area, but there are a couple of shifter packs who claim Silver Rapids wasn't settled until more people came together and built the town, and that before it was only a coven."

"That's so fucking cool," Sammy breathed.

The server dropped a plate off at the booth across from where they sat, and Silas waved when he noticed Jared, the bookstore owner, sitting alone. He couldn't be more than ten or fifteen years older than Silas and Finn, but his shock of thick, white hair and full white beard made him appear older.

He nodded once in acknowledgment, before tucking into his breakfast. Jared was a loner, but he'd always been kind.

"Are you ready now?" the server asked when she made her way back over.

As expected, Sammy ordered a stack of chocolate chip pancakes, but Silas wasn't in the mood for something so sweet.

"Is there a special this morning?" he asked.

"Oh, um, yes. It's Nashville hot chicken and waffles," she said. "The chicken's really spicy, though. I'm supposed to warn people."

Silas groaned. It had been ages since he'd let himself have hot chicken. "I'd better just stick with the eggs and bacon, then. With an extra side of hash browns and sausage. And biscuits, please."

"Eating light this morning?" Sammy asked as she walked away.

Silas winked, mostly just so he'd make that pinched face he did when he was pretending to not like something. "Careful love or I won't share my biscuits with you. And yes, actually, that is light. When you're as big as I am, you've gotta eat."

Sammy blushed, and Silas would love to know what he was thinking. He always reacted in some way whenever Silas talked about how tall he was. Maybe he was self-conscious about his height?

He shouldn't be. Sammy was delightfully compact.

Silas loved that he was small and yet sturdy enough to be thrown around without worrying about hurting him. He imagined Sammy's thighs would be a good handful, something thick to hold on to when Silas folded him up like a parcel and drove his cock deep inside...

"Why didn't you order the hot chicken?" Sammy asked.

Silas blinked, reorienting himself back to reality. "Huh?"

"The hot chicken, it sounded like you wanted to order it but changed your mind. Why?"

He contemplated deflecting for a heartbeat, but Sammy

had shared something personal, hadn't he? Silas could do the same. "I liked it *too* much at one point and regretted it a whole lot later if you know what I mean. I'd rather not have a repeat."

The corner of Sammy's mouth tipped up, and he snorted. Silas adored the unfiltered sound so much, the story spilled out of him before he could stop it.

Anything to hear Sammy laugh again.

"Years ago, when Finn, Sheppard, and I were in the military together, I ate one too many spicy chicken sandwiches before we went out on a training exercise in the middle of nowhere, New Mexico. My choices came back to haunt me... explosively."

Yeah, this is how you'll woo him. Tell him all about the raging diarrhea that still haunts you ten years later. He'll be begging to make out with you after this.

But as Silas spoke, Sammy chuckled, eyes bright, and Silas was a glutton for it. He continued, "So I stepped away from the team to take care of things, but my belt ended up tangled in my gear as I squatted down, and I tipped over ass first... into a cactus."

Sammy was full-on belly-laughing now. It was one of those contagious half-wheeze laughs, and Silas couldn't help joining in, even though he was sharing one of the most embarrassing things to ever happen to him.

Still laughing, he finished, "And the worst part was, some of the cactus spines were so big they'd embedded too deep in my ass, so my skin was healing around them instead of purging them. Finn refused to pull them out, so we had to call the medic. He was cute—I'd wanted his number but couldn't bring myself to ask him out after he'd dug around back there with a scalpel."

Sammy was laughing so hard tears formed in the corners of his eyes. Silas had never seen him like this—loud and unguarded. It felt like he'd pulled back a curtain; like he was seeing something not many others were honored with.

This relaxed, carefree version of Sammy was entrancing, and Silas felt gravity shift again, just a little. Except this time, it wasn't the mate bond.

It was his heart.

Silas passed him a napkin while Sammy wiped at the corners of his eyes. "That's the best story I've heard in a long fucking time," he said, still chuckling. "I'm sorry your run-in with the cactus cock-blocked you with the cute medic," he teased.

Silas shook his head, drunk on the moment. "I'm not. It doesn't matter. I'm right where I want to be."

Careful, Silas. Careful.

Warm embers shone in Sammy's eyes. They'd cultivated those together. "If you ever decide you want to try hot chicken again, make sure I'm the prickliest thing nearby. Your ass is safe from me."

Well, that's a shame.

The joke was on the tip of Silas' tongue, but their angsty teenage vampire server appeared just then with their food. It was probably for the best, anyway. Silas had already pushed his luck far enough this morning, and he didn't want to dampen the heat building between them again.

They tore into their breakfast, with the warmth from

those embers in Sammy's eyes lingering. He was still keeping secrets. Big ones, if last night was any indication.

He'd shared one, though. That was a start.

Silas knew he was playing with fire by opening himself back up to this push-and-pull dance with Sammy. He knew he'd be burned again before they were done, unable to stop himself from falling hard and fast.

But as long as Sammy stayed, as long as he didn't leave, Silas could keep him safe. He could wait him out. He'd dance for as long as Sammy needed; he'd dance forever.

The flame hadn't gone out, after all.

CHAPTER 6
SAM

S am stared out the truck window and pondered the merits of lobotomy.

They'd finished breakfast a few minutes ago, and were on their way to Monroe to pick up his car and any of his clothing or important belongings that were salvageable.

The drive was quiet, giving Sam plenty of room to catastrophize the morning's events. That was saying a lot, considering someone wrecked a car into his apartment last night.

What the fuck had he been thinking, telling Silas the truth about his job? He had a plan, goddammit.

He'd quickly finish editing his latest audio recording while Silas was busy outside, they'd go get his car and some clothes that fit him and didn't smell so fucking good, and then he'd leave.

Where he went when he left was future Sam's problem. He just needed to go, before he spent any more time around Silas and his big brown eyes and rumbling laugh.

When he woke up this morning, cozy and comfortable in Silas' bed, everything that'd happened the night before rushed back. The feel of those giant arms holding him close when Sam was so vulnerable would be burned into his body forever.

He wouldn't be surprised if he found tattooed hand-prints where Silas had touched him.

Sam wasn't new to sex. Blowing off steam through casual hookups had gotten him through those first few years on his own after moving Jaime and Alfie out of their dad's house.

He'd never resented his choice to leave; never balked at making sure Jaime knew he was cared for. He fucking deserved that. Sam had twelve years with their mom, but Jaime only had eight. None of it was fair, but he'd done his best to make sure his brother knew what real love felt like.

Still, it'd been a lot for him to manage at nineteen, and he'd needed an outlet. So what had happened last night with Silas shouldn't have phased him. It hadn't even been sexual.

Maybe that was the crux of it, though. Sam was familiar with casual physical touch, but not intimacy.

Everything with Silas was intimate.

Hell, talking about chocolate chip pancakes felt inti-mate. And that just wasn't going to work, since Sam had sworn he'd stay away and keep his issues with Cain to himself.

Hidden. Forever.

But then Silas had stormed in on him, catching him in the act of editing audio on his phone with his stupidly good hearing and confusing Sam by standing very close, sweaty from chopping wood and making him have *feelings*.

When Silas had pleaded with him to be honest for once, Sam had sort of... folded.

He blamed those goddamn sleeveless hoodies; Sam couldn't think clearly with Silas' big, beefy biceps just there to look at, for *free*.

Who the fuck cuts the sleeves off a hoodie, anyway? What was the point? Especially when Silas was in his partial shift, and the garment barely stretched across his shoulders at all.

And *why* did he insist on wearing one all the time? Did he walk around in public like that? He'd have everyone within a twenty-mile radius lined up to get a look-see.

Irrational jealousy burned in Sam's chest at the thought. At least Silas hadn't worn one to breakfast.

Maybe Sam would throw them all out before he left.

The awful truth was, though... Sam felt better for telling Silas about his job. Lighter. Like by sharing a part of himself he'd kept hidden, it was set free.

He'd never needed the world to know or accept him, but he'd also never intended to keep his job a secret for so long. Somehow, though, it'd just built and built and turned into this *thing* that felt like too much to share with Jaime or anyone else all at once.

A part of him had almost hoped Silas would shame him for it. At least then, he'd have an easy reason to tell him to fuck off and never think about him again.

Of course, Silas hadn't done that. He hadn't given him one of those "to each their own" reactions, either.

He'd *liked* it.

The heat burning in his gaze hadn't lied. But even more

than that... he'd asked Sam if he was happy doing it. Like the way it made Sam feel mattered more than Silas' opinion of it.

Sam had never experienced that with anyone. He'd never known what it felt like to have someone focused on making sure *he* was taken care of, not the other way around.

He hated how much he loved it.

Silas' phone rang through the truck speakers and broke through Sam's inner turmoil. "Not again," he groaned. "Why does the world fall apart when you and I get breakfast? Can't we eat in peace?"

Silas chuckled. "It's Sheppard, not Finn. No cross-state rescue missions on our agenda today."

Sam smiled. He liked hearing Silas' laugh. Listening to him talk about pulling cactus prickles out of his ass while having explosive diarrhea would be the highlight of Sam's whole year.

"Hey Shep, I'm here with Sammy. What's up?"

"Silas, Sam. So, Gabe called. Something's come up, and he'd like you to come into the station."

Sam tensed up. "I'm not stepping foot into that building without a lawyer."

He knew Sheppard was a good guy, but he clearly had a thing going on with the DA. He may trust them, but his judgment was skewed. Sam would never forget the way those detectives had Jaime cornered, traumatized, and still coated in a dead woman's blood.

Fuck them.

"Uh, it's actually not about last night. He was asking for Silas to come in."

Silas' brows knit together. "Me? Why does he need to talk to me?"

Sheppard sighed. "Gabe isn't the one asking for you, someone else is. They found him nearly dead on the side of the highway about an hour ago. When he woke up, the only thing he'd say was your name, Alpha Silas. Over and over." He lowered his voice. "He's a shifter, Si. And he smells like Salt Creek."

~

Sitting next to Jaime back inside the Monroe police station was a trip down memory lane Sam did *not* want to take.

"Is this weird for you?" Jaime asked, shifting uncomfortably.

"Super fucking weird," Sam said. Turning to look at him, he continued, "We don't have to stay if it's upsetting you. I'll wait with you outside."

Jaime shook his head. "No, I'm good. Thanks. I'd rather know what's going on firsthand, you know?"

Sam did know. It was the only reason he'd agreed to come; agreed to sit and wait while they brought out this Salt Creek wolf who wouldn't say anything except Silas' name.

The timing was suspicious as fuck, with Sam being back in Silas' orbit after the wreck last night, but he couldn't voice that out loud or he'd risk tipping someone off that he was more involved in Cain's business than he should be.

Yes, it was true he wasn't aware of anyone who wanted

him dead, but the fact that he owed an outstanding favor to a creep like Cain was probably something Jaime and Silas would have considered *relevant* in the grand scheme of things.

Sitting on Sam's other side, Silas could almost pass for relaxed if not for his incessant knee jiggling. Finn alternated between shooting looks that could kill at anyone who walked by, and giving Silas those sad puppy eyes.

Sam exhaled and knocked his shoulder into Silas'. "It'll be ok. We've gotten worse phone calls. Besides, we actually got to eat breakfast this time. Although it's probably best we hadn't before, in hindsight."

Silas laughed and leaned back, his shoulders relaxing. He casually rested his arm behind Sam along the bench.

Casually. It was all very casual.

If Silas could be casual, so could Sam.

Casually, he leaned into where Silas' arm rested. Because he was cold, dammit. That's all. And if he was sitting in this stupid police station he might as well at least be comfortable.

That rumbling noise Silas sometimes made started up.

Jaime coughed, and Finn put a hand over his mouth to cover a shit-eating grin.

"Are you sure you don't need to go to the bathroom?" Sam asked.

Silas cleared his throat, but the rumbling didn't stop. "Uh, no. That's not my stomach."

Well, that was vaguely alarming. "If that's not your stomach, then you should get that checked out. That's not normal."

Jaime and Finn snorted at the same time. "I told you they purr," Jaime whispered, schooling his features.

"I thought you said that was a sex thing," Sam replied.

"Jesus Christ." Finn stood up and paced away, the laughter he failed to choke down echoing through the waiting area.

Jaime blushed. "No. You assumed it was a sex thing. Which... kind of. But hey, every guy's different. Apparently, Silas just purrs more than Finn."

"Alright, can we please not compare purrs?" Silas begged, a pained look on his face.

"Please," Finn echoed, sitting back down next to Jaime.

"Hey, I didn't start this. You're the one purring in a public lobby," Sam grouched, folding his arms. And if he tucked a little bit further into Silas' *casual* arm while he did it, well, that was his business.

Silas purred louder.

Sheppard and the DA appeared from a back hallway. "Ok you four, he's cleaned up a bit and ready to see you. Just try not to startle him too much."

"Goody..." Sam mumbled.

Sam hated him immediately.

Like, *actually* hated him.

He hated his stupid heart-shaped face and button nose and the starry-eyed way he stared at Silas, like by sweeping in and saving the day, Silas had made everything in the world right again.

"Alpha Silas," the petite, dark-haired man breathed.

Gag me.

"Um, it's just Silas."

Sam hated the gentle way Silas spoke, being careful not to *startle* the doe-eyed pretty thing.

"Now that Silas is here," the DA said, "can you tell us your name? Or how you ended up out on the highway? Or where those scratches all over your arms came from?"

God, even his *don't worry, I'm your friend and here to help* schtick wasn't as irritating as the way the newcomer's eyes kept darting back to Silas.

"It's not safe here," he said, shaking his head back and forth frantically and pulling his sleeves down to cover the deep gashes along his forearms. "We're not in Alpha Silas' territory. He'll find us here. He'll find me here."

"Who will find you?" Sheppard asked. "Cain? Is he the one who did that to you?"

The wolf just shook his head again, trembling. "We're not safe until we're in the alpha's territory. Please."

Silas sighed, pinching the bridge of his nose. "Do you have somewhere you can go? Family or friends who aren't in Salt Creek?"

The newcomer shook his head again. "No one. They're all—I don't have anyone. And he'll find me, anyway. He'll find me outside of your territory. It's the only place that's safe."

Silas' brows pinched. "I don't know what you mean, I haven't established a territory."

"I think you have though, Si," Finn said quietly. "I think he means Silver Rapids."

The wolf nodded frantically. "Yes. He can't find me there. Asylum, Alpha. Please, I invoke asylum."

Something odd rippled through the wolves in the room, a shimmer of energy at this stranger's demand. Silas, Finn, and Sheppard all stood taller, like an invisible string had yanked them to attention.

Sam and Jaime shared a look of caution.

Another heavy sigh left Silas, and Sam knew what he was about to offer before he even spoke.

He'd just done the same thing for Sam, after all.

"You can come and stay in Finn's old room until you're up to talking or until you find somewhere else to go. How's that sound?" Silas said.

The stranger nodded his head quickly. "Thank you. Thank you, Alpha Silas."

Sam's chest felt tight, like fingers had reached in and were squeezing, twisting his heart around. *Of course,* Silas stepped in and offered the beautiful wolf a place to stay. *Of course,* he had to make everything better. It's just what he fucking did.

For everyone.

Sam had never been special. It'd never been about knowing him, or caring for him, or asking if the things in his life made him happy. It'd been about keeping a watchful eye on him. That's all. How he'd managed to forget that in less than twenty-four hours, Sam had no idea.

He wouldn't forget it again.

Silas would probably carry this sweet, innocent-looking thing into the house the same way he'd held Sam. He'd probably ask Sam to move to the guest room so Silas could care for the wolf in his room.

In *his* bed.

And this other man was already far more docile and willing to be saved. Did Silas like that? Would he have preferred Sam if he groveled and simpered and batted his eyelashes in that soft *help me* way?

Stop. Stop it.

It'd never mattered, anyway. Sam would be gone in a day or two, leaving the brown-eyed beauty and Silas alone to their own devices.

The thought tasted like bile in the back of his throat. He shouldn't have eaten all those pancakes.

The DA looked reluctant to agree to Silas' offer. He motioned for them all to step out of the room with him. "Give us just a minute, please," he said to the newcomer.

Sheppard, Finn, and Jaime all filed out ahead of Sam.

Silas put his arm out as if to guide him through the door together, but Sam sidestepped the gesture and walked ahead.

Once out in the deserted hallway, they all gathered close, speaking in hushed tones. "Detective Sutton isn't going to be happy when she hears we picked up a half-alive person on the side of the highway and let him go home with you," the DA said. "Not when we're looking for someone who fits that description concerning last night's wreck," he motioned to Sam.

Silas shuffled a step closer, but Sam lifted his chin and leaned away from the contact.

"He's a shifter, though," Jaime said. "If he was injured last night he'd be long healed, wouldn't he?"

"I'd think so, but honestly, I've never seen anything like that," Silas said. "Even if he was cut up right before you found him, he should be healing, and he's not."

Sheppard shook his head. "The entire situation is strange. Invoking asylum is archaic. Old magic. Most people wouldn't even know to do it."

"Magic?" Sam asked.

Sheppard nodded. "There's so much about pack dynamics that we just don't know anymore. Traditions that used to be a part of everyday life, or to aid in power struggles among pack territories. There are still some packs that maintain that knowledge, but they probably wouldn't be keen on sharing it."

"Even so, his injuries don't look like they came from a car wreck," Finn said. "They look like claw marks."

"So you think Cain did that? And then dumped him on the side of the road, half dead? Why?" The DA asked.

Silas shook his head and subtly pressed his arm into Sam. "I'm not sure, but I don't feel great about leaving him to fend for himself if he's fleeing Salt Creek. He can rest until he's up to talking or finds somewhere else to go."

Sheppard sighed. "Buck will be in town in a few days. I had planned to let him settle in first, but if you're comfortable keeping an eye on this guy until then, Buck can step in when he arrives."

Who the fuck was Buck?

Silas stared at Sheppard for a moment before the confusion on his face cleared. "Fuck, I forgot all about that."

"Who's Buck?" Finn asked, and Sam felt a little better that he wasn't the last one to find something out. Again.

"I completely forgot to tell you after I got back last night," Silas said before Sheppard cut in.

"I've hired someone new to join the team. He's on a trial run to start, but if he's a good fit, he'll be our primary lead on traveling jobs."

Finn reached over to take Jaime's hand. "And you trust him?" he asked.

Sheppard nodded. "With my life."

Finn gave him a hard look for a few seconds before his forehead smoothed out. "Alright," he said, nodding.

Not for the first time, and certainly not for the last, Sam was glad Jaime had fallen in love with a man who could protect him with claws and teeth, even if they hadn't started on the best of terms.

The DA still looked wary. "We don't have any proof he was involved in the wreck, and he hasn't done anything wrong, but I still think it's odd."

"What *do* you have to go on from last night?" Sam asked.

The DA sighed. "A couple of your neighbors saw someone run off into the trees immediately after the wreck. They all described them as a young, thin male. Possibly a teenager, with light blonde hair." Clearly, he wasn't as tight-lipped as Detective Sutton.

"That doesn't match, then. This guy's got dark hair, and he's not a teenager," Silas said.

DA Rivera shrugged. "Eye witness accounts aren't usually very reliable. There was also a cell phone left in the passenger seat," he said. "It's password protected, and the warrant took a bit to put together so we don't have an identity yet, but I don't expect it will be long. It'll be something better to go on."

Sam nodded. "Good. And my apartment? Is it still blocked off?"

The DA grimaced. "Yes, it's going to be a few more days on that, too. They're sorting through the debris to make sure we don't miss something that came from the car."

Great. Fucking *great*.

"And my car?" he asked through gritted teeth.

DA Rivera shook his head. "That whole section of the complex is closed off."

Sam hated feeling trapped, and he hated the idea of staying to watch Silas take care of someone else, but he wouldn't become even more of a burden to Jaime than he already was.

Until he had his car back, he had nowhere else to go.

They ushered the injured wolf—Riley, he'd said his name was—out of the police station. On their way to the truck, Silas hooked Sam by the elbow and pulled him aside.

"If you're not ok with this, tell me. We can figure something else out," he said, leaning close and speaking low.

We can figure something else out.

Meaning Sam could find somewhere else to go.

He pulled his arm from Silas' grip and turned his back so he wouldn't see how much that hurt, even though it shouldn't. "It doesn't matter. It's your house; I'll be gone in a few days anyway."

~

THE RIDE BACK TO SILAS' was possibly the most awkward half-hour Sam had ever endured.

After the police station, they'd stopped off at a store for Sam to pick up a few changes of clothes and some toiletries that Silas didn't already have. He'd thrown in a couple of things for Riley, too, since *apparently* he'd be staying at Silas' now, and Sam wasn't a complete asshole.

Sam had insisted he was fine to run in on his own, but Silas had followed anyway. Since they'd only be a few minutes, they'd locked Riley in the truck with the heater running and a window cracked.

It had taken every ounce of restraint Sam possessed not to ask if they should leave out a bowl of water, too.

Once back on the road and headed for Silver Rapids, he flat-out refused to engage in the small talk Silas tried to make with them both, and Riley only gave soft, one or two-word answers from where he sat curled up in the back seat. Otherwise, he'd just stared out the window until they pulled into Silas' driveway.

Sam was going to get a crick in his neck from how tense he'd been, pointedly *not* looking at Silas, who kept shooting worried glances his way the whole drive.

Maybe he was trying to figure out how to politely kick Sam out so he could be alone with Riley.

The thought made the backs of Sam's eyes burn.

He all but dove out of the truck when Silas came to a stop, putting as much distance between them as he could so he wouldn't witness Riley's grand entrance into Silas' home.

Had it only been last night that Silas carried Sam up the

stairs to bed? It felt like a lifetime ago, even if he could still feel where Silas' hands had been.

But because Sam was born only to suffer, he had to stand and wait for Silas to unlock the front door, with Riley walking up the porch steps close behind.

Silas pushed the door open over Sam's head, and he darted for the stairs so he could shut himself in the guest room before Silas had to ask him to move there.

"Riley, make yourself comfortable. We'll be down for lunch in a few minutes," Silas said. Then, the sound of his footsteps hurried upstairs after Sam.

Before he could open the door to the guest room, though, a large, calloused hand caught his arm and pulled him back into Silas' room. The *snick* of the door shutting echoed loud in the quiet.

"Would you *stop* running away from me? What is the matter? Everything was fine, and then, what? What happened? What did I do wrong?" Silas asked, his voice distant thunder and boulders.

Sam tilted his chin up in that haughty way he knew burrowed under Silas' skin. "I don't know what you're talking about. I'm fine."

Silas' eyes narrowed, and a clawed finger came up to point at him. "That. Don't do that. I thought we were past lying to each other."

Sam felt pinned beneath Silas' gaze, squirming around with nowhere to go. He always saw too fucking much.

"How do you know you can trust anything that guy says?" Sam whisper-shouted, the words spilling out. "This could all be some plot Cain orchestrated. *Send over the pretty wolf in distress who's begging for Alpha Silas' help; he won't be able to resist.* And you're falling right into it! You brought him *home!*"

Silas carded his fingers through his loose hair, tugging on the ends. "I don't trust him, but he invoked asylum. There are rules about that. I think. I'm just trying to..." he paused, shuffling a step closer to Sam, his eyes pleading for understanding. "My parents depended on others to make their escape safe. I won't turn away someone looking to do the same. But if you aren't comfortable with it, we can figure something else out."

Shame flared up the back of Sam's neck. Silas would always do the good thing, the right thing, and Sam clearly had no place in that.

Silas would find somewhere else for him to go.

"Fine," he choked out. "Give me a few days to get my car back, and I'll leave you two alone so you can give him your clothes or tuck him into your bed or light a bunch of candles and dance around the living room together, or whatever other kind of romantic shit you want to do. I don't care."

Silas' face knitted in confusion. "What the fuck are you talking about? *Romance?* Sammy, the man looks like one strong gust of wind would blow him away. We're just giving him a place to sleep until Buck can take over. That's all."

"Why bother sending him away? He's already safe right here with you, *Alpha Silas,*" Sam seethed.

He hated the words coming out of his mouth. Hated that he sounded like a jealous, insecure ex-lover, but he couldn't stop. "Hey, maybe he's that *mate* you've been looking for. Once I'm gone, you can—"

Sam didn't get to finish his sentence.

In one large stride, Silas had Sam pinned back against the wall, all the air in his lungs whooshing out from the hot press of Silas' torso against his.

"Let me make one thing very fucking clear, love," Silas growled into Sam's ear.

Goosebumps erupted along his arms, and he felt every place their bodies touched spark and flare with electricity. Silas' forearms were pressed up by Sam's face, bracketing him in and forcing his gaze up so he had nowhere to look except right into Silas' near-black eyes.

"The only reason Riley is here right now is because Sheppard doesn't have someone else to keep an eye on him. I won't have his death on my conscience if I could have done something to prevent it."

Sam's gaze drifted to Silas' lips as he spoke. If he leaned forward just slightly, his kiss would fall between Silas' pecs.

His cock chubbed up at that simmering image.

"So that's why you took me in, then? Because you're the hero alpha, and I was the lost little lamb you wouldn't have on your conscience? Well, I'm sorry if I've disappointed you, but Riley seems much more receptive to the hero schtick. Maybe you should try tucking him into your bed and see if he's better at being saved than I am."

Flames danced in Silas' gaze, and he leaned down so their foreheads were pressed together as he spoke, canines flashing. "You are no lamb, Sammy Lamont, and I don't ever want you to act like one for my sake. You're as much a wolf as I am. And I brought you into my home, into my bed, because it was the only option I could even remotely tolerate.

Because it was fucking inevitable. Because having you—just as you are, with all those sharp claws and biting words and secrets—right here with me has always been inevitable."

Silas brought a claw-tipped hand up to trace the delicate curve of Sam's ear, the gentleness in stark contrast to the intensity in his eyes.

"And he is *not* my mate."

Then Silas was gone, shutting the door behind him and stealing all the air in the room, leaving Sam bereft and hollow in his wake.

CHAPTER 7
SILAS

It took Buck four more days to arrive.

Sammy was subdued after their confrontation. Silas was afraid he'd scared him off again, that he'd revealed too much, too soon, but Sammy hadn't run. He hadn't tried to avoid Silas, either. He just seemed reflective; like he needed space after the whirlwind of the last couple of days.

When Silas had finally realized Sammy was upset because he was comparing himself to Riley, imagining that Silas would treat the Salt Creek shifter in the same way he'd cared for Sammy, he'd needed to clarify.

Hey, maybe he's that mate you've been looking for.

Almost.

With the lightning-bright feel of Sammy's body all pressed up against his own and those ten-thousand leagues deep green eyes staring up at him, Silas had *almost* corrected him.

He'd been a heartbeat away from proclaiming that he'd already put his mate in his bed where he belonged, and no one else would ever be welcome again.

But the sound of Sammy's rejection last spring still rang in his ears whenever he laid down to sleep, like a haunted lullaby.

I don't want you.

If Sammy knew he was Silas' mate and still turned away, he would never recover. So, he'd kept his mouth shut.

It was not lost on him that this was directly in contradiction to the advice he'd given Finn when he'd had his own crisis over revealing the truth about shifters and the mate bond to Jaime, but it'd been obvious to everyone except each other that they were already head over heels in love.

Plus, Jaime and Sammy were not the same person.

Still, Silas may have gone a little overboard in clarifying. His response had been reserved compared to how his wolf had wanted to demonstrate his feelings for Sammy, though.

He's ours. Ours.

Bring him firewood and toothbrushes and conditioner and give him our knot so he knows he's our mate.

Show Sammy he is our mate.

Show him.

Silas' preferred method started with shoving his tongue down Sammy's throat to stop the nonsense spewing out of his mouth, and ended... Well, actually, he and his wolf hadn't really disagreed in that regard.

But in the following days, he gave Sammy the space he needed, recognizing how overwhelming everything had been since the wreck.

Silas had insisted Sammy stay in his room for now, and the quietly pleased look on his face followed by a tentative "ok," was worth the backache from sleeping on the lumpy pile of laundry a hundred times over.

The guest room was also situated between his bedroom and Finn's old room, where Riley was staying. Silas wouldn't be able to sleep if he wasn't physically separating Sammy and the Salt Creek shifter, so it made sense anyway.

It makes the most sense to sleep in our bed with our mate, his wolf grumbled.

It's truly a joy to share a brain with you, Silas grumbled back.

Riley may appear non-threatening, but Silas would never take that chance, even if all the waif-like shifter had done since he'd arrived was sleep for nearly seventy-two hours straight.

Every time Silas went to drop off food and water, the previous plate would be licked clean, and all the water gulped down, but Riley would be fast asleep again. He was starting to look a little less like a tumbleweed blowing in the wind and more alive than he had when he'd first arrived, but the claw marks on his arms weren't healing.

"Some are scarring over, others still look fresh. I've never seen anything like it," Silas told Sheppard over the phone a couple of days later.

Sheppard sighed. "I'll make some calls. Shifter doctors are pretty rare, but maybe someone will know how to help."

"He's eating and sleeping fine, at least. Maybe that's all he needs?"

"Maybe," Sheppard said. "I'll let you know what I hear."

Other than waking up to eat every few hours, Riley hadn't done anything. He hadn't even explained why he'd left Salt Creek.

How Sammy could have misconstrued the situation as *romantic*, Silas would never understand.

Sometimes he forgot how much more information he was privy to with his nose and ears and heightened senses. It was obvious to him that Riley wasn't attracted to him, and he certainly had no interest in the shifter.

But Sammy couldn't glean that with his human sense of smell the way Silas could. And while it was clear that Riley wasn't interested in him, Silas couldn't help but notice that Sammy definitely was.

Especially when he wore one of his old sleeveless hoodies.

He may or may not have pulled a few more out of the depths of his closet to wear around the house just to get a rise out of him. Although that decision backfired spectacularly when Sammy seemingly caught on to Silas' game, and started playing one of his own.

After their first morning of taking turns using the shower in Silas' room, Sammy started wearing fewer and fewer clothes as he emerged from the steamy bathroom. The first time, he smirked as he walked past shirtless, with a pair of fitted grey joggers slung low on his hips.

The imprint of his cock hanging heavy would be burned on the backs of Silas' eyelids forever.

Newly enlightened, or maybe burdened, with the knowledge that Sammy was thick *everywhere*, Silas took himself in hand under the hot shower spray and painted the tile with stripes of cum.

He wished he'd come all over Sammy's soft belly instead, marking him. Then, he'd lap it up before following that happy trail all the way down to drink his orgasm from the thick cockhead he'd been teased with.

The next day, Sammy emerged with his hair still dripping wet, naked except for a towel wrapped around his hips.

Stunned into stillness, Silas tracked the beads of water as they slipped down the broad planes of his skin like a predator locked in on the hunt.

Peering over his shoulder, Sammy smirked again. "Sorry I took a little longer this time, hopefully there's enough hot water left."

Silas gulped and wordlessly strode into the bathroom, shutting the door behind him before he suggested they shower together from now on.

To conserve hot water, obviously.

He nearly had to chain himself to the sink when he scented what remained of Sammy's own shower jerk-off session still lingering in the steamy air.

What had he thought of to bring himself over the edge? Had his cum slipped down the same rivulets Silas' had the day before?

He hoped so.

Silas wanted to put his mouth where Sammy's had been on his morning coffee mug; he wanted to bury his face in his pillow after Sammy slept on it, and wrap himself in the blanket Sammy left on the sofa, feeling his lingering warmth against his skin.

He wanted to lick where their cum had sprayed all over the tile, so he knew what they tasted like together.

Fuck. Silas was going to rub himself raw like a horny teenager if he didn't stop thinking about it.

This push and pull between them had Silas' wolf clawing and scratching to be set free, to take what was his, but Silas' functional brain knew better.

The embers they stirred together were still tender, and Silas wouldn't chase Sammy off again by thinking with his dick, especially once he noticed the quiet little things happening around the house. Considering Riley was asleep most of the time, they could only be attributed to Sammy.

After grumbling all day about his second night sleeping on the lumpy pile of clean clothes in the guest room, a plight Silas was well aware he could remedy on his own, he went to bed that night only to find they had all been folded and stacked neatly on the dresser, waiting to be put away.

Silas would search for his water bottle to refill, only to find it'd already been topped up. When he stepped into the bathroom after yet another teasing display from Sammy, he found a fresh towel hung over the air vent, clean and warm and ready for him.

Just this morning, a steaming mug of coffee had been waiting for Silas on the kitchen counter, with the exact amount of creamer he preferred already poured.

He'd nearly wept.

Sammy looked after the people he cared for through his

actions, rather than flowery words. Silas had clocked this months ago after Sammy revealed that he'd stayed away from Jaime because of a stalker.

So he was awed by each small act of kindness, warmth spreading through him with every find that was altogether different and deeper than the burning desire he felt seeing Sammy in nothing but a towel.

Was this what it would feel like to be loved by Sammy, even just a little?

It gave Silas hope.

Hope that Sammy felt *something* for him, and maybe, someday, that little bit of something could turn into more.

Which made the day they picked up Sammy's car even more terrifying.

"That was the detective," Sammy said after he'd stepped away to take a phone call. They'd just finished takeout from Andi's for dinner on the third evening since he'd come to stay. "I can have my car back now. And go through my things."

Silas held his breath, unsure how to casually convey that the thought of existing in this house without Sammy made it hard to breathe.

"Cool," he settled on, before clearing his throat. "Want me to come along and help? We can go in the morning. I'll call and have Finn or Sheppard come over to keep an eye on Riley."

"Yeah. Yeah, I think that sounds good," Sammy replied, and Silas told himself not to read too much into the reluctant hesitation in Sammy's voice, like maybe he wasn't that keen on leaving either.

ALMOST NOTHING WAS SALVAGEABLE.

Between the damage from the initial crash and being exposed to the elements for four days, there was very little left of Sammy's worldly possessions that could be saved.

His bedroom had also been on the front side of the small apartment, just off the living room, and a portion of the exterior wall had collapsed, either from the initial crash or when they pulled the car out.

If Sammy's belongings hadn't ended up smashed under debris, they'd been damaged from freezing and thawing as daytime and nighttime temperatures fluctuated. He'd scrounged a few boxes worth of clothes, toiletries, and pictures and mementos that weren't broken—including the painting Jaime had done of Sam's beloved dog, Alfie.

Otherwise, he left everything to be demolished and thrown out.

Sammy had been on the phone with his insurance company and the apartment complex off and on for the past few days, trying to get his security deposit back and filing all the appropriate claims, but none of that happened quickly.

He'd rooted around for his laptop and recording equipment, only to find it all completely busted under what was left of the coffee table.

"The first time you called me, I let it go to voicemail," Sammy said, his voice muffled in the biting wind rushing through the open walls.

They'd had a little snow overnight, but nothing like what

had usually accumulated by this time of year. A big weather system was supposed to move in soon, though.

Silas peered up from where he was rummaging through the books that'd become damp and then froze in the recent snow. "The wreck hadn't happened yet?"

"No, not yet. I wasn't in the right headspace to talk to you. I left my phone in the kitchen," Sammy gestured behind Silas, away from the heart of the damage.

Silas stayed quiet, sensing Sammy needed to talk through those moments in his own time.

"But I kept hearing something scrounging around on my front doorstep," Sammy continued. "It was freaking me out. I thought it might be... I didn't know what it was. So I walked over to the living room window to peer out."

Silas sucked in a breath.

"And then you called me again."

Silas couldn't place the look on Sammy's face. Grief, maybe? Fear? Gratitude? He was composed, and then he wasn't; the swell of emotion was sudden, crumpling his features.

He began to sob, standing among the rubble that had been his home.

Silas strode over and wrapped him up in his arms, curling in as if he could engulf Sammy and shield him from the fear of what could've been.

"I walked back into the kitchen to answer it. If you hadn't called me again..." Sammy choked out, fingers bunching in Silas' hoodie. "I would've... I'd be..."

"Shh. Shh. It's alright, love. Let it out," Silas crooned, petting the back of Sammy's head while he continued to cry.

Fuck. He should've realized how emotional this would be. He'd only been focused on whether or not Sammy would actually come home with him after this, or whether he'd drive off and Silas would never see him again. He should've known this would be difficult.

"Why did you call me again? Why did you keep calling?" Sammy asked, the tears in his eyes reflecting like the rarest emeralds.

Careful, Silas.

He had no intention of lying to Sammy, he just wasn't sure he could explain the overwhelming sense of urgency and dread he'd had that night. It'd felt like if he didn't get to Sammy *right now*, nothing else would ever matter again.

"I... sensed something. I don't know if I can explain it. I just knew I needed to come see you. I started calling when I was on my way, and got worried when you didn't pick up."

There. That was all true. It wasn't even close to the entirety of what had happened that horrible night, but it was true.

Sammy's hands grasped Silas' hoodie tighter. "However you knew, thank you. And thank you for letting me stay with you. I don't think I said that before, and I should have."

Silas' chest began to rumble, and he held on tighter. "Oh Sammy, you don't have to thank me for that."

Sammy released his hold on Silas and stepped out of his arms, wiping at his eyes. "I'm sorry. I didn't realize everything would be so overwhelming. I guess I didn't think it would be like this," he said, gesturing to the destruction around them.

Silas guided him out of the rubble, grasping his waist so

that he wouldn't trip. "I didn't either. I wasn't paying attention to the damage when I got here, I was just focused on getting to you."

Sammy chuckled, some levity back in his voice after the emotional upheaval. "You broke through the wall. For a second I thought it was another car."

Silas chuffed. "Walls won't stop me, love."

All the walls you throw up around that heart of yours won't stop me. I'll wait forever for them to crumble.

Sammy stopped walking and looked up at him, almost like he'd heard Silas' thoughts. He opened his mouth to speak, and suddenly Silas was terribly afraid of what he was going to say next. They'd already gone through the wreckage, all that was left now was to get his car and drive it wherever Sammy wanted to go.

"So, can I—"

Before Sammy could finish his question, though, Silas' phone rang.

Sammy huffed. "I'm starting to take that personally. We can't go anywhere."

Silas wanted to kiss the adorably put-out look off his face. "It's probably just Finn telling us to be back for lunch soon because he's made something delicious."

It wasn't Finn's name on the caller ID though, and a smile was already stretching Silas' face when he hit the speaker button and answered, "Hey Mom, how are you?"

"When are you boys coming to see me?" she asked instead of a greeting.

Silas chuckled and threw his arm over Sammy's shoulders. "Today or tomorrow at the latest, I promise. We're just waiting on this new guy Sheppard hired to arrive, and then we'll be there."

"Good. I've made a massive trip to the grocery store, so tell Finn he can cook us all something wonderful with whatever he finds. And I got those cheddar brats you enjoy so much. And we'll have a roast for lunch on Sunday."

Silas groaned. "Fu—I mean, *heck* yes, that all sounds wonderful."

"Your father cleared out your old rooms so Finn and Jaime and you and your... Sammy will have somewhere to stay."

Shit.

Silas had been meaning to ask Sammy if he would come, he just hadn't found the right time. The words became all tangled and mushed up in his head whenever he thought of taking Sammy home to meet his parents, especially when he wasn't even sure if Sammy was going to stick around or leave again.

"Uhh..." Silas palmed the back of his neck and found Sammy's gaze peering up at him in question. "Thanks. Yeah, I'll talk to him. We're all looking forward to coming," he said, cringing.

"We're so excited to meet them both," she said, and the warmth in her voice made Silas want to melt into the ground.

"Can't wait. I've gotta go, but I'll text you guys the plan when we know what time we're leaving," he said.

"Alright. We love you. See you soon," she said, and the silence after Silas hung up was so loud you could hear a pin drop.

"So, that was your mom," Sammy said.

"Uhh, yeah." Silas cleared his throat. "She, uh, I mean Finn and I usually visit together you know, since he basically lived with us growing up. He's family. And he's bringing Jaime to meet them, and so I thought, I mean if you wanted to, since he's coming, I thought you could come along too?"

Fucking hell. Silas had flirted with and wooed plenty of pretty men before, and *that* was how he asked his goddamn mate to come home and meet his family? Really?

"Oh," Sammy said, the hurt on his face schooling into disinterest almost faster than Silas could clock it. "Just because they invited my brother doesn't mean I need to come, too. I'll be fine. I need to look for apartments in Anchorage anyway so that I know where I'm going once I get my security deposit back. I'll just do that when you all leave."

Fuck. Fuck, fuck, fuck.

Sammy tried to brush past Silas, but he grabbed his hand to stop him, squeezing. "I'm sorry. I didn't mean for it to come out that way. I would have asked you to come regardless of whether Jaime or Finn were too, Sammy. I just never found the right time," Silas said, his throat scratchy. "I want you to come. I want you to meet my family."

He felt a bit like he was flaying himself open to be poked and prodded, but somewhere along the way, Silas had realized that Sammy's front of callous indifference was just that—a front. He was never going to be the one who was vulnerable first, which meant if Silas ever wanted to break through his walls, he had to be the one to take that terrifying first step.

And he would take it, over and over, until Sammy realized there was nothing Silas wouldn't do for him.

So he was fully prepared for Sammy to pull away and brush him off again, but his heart nearly tripped and fell out of his chest when instead, Sammy halted.

"You want me to come?" he asked.

Silas' voice shook ever so slightly. "Yes. I want you to come."

Sammy toed at the ground, almost bashful. "And... they're expecting me? They want me there?"

See? Behind those claws, he was all fluff.

The rumbling began in his chest again. Silas threaded his fingers through Sammy's and tugged him closer. "They're so excited to meet you. *I'm* excited for them to meet you."

Sammy wasn't staring at his feet anymore, but he wasn't looking at Silas either. His gaze darted around like he was struggling to be casual just as much as Silas was.

Fucking hell, who were they trying to fool? They couldn't be *casual* while holding hands, interlocked-finger style.

"Ok. I mean, sure. I'll come," Sammy said, shrugging his shoulders.

Silas let out the breath he'd been holding. "Ok. Good. Great. I'll tell them."

He really shouldn't push his luck, but the words *I need to find an apartment in Anchorage* were still screaming their way through his mind. "And there's no rush to leave, Sammy. You can stay with me until you get your security deposit back. Or longer, if insurance drags their feet. I'd rather you stay, than move to Anchorage," Silas said.

Please don't move to Anchorage.

Sammy did look at him then, assessing. "Ok."

Silas felt his heart skip around again. He smiled, and even though the wreckage of Sammy's apartment was still behind them, the day looked a little brighter. "Ok."

And then Silas' phone rang again.

Sammy threw his hands up in the air, turning toward their parked vehicles. "I'm going to chuck your phone into the lake one of these days," he grumbled, and Silas loved this playfully grouchy version of him so much he'd probably let him.

Silas trailed Sammy back to the truck, chuckling, and answered without looking at who was calling.

"Hello?"

He halted at the rough sound of Sheppard's voice, decidedly *not* casual. "Silas. Buck is here, and Gabe stopped by for an update. You should come back right now and hear this."

"Fuck. Alright, we're leaving now."

They hung up, and just as Silas stepped into his truck, he caught movement out of the corner of his eye—a bright flash of light gold that looked out of place among the trees surrounding Sammy's apartment complex.

Quickly, he turned to look, catching the vague shape of a person disappearing into the forest.

Stay with mate.

Stay with mate.

Despite his wolf's warnings, Silas debated following the unseen observer. What if that was the driver who'd wrecked into Sammy's apartment? Or maybe the stalker Sammy assured wasn't a problem anymore?

Staywithmatestaywithmatestaywithmate.

Alright, I'll stay. I'll stay.

The internal panic that surged at the thought of leaving Sammy to track their observer eased with his assurances that he'd stay. Shaking it off, Silas shut his door and made sure Sammy was safely in his car before driving away, leading them back to Silver Rapids.

CHAPTER 8
SAM

I think I've been body snatched and I need your help. Call me, please.

Sam quickly tapped out a text to Lana before the last traffic light leaving Monroe turned green.

He needed to speak to someone who didn't purr, know when he was a little gassy after eating too many cheese quesadillas, or turn into a giant, hairy, *attractive* beast man, or else he might go mad.

Silas wanted Sam to meet his parents.

Even more alarming, Sam wanted to meet Silas' parents.

Worst of all, *Sam had agreed to meet Silas' parents.*

They hadn't even fucked yet. They hadn't even kissed yet.

They'd *held hands!*

What the hell was this? Four days ago, Sam was doing

everything he could to avoid Silas as much as possible, and now he was meeting his family?

Had he slipped into a *Seven Brides for Seven Brothers* alternate gay universe? Had Silas come to claim him as husband and husband, forever bound in flannel and chaste hand-holding?

Except without all the cooking and cleaning and misogyny. Sam would die before he dated a man who didn't know how to take care of himself.

You folded Silas' laundry two days ago. And the man thinks it's acceptable to use two-in-one shampoo and conditioner.

Sam had actually wept when he saw the bottle in the shower.

The fact that Silas' hair was somehow still soft and shiny and gorgeous while Sam's felt simultaneously dry and greasy after only four days of use was an even more upsetting mystery than where all the sleeves to those stupid hoodies had gone.

The lobotomy. Where was the lobotomy when he needed it most?

And some real fucking shampoo and conditioner, *please.*

Once again, they were flying down the highway back to Silver Rapids for the most recent emergency. Except this time, Sam followed behind Silas in his car.

He really should be more concerned about whatever heinous new detail was about to be unveiled, which would probably lead right back to Cain, but he was so out of his depth with Silas and desperately needed a second opinion.

He answered the phone call on the second ring. "Ok, I'm

going to explain a situation to you and I want you to help me figure out what's going on," Sam greeted in a rush.

"Well, I know you haven't been body-snatched. No one else would ever ask me to be their voice of reason," Lana replied.

Sam rolled his eyes even though she couldn't see. "So there's this guy."

He cringed at the screech ringing through the car speakers. "EEEEEEEEE!!! I knew it. I knew you were keeping something from me. Tell me everything. What's his name? Is he rich? How big is his dick? Oh God, is he one of those flannel-wearing mountain men? You live in Alaska, of course, he is. Is he this "Alpha" guy you've been having mind-blowing orgasms thinking about for the last few months? Because I've kept tabs on your recent uptick in subscribers, and you're good, but you're not *that* good. That shit is real."

Sam blushed. "Hey, I can fake moan with the best of them."

"That's not fake."

Sam shouldn't be surprised she'd caught on that he was using... *source material* when scripting his recent audios. In fact, most of them weren't even scripted at all. He'd just let himself imagine Silas in all the many ways he wanted, and hit record. His audios were doing well because of it— listeners loved to hear real pleasure.

Which wasn't always a reality for him.

Not because he didn't enjoy the process or was incapable of experiencing pleasure through performing, but because the minute he made orgasming a source of income, it inherently became *work*. And sometimes that meant performing even when he wasn't feeling all that hot and bothered.

In fact, depending on the scenario he was acting out he sometimes used several microphones to record vocals and ambient noise at once and then layered in the, well, *slick* sound effects afterward on a separate track. It created a more polished product, but meant he was focused on ensuring all the moving parts were in place rather than the thrill of the moment, so to speak.

Sam huffed. "Whatever. That's neither here nor there. So yes, I met this guy a few months back. We were... chatting."

Chatting wasn't the right descriptor for the intense chemistry and intimacy that had ignited between them last spring, but he didn't think he had words to explain that.

"And then there were... *circumstances* which made it so we kind of stopped seeing each other until a few days ago," he finished.

"What *circumstances* kept you apart? Did he ghost you? Ohhhh, did you ghost him?"

"Umm..."

Well, I borrowed money from his uncle, who's this evil crime boss wolf-man guy. Silas can turn into a wolf-man too, except it's actually hot when he does it? Anyway, I didn't know he was Silas' uncle at the time, but now I owe him a mysterious favor and Silas has been trying to stay away from him his whole life, so if I stick around I'll only be bringing more hardship with me. Which he definitely doesn't want. Oh, and I needed the money because I did something I deeply regret, and this shitty guy I met in a bar named Derek knows about it and blackmailed me over it for a year, and I gave him all my savings to keep quiet. Also, someone crashed a car into my apartment and then ran off and I'm not sure yet if it's related.

"...Nothing all that interesting, but it was a me thing. Sort of. I knew someone who used to know him, and thought it would be best if we stayed away from each other so it wouldn't become awkward."

"You knew someone who used to know him? Like an ex?"

Sam guffawed. "God no. His uncle."

"So you were dating his uncle? Yes, I can see why that would be awkward."

"NO! I wasn't *dating* his uncle."

"Ok. So you knew his uncle, and that's a problem because...?"

Sam sighed. "Look, I can't explain any more than that. It was just best that I stayed away. But now I'm living with him, and he's asked me to meet his family, and I don't know what to do about that. Tell me what to do about that! What is this?"

"Wait. Wait, wait, wait. You're living together? I thought you said you weren't talking. What changed?"

Sam cringed. "We aren't *living together*, living together. Something happened to my apartment, and I needed somewhere to stay. And he showed up and helped me, and was wearing this stupid sleeveless hoodie that made him so unfairly hot, and I had to take an anxiety pill, so I was all sleepy and I may have said his wood was really big and then he tucked me into his warm bed."

A few beats of silence passed before Lana spoke. "There's so much to unpack there, it's going to take me a fucking minute. But... Do you want to stay with him? Do you like being around him?"

Sam squirmed in his seat. "Yes. Yes, I do, but I've kept away for a reason. How can I just let all that go?"

Lana sighed. "Well, obviously I don't understand all of the circumstances, and I know you haven't ever been one for serious relationships before. But maybe that was less of a you thing and more that you just hadn't found the right guy. If you've been hung up on him for months, even after staying away, I don't think you should ignore that."

"Even if he deserves better than all the baggage I bring to the table?"

"If he's been hung up on you this whole time too, which it sounds like he has, considering he showed up for you when you needed someone, invited you to live with him, *and* wants you to meet his family, then it doesn't seem fair to make that decision for him. Whatever's going on, it should be something you both have a choice in."

Sammy felt tears spring to his eyes again. Fucking hell, when did he become such a crier? "But... What if he *does* decide it's too much? What if he decides he doesn't want me? That I'm not worth it?"

What if he finds his mate and leaves, and I'm left with a gaping hole where my heart used to be?

Lana's voice softened. "Oh, Sam. You've got it bad, don't you?"

He wiped at his face. "I should go. We're almost back to his place."

"Hey, you're *so* worth it. You love deeper than anyone I know, and the very small number of people you give it to are lucky to have you. Plus, you're fucking hilarious, and you look great with a beard. If he doesn't want you, that's his loss. If he makes you feel like a burden then fuck him. Actually no, fuck his uncle, like really. In retaliation."

Yikes.

Sam let out a wet laugh. "Thank you. Really."

"Whatever you decide, let me know you're good, ok? And don't think I've forgotten about everything else you said. You still owe me an explanation on your apartment and these mysterious circumstances and how big his wood is."

Sam smiled. "I will. You take care, too."

He hung up the phone just as they turned down Silas' street. When the little craftsman house came into view, Sam was struck with the feeling of *home;* more so than he'd ever felt in his apartment.

Maybe that had more to do with the man who lived there.

Sam had thought a lot about Silas over the last few days —and not just those scorching looks they exchanged every time he stepped out of the shower.

How do those sleeveless hoodies feel now, hmm?

He thought about the way Silas put the last handful of shredded cheese in Sam's quesadilla, even though it was obvious he wanted more for himself, too.

He thought about the way Silas kept adding blankets he'd find to Sam's bed so he'd stay warm throughout the night, and about the way it wasn't really Sam's bed at all—

but Silas had given it up anyway because he wanted Sam to be comfortable.

Sam thought about the quiet joy he'd seen on Silas' face every time Sam had done something nice for him, and the fear in Silas' eyes when it was time for Sam to pick up his car —like the world would have fallen apart if he'd decided to leave.

Most of all, though, Sam thought about the words Silas had growled in his ear the first day they'd brought Riley to stay, and how much fire had been in his gaze with their bodies all pressed up against each other.

I brought you into my home, into my bed, because it was the only option I could even remotely tolerate. Because it was fucking inevitable. Because having you—just as you are, with all those sharp claws and biting words and secrets—right here with me has always been inevitable.

He'd fought himself so hard to stay away all these months, and for what? To be sad and alone?

The audio he'd posted a few days ago was doing well; he'd probably be able to pay Cain in full within the month. Then all of that could disappear. Sam would bury it, alongside what he'd done to wind up in Cain's clutches in the first place, and he could move on.

He could choose to be happy. He could choose to be with Silas—if Silas wanted him back.

Maybe he wasn't looking for a mate. Surely, it was rare to find one? Silas may never meet his at all. Maybe he'd be happy with what they could build together, even without that connection.

They'd never know unless they tried.

As he pulled into the driveway behind Silas' truck, Sam surfaced from his swirling thoughts at the sight of Finn, Jaime, Sheppard, DA Rivera, Riley, and someone he didn't know all standing in the front yard.

Oh goody, sleeping beauty woke up.

So maybe Sam hadn't *quite* gotten over that yet. Whatever. He'd never claimed to be the bigger person.

The second he opened his car door their loud chatter surged in, and Sam realized something was wrong. Sheppard was standing between Finn and Jaime and Riley and the stranger, with both arms outstretched, like he'd just pulled apart two brawling drunks at a bar.

Sam saw the stranger, who had to be Buck, pulling Riley away from Finn and Jaime. Had Finn attacked him?

Except it wasn't Finn that Sheppard had a hand up to stop—it was Jaime. Finn also had a firm hold on Jaime's shoulder and was pulling him away the same way Buck was with Riley.

And Jaime was... yelling? "You stay the fuck away from my brother! Get him out of here!"

"What the hell is going on?" Silas asked, striding over to the tense group and positioning himself in front of Sam in that same irritating way he had when they'd confronted Cain last spring. He was even larger in his partial shift.

Sam elbowed his way around him, just as he had then. "I can't see anything when you do that, you Oaf."

"So, uh, Riley's awake," Finn said, gesturing vaguely at where he was standing a little ways away. "And Buck is here."

Sam's eyebrows shot up as he took in the deer shifter for the first time.

How the hell are all of these people so damn attractive?

Buck was ripped.

Like, the guy had muscles on top of muscles. He wasn't much taller than the average man, but he had shoulders for days, and tattoos covered his arms and neck. His dark hair was cropped close, and his gaze darted between all of them like someone who'd gone up against worst odds before, and still come out on top.

Jaime's face was red in anger, and he pointed his finger at Riley when he said, "That cell phone was his. He was there—he was in that fucking car!"

PLEASE DON'T PET THE MOOSE

SAM

FIVE MONTHS, TWENTY-THREE DAYS, AND THIRTEEN HOURS AGO

"Hey Sammy, wait up!"

With his face still stinging, Sam ignored the call and pushed his way out the front door he'd stormed into just minutes earlier, rushing down the path to his car.

What the fuck had he been thinking, barging into someone else's house that way?

The text he'd received from Cain an hour ago flashed through his mind.

UNKNOWN NUMBER

I see Finn from Private Security Solutions is looking after your brother well. Maybe a little too well?

156

Along with the message, he'd sent a photo of Jaime and one of the bodyguards—the blonde one—standing close to each other outside his cabin. Standing *very* close to each other.

It'd scared the shit out of him—that's what he'd been thinking. He didn't want Cain or any of his criminal connections anywhere near Jaime. How had he known who his private security was, anyway? Were they somehow connected?

Surely not.

Sam had nearly run to his car after he'd read the message, tracking down the Silver Rapids address he was given for where Jaime was staying after the attack at his cabin the night before.

He'd planned to pull Jaime out, make sure they hadn't hurt him, and then... Well, he hadn't figured the rest out yet. He'd just needed to get Jaime away from anyone associated with Cain, and if that meant firing the security detail he'd bargained with the Devil himself to afford, so be it.

Upon bursting into the stranger's house and rushing up the stairs to find Jaime wrapped up in bed with that same bodyguard, he may have overreacted.

When he'd watched that security guard turn into a giant, hairy beast-man, he'd *definitely* overreacted.

Or had he? It wasn't his finest moment, for sure—but come on. The dude looked like he'd come straight from eating grandma, and not in a fun way.

"Wait, please don't go," the other wolfman-werewolf-*whatever* said, still following Sam to his car. The big one. Silas, maybe?

Sam ignored him again.

The sight of Jaime's hurt and angry face moments after hitting him still smarted, even more than the burn on his cheek, and he didn't need the bigger hairy oaf to rub salt in the wound.

Really, could this day get any worse?

Just as he made it to his car and almost had the door open, a giant hand reached out and held it shut. "Wow, you're fast for such a little guy," the big one said, panting over Sam's shoulder.

Apparently, it can.

Sam turned and glared; that look usually made the people who tried to sell him things from those little huts in the mall go away. "Excuse me?"

The giant oaf rubbed the back of his neck. "Fuck—I mean, shit—fuck! I mean, I'm sorry. I wasn't trying to offend. I like it. Your height, that is. Compact. Nice. You should see me try to get on a plane, it's an absolute nightmare. I have to buy two tickets. I bet you don't have that problem. That's good," he said before he snapped his mouth shut like he just realized he'd been rambling like a complete idiot.

It was on the tip of Sam's tongue to tell him just that. Anyone else, and he would have without a thought. But the way this giant man stood there, looking down at him with that *I'm sorry, please like me* look on his face with one fang peeking out, struck something deep in Sam's chest, and gave him an overwhelming sense of déjà vu.

Sam shook off the strange feeling. This day was already weird enough. "Great, glad you approve. Wanna know my shoe size, too? Do you have a ruler handy for a little one-to-one comparison?"

The giant oaf's face split into a smirk, and again, Sam had the strangest sense that he'd seen it before. "I came out here to apologize for how all that went down in there, but I'll never pass up an opportunity to get to know you better," he said with a wink.

A fucking *wink*.

Now it was Sam's turn to feel on the back foot, heat creeping up the nape of his neck. "That's not—I wasn't—stop that. I'm leaving. Move." He shoved at Giant Oaf's arm, who didn't even give Sam the courtesy of pretending like he had to brace against the move.

Continuing to hold the car door shut, he only stepped closer to Sam. "Look, that was a shit show. Can we start over? I'm Silas." He stuck out his other hand.

Again, any other time, Sam would have sneered and walked away. Instead, he found himself reaching for it without a thought; like they were always meant to meet right there, with Sam's cheek burning and that stupid, crooked grin on Silas' face.

Something hot and bright zipped up Sam's arm when Silas' warm grip dwarfed his own.

Maybe it was time for a health physical.

He cleared his throat, soothed by the contact. "I'm Sam. And I was just as much of an idiot in there," he said, pointing back toward the house. "It's clear Jaime doesn't want me here, so I'll leave. As long as he's safe and happy, I won't tell anyone about... whatever you are. You don't need to threaten me. I don't really give a fuck, to be honest. Now please, can I get in my car?"

Giant Oaf frowned. "I would never threaten you, and I don't blame you for how you reacted. I'm sorry you had to find out that way. How's your face feeling? You should ice it. And put a coat on, it's chilly."

"You're sorry I found out my brother is fucking his security guard, or that you all can turn into giant, radioactive beavers? And my face is fine; I'll wear a coat if I want to," Sam huffed, crossing his arms. The wind was a bit nippy, but he'd be damned if he admitted that now.

"It's not—wait, *beavers?* You think we look like beavers? Really? Have you ever taken an outdoor safety course? Wildlife identification? You do know the moose aren't friendly, right? They kill way more people than bears or wolves do. They're the big, four-legged horse-looking things. Some of them have antlers. They're grumpy assholes, and they'll trample you in a heartbeat," Giant Oaf said in a rush. As he was speaking, he raised his arms and mimed a set of moose antlers on his head, turning this way and that.

Sam gaped.

Who was this guy? What the fuck did he care if Sam had taken an outdoor safety course? How had this conversation even started?

"Yes, I know not to *pet* the fucking moose. And my inability to identify you when you're a giant, hairy creature has nothing to do with my *wildlife identification skills*, and everything to do with the fact that you need a bath and a goddamn hairbrush. Now, for the last time, move!"

The giant oaf finally stepped back when Sam pushed, releasing his hold on the door.

Sam peered around, the loud echo of his outburst reminding him they were speaking outside, where anyone could hear. Where *Cain* could hear.

Clearly, he was having Jaime followed; was he doing the same for Sam?

"Are you alright?" Giant Oaf asked, glancing around like Sam had just done, as if to look for the threat he couldn't see. "Is there someone following you? Or someone you're expecting to meet here?"

Sam tensed. Big Moose Man saw too much, and he hated it. "No. Right, I'm leaving. You know, in case any moose are lurking nearby," he said, unable to help the snark.

Finally able to open the car door, he stepped inside and hit the lock button the second it closed behind him.

The giant oaf was staring at Sam with a strange intensity; it tugged on him, demanding his attention. Almost as if he couldn't help it, he rolled down his window instead of immediately driving off the way he'd planned. "I still expect regular reports on my brother's well-being."

Silas leaned down, resting an elbow on the window. His eyes were gentle. "They're not just fucking, you know. Finn will protect Jaime with his life. I promise you don't have to worry about his safety when Finn is around. I'll swing by your place tomorrow morning to update you, how's that sound?"

Sam stiffened at the soft understanding in his voice. Too much. He saw too much. "A phone call would be sufficient."

Silas smirked. "But how will I know if you're staying away from the moose that way?"

Sam rolled his eyes. "You're ridiculous," he mumbled, putting the car in reverse and backing out before he found another reason to stay and talk to the giant man with familiar, knowing eyes.

He felt the weight of that stare the whole way back to his apartment, well after Silas had disappeared from Sam's rearview mirror. And even though he knew he was driving in the right direction, he couldn't shake the feeling that he was going the wrong way.

CHAPTER 9
SILAS

"That cell phone was his! He was there—he was in that fucking car!" Jaime said, voice filled with rage.

Silas saw red.

Like he'd flipped frequencies on a radio, multiple voices surged into his head, all shouting over each other.

Get him out!

Jaime is hurt!

Danger. He's dangerous.

Calm down.

Protect pack.

Protect mate.

Calm down!

Make him leave!

The onslaught of thoughts was overwhelming—some were his own, and some belonged to Finn and Sheppard, their proximity and stress bringing them together the same way they had the night Sam's apartment had been destroyed. All of it culminated in a roar in Silas' mind, building until it blocked out all other thought.

His pack was hurt. His pack needed him. They needed an alpha.

He turned to where Buck held Riley by the arm. "*Explain*," he commanded in that deep, rolling thunder voice he rarely used.

Riley trembled and dropped to his knees, baring the nape of his neck to Silas. "Please, Alpha. I didn't—" Riley choked, his words clogging in his throat. "*Please*, don't hurt me. I'll leave. I'll go, and you'll never see me again."

Silas recoiled.

The cacophony of pack thoughts switched off like he'd yanked out an old television cord, memories of so many kneeling before his uncle flashing through his mind in their wake—memories of his *father*, bloody and defeated while Silas and his mother could only watch, terrified and helpless.

Silas vividly recalled the way his uncle's yellow eyes had glowed as he'd relished their subordination.

Nausea roiled his stomach.

"Get up," he croaked. "Get up, get up. I'm not going to hurt you. I'm not him, fucking hell." Sweat pricked along the back of his neck. "Or stay there. Do whatever you want, I don't care—just—"

A warm hand pressed on Silas' back. Strong and comforting.

Sammy.

"No one's going to hurt you, Riley. Please stand up and explain," he said. It was probably the first time Silas had heard Sammy directly address the Salt Creek shifter. His voice was confident and sure, but not unkind.

Matematematemate.

Jaime continued staring daggers at Riley. Silas noticed he was cradling his hand and remembered from their jumble of shared thoughts that someone had said Jaime was hurt.

Well, that scene was familiar.

"Keep that one back," Buck said as he helped Riley stand, pointing at Jaime. "He's scrappy, and he's going to hurt himself."

Finn growled, and Silas' hackles raised at the noise; it was nothing like the good-natured grumbling that was typical between the three of them.

"Watch it, Bambi," Finn said.

"Alright, enough posturing," Sheppard said. "We've already given the neighbors enough to gossip about for weeks. You—" he pointed at Jaime, "go find some ice for your hand. You two—" he pointed to Buck and Riley, "come sit inside with me and Gabe so we can have this conversation with a bit more privacy. And you—" he pointed at Finn, "stop growling at the new guy."

Finn and Jaime went into the house in search of an ice pack while the others trailed behind at a respectful distance.

The whole time, Sammy's hand remained warm on Silas' back. It grounded him more than he'd like to admit.

"Are we sure it's a good idea for them to be in the house together? Won't they break the furniture?" Sam asked.

Silas gave a shaky laugh. "That couch is over ten years old—it's seen things. Let them break it. I should get a new one anyway."

Sammy moved until he stood in front of him and leaned his shoulder into Silas' chest. "*Please,* nothing with built-in cup holders," he said, making an exaggerated shuddering motion. "And get something with a little color. Greige is depressing."

Silas grinned.

His voice had stopped shaking, and gravity shifted a little bit more with each of Sammy's attempts to pull him back from those awful memories. "You'll just have to come shopping with me, then, so I don't choose whatever *greige* is," he said.

"Alright," Sammy said, easy as breathing, and Silas wondered if his eyes had ever been so warm.

Silas pulled him a little bit further into his arms. "I hate using that voice," he whispered. "He used to do that to my parents a lot. And me, too. Just because he could. It scares me."

Sammy was quiet for a moment before reaching up to tuck a strand of hair that had escaped Silas' half-back bun behind his wolfy ear. "It's not the same," he said. "You're not the same as him. Riley's clearly dealing with some shit; his reaction had little to do with you and everything to do with what he already knows."

Silas nodded, looking down at his feet. "But what if I do get that way? What if it turns out I'm just as bad as him; what if the power goes to my head? I don't ever want to be like that."

"Look at me," Sammy whispered. His eyes were so tender; usually hidden behind thick walls, the vulnerability shined so brightly now. "That will never happen. There are far too many people who love you and would never let you become that. *You* would never let that happen, either; there's too much goodness inside you."

Silas felt each word crackle and pop like blazing embers in his heart. "Sammy..." he said, slowly leaning down into his space.

Silas was torn between explaining that none of it mattered anyway unless Sammy was one of those who loved him, and kissing him silly. Their lips were so close Silas felt each of his shaky exhales against his own, their eyes darting back and forth between each other.

"Sammy..." he repeated, the hunger burning in Sammy's gaze deciding for him.

Silas took hold of his chin, tipping his face up while Sammy's eyes fluttered shut, and he wished he could frame this moment, a keepsake to tuck next to his heart forever.

He closed the scant distance between them, the ghost of Sammy's lips against his own magnetic before muffled shouts rang out from inside the house.

They startled at the noise.

Sammy quickly stepped back, clearing his throat. "We should go see what this is all about before Finn and Buck start growling at each other again."

Silas blew out a breath, raking a hand through his hair. "Sure. Yeah, let's do that."

He followed Sammy inside, unable to think with the scent of toasted marshmallows coating his throat.

There are far too many people who love you.

Would Sammy be one of them someday?

~

Despite the accusations made against him, Silas felt a little bad for Riley right now.

They'd moved the kitchen chairs into the living room so everyone would have somewhere to sit. Silas stood just to the side of Sammy's chair, where he and Jaime sat across from Riley, staring with varying levels of dislike.

He shuddered at the thought of being on the receiving end of their combined ire.

Not that Riley had anything to worry about with the way Buck hovered next to him like a guard dog. Or a guard deer? Whichever it was, he was taking his first assignment seriously, and Silas respected him for that.

Finn was still grumbling, though.

"Alright, Riley, let's talk about the cell phone," DA Rivera said. "You thought far enough ahead to buy a burner and pay with cash, but we have you on surveillance in the shop. We know you were the one who purchased it."

Silas wondered how much of that would actually hold up in court and why the DA was here and not the detective, but in the end, he didn't give a fuck about the legal side of things.

He shifted closer to where Sammy sat.

Riley stared at the DA for a long moment, face unreadable. "Yes, it's mine."

DA Rivera looked a bit taken aback that he hadn't tried to deny it. "Ok. So how did it end up in the car that ran through Sam's apartment?"

Again, Riley thought for a moment before coolly replying, "Because I did it. I was driving the car."

A low growl started in Silas' chest.

He shifted even closer to Sammy, putting a hand on the back of his chair. It took effort, but his voice was his own when he asked, "And then you came begging for my help? You asked for asylum and took shelter in *our* home after you tried to kill him?"

Silas wasn't entirely sure what Riley had done by invoking the old magic. It'd just felt wrong to leave him to fend for himself—like the shifter was his to look after. He'd been too preoccupied with Sammy to pay further attention to the feeling, aside from giving Riley a place to rest until he was healed enough to leave.

Obviously, things had changed.

Riley scooted closer to Buck on the sofa. He was still shaking a little, but at least he remained upright, face stony. "I didn't realize—I'm sorry. It wasn't personal. I didn't want to hurt him. I didn't want to hurt you," he finished, turning to Sammy.

"What the fuck does that mean, you didn't want to hurt him?" Jaime snarled.

Maybe Silas could read Sammy better now, but he swore he sat a little straighter, his chest puffed up at being the one Jaime defended with all of his brash boldness this time around.

And with his fist, if the ice pack cradled to his knuckles was anything to go by.

"We were just meant to keep track of Alpha Silas," Riley said, sighing. "I couldn't get into Silver Rapids because of the territory line, but there was a scent trail leading away from town. It was strong enough to be recent, so I followed. It led me right to your apartment."

Fuck. Fuck, fuck, fuck.

How stupid was he? Not only had Silas been away for an entire week, but he'd left a goddamn yellow brick road right to Sammy's front door.

And he still had no idea what territory boundary Riley was talking about. Silas, Finn, and Sheppard each took turns running patrols around the area, but they hadn't intentionally marked anything.

After a shaky breath, Riley continued. "I reported what I found, and that was supposed to be it. That's all that was meant to happen, and then he'd let us go."

Sammy narrowed his eyes.

"I don't know what changed. He ordered me to bring you to him," Riley said, looking at Sammy. "I didn't want to hurt you—I tried to fight the order and turn the car around, but it was too strong. Before I knew it, I'd lost control and crashed into your apartment. I thought you were dead, so I ran off."

Riley looked strung out and exhausted. Buck passed him a glass of water and whispered something low.

Torn, Silas squeezed Sammy's shoulder.

On the one hand, he very much understood how powerless Riley would've felt in those moments and how limited his autonomy would've been when Cain wielded his awful commands. On the other, he wanted to throw the man out and order him to stay as far away from Sammy as possible—forever.

Whether that was back with Cain or in prison, again, he didn't give a fuck.

"What do you mean you tried to fight the order?" Sammy asked. He didn't sound angry, more… confused. "Did you get out of the car?"

Riley swallowed. "No. No, I didn't. I drove down the road, tried to stop, and lost control of the vehicle."

When he finished, the crackle of the fireplace filled Silas' head, alongside the memory of how terrified Sammy had been when he couldn't shift the cabinet off his legs.

Silas felt the immense weight of every decision they'd all made leading up to that moment.

So many alternate, unthinkable scenarios ran through his mind; what if Finn hadn't called him to ask if he was ok? What if he hadn't called Sammy right after? What if he'd stopped calling after he didn't pick up the first time? What if he'd returned to Silver Rapids a day or even a few hours later?

A shudder passed through him.

"What happened to you after that?" Sammy asked quietly.

Riley squirmed. "I reported back to Alpha Cain."

"So he was the one who did that to you?" Sheppard asked, gesturing at the still-healing wounds all over Riley's arms. They looked so wrong to Silas—so out of place on a shifter.

Riley nodded. "I told him you were dead. That I'd accidentally killed you. Afterwards… he threw me out of the pack. I don't remember much after that; I don't know how I ended up where they found me. But when I woke up, I knew coming here and pleading asylum was the only thing I could do."

"What did you mean when you said he'd let you go if you did what he asked?" Sheppard asked.

Riley sighed. "Alpha Cain promised he'd let me out of the pack. That he knew someone I could work for in Anchorage, and he'd find me a job and a place to live," Riley answered.

"And you believed him?" Jaime asked, incredulous.

"Yes," Riley said, his hard expression finally slipping. "Yes, I did."

To Silas' surprise, Sammy took a deep breath and said, "I believe you. I believe you didn't want to hurt anyone and that you felt like you had to because you wanted out."

Riley blinked. His face was still stony, but he sounded genuine when he said, "I'm sorry."

Buck reached over and gently patted Riley's back in stilted movements like he wasn't familiar with comforting gestures. Addressing the group, he asked, "What about his arms? Why aren't they healing?"

"We don't know," Sheppard said. "But we've contacted a shifter doctor who lives off-grid way up in northwest Alaska. He travels from pack to pack in the most remote regions when he's needed. We've sent him a message asking for help but haven't heard back yet. Apparently, he sometimes goes weeks, even months, without communicating with anyone."

"Sounds like a dream," Finn deadpanned.

"You'd miss fresh produce way too much to live off-grid," Jaime teased back, smiling.

"We'll let you know as soon as we hear from him," Sheppard said to Riley before turning to DA Rivera and Silas. "Can I speak with you both?" he asked, motioning for them to step outside.

Squeezing Sammy's shoulder again, Silas followed them into the backyard. The wind muffled their voices enough for a bit of privacy.

"I don't particularly want him around, but I'm not sure I'm comfortable with him being criminally charged for something he was, at minimum, coerced into," Sheppard said.

Silas' wolf grumbled. "As long as he's nowhere near Sammy, I don't care what happens to him."

DA Rivera gave Sheppard a pleading look. "Cam, I'm a fucking District Attorney, not a detective. I shouldn't even be here. Technically, this conversation never even happened. But once Sutton gets ahold of those surveillance tapes for the phone purchase—which she will—we could potentially be looking at attempted manslaughter, if not attempted murder."

"That's bullshit," a deep voice called out. Silas turned to see Buck striding over. "You have no idea what it feels like to fight one of those orders. It wasn't his choice."

Sheppard clapped the deer shifter on the shoulder as he joined them.

DA Rivera looked exhausted. "Look, I know there are bigger things at play here. I can see about offering him some sort of deal once he's charged, but I can't keep covering this shit up. I can't just let him go. I'll lose my job, and then someone else will come sniffing around asking questions. Is it really worth that?"

Guilt washed over Sheppard's face. "I'm not asking you

to let him go. Just... wait? At least until we hear if the doctor is coming. Maybe something from the investigation into Cain will shake out in the meantime."

The DA shot Sheppard a look like he'd said more than he should've.

"How is that coming along? Will you be able to arrest him soon?" Silas asked. What a relief that would be for them all.

Rivera pinched the bridge of his nose. "I really can't share any more than I already have, I'm sorry. And I can stall on arresting Riley for a few days, tops. But he can't be left alone. If he runs, I'll have hell to pay."

"I'll watch him. I'll make sure he doesn't run," Buck said.

Sheppard nodded. "I have the safe house here in Silver Rapids already set up. He'll be close, and we'll keep an eye on him."

The DA gave Sheppard a look Silas couldn't read. "I'm trusting you with this, Cam."

Silas cleared his throat in the quiet that followed. "We planned to go visit my parents for a couple of days, but if you need Finn and me around to help out, we can stay."

"No," Sheppard said. "Go. You two deserve it. Tell Meera and Cal hello for me. Buck and I can handle Riley."

Silas nodded and walked with Buck back into the house, leaving Sheppard and Rivera to work through whatever *that* was.

"Sorry about the tense start," Silas said. "Things aren't usually like this."

Buck grunted. "A lot going on. I get it."

Right. Another yapper.

Just as they reentered the living room, Jaime turned to Riley and asked, "If you wanted to go, if you didn't want to hurt anyone, why stay? Couldn't you just leave?"

Silas knew the answer to that question all too well.

Riley's face hardened. "And go where? The rest of my family left the pack years ago and have been no contact ever since. I don't blame them for that, but you have no idea what it's like to leave the only thing you've ever known. I don't have a driver's license or proof of an education. Where would I get a job? Where would we live? Where would I buy clothes to go to an interview, and how would I get there? Running is hard, but so is everything else after that. I stayed because he promised me a job, connections, and somewhere warm to sleep at night."

Sammy gave Riley that same assessing look from earlier.

Jaime grimaced. "I am sorry you were in that position. I'll never forget the terror I felt staring at a car hanging out of my brother's apartment, but I am sorry for what you've gone through, and I wish you better days."

Silas turned away. He didn't have words for Riley just yet. He deeply understood the man's circumstances but couldn't bring himself to forgive so easily.

Finn and Jaime left shortly after to pack up their things, agreeing to meet just out of town to make the drive to Silas' parents.

Buck and Riley left for the safe house with Sheppard, and DA Rivera headed back to Monroe, presumably to hide what they'd discovered from Detective Sutton for a little while longer.

He and Sammy ate a quick lunch, and also packed their bags, making sure the house was secure for the few days they'd be away.

There was an ebb and flow to their movements when they were close; never quite touching, but drifting near enough to to feel each other's warmth before pulling away.

Like the moon drawing in the tide.

It felt so domestic and wonderful to do mundane things with Sammy at his side. Silas' heart ached in want.

"How far away do your parents live?" Sammy asked as they loaded their bags.

"Not very far, but it's an elevation climb up the mountain," he answered.

"Do you visit often?"

Silas smiled, stepping up into the truck and buckling himself in while Sammy did the same in the passenger seat. "As often as I can. It's so peaceful up there; we don't have to hide our shifts at all. It's a much-needed relief most of the time."

Sammy cocked his head to the side. "Do people not hike in the area?"

"No," Silas chuckled. "The list of people who know how to find my parents' house is very, very short. You can't find it at all, actually, unless you've been there before."

"You mean, it's not on Google Maps or something?"

Silas grinned. Sammy had loved the tidbits he'd shared about the history of Silver Rapids and the paranormals who settled it. He would probably love this, too. "You remember when I told you Andi's a house witch?"

Sammy nodded.

"Well," Silas continued, putting the truck in reverse and backing out, "my parents knew a house witch back when we left the pack. She helped us out a lot with the home we moved into, adding all kinds of layers of protective magic on the structure itself and us. So, you can't find it unless you've already been there."

"You mean, like, magic? *Magic* magic?"

"Yep, magic, magic," Silas repeated, turning onto the highway. "So we hardly ever bring anyone new over. Finn was the first, then Sheppard. My parents have invited a couple of family friends over throughout the years. And now, you and Jaime."

Sammy spluttered. "But... but, why?"

"Well, they didn't want to leave Alaska but were afraid my uncle would track them down, so—"

"No," Sammy interrupted. "Why bring *me*? Jaime, I understand, he's Finn's mate. But why me?"

Silas held his breath. Was this the moment? Could he really blurt out that Sammy was his mate while driving down the highway on their way to see his parents?

Well, you're kinda my mate, too, so I figured, why not?

God, it sounded even worse than when he'd fumbled through inviting him in the first place.

Silas hadn't even shared the way he felt yet. He wouldn't want Sammy to think he only pursued him because of the bond when it was so much more than that.

Besides, he wasn't even sure if Sammy returned his feelings beyond physical attraction.

I don't want you.

And... things were going well. Sammy was opening up more and more; if they hadn't been distracted earlier today, they absolutely would've kissed. Silas had to adjust in his seat just thinking about it.

Maybe if he waited while they continued to build the foundation of their relationship together, brick by brick, Sammy would be more inclined to be with Silas when he eventually shared the truth of the bond.

Silas reached out and took Sammy's hand. "Because I want you there, and I trust you. It's also the safest place I know, and I think we'll all breathe a little easier knowing we can relax for a few days, yeah?"

Sammy squeezed his hand. "Yeah," he said, his voice rough. "Ok."

CHAPTER 10
SAM

Because I want you there, and I trust you.

I trust you.

I trust you.

Sam was in so deep he couldn't see the surface anymore.

He had to leave. It was the only option.

He had to go far, far away because Silas was beautifully whole, warm, and kind, and wouldn't deserve any of the turmoil Sam inevitably brought upon him.

He wouldn't *want* any of what Sam brought upon him.

He wouldn't want Sam.

He had to go because every day he spent with Silas, every minute in his presence, every casual-not-so-casual brush of their hands felt like Sam's heart was leaking out through the cracks in his chest. He was certain if their almost-kiss had gone any further, he would've burst at the seams, spilling every bit of his wretched soul out on the pavement for Silas to see.

Sam had to go because Silas trusted him and wanted him to meet his family so much he'd shared a precious secret. He'd been trusted with a secret before, and he'd fucked that up so thoroughly he'd given nearly everything to try and fix it.

Jaime had deserved better. Silas deserved better, too.

Sam was so caught up in his distraught thoughts he nearly missed it—the *magic* magic Silas spoke of.

While the drive from Silver Rapids had been short, they'd climbed in elevation quite significantly, and the dirt road they traveled down was thick with snow. The path was barely accessible, even with snow tires, and when they reached a point where they couldn't go any further, they came to a stop.

Finn and Jaime pulled in close behind.

"Come on, love," Silas said, grinning. He motioned for Sam to exit the truck with him, his face already flushed from the cold and excitement. "I can't wait to show you this."

By the time Sam was unbuckled and opened the door, Silas was already on his side of the truck, reaching up to help him down. Wrapping his gloved hand around Sam's, Silas pulled him across the road and pointed out toward the nearby mountain range.

"There," he said, "on the far side of the valley near the bend in the river, at the base of those foothills. Can you see it?"

Sam squinted, scanning for something that disrupted the tree-studded plain. "I can't see anything," he said, shaking his head.

Silas stepped up behind him, wrapping an arm around

his middle while he pressed his body flush to Sam's. He pointed his other arm out over Sam's shoulder, guiding his gaze just slightly to the left.

Right in his ear, Silas said, "It's just there, past where those trees have fallen in the river. Look for the smoke coming from the chimney."

Sam couldn't focus on anything except the hard press of Silas all along his back. The way his arm banded around his middle had all sorts of visions of Silas holding him like this while he drove his cock up into Sam from behind.

Would Silas fuck slow and deep, drawing out every bit of pleasure he possibly could before finally tipping Sam over the edge? Or would he drive into him hard and fast, over and over, until Sam was screaming?

He felt like he was burning up from the contact, even through all the layers Silas had bundled them into before they'd left the house. But... yes. Blinking the haze of lust away, Sam caught sight of the barest hint of smoke curling toward the sky.

Following it down, he squinted at the slight shimmer in the air, almost like sunlight reflecting off water. "I think I see something..."

"That's where they live," Silas whispered in his ear.

Sam gasped as the shimmer dissipated, revealing the most picturesque cottage he'd ever seen. "Wow," he said, breathless. "They live all the way out there? That's amazing! How do we get there? How did you get to school every day? How do they get groceries? Where does their water come from?"

Silas laughed and released him, stepping back. Sam felt

suddenly naked in the cold without the warm weight of him. "When the snow's gone, there's a small road you can take up to the house, but otherwise, we shift and run, which only takes a few minutes. If we can't run in the winter, we take the snowmobiles."

Sam looked back over his shoulder to see Finn had already parked one truck inside a shed he'd missed when they first arrived and was pulling the second in next to it. Two snowmobiles were sitting next to the shed, and Silas began helping Jaime stack their bags onto the covered sled attached to the back of one.

"They shop for groceries in bulk and haul it all to the house using the sleds, and they get water from a private well. They heat the house with gas, plus the wood-burning stoves."

Sam was fascinated by all of it. He'd love to live this way someday; completely removed from people, alone out in the middle of the Alaskan taiga where he and Silas could—

Stop.

His chest ached in wanting that fantasy to be a reality. Thankfully, the loud whir of the engines rumbling to life cut off Sam's thoughts. He helped gather the last of their things from the truck, securing everything onto the sled.

"The terrain getting down into the valley is a bit rough," Silas hollered over the sound of the engines. "Wear this."

He passed Sam a helmet with a snow visor.

"You aren't wearing one," Sam accused.

Silas grinned, flashing his teeth. "Thinking of shoving me off? Can't get rid of me that easily, love. Super healing noggin, remember?"

Sam was glad for the excuse to push the helmet down over his head so the visor covered his blush. He fumbled with the strap for a few seconds before Silas stepped close, reaching to take over.

"Let me." Silas' fingers gently brushed the delicately soft skin on the underside of Sam's chin, lightly scratching against the stubble of his beard as he made sure not to pinch when he secured the clasp.

"There," he said, hooking his palm around Sam's nape. His hand was so large his thumb brushed along the front of Sam's throat, over his Adam's apple. "All secure."

Sam had never once considered it a turn-on to have his neck held during sex, had never trusted anyone with his safety that much, and certainly had never allowed anyone close enough for that level of intimacy. And yet, Silas had once again broken through Sam's defenses—not with force, but with gentle strength.

At that moment, Sam would do anything Silas asked of him with his giant hand wrapped around his throat and those eyes that peered down like he was something to be treasured and protected.

"We should go, we'll lose the light," Finn shouted from where he and Jaime were mounted on their snowmobile, ready to depart.

Silas released him, and again, Sam felt unfinished without his touch. Throwing a leg over their snowmobile, Silas held his hand out to help Sam on behind him. "Hold on to me," he shouted.

Sam locked his arms around Silas' middle as they took off, happy for the excuse to cling on to his sturdy warmth while Sam scrambled to sort through his overwhelmingly big feelings.

It was both wonderfully profound and horrible to realize that holding on to Silas was all he'd ever really needed.

~

"You made it!" a stunningly beautiful woman exclaimed, jogging down the porch steps and throwing her arms around Silas the second he dismounted the snowmobile.

As Sam pulled off his helmet, Silas lifted her in one of those giant bear hugs that were as much a part of him as the furry ears on top of his head. "Of course we made it. Sorry we were a few days delayed," Silas rumbled.

A man who Sam supposed was Silas' father pulled Finn into a similarly all-encompassing hug.

Sam blinked. He'd never seen Finn look so soft, like a boy who just needed to be held. Was that the Finn Jaime had fallen for so completely?

The beautiful dark-haired woman with Silas' deep brown eyes stepped over to him. "Hello Sam, I'm Meera," she said, smiling. Her canines were proportionally smaller than Silas and Finn's, and her dark, furry ears were more pointed—not quite as blunt as Silas'.

But what Sam noticed most, what stole his breath like a fast-pitched baseball right to the chest, was the way her eyes crinkled in the corners when she smiled, exactly the way his mom had.

The wave of familiarity-driven grief was sudden and entirely unexpected. "Nice to meet you." He coughed to clear the crack in his voice, blinking rapidly. "Thank you for having me, or I mean, inviting me. I've never seen a house more beautiful than this," he said lamely, his words tripping over each other while he collected himself.

It was true, though; the house really was the most gorgeous he'd ever seen.

Tucked into a small clearing, the cottage looked like it'd been pulled straight from a fairytale. A steeply pitched roof sat atop two stories, with warm light pouring out of each pitched dormer window and smoke curling from the large center chimney. It looked cozy and welcoming, beckoning him inside from the cold.

Silas wrapped an arm around his waist, and Sam had never been more grateful for the shared strength.

"We're so glad you came, we've been looking forward to meeting you. Silas talks about you all the time," she said, beaming again.

"Uh yeah, hey, come meet my dad," Silas said, palming the back of his neck. Sam had the overwhelming urge to kiss the blush off his cheeks.

They turned in time to see Silas' dad release Jaime from the bear hug he'd wrapped him in, and Sam thought he'd start crying all over again.

Fucking hell, he'd expected Silas' family to be *nice*, but he hadn't been prepared for just how wretchedly wonderful they were.

"Call me Cal. It's so nice to finally meet you, I feel like we know all about you already from Silas," his dad said, squeezing Sam in his large embrace.

Yeah, definitely where Silas learned to hug.

"It's nice to meet you too," Sam responded when he could take a breath.

"Alright," Meera said, clapping once. "Everyone inside, out of the cold. Boots off, don't you dare track snow onto my rug."

They unloaded the sled and filed in through the front door one by one, removing their snow-covered outer layers and boots as requested.

Piling their bags by the stairs, Meera herded everyone in, where she had coffee and tea waiting. The kitchen was open to the living area, and while it was small with all of them crowded in close, it wasn't cramped.

"Welcome to the family, Jaime," Meera said, her eyes glistening as she held up her coffee. "We were overjoyed to hear Finn had found you. It's lovely to have another son to embarrass and ply with too much hot chocolate. And we're so glad we finally get the chance to know you better, Sam," she finished, softly smiling at him.

Everyone held their cups up and drank to Meera's loving toast.

Sam couldn't make eye contact with any of them afterward, moving through the motions of sipping his coffee as they all settled into the living room to relax before dinner.

His skin lit up when Silas leaned in close, brushing their arms together. "Are you alright?" he asked, voice low.

"Yeah," Sam said, still not looking at him. "I think I just need to use the bathroom."

Silas' brows knit together, but he pointed Sam down a hallway off the living room.

Excusing himself, Sam hurried down the quiet corridor

and shut himself in the small half-bathroom, immediately feeling better with the door between him and the over-whelming feelings that waited on the other side.

He heaved a deep breath.

Cal and Meera were warm, wonderful people. They clearly loved Silas and Finn very much, and in a gesture Sam still hadn't fully wrapped his mind around, they'd opened their home to him and Jaime. They'd welcomed Jaime into their family as another *son*.

So why am I about to cry?

Because that may be the first motherly love Jaime could remember, and that was so fucking unfair, Sam wanted to scream.

He remembered *their* mom. He remembered how much she'd loved them, how she'd looked at them like they were her whole world. She'd been theirs, and she was taken slowly and cruelly, the way cancer stole so many.

He wanted to cry because no matter how hard he'd tried to be enough for Jaime after she died, he never had been. Because that burden should've never been his in the first place.

Because their father should've been stronger. Should've loved them more. Should've loved them enough to climb out of his own grief and help them through theirs.

Sam wanted to cry because Silas' dad would have been strong enough. He'd risked everything to save his family from Cain's power and influence. Sam's dad hadn't even been strong enough to remember to go to the goddamn grocery store.

And that's why none of this can be yours.

Yes. That.

That was why Sam wanted to cry, most of all.

Because Jaime had found a lovely, wonderful family, and Sam couldn't be a part of it. Because Silas was a part of that family, and he was everything Sam could've ever wanted, but he couldn't keep him.

Sam's mother hadn't been strong enough to live, and his father hadn't been strong enough to love them. Sam had already failed Jaime once; this time, he had to be strong enough to walk away, or else he'd be just another failure. He had to leave, or else he'd drag the one thing every single lovely person in the other room had been running from right back into their lives.

Sam could never bring Cain down on this family.

Splashing water on his face, he took several deep breaths and prepared to do what he'd done so many times—lie.

He'd tell Silas he was sick and needed to leave. He'd ask to be brought back to the house, where he'd gather his things and drive to Anchorage. He'd find a cheap motel to stay in until he had his security deposit back, and then he'd do his best to close up the jagged rift left in his heart from knowing Silas, from feeling what could have been with him and his family.

Sam took one last look in the mirror, his hollow gaze staring back. "At least I look terrible enough to pull this off."

He turned and opened the door, ready to shore up his walls all over again, only to come face-to-face—or really, face-to-chest—with Silas' dad.

CHAPTER II
SAM

"Oh, um, sorry," Sam said, caught off guard. Cal smiled, and it was so similar to Silas' he could barely look.

His hair was greying, but Sam could tell it had been brown, several shades lighter than Silas', and he wore it in the same shoulder-length half-back style tucked around his wolfy ears. "I thought you might be in here panicking over that toast, so I came to talk you out of whatever drastic plan of escape you've conjured up."

Sam gaped. "Well— I—"

Clapping him on the shoulder, Cal pulled him from the doorway and directed him further down the hall. "Come on. Let's go talk somewhere that's not the bathroom."

Cal directed Sam into a small room at the end of the corridor. Bookshelves lined the wall, with pictures of Silas, Finn, Cal, and Meera scattered throughout. There were two soft-looking armchairs sitting on either side of a large window overlooking the valley they had come through on the way here, and a wood-burning stove squatted in the corner, crackling merrily.

Sam had never seen a cozier room.

"Please, sit. I'd offer you something to drink, but I'd have to go to the kitchen to get it, and I don't want us to be interrupted," Cal said.

Sam stiffly perched on one of the chairs while Cal took the other across from him.

He couldn't decide if he was about to be scolded or interrogated. Was it possible that Cal knew of his involvement with Cain? Would he ask him to leave immediately? To never darken his son's doorstep again?

Sam's trepidation must have been written all over his face because Cal chuckled and said, "Whatever you're thinking, the answer is no. I'm not about to do that."

Sam huffed. "How do you know what I'm thinking?"

Cal smirked. "A lifetime of reading people. Now, I apologize if Meera's toast upset you. She didn't mean to make it sound like we were taking Jaime from you. Only that we're expanding your family if that's something you want."

"How did you know the toast upset me?"

Cal's whiskey-brown eyes glinted, the warm twin to Cain's cold, yellow gaze. "Again, a lifetime of reading people. And I'd imagine you'd be fairly defensive over your brother since you were the one who provided for the both of you from a very young age."

Sam blinked. "How do you know that?"

He smiled softly. "Silas has told us a great deal about you, Sammy. Or is it Sam?"

Sam shifted in his seat. He opened his mouth to say that Sam was fine, but for some reason, what came out instead was, "I don't mind Sammy, from him. Or you."

"Alright then, Sammy. So, how were you planning to leave? You don't have the convenience of four furry legs to carry you across the valley, and I'm confident Silas can outpace a snowmobile."

Sam studied Cal's face. He appeared genuinely curious; Sam didn't think he was trying to prove a point or having fun at his expense. "I was going to lie and say I didn't feel well and ask him to take me back to Silver Rapids," Sam said.

He felt better and worse for having told the truth.

Cal nodded, somber. "Would you have been there when Silas returned?"

Sam looked away, out through the trees where the river lazily cut across the landscape. "No," he whispered.

"Hmm. Has Silas told you the story of how his mother and I fell in love?"

He turned back to Cal. "No, he hasn't."

A sly grin stretched Cal's face. "She was betrothed to another man before we met."

Sam tucked one socked foot up underneath him, settling further into the chair that was as comfortable as it looked. "She was in love with someone else?" he asked, scandalized.

Sadness clouded Cal's face. "No, it was not a love match. The betrothal had been organized by their parents. She's the daughter of an alpha of a prominent pack in the southwest, and her betrothed was the alpha son of an alpha here in Alaska. She fully intended to honor the betrothal, even after we met and realized we were mates."

"What happened?" Sam asked, his voice hushed.

Now, it was Cal who looked out through the forest surrounding their home. "It became impossible to hide the bond any longer." Looking back at Sam, he continued, "The scent becomes apparent as the bond grows. Usually, when a couple is aware of it or accepts it. She explained the situation to her intended, and he agreed to release her from their betrothal, on one condition."

Dread filled Sam's stomach. He had a terrible feeling he already knew the outcome of this story. "It was Cain, wasn't it? She was meant to marry him," he whispered, afraid that speaking his name in this secret, sacred place would allow him in.

Cal nodded. "My mate was betrothed to my brother."

"How did you stand it?"

"Every day was a choice between begging her to run away with me so we could be together and hiding my feelings so she wasn't in danger of his ire. I chose her safety until it wasn't a choice anymore," he said, and Sam felt flayed open beneath his gaze.

"What was the bargain?" Sam asked.

Cal looked at his hands before meeting Sam's eyes once again. "That if our union bore an alpha child, Cain would have a say in their upbringing. He would train them to be his successor. Not many are born in a pack's generation. If we had an alpha child before Cain, the odds of any of his children also being an alpha were very low. It was a bargain based on risk and chance."

"And... Cain won?" Sam asked quietly.

Cal smiled and shook his head. "No. He didn't. Silas has always been our greatest joy."

Silence stretched between them.

Sam couldn't help but feel like Silas' dad was telling him all of this to make him even more convinced he needed to go so that Cain was no longer in their lives.

"So, you did the right thing, then, by leaving. You protected them."

"Yes, eventually. But that wasn't an easy decision to make and it wasn't one I would've made on my own. It took me six years, Sammy," Cal whispered into the quiet.

"But you did. You were strong for them."

A single tear tracked down Cal's face. "Do you know how many times I let Cain make my child cry in those six years? How many times I held my terrified mate, telling her that leaving was a death sentence? When really, I was just scared to try. Scared to trust. Scared to fail."

Sammy was confused. "You're here now, though. You're free of him. That's what matters."

Cal smiled. "What matters is that we chose each other. We trusted each other—despite him. *That's* how we got away. Men like Cain will do everything in their power to maintain control—and that includes isolating those they know would be their greatest challengers. We're stronger together."

Sam blinked. What was he saying? "I don't understand."

"Wolves aren't meant to be alone. We're meant to lean on each other. Don't isolate yourself, Sammy," Cal said before standing. "Now, come on, we should get back out there. I can hear Silas worrying from here."

Sam stood with him. "Wait..." he began, barely able to speak the words aloud. "What if it'd been in your power to keep the ones you love from being hurt? Would you have done it, even if it meant losing them?"

Cal turned back toward him, so much understanding on his face Sam could barely stand it. "Cain's greatest weapon and biggest deceit was convincing me that his actions were dependent on my obedience. But we can't stop other people from hurting those we love by expecting them to hold up their end of some terrible bargain. They only lose power when we trust the ones we love, and choose each other."

Cal opened the door for Sam, and they walked together toward the bustling sounds coming from the living room, his head still buzzing.

"How did you know I was thinking of leaving?" Sam asked.

Cal looked down at him and winked. "I'm not sure what you're talking about. But if I did, I'd say—a lifetime of reading people."

Sam narrowed his eyes, ready to call him out on his weird mystical bullshit, but suddenly Silas was in front of them, eyes full of worry.

"Are you ok?" Silas asked, looking back and forth between Sam and his dad.

Hot shame crept up the back of Sam's neck at seeing the concern on his face. How could he have contemplated leaving without saying goodbye?

"I'm ok," he said. "Really," he added with a smile, reaching out to squeeze Silas' hand.

His face relaxed, and they followed his dad back out to

the living room. "Good," Silas said. "Now, help me decide what Finn should make for dinner."

THE REST of the evening flew by.

Cal and Meera handed the kitchen over to Finn, who rubbed his hands together before diving in to prepare cilantro-lime rice bowls with pico de Gallo, seared steak, and homemade tortillas.

Jaime was on vegetable chopping duty, and Sam couldn't help but laugh every time Finn had to fend Silas off from sneaking *"just a bite"* of steak.

"You have to let the meat rest, you animal," Finn grouched.

"That's what he said," Silas shot back, turning to wiggle his eyebrows at Sam.

By the time dinner was done, his face hurt from how much he'd laughed at their antics, and his belly was full to bursting.

"Fantastic as always, Finn," Cal said.

"Yes, thank you for making dinner. Now, you all shoo while we clean up," Meera said.

"Are you sure?" Jaime asked.

"Yes, go find a movie to watch. We won't be long," Cal said, gathering the plates to start the wash.

Back in the living room, Finn and Jaime collapsed onto one side of the large sectional, and Silas settled on the other, stretching his legs out.

Sam hovered for a second, unsure if he should sit next to

Silas or in one of the open armchairs, but Silas reached out and pulled him down next to him, tucking Sam under his arm.

"This ok?" he asked quietly.

Sam angled his head up to look at him. "Yeah," he replied, nodding. He wiggled in a little closer, because he wanted to.

Silas began purring.

"*Ugh*, dude, you've gotta shut that off in mixed company," Finn grumbled, chucking a throw pillow at Silas.

Silas dodged the pillow and whipped the remote through the air right back at him, hitting Finn square in the chest. "Find us a movie, you grouch."

"If you two break another remote, it's coming out of your Christmas presents this year," Cal said from the kitchen.

"Sorry," Silas and Finn replied in unison.

Sam looked at Jaime, and they grinned at each other. He couldn't remember ever feeling happier than this.

When Cal and Meera joined them, sitting in the armchairs angled in front of the sofa sectional, Finn put on a movie about a guy who was left at the bottom of the ocean without oxygen for a concerning amount of time and somehow still survived.

Jaime pulled out his e-reader five minutes in.

Exhaustion weighed Sam down after the emotional turmoil of the day, but at the same time, he was buzzing from the casual intimacy of sitting next to Silas on the couch. Tucked right up next to him, Sam could only pretend to watch the movie, when really he couldn't focus on anything except the places their bodies touched.

He felt like a naughty teenager as they sat just behind Silas' parents, playing footsie. Or shinsie? Sam's legs were nowhere near as long as Silas', so he ended up draping one across Silas' and giving up.

He forgot how to breathe when Silas began drawing slow circles on the nape of his neck with his thumb; an arm stretched behind Sam along the cushion.

So Sam returned the favor, covertly tracing patterns on Silas' thigh, just high enough to make him shift in his seat, angling a knee up.

Sam smirked. He'd never done *this* before, whatever this slow form of torture was.

By the time the movie ended, Jaime was sound asleep, curled up next to Finn. They all whispered goodnight, and Sam shouldered his bag and followed Silas up the stairs.

A hush fell over the house, and the sound of the wind blowing through the chimney and rattling the wooden exterior made him feel strangely vulnerable.

Perhaps it was silly of him, but he'd expected Silas to point at whichever room he'd be staying in and bid him goodnight. He wasn't prepared for Silas to whisper, "Mom and Dad's room is down the hall, and Finn and Jaime's is across from ours. We're staying in my old room."

Silas' door creaked when he opened it, and he flicked on a warm lamp before setting their stuff down and shutting them inside.

Sam stood in the center of Silas' childhood bedroom, taking in the sparsely filled bookcases that sat on either side of the window, a few knickknacks still scattered along the shelves. Glow-in-the-dark stars were haphazardly stuck along the ceiling like there had been a lot more at one time, but some had fallen in the years since they were placed there.

His eyes fell to the full bed pushed up against the wall, covered in a pillowy, dark blue duvet and a soft quilt draped over the footboard, and then to the twin blow-up mattress made up on the floor.

Right. Well, this would be an uncomfortable night's sleep.

He dropped his bag to the side and turned to look at Silas. "Since you'd probably pop that mattress by just looking at it, I'll take the floor."

"No, you won't," Silas rumbled, and he stepped up to Sam, took his face between both hands, and kissed him.

CHAPTER 12
SILAS

Kissing Sammy was like coming home.

Silas held his face between his hands, marveling that his beard was softer than he'd imagined and his lips were just as soft as he'd dreamed they'd be.

Silas kissed Sammy like it was the most important thing he'd ever done, because it was.

When he finally surfaced to take a breath, he refused to open his eyes, afraid of the rejection he might witness, so he continued to cradle Sammy's precious face, squeezing his eyes shut while he bumped their foreheads together.

Their chests pressed against each other with every heaving breath, and Sammy had the power to kill him right there with just one word.

"Silas?" Sammy said, breathless.

He was still afraid to look, so Silas nuzzled his cheek into Sammy's hair, luxuriating in the sweet, hot scent. "Hmm?"

"Kiss me again?"

Silas slammed his mouth back onto Sammy's, the force of it tipping him backward, so they stumbled together until Silas caught him.

Sammy moaned into the kiss, low and husky. Silas licked and sucked at his bottom lip until he opened, and with the first dive into his hot mouth, embers sparked and crackled in Silas' vision.

"Come here," he growled, frantically grabbing at Sammy anywhere he could reach, pulling him as close as possible. Hooking his hands under Sammy's thighs, Silas hauled him up into his arms, and Sammy wrapped his legs around Silas' waist, locking them together.

"Yes, more. More," Sammy moaned, pressing open-mouthed kisses down along his throat and grinding his hardening cock between them, which happened to be the perfect angle for Silas to rut up along Sammy's ass through their joggers.

"*Fuck*," Silas cursed, finding Sammy's lips with his own again.

He quickly shifted back into his fully human form and walked them backward toward the bed, tripping and stumbling when he shuffled around the stupid plastic monstrosity on the floor.

A loud *pop* and *wheeeeeeze* echoed through the room when he accidentally stepped on the blowup mattress, deflating like a balloon beneath his foot.

Sammy chuckled into his mouth. "You did that on purpose," he crooned, fingers tangling and lightly pulling in Silas' hair.

Silas smiled, catching Sammy's bottom lip in his extended canines in return, tugging ever so gently.

He hadn't popped it intentionally, but he wouldn't mourn the loss.

"Good riddance," he murmured before twisting so he took the brunt of the impact when they tumbled onto his bed.

The box springs squeaked as Silas adjusted so Sammy was spread out on top.

Sammy began laughing again and pressed his face into Silas' chest to muffle the sound. "Oh my God," he whispered. "Your whole fucking family has super hearing. I won't be able to look them in the eye in the morning."

Silas pulled Sammy's face back up to his and coaxed his lips open, leading him into a messy tongue-first kiss that melted his brain and lit them on fire.

Sammy moaned again, deeper this time, and ground his hips down at just the right angle to draw out a helpless sound from Silas, one he was certain he'd never made before.

"The house... muffles the noise," he panted through sloppy kisses.

"Huh?" Sammy said, busy dancing his fingers along the line of exposed skin where Silas' hoodie had ridden up.

"The house," Silas responded, sucking in a breath when Sammy dropped down to put his mouth where his fingers had just been, tonguing wet kisses along Silas' hairy stomach. He ran his claws through Sammy's hair, tugging gently.

He nearly came in his pants at the sight of Sammy's lust-filled gaze peering up at him from where he perched on his thighs. Silas shifted one inward so that the meat of it pressed on the prominent tent in Sammy's pants.

He'd remember the punched-out whine Sammy made at the friction for the rest of his days.

What had they been talking about? Oh, yeah. "The house muffles the noise in our rooms. I'm not sure how it works, but I'd have to try very hard to hear what's happening on the other side of that door. And I'd rather listen to you," Silas finished with a growl, digging his thigh in as Sammy rocked his hips down onto it in rhythmic thrusts. "I'd rather hear you moan and rut that fat cock of yours until you spill in your fucking pants. You want to, don't you, love? You want to ride my thigh until you come all over yourself?"

Sammy's gaze drifted down to the massive tent in Silas' own pants. "So...*hnnf*, so they can't hear us?" he asked.

Silas tugged lightly on the ends of Sammy's hair again. "No, and they aren't trying to."

The only warning Silas had was a flash of green as Sammy peeked up at him. "Good," he said before he dropped down again and opened his mouth around Silas' still-clothed cock.

He swallowed a shout. The walls may muffle sound, but he wasn't keen on testing their limits.

The sight of Sammy nuzzling and kissing along his covered shaft, combined with the humid heat through the layers of clothes separating them, was like nothing he'd ever felt before. No one had ever wanted him enough, been desperate enough for his cock to worship him that way.

Sammy hooked his fingers into the waistband of Silas'

joggers, teasing the soft skin. He peered up and raised an eyebrow in question.

"Yeah," Silas said, nodding his head vigorously and jerking his hips up in anticipation.

Instead of taking his cock out right away, though, the little brat wrapped his mouth around the tip through his pants and exhaled.

"Fuck," Silas said hoarsely.

Then, faster than he could blink, Sammy yanked his waistband down and pulled him out, jerked him once, fully exposing the thick, broad crown from its foreskin sheath, and sucked the head into his mouth in the same move he'd just done through his clothes.

"*Fuck!*" Silas whisper-shouted again, desperately trying to keep his voice down. He cupped the back of Sammy's head with one hand and tangled his fingers in the collar of his shirt with the other, holding him steady.

Sammy kept a firm grip on his shaft, jerking him while he lapped and sucked at what Silas slowly fed into his mouth. Pulling off with a *pop*, Sammy dragged his tongue from base to tip, teasing at the little v-shape just under the head.

"Shit," Sammy said, catching his breath and staring at Silas' cock. "I mean, I could feel you were big, but fucking hell."

Before Silas could respond, Sammy wrapped his lips around him again, swallowed as much as he could down his throat, and moaned.

Silas felt the noise travel through his cock, sparking up the base of his spine like a live wire. He really was in danger of coming now, far too riled up from the hot, sweet little moans Sammy kept making as he tongued and worked at Silas. His husky voice was fucking sinful. No wonder people paid to hear his pleasure.

But Silas didn't just want his voice; he wanted everything.

"Sammy," he panted, digging his fingers into the hair at his nape. "Sammy, come here."

Sammy peered up at him. "Make me," he quipped, thumbing at the precum weeping from his cockhead.

Something that'd laid dormant in Silas snapped its eyes open at the challenge, rearing its head.

Make me.

"Alright, love," he growled.

Silas yanked him up and rolled, not being as careful as he should've been to avoid squishing him. He manhandled Sammy, who, to be fair, had only latched back onto Silas, sucking and biting marks wherever he could reach until he was caged in underneath him.

Planting his knees on either side, Silas braced himself on one forearm and pushed Sammy's shirt up with his free hand, exposing the soft skin along his stomach.

Sammy also reached down and dropped his joggers just far enough to pull his cock out. It bobbed heavily before resting against his stomach, and Silas' mouth watered at the sight.

Just as he'd thought, Sammy was thick and already leaking along his lower belly.

Then, Sammy took Silas in hand and guided him so he could hold their cocks together, pumping once, twice.

Another one of those embarrassingly needy sounds escaped him at the delicious friction.

"So fucking hot," Sammy mumbled, arching up into Silas. "I've never been with an uncircumcised guy. Love the way you feel."

Silas growled and dropped more of his weight down onto Sammy, halting his movements. "I'm not the jealous type, but if you start talking about another man's dick right now..." he trailed off, nipping at Sammy's exposed collarbone.

Sammy pulled his hand from between their bodies and bracketed Silas' face in his grip, locking their gazes together. There was fire in his eyes—fire and raw need and vulnerability when he said, "You're all I can think about. All I've thought about for so long. And I *am* the jealous type, so if you don't feel the same—"

Silas shoved his tongue down Sammy's throat in answer, and he melted underneath him.

Yeah, shutting him up like that was his favorite option so far.

"What do you want, Sammy? Tell me what you want," Silas said between heated kisses, edging closer and closer to spilling all over Sammy from just the feel of their naked skin sliding together, hastily exposed between rucked-up shirts.

Sammy wrapped his arms around Silas' torso, pulling him down. "I need you all around me."

Silas let himself be yanked and positioned where Sammy wanted him, with their hips aligned so that their cocks slid together in a meltingly hot friction and Sammy's legs wrapped around his waist.

Because of their height difference, Silas had to hunch

down to take Sammy's mouth back in a wet kiss as he set a frantic pace, rocking them together.

He'd never frotted with anyone before, never really cared to linger over the scent of a partner's skin or the way they felt pressed up against him or the sound of their hitched breaths—but Silas was consumed with it all now, here, with Sammy.

He wanted to document every place he touched that caused Sammy to knit his brows together; he needed a record of what his mate felt like shivering underneath him in pleasure.

His mate.

Silas had Sammy in his arms, in his bed.

Finally.

Mate feels perfect, mate smells perfect, mate tastes perfect.

Sammy is ours.

Mate is ours.

Oursoursoursours.

Sammy tipped his head back and softly cried out when Silas began rutting them together harder, and he sucked and tongued at his exposed neck to keep from repeating the triumphant declarations out loud.

Yes, wolf. He is ours.

The swell of emotion tipped him over the edge, sudden and overwhelming, and Sammy fit his mouth back over Silas' just in time to swallow his cry, the involuntary kick of his hips shooting ropes of hot, sticky cum between them.

When he was finished, Silas made to pull away, to reach down and tug Sammy's orgasm into his palm, but Sammy's legs gripped him tighter, his arms locked around his torso, holding fast.

"*Silas.*"

Sammy said Silas' name like a plea, an acute need, something critical for survival.

Silas pressed back down, ignoring his own overly sensitive cock and the cum drying tacky in the hair on his belly. "I'm here," he rumbled. "I'm right here, love."

Dropping his elbows just above Sammy's shoulders on the bed, Silas braced one hand on the headboard and cradled Sammy's face to his chest with the other. Guided by his husky, muffled moans and bitten-off, high-pitched whines, Silas continued to grind into Sammy's thick, cum-slick cock the way he needed.

"*Oh,* oh fuck, like that. Yes, like that!"

Sammy buried his face in Silas' chest when he came, moaning and hips twitching, digging his fingers into Silas' back.

His rumbling purr was loud in the quiet, and he pulled Sammy's scent deep into his lungs, thicker and richer from their exertions and his fresh orgasm, like dark chocolate and coal fire.

Silas held Sammy through it, cradled underneath him until their breathing evened out and the sweat along Silas' back cooled. Shifting his weight to the side, he pulled Sammy further up the bed so they were lying face to face on the shared pillow.

Silas traced a claw along the curve of Sammy's ear. "Wow," he whispered.

Sammy's eyes snapped up to his, almost bashful. There were no walls in sight. "Yeah, wow," he parroted warmly.

They both started chuckling, and then Sammy's face was back in Silas' chest to muffle his laugh. "Were you serious about the magical walls, or were you just saying that to make me feel better about getting off in your childhood bedroom?" he asked, nuzzling his beard into the hair there and kissing along his pecs.

Silas hummed, raking his claws through Sammy's hair. "I was serious about the walls. As a kid, it was a fun quirk; Finn would run into the other room, shut the door, and shout at the top of his lungs, and I'd stand in here and could barely hear him. As teenagers, we appreciated it for other reasons. I'd have clawed my face off if I had to listen to him jerk off."

Sammy's face screwed up in a grimace. "Eww, don't. I can't think about that. My brother's in there with him."

Silas chuckled. "Come on, let's get cleaned up and changed."

They shuffled around each other as they readied to go to sleep, trading places in the hall bathroom. Silas stayed in his human form since the bed was already cramped enough as it was, let alone with the added bulk of his partial shift.

He hadn't wanted to deal with the whole knotting thing for their first time together. Startling Sammy with an unreasonably large dick was not how he'd wanted things to go. Thankfully, he'd kept himself in check.

Maybe I should ask Finn how he broached that subject with Jaime... because the last time he'd brought up knotting with his best friend had gone *so well.*

Silas made Sammy take the wall side so that he wouldn't

accidentally push the smaller man out of bed in the middle of the night. "It's been so long since I've slept in a full bed, I'd feel awful if I kicked you out," he said, pulling the covers over them both.

"Yeah, well, don't roll over and suffocate me, either. Being squished by you during sex is hot, but I don't want to die that way," Sammy said.

Silas tracked the blush that crept up the back of his neck. Reaching out, he ran a thumb along Sammy's cheekbone. "I'll try not to squish you... when we're sleeping," he said, smirking at the deadpan look Sammy shot him before swatting his chest.

"Turn off the lamp. I'm tired," he said, yawning.

Silas reached back and flicked it off. They shifted, settling with Sammy's back to Silas, just far enough apart so they weren't touching.

He hated it.

The wind had picked up even more, whistling through the trees and causing the house to shift and creak in the quiet. Silas had always loved the sound of windy nights; they made him wistful. They made him long to hold someone close and to be held tenderly in return.

Slowly, so that Sammy could pull away if he wanted, Silas shifted forward and reached his hand out, resting it on Sammy's waist. Silas felt his sharp inhale, but he didn't pull away, so he scooted forward a little more until he had Sammy spooned up against him in a long line of warmth and comfort, with an arm draped around his waist.

"You're all I can think about, too. For so long, Sammy..."

Silas whispered, unable to stop himself from nuzzling into the back of his hair.

It wasn't enough; it didn't even come close to all he wanted to say. But Silas was still unsteady after coming so hard, and he wouldn't want Sammy to think his confessions were made from lust. So he contented himself with the way their scents combined and his mate's steady breaths.

Sammy threaded his fingers through Silas', right over his heart, and together, they drifted off to sleep.

CHAPTER 13
SILAS

The next two days were some of the best Silas could remember.

He woke up the first morning wrapped around Sammy. He really had nearly squashed him, but when Silas loosened his hold and gave Sammy a bit more room to breathe, he'd made the most adorable *humph* sound, still half dreaming, and rolled into Silas' arms again, hooking their legs together and drifting back to sleep.

Silas felt like a giant hound, unable to move because a kitten had curled up in its fur for an afternoon nap. He wasn't complaining, though.

Except they both had morning wood.

Just as he'd decided to nudge Sammy awake so they could take care of that problem together, someone banged loudly on the bedroom door.

"Breakfast will be hot in fifteen minutes, and then we're

going running! Sort yourselves out!" Finn shouted, loud enough to be heard through the walls.

"I'll sort *you* out," Silas grumbled back, even though Finn wouldn't be able to hear.

"Oh my God, he's a morning person, isn't he? You can hear it in his voice," Sammy said sleepily, shuddering. "If I'd known that, I would have protested harder when he and Jaime got together."

He pulled the covers further up over his head.

Silas chuckled, rubbing his cheek through Sammy's hair. "Come on, love. Food awaits. And then we'll go for a run. It's actually a lot of fun," he said, tossing the duvet back and swinging his legs to the floor.

Sammy grabbed the covers Silas had discarded and wrapped himself up even more. He looked like the most adorable grumpy burrito Silas had ever seen.

Fuck, I hope Finn is making breakfast burritos with those leftover tortillas...

"I don't know who you think you shared a bed with last night, but it certainly wasn't someone who would agree to go *running*. In the *morning*. When it's *cold*."

Sammy spit the words like Silas had suggested they spend the morning kicking puppies.

He chuckled. "You won't be running, love. You and Jaime can take the snowmobiles. But the rest of us need to stretch our legs, or else we'll get grouchy. Well, Finn will get *more* grouchy."

Sammy mumbled something under his breath inside the blanket burrito, so Silas reached over to gently prod him until he got out of bed—only to discover that Sammy was ticklish.

And that he *giggled*.

A sly grin stretched his face, and Silas all but tickled Sammy out of bed and down the hall to the bathroom. His laughter ignited little gas lamps of warmth in Silas' mind, a path to follow home.

～

IF SOMEONE HAD ASKED him a year ago what his favorite thing to do was, Silas would have said running in his wolf form with his family.

And then eating a lot of food.

The rush of speeding through the valley on all four legs, stretching out his gait as far as he could while he and Finn danced in and out of the shallow river rapids or barreled through a drift of fresh snow, his parents moseying along behind at their own pace, was unparalleled.

Until today.

Today, he experienced what all of that felt like with his mate right alongside him.

That was his favorite thing.

Watching Sammy slowly wake up over a cup of coffee and a stack of Finn's chocolate chip pancakes was a close second, though.

Silas and Finn loped along behind the snowmobiles for a few minutes while Sammy and Jaime adjusted to how they drove. When Sammy began *accidentally* kicking up snow all over him, Silas picked up the pace, nipping at Finn's heels until he joined.

Yipping at Sammy as he passed, Silas bolted ahead faster than he'd pushed himself in a long time.

And maybe he was showing off a little, so what?

Hours later, when his legs were pleasantly sore and Silas felt like he wouldn't be able to get back up if he laid down, they called it quits. Lazing around the house for the rest of the day, they binged a season of *The Great British Bake Off* and ate cheddar brats for dinner with a mountain of mashed potatoes on the side.

Sammy passed out on the couch afterward, and Silas carried him up to bed, just like he had the first night he'd brought him home.

Curled up in a too-small, cozy bed with Sammy after spending a full day with his family, Silas' wolf felt more content than he could ever remember. Their two sleep-warm scents intertwined to tell a story of a day full of laughter and flushed cheeks and happiness.

Pack.

Yes. Together, they smelled like pack.

His parents had always smelled that way. Or, well, like *family* at least. And when Silas nervously walked into a classroom full of strangers on his first day of human school, only to be surprised by another shifter like him hunched in the back of the room, he'd immediately smelled like he belonged, too.

Stomping up to Finn on the playground, Silas asked, "Who's pack do you belong to? Why are you the only shifter in our class?"

Finn had blinked at him, ducking his head. "Um, pack? It's just me and my mom. She's normal. Not like me. Or you. I *can* smell you, but I'm not supposed to. It's not normal. I'm not supposed to, you know, *change*."

He'd whispered the last word like it was a dirty secret.

"Change?" Silas had asked, not understanding. "You mean when you shift into your wolf?"

Finn had nodded, shooting glances around like someone could overhear. "It's not normal," he'd repeated.

Then it was Silas' turn to blink. "But it's the way we are. It's a part of us, how could that not be normal?"

Finn hadn't responded; he'd just given Silas those big, brown puppy eyes—the ones he'd never really grown out of, and right then, Silas had declared that they were friends.

"You can be *my* friend," he'd said, careful not to use any of his alpha instincts. His parents had said he wasn't supposed to show them to anyone, not for a long time.

"You can come to my house," he'd continued. "I'll show you how to find it with your nose. It's hidden, but not if you know where to look. And we'll run together, and I can show you how to hunt, and you can be pack, too."

He'd nodded as if deciding such a thing were that simple.

In the end, it had been. They'd quickly become inseparable, with Finn spending as much time as he could with Silas and his family at the house that was hidden unless you knew where to look.

Finn became his brother, his best friend.

His pack.

When they met Sheppard and Renner in the military, they'd felt like pack, too.

Silas' parents encouraged him to join, saying it would be good for him to learn to take orders and direction from others, especially in a specialized shifter unit. He'd agreed, but only with the assurance that Finn would go with him.

In private, even out of earshot of his best friend, they'd told him it would help keep the alpha instincts subdued.

Silas had learned all of what they'd hoped; he'd rarely struggled to keep himself in check after that. He'd also learned what it felt like to have a broken heart, to lose a friend. They'd come back broken after Renner died—Sheppard most of all—and had rebuilt together, just the three of them.

Silas hoped whatever was happening between him and the DA, Sheppard wouldn't be hurt again.

Even still, Silas was grateful his parents had encouraged him to leave home and try new experiences. It made realizing Silver Rapids was where he belonged all the sweeter.

They'd been terrified for him when he and Finn moved into the tiny town, in a house anyone walking down the street could easily spot. Silas had convinced them it would be alright; the Salt Creek den had still been hours north at that point, having only established the new outpost within the last couple of years, and not even Finn and Sheppard knew he was an alpha.

Those instincts had gone dormant.

Silas hadn't missed them, and he hadn't blamed his parents for their absence. They loved him very, very much. It'd never been about hiding a part of who he was; even from a very young age, Silas understood it was meant to keep him safe.

He remembered flashes of the night they'd fled, terrified of what his uncle's ultimatum would mean for them all.

Sitting out of sight at the top of the staircase, confused and scared and quiet as a mouse, Silas had listened as they'd argued over what they should do.

He remembered the fear in his father's voice when he'd begged his mother to understand that their plan wasn't foolproof, that he may not be able to protect them if they were caught, that he was *scared*. His mother had explained through broken sobs that she wouldn't survive Cain taking Silas away, her words muffled by his father's shirt.

Silas remembered their horrified faces when he'd been unable to stifle his own tears, and they'd rounded the corner at the base of the stairs to find him crying alone.

He remembered his father, whom he inherited his size and build from, had taken the stairs three at a time, scooped him up into his lap, and chuffed into his hair. "It's alright, baby. *Shh*, it will be alright. We'll protect you," he'd said, the deep rumble of his voice as comforting as ever.

His mother's scent had surrounded him when she'd wrapped her arms around them both, making Silas feel whole and loved and safe.

"I'm scared," he'd whispered into the space between them. "I don't want to go live with Alpha Cain."

"You are *ours*, and we will never let him take you from us," his mother had said, a snarl in her voice. "But to make sure of that, we need to go live somewhere else."

"You mean, leave the den?" he'd asked.

"Yes, baby. We'll leave the den and take you somewhere safe. How does that sound?" his father had asked.

"But you're coming with me, right?"

"Of course," they replied together.

His father bent his head low, curling even more around Silas. "We'll have to keep some things a secret for a while, Si. I know it might get uncomfortable, but to keep you safe, we'll have to hide that you're an alpha from strangers. Just until we know it's safe," his father had said.

"Oh. Would... would someone want to be my friend, then? If I'm not going to be alpha? Like in the library today— he's my friend," he'd said.

His mother had pressed a kiss into his hair, smelling of fresh tears. "Yeah, baby, I think you'll find a friend. Let's go pack up now. You can pick out your favorite shirts and socks with me."

His father had tucked him into the backseat of the car under the cover of dark and pushed from behind while his mother steered them out of the compound. When they'd finally started up the engine and driven away, Silas was lulled to sleep by the steady rhythm of the road, and dreamt of a friend.

THEIR LAST MORNING visiting his parents was cold and sunny.

Silas squinted against the bright reflection off the snow as he brought his axe down over and over, logs tumbling to the ground with each swing.

Crack

Crack

Crack

He'd been outside splitting wood for half an hour or so when footsteps approached from the house, their steady, heavy crunch so similar to his own. "Is everything alright?" his father asked when he'd made his way over.

Silas halted his next swing and turned, wiping at his brow. "Yes," he answered honestly. The image of Sammy, curled up in his arms and still deeply asleep when Silas woke earlier this morning, flashed through his mind. "Yes, everything's good. Really good."

"I'm glad," his dad replied, eyes twinkling. He picked up the second axe leaning against the splitting log and joined Silas in adding to their pile of kindling. "But I know you. When the wood pile is growing, something's on your mind."

Silas had noticed his parents' firewood supply was low, so when he'd been unable to fall back asleep this morning, thoughts spinning, he'd opted to come and replenish it before they returned home.

After years of splitting and hauling firewood together, they fell into an easy rhythm, the sounds of their chopping and stacking a familiar soundtrack in Silas' mind.

"Could you read Uncle Cain's thoughts back when we were still in the pack?" Silas asked after a few swings, his breath billowing out in the cold morning air.

His dad stopped and turned to him. "Read his thoughts? Like, hear the things going through his head?"

Silas nodded, resting the heavy end of the axe on the ground.

"No. Never."

"Have you ever heard of telepathy developing in a pack?"

His father's eyebrows knit together. "Maybe in an old bedtime story. When your uncle and I were boys, your great-grandmother used to tell us tales of how shifters came to be—how the ancient packs had all sorts of magic at their fingertips and that they could communicate with each other without speaking. But those were just stories. Why do you ask?"

Silas shook his head, looking at his feet. "It's not just a story," he said quietly. "Ever since I told Finn and Sheppard I was an alpha last spring, it feels like I woke something up. Or shifted something, somehow. I can't explain it, but we all feel it. We can hear each other's thoughts now. Not all the time, and not super clearly. We can't speak to one another directly; more like, we feel the big emotions the others are feeling."

Silas' dad blinked in surprise. "I've never heard of that happening, but I suppose if it had, that's something a pack would keep secret. Have you looked into it further?"

Silas nodded. "Sheppard's contacted a shifter doctor from way up north to help figure out why Riley isn't healing," he answered. "If we trust him, I may ask if he knows anything about it."

His dad nodded. "Your mother has family you could call, too. It wouldn't hurt to see what they know."

Silas sighed. "Yeah, I'll do that. It's been a lot. I haven't wanted to deal with any of it, but now..." He peered up at his bedroom window, wondering if Sammy was still asleep or if he'd already readied himself for the day. "Now I feel like I can."

He picked his axe back up, and they resumed their firewood splitting.

"You don't need to help with this, you know," his dad said after a while, gesturing with an arm full of logs.

Silas smiled. "I know, but I like to. It's a lot of work to live out here."

"Yes, it is," his father said, chuckling. "It's something your mother and I have been discussing more and more, but that's a topic for another day. Now, why haven't you told Sammy he's your mate?"

The question startled Silas, and he fumbled the firewood he'd already stacked, knocking part of the pile over.

How had his dad known Sammy was his mate? He was fairly certain the bond wasn't detectable yet, and sure, he'd chatted his parents' ears off about him in passing phone conversations and visits, but he'd never come right out and said it.

He wanted Sammy to be the first person he told when the time was right.

"What?" Silas asked, even though he'd heard him perfectly well.

His father simply raised an eyebrow in response—the meddling snoop.

Silas narrowed his eyes. "Is that what you spoke to him about when we first arrived?" Surely not; there were boundaries even a nosey nelly like him wouldn't cross.

"Of course not," his dad said. "I could tell your mother's toast had upset him, and when I went to check on him, I overheard him talking to himself about looking frightful enough to pull off an escape. We spoke, and it was clear that the root of his angst was only partially due to your mother's words, and that you mean a great deal to him. It was also clear that he has no idea how much he means to you."

Silas peered out through the trees, knowing it would be useless to deny. "He's only just let me back into his life," he said quietly. "I won't rush it. I won't rush him. Just because I know he's... the one for me, I won't force that on him."

His dad clapped him on the shoulder. "You want him to choose you, too."

Silas nodded once.

"Oh, to be young and an idiot in love," his father said with a sigh.

"Hey, I'm not an idiot," Silas grumbled, toeing at the ground.

"You both are."

Silas studied his father's face. "How did you know? That he's my... *you know*."

His dad rolled his eyes. "You are my son. He's also the first man you've ever brought home, Silas. Of course, he's your mate."

"We don't bring just anybody here. It's not safe."

"Exactly," his father said with a sly smile. "And yet, you didn't think twice about inviting Sammy, did you?"

No. He hadn't.

"Now, come inside and get cleaned up. Finn is already helping your mother with the roast. And I won't meddle..."

It was Silas' turn to roll his eyes.

"*...but* I wouldn't recommend waiting too long to tell him the truth. I'm afraid you'll regret it if you do."

HOME

SILAS

*FIVE MONTHS, TWENTY-SIX DAYS, AND THIRTEEN
AND A HALF HOURS AGO*

"JAIME! Jaime, open up!"

Silas screeched to a halt, all four legs tangling and jumbling together as he tripped over himself and rolled, crashing through the forest undergrowth and tumbling into a tree.

GOBACKGOBACKGOBACK!

HE'S THERE!

WE FOUND HIM!

GO BACK!

Panting, he stood and shook the dirt and leaves from his coat.

He'd heard the shouting from a long way off, farther than sound usually carried through the thick vegetation. He'd been running the perimeter of his house while staying well out of earshot of the activities he very much did *not* want to overhear Jaime and Finn getting up to the night before.

When he'd left them after dinner, it'd been clear they'd both finally pulled their heads out of their asses and opened their eyes to how much they wanted each other.

Silas hadn't been able to get out fast enough; the smell in the kitchen alone would haunt him.

GO BACK!

GO BACK!

GO BACK!

He turned and followed the sound of those shouts.

He knew that voice. He'd heard it a few days ago over the phone, yes, but it was more than that. In person, it struck him deeper, kicked him in the diaphragm right as he was about to take a breath, demanding his full attention.

The sound of those shouts yanked on a cord tied to his ribs and made his wolf whine and snarl and claw to be set free. Yet, it also soothed his aching and weary soul in a way he hadn't known he'd needed.

That voice said, *this way, to me, you know what direction you should run in now. No more wandering. To me! To me!*

Spurned on by the overwhelming need to see the person that voice belonged to, to see him *again*, because it was so familiar it couldn't be the first time they'd met, Silas ran faster than he'd ever run before.

Flashes of memory, fuzzy and distant, burst through his mind.

What should we read next?

I wish I could fly way up high to see everything!

His wolf spurred him on, aching to go faster.

Finally back at the house, he shoved through the door.

Upstairs. He's upstairs, go! Go!

More than one person's voice rang out, startled and angry.

Shifting out of his wolf form, Silas tripped up the stairs as he threw on a pair of pants and a sweatshirt, not even pausing to properly get his legs through the foot holes first.

Oursoursoursoursours.

He paced down the hall, drawn in by the sound of that voice like a homing pigeon. It was *his*. He knew that. Silas could forget his own name and still know he belonged to the speaker of that husky, low timbre.

The scent of crackling embers and toasted marshmallows clogged his throat. It conjured images of him as a boy, so much smaller than he was now, wandering through tall wooden shelves filled with books. An illustration of a red fox flashed through his mind, along with the sight of a small boy sitting cross-legged on a rainbow-colored carpet.

Silas rounded the corner of Finn's bedroom door. Like something he'd forgotten, only to remember hours later, *oh yes, that's right, it's you,* his mate stood before him.

A stranger, yes, but also not.

The person Silas had been looking for his whole life.

What's your name? Can we be friends?

Sure! I'm Sammy. What's yours?

Words bubbled up on the tip of Silas' tongue, ready to spill out.

Hi, my name is Silas and you're my mate and I remember you, do you remember me? You were my very first friend. Do you still want to learn to fly? I know we don't know each other yet but you smell like toasted marshmallows, they're my favorite, so maybe I can chop us some wood and build you a warm fire and then I'll give you everything you've ever wanted.

Before he could voice them, though, Jaime, standing next to Finn, hit Silas' mate in the face.

Silas jolted forward. *Mate is hurt!*

Somehow, he had the wherewithal to know if he growled at Jaime, Finn would throw him through the wall and then feel really bad about it, so he held it back. Stepping in front of his mate to block him from the danger, Silas tipped his face up—*he's so short! Perfect for wrapping up to keep warm*—to check and see if anything was broken.

His nose looked unhurt, straight, and dusted with freckles that disappeared into his strawberry blonde stubble, a shade lighter than his fox-colored hair. Shockingly green eyes narrowed at Silas when he tipped his face side to side, watching the flush from the hit bloom on his cheekbone.

He's beautiful.

By the way his mate was looking at him, though, Silas knew one wrong move, and he'd also chuck him through the wall.

Only he didn't look like he'd feel bad about it.

Hot.

Time seemed to stop while Silas fully took him in, the most gorgeous man he'd ever seen.

Matematematematemate.

Sammy.

Home.

Yes, he'd finally found his way home.

CHAPTER 14
SAM

Sam sat in Silas' room, showered and ready for bed, only a few hours after they'd returned to Silver Rapids. Yet, the last few days felt more like a dream than any reality he could believe.

His phone chimed, alerting him to a text. Smiling, Sam opened the message.

LANA

So??? Did you meet the parents? How'd it go!?

SAM

They're upsettingly wonderful people.

That's good, though, right? I mean, marry for love and all that bullshit, but I don't want to deal with someone's monster of a mother for the rest of my life.

The irony of Silas' mother being the farthest thing from a

228

monster-in-law was not lost on him.

Yeah, it's good. They live in a beautiful area. There's no one else around. We took the snowmobiles out for a few hours one day. I had a great time.

I'm so glad. Are you still happy staying with Mr. Mountain Man?

Sam's thumbs hovered over the keyboard, unsure how to articulate what he felt.

Cozy in his pajamas and under the spell of *what could be,* recalling that first night with Silas and the days since felt like he was watching his life play out inside a snow globe.

In there, he was happy—more than happy—and could laugh and fall asleep next to the only person who'd ever made him feel truly safe, like he could be prickly and soft all at once and know that Silas still wanted him.

Sam had never had that before. He'd never let himself have that before.

Inside that snow globe with Jaime, Silas, and his family, he felt like he belonged. In there, he felt like *Sammy.*

But he wasn't in that snow globe anymore, and nothing was more of a stark reminder than closing out of their messages, still unsure how to respond, and opening his banking app, only to find several green *pending* numbers glowing so brightly his eyes watered.

Or maybe he was crying.

His security deposit had been returned while they were at Cal and Meera's house, along with the payout from his home and property insurance claim from the wreck. The most recent paycheck from his subscription account had cleared, too. It was the highest-grossing month he'd ever had.

He could pay Cain back.

Sam could demand he accept the money, forget the unfulfilled favor, and actually be free of him.

He could move to Anchorage and leave the past behind the way he'd said he would from the start. He could take his history with Cain and go, so it never touched Silas and his family and their beautiful hidden home ever again.

Except those plans didn't make him happy. They made him hollow.

Or, you could stay. You could stay with Silas. With his family.

Sam couldn't stay with Silas and never tell him the truth, though.

That ship had sailed the moment Silas kissed him. Or maybe it had been when he'd held Sam while he came in his arms, or when he'd made Sam laugh about cactus diarrhea, or when they'd cried together after finding out Jaime and Finn were ok, or when he'd held his arms up over his head like antlers and told Sam to please be careful around the moose...

Sam blinked away the tears filling his eyes.

Too much; there'd been too much vulnerability and intimacy and that other big four-letter word—the one Sam couldn't bring himself to say just yet—to choose to stay with Silas and never tell the truth of what he'd done.

What matters is that we chose each other. We trusted each other—despite him. We're stronger together.

Cal's words bounced around in Sam's head while he tapped out a reply to Lana, not wanting to leave her waiting.

I am happy here, just not sure about the rest. Tired from this weekend, going to get some sleep.

Her response came through quickly.

Remember what we talked about. You're not baggage. And please let yourself be happy. 🤍 Night!

Sam flicked through the dashboard of his subscription account on autopilot, thoughts of staying and leaving and what it meant to be happy, what it meant to choose Silas, on repeat.

"Are you working on your audio recordings?" Silas asked.

Sam jolted up from the edge of the bed, unsure how long Silas had stood there.

Leaning against the doorframe, his hair was still damp from the shower, and he was wearing soft, threadbare pajama bottoms with one of those sleeveless hoodies.

"Not really," Sam answered, tracking the way Silas' chest bunched when he crossed his arms. "Just checking on how the latest upload is performing."

"And? Is it doing well?" Silas asked, padding over to loom in a way that was *not* sexy. It was just the effect of those stupid cutoff hoodies—they scrambled Sam's brain.

Really, though, it looked even more ridiculous on him now in his half-shifted form, stretching across his massive chest and highlighting just how large his biceps were.

"*Umm...*" Sam said, trying to remember the question, head fuzzy from the way Silas' arms flexed. Was he doing that on purpose? "Yeah, it is. The alpha ones have been blowing up."

He clipped his mouth shut, eyes widening in realization. He had *not* meant to say that out loud.

Fuck. Fuck, fuck, fuck!

"Alpha?" Silas rumbled, eyes flashing, voice so low Sam could barely understand him. "Who is that? Who's *Alpha?*"

Sam gulped, trying to look anywhere except at Silas. Was he jealous? Was that hot?

Who was he kidding, of course, it was hot.

"Just... it's nothing," he said.

"*Show me,*" Silas growled, stepping closer so that Sam was forced to sit down on the bed again, head tipped back to maintain eye contact. Silas stood between his legs. "Show me who that is."

Sam was torn between leaning away so he wasn't distracted again by how good Silas smelled fresh out of the shower and pressing forward to bury his face in Silas' stomach.

"It's not someone else," he said, fumbling with his phone to pull up the app.

As hot as Silas' jealousy was, Sam balked at actually letting him believe he had competition—not after their past couple of days together. "There's no one to show. It's just, like, a thing I say sometimes. If I put it in the title, the audios do better."

Sam held up his phone, showing Silas the title of his latest recording.

God, what the hell was he doing? Telling Silas about his

job was one thing, but sharing an audio with him? That was entirely another.

Slowly, Silas took the phone, cradling it in his hand like it could shatter at the slightest touch. *"ThatNeedyBoyVA?"* he read aloud, eyes darting back down to Sam's in question.

Face hot, Sam cleared his throat. "Um. My name. My creator name."

Reaching out, Silas palmed the nape of Sam's neck with his free hand, keeping his head tilted back. *"Big Alpha Cock Fills Up My Tight Hole and Makes Me Cry,"* he read aloud again, sounding dazed, words slurring through his canines.

"Yeah," Sam croaked.

Silas' thumb flicked to scroll further down.

Fuck, could he see Sam's other audios on the same page? He couldn't remember for sure, but he didn't need Silas reading them all aloud like some fever-dream-induced bedtime story.

Sam snatched the phone back. "See? No one else. Now, I'm tired. Let's go to sleep."

He made to scoot back on the bed, but Silas's hand on the back of his neck held him in place, clearly not finished with their conversation. "Who is it, then? Someone you think about when you record?"

"Nope," Sam squeaked, studiously avoiding Silas' gaze.

Get a grip. You're a better liar than that.

Silas traced his thumb up the front of Sam's throat. "Sammy, who do you think about when you record? Who do you call Alpha?"

Sam narrowed his eyes. "I told you, it's no one."

"Hmm..." A wicked grin stretched across Silas' face. "You're lying."

"I am *not*," Sam huffed, trying to ignore the way Silas' hoodie rode up, exposing his prominent happy trail. He wanted to put his mouth there again. "And why do you wear those stupid things anyway?"

Silas arched an eyebrow at his deflection. "These?" he asked, pulling at the hoodie.

"Yes, *those*. I can't believe you leave the house in that. What's the point if they can't even keep your arms warm?"

Silas' eyes flashed again. "The *point*," he said, head cocked to the side with the most infuriating smirk on his face, "is it drives you crazy when I wear them. I fucking love when you're all riled up with nowhere to go. Now, who's Alpha?"

Sam gaped, outraged. He pushed Silas back so he could stand, chest to chest. "It does *not*—if you think I give a damn about you wearing that stupid hoodie—"

Faster than Sam could react, Silas spun him around and pinned him face down into the duvet, ass in the air. His feet were still on the ground, and Silas was folded all the way down so that his chest pressed into Sam's back.

"I can smell it, you know," Silas groaned into his ear, his breath hot against Sam's cheek. "When you're so turned on, you can't tell if you want to fuck me or fight me. Come on, love. I'd enjoy either more than you'll ever know."

Sam squirmed beneath him, trying and failing to reach out of the cage of Silas' arms for leverage. "What the fuck are you doing?" he spat.

The way he was grinding his ass back into Silas' rapidly

hardening cock may have taken some of the bite out of the question, though.

Silas nipped at Sam's ear. "You're being a *brat*, so I'm putting you in timeout until you've learned your lesson."

Sam's cheeks flamed. So Silas *had* caught a glimpse of his other audio titles.

No one had ever dared call him that. There was only one person in the world Sam would *let* call him that and not gouge out their eyes for it. Still... "You can't treat me like a misbehaving child," he snarled, even though his cock was filling so fast from Silas calling him a *brat* he felt lightheaded.

Silas chuckled, and the sound simmered low in Sam's belly, right where he ached to be filled. "How about you tell me who Alpha is, and I'll show you how naughty brats should behave. If you want that?"

Sam panted into the mattress, head spinning.

Do I want that?

Yes. In bold fucking underlined letters, yes.

The never-ending questions that'd been floating around in his head had melted away, and all that remained was an unrelenting need for whatever Silas was willing to give.

He'd already chipped away at so much of the wall erected around Sam's heart. What was the point in keeping the fact that he'd been thinking of Silas for months and months a secret anymore?

Sam reached out and squeezed the hand Silas had braced by his head. "Yes," he answered through gritted teeth. "Ok."

"Yes, what, love?" Silas asked, dancing featherlight kisses along the nape of Sam's neck.

Sam blew out a petulant huff, wiggling back on Silas' cock again until he growled. "Yes, please. Show me, *Alpha*."

Silas' chest rumbled, the sound vibrating through him. He was still partially shifted, and Sam reveled in the feel of him all around, larger and thicker and *everywhere*.

"That's right, Sammy. I'm your alpha. Your only alpha," Silas said right into his ear.

He kicked Sam's legs further apart and took hold of his arms, pinning them behind his back. "I want you to say it. Say that I'm the one you think about when you scream for them. Tell me I'm who you imagine filling you when you make yourself come. Say you've been thinking about me for as long as I've been thinking about you."

His voice was a growling mix of pleading demands, and Sam was a slave to it. "You're my alpha," he said, groaning and rocking into Silas. "It's you. It's always been you."

"You bet it's fucking me," Silas said, triumphant. He bit at Sam's shoulder. "Now, you'll stay just like this. If you move, I'll stop. Yes?"

Sam nearly keened. What the hell was Silas doing to him? "Fine," he panted, trying to reel himself back in. He'd never felt more exposed, more vulnerable. "But get on with it."

Silas smiled, pressing his teeth into the crook of Sam's neck before kissing his way down his back. Kneeling behind him, Silas pushed Sam's shirt up until it hung around his shoulders and adjusted his arms to keep it there. It blocked any view Sam had of where Silas knelt behind him, leaving him helpless to predict his movements.

"What—what are you doing?" Sam asked.

Silas drug his fingers down the newly exposed skin along Sam's back, careful not to prick his claws, and smacked a hand on one of Sam's ass cheeks—hard.

It'd been dampened by the sweats he still wore, and Silas soothed it immediately by gently running his hand over the area, but it still smarted in all the ways Sam hadn't known he'd enjoy.

"I'm showing you how naughty brats should behave, remember?" Silas said, hooking his fingers in Sam's joggers and boxer briefs and pulling them down, not bothering to free his feet.

Sam could only whimper, turning his head to muffle the sound into the bedding.

"Now that won't do, love," Silas cooed, the hot exhale of his breath against Sam's most vulnerable parts making him shiver. "I want to hear you. I want you to make every little noise you'd share with your subscribers, except this time—it's all for me."

He'd pressed the last few words right into the swell of Sam's ass, where he was still sensitive from the slap. Nipping and soothing the bites with his tongue, Silas worshipped the soft skin along his thighs and cheeks, trading one open-mouthed kiss for each of Sam's sighs and hitched breaths.

"Si—Silas, please. Do *something*," Sam begged, his cock aching where it hung heavy and full from the teasing attention. He'd never been taken apart like this before.

He'd never *wanted* to be taken apart like this before.

Silas nipped harder, causing Sam to yelp and squirm. Then he grasped Sam's ass in both hands and pulled his cheeks apart with his thumbs, exposing him fully to the cold air.

"*Fuck*, Sammy. You're perfect. So perfect. I want to hear you, remember? Don't hold back, love," Silas said, and then he licked over Sam's opening.

Sam cried out, melting into the mattress with each swirl and lap of Silas' tongue. He reached forward between Sam's legs and tugged lightly on his balls, leaving his cock touch-starved and aching.

"Oh God, oh my God, Si—I'm, *oh*, I need more. Please. Please fill me up."

Sam rocked back, letting out a small, high-pitched moan each time Silas drove his tongue as deep as he could inside Sam's hole. It was too much and not nearly enough. He wanted to be full of Silas, stuffed to the brim with his cock, with everything he could give.

Surfacing for air, Silas cursed again. "I fucking love how you taste," he groaned. "And the way you sound begging on my tongue, and the way you squirm..." he smacked Sam's ass. "Which you're not supposed to be doing."

Sam pouted when Silas stood, yanking open his night-stand drawer and fishing around for something. Hurrying back over to kneel behind Sam again, Silas kissed all over his backside to the unmistakable *flick* of opening a bottle of lube.

"I'm too riled up to shift back, and I can't fuck you like this. Not yet. But I'll give you what you need, love," Silas said gruffly.

Sam whined again and opened his mouth to ask why Silas couldn't fuck him in his partial shift, because *that* sounded like everything hopes and dreams were made of, but he let out a punched-out moan instead when Silas began massaging the slick pad of one finger over his hole.

"You're already so relaxed, so open for me. This will be nice and easy...*ah*, there it is," Silas said as one finger slid inside with almost no resistance—like Sam's body welcomed it home.

Thankfully, he'd remembered to put his claws away.

Sam's voice broke into a husky moan, reeling from the way Silas' finger filled him, finally giving him *something*. One of his fingers felt like two of Sam's, and the thick ring of muscle sucked it inside, eager for more.

But it wasn't enough. Not even close.

"I want more, *please*, Silas," Sam begged. "I need more."

He tried rocking back onto Silas' finger to feel it deeper, clenching down, but Silas *tsked*, pulling out. "*Ah, ah, ah,* remember? You move, and I stop."

"*Fuck*," Sam pouted. "Just—fucking—fuck me already!"

Another hard smack, this time on the other cheek, made Sam cry out.

"Want another, brat? Or will you do as you're told and stay still?"

Sam huffed and clenched his hands into fists but kept his arms where Silas had put them, crossed behind his back.

Silas gave him two lube-coated fingers all at once as a reward, and Sam keened at the delicious stretch.

"See? Doesn't it feel better to listen and do as I tell you?"

Sam was beyond snark now, beyond anything really besides tiny, reedy moans each time Silas fucked his fingers in and out, curling them experimentally until he found the spot that made Sam jerk involuntarily and precum drip from the head of his cock in long strings, leaking onto the duvet.

"Oh—oh—oh, Silas. *Silas!*"

"*Shh*, it's alright love. I can't give you my cock right now, but we'll make this good together, yeah?" Silas' words came out thick and slurred through his teeth.

Sam still strongly disagreed with that, but Silas stuffed three fingers inside his ass, and there was less to complain about. Curling them purposefully now, Silas firmly massaged over his prostate, milking him while he tongued at Sam's balls, pulled up tight the longer this went on.

Silas still hadn't even touched Sam's cock, and yet he felt an orgasm building, one of those once-in-a-blue-moon full-body experiences that were so intense they left him completely drained—literally and figuratively.

Usually, it took Sam a whole lot of self-induced edging, finding the right spot with a prostate vibrator, and a fantasy about Silas drilling him through the mattress to get there.

All it took Silas were three fingers and the word *brat*.

"Silas, I'm going to come from that. You're going to make me come doing th-that—" Sam panted, overwhelmed and wanting to scramble around in the sheets but unable to move because then Silas would *stop,* and the world would rend in two if he let up now.

Silas chuckled again and continued massaging three fingers *just there* in a near-constant press. "Brats ask permission before they come, they don't declare it."

A high-pitched "*ah!*" whooshed out of Sam when Silas

reached between his legs and finally, *finally* wrapped a slick hand around Sam's cock.

"Well? Ask me nicely, love, and I'll let you come," he said, tugging lightly.

Sam was trembling all over from the combined stimulation, feeling the shudders begin to wrack his body. *"Please?"* he begged. "It's—Silas, I'm close. I can't—*hnngh.*"

Silas released his cock, smacked his ass, and took hold of him again, pumping firmly. "Ask *me*, brat. Ask your alpha if you can come," Silas said through a snarl, the deep voice of the alpha rumbling through Sam.

"Oh, fuck! Please, Alpha, can I come? Please let me come, please, please, *please!*"

Silas maintained the same steady pace as he massaged over Sam's prostate, but he *pushed* down more firmly inside him at the same time his hand did this twisting-tug motion on Sam's cock. "Yes, Sammy, come. Come all over our bed."

Sam's vision whited out. His whole body seized as he came, and instead of spurting out in regular intervals like usual, his cum streamed out the head of his cock in one continuous flow, dribbling all over the duvet.

He had to be screaming. Or maybe his throat was so raw by now he wasn't able to make any sound at all.

Sam blinked and found himself on his back, lying in the wet patch he'd just made and staring up at Silas.

He looked completely feral.

With one leg hiked up on the bed over Sam and canines bared, Silas furiously jerked his cock with one hand and squeezed the base with the other. The way his foreskin moved as he worked himself fascinated Sam—he hadn't realized how fucking hot that would be until seeing Silas' cock for the first time.

To be fair, it could just be that *Silas'* cock was fucking hot, no matter what.

Blearily, Sam reached up to wrap his hand around the quickly swelling base, not really knowing why, except that he needed to feel it.

Silas cried out, his brows pinching together at Sam's touch. He roughly took hold of Sam's hand and squeezed it around the knot, hard, harder than he would have thought pleasurable, and then Silas roared.

Cum rained down on Sam's chest and belly.

Silas collapsed on top of him, barely supporting his weight so that Sam felt truly pinned. Which was good, because he'd fly apart without Silas holding him together.

Sam wrapped his arms and legs around him, clinging on as they came down from that debilitating high.

They were both panting, raw, and worn out. When his breathing finally evened out, Silas groaned as he lifted up and off Sam. "Don't move, love, I'll grab what we need to clean up," he whispered, dropping a gentle kiss to Sam's forehead.

After everything they'd just done, Sam shouldn't have been so taken apart by it.

Silas wasn't gone long, and when he came back, he gently wiped Sam off with a warm washcloth and tucked him back into his pajamas. Tossing the rag into the hamper, Silas scooped him up and arranged them so they lay up on the pillows, with Sam resting mostly on top of Silas and the warm duvet pulled over them both.

They'd deal with the wet patch at the foot of the bed tomorrow.

After several long minutes filled with the sound of their steady breaths and Silas' nails gently scratching along Sam's scalp, Silas whispered, "I know you were thinking about leaving. When we first arrived at my parents' house, and just a few minutes ago. You have a look when you're about to bolt."

Silas' words caught Sam off guard after their mind-blowing sex, but he wouldn't deny it, not when there was no point. Sam couldn't bear to see the disappointment in his eyes, though, so he tucked his face into the crook of Silas' arm, hiding from the truth.

Silas held him tighter. "I'll never give up, you know."

Sam turned to peer up at him, wishing he had the courage to tell him he should—he deserved so much more than what Sam would drag into his life. "Silas—"

"No," Silas interrupted with that rumbling dominance that had only ever demanded that Sam stand tall and never cower.

Demanded that he stand *with* Silas.

"No. You can push me away all you like. You can run. But I'll never stop looking for you. I'll never stop hunting you, choosing you. I'll never stop waiting for you to choose me, too."

Sam shook his head, tears falling quickly, choking him.

He couldn't respond. What was there to say?

He didn't know what it meant to choose Silas. Everything in Sam ached to beg for his forgiveness, to lay his heart and transgressions out before them both and ask to be loved anyway, to try and make a life together despite all of Sam's lies and fuck-ups and *mess*.

Sam didn't care anymore that he wasn't Silas' mate.

One year, one month, one *day* would be more than he'd ever hoped to have as the man Silas loved. If that's all they were destined for before Silas found someone else, someone better, he'd take it.

And when he was alone again, he'd hoard his memories of belonging to Silas the way a dragon collected gold—wallowing in it, an eternal guard of his most precious riches.

But how fucking selfish would it be to expose Silas and his family to Cain all over again, for at most a few years of feeling whole?

What if choosing Silas meant choosing to give him happiness and forsaking his own?

Words still evaded him, so Sam pressed kisses all across Silas' chest, right over his heart. He wiped at Sam's tears and turned him so they were spooned together.

Silas fell asleep that way, holding Sam tight like he was afraid he'd disappear while they slept.

Sam's thoughts kept him up until well after midnight, though, long after Silas' breaths became even and deep with sleep. Again, he thought of what it meant to choose Silas, to make him happy, warm, and safe—just like he'd done for Sam.

Ever so gently, Sam shifted out of Silas' embrace without waking him. Reaching for his phone, he pulled up the text string that had always made him want to vomit. Thumbs shaking, he tapped out a single message, hitting send before he could overthink.

Then, Sam curled back into Silas' arms; they fit around him like they were made to hold each other. He lay awake for a long time, soaking in every sensation and committing to memory the feeling of being surrounded by Silas.

CHAPTER 15

SAM

Halloween dawned crisp and overcast.

A snowstorm was forecasted later that night, but the air felt oddly still that morning, foreboding in a way Sam thought fitting.

Cal's words spun round and round in his head while Sam had stared at his phone for the last four days, waiting to see if Cain would text him back. He hadn't yet, but in the end, it didn't matter.

Sam knew what he had to do.

He was thankful he had one more good day to soak up, though. One more day filled with laughter and family. One last treasure to hoard.

Silas had invited Jaime and Finn over to celebrate and hand out candy to trick-or-treaters, and the two of them would arrive in a few minutes to set up.

Jaime had big decorating plans, and it'd warmed Sam's

heart to hear the giddiness in his voice as he listed off every-thing they were bringing over.

He was soaking that up, too.

Silas had told Sam about the Halloween plans the day after he'd confronted him about leaving. The desperation in his voice was palpable as he said Jaime was looking forward to spending the holiday together. Underneath his forced casual tone, Sam knew that Silas was hoping he'd bought at least a few more days before Sam made a decision.

He regretted everything he'd ever done to make Silas think he *wanted* to leave.

They'd tiptoed around each other since they'd returned home, both of them holding their breath while they waited for the other shoe to drop. It seemed Silas was doing every-thing he could to entice Sam to stay without forcing the issue.

Sheppard had called with an update on Riley and the wreck, saying that even though DA Rivera had been there, but not *really* there, for his confession, the investigation had gone in a different direction after receiving "new information."

The DA hadn't shared what that was but implied that it appeared as though more than one person may have been involved. Sam speculated that they'd been investigating Cain for months and had found a way to tie him to the wreck.

It left Riley in a state of limbo, resting in the Silver Rapids safe house with Buck and waiting for the doctor. Given the uncertainty, Silas had made it clear that the best place for Sam to be was with him until everything was sorted out.

Sam hadn't disagreed, but kept the rest of his thoughts about Riley to himself for now.

Mainly, that Riley had lied.

He'd taken the blame for the wreck far too easily.

When Sam had lightly pressed him for details, Riley clearly had no idea what'd happened that night. He claimed he'd driven down the road and wrecked right away after changing his mind and attempting to turn back, but Sam remembered seeing the car idling outside for some minutes before the engine revved, followed by the crash.

He was also fairly certain someone had tried to come inside his apartment first, or intended to, before changing their mind. He'd heard shuffling on his porch several times before the accident, and that wasn't considering the hours he'd had headphones on.

So, Sam didn't believe Riley, but that left him wondering why he'd fold so easily and take the blame. Did he want out of Salt Creek so badly that prison was a better alternative? Was he protecting someone? Had Cain ordered him to take the fall for the wreck, should he be asked about it?

Between his spinning thoughts about leaving, waiting for Cain's response to his message, and Riley's motivations for lying about the wreck, the days had slipped by in a blur.

The tentative balance he and Silas had created carried into the bedroom as well. They didn't discuss their intense sex from the night they'd returned home, and in an unspoken truce, neither of them had initiated in the days since, either.

They'd clung to each other, though, every night. Sam was terribly afraid he'd never be able to fall asleep again without the safety and peace that came with dreaming in Silas' arms.

Sam was sitting on the living room sofa, wringing his hands, when Silas trotted down the stairs, wolfy ears swiveling, probably listening for Jaime and Finn's truck.

"They're pulling into the driveway now... Are you alright?" Silas asked, brows pinching.

Sam looked up and forced a smile. "Yeah," he said, clearing his scratchy throat. "I'm fine. Let's go help them unload."

Silas only watched him with those eyes that always saw all of him.

He'd never hated it.

~

THE DAY WENT by too fast.

One minute, Sam was caught drooling over the way Silas' shirt pulled up when he extended his arms over his head, hanging decorations, and the next, he was hugging Jaime goodbye, holding on a little too tight and a second too long for Silas not to clock it.

He'd carved pumpkins and hung string lights all over the house, anywhere Jaime pointed, and he'd even worn one of Silas' flannel shirts as part of the make-shift Woodsman costume Jaime had all but shoved him into.

Silas' reaction to seeing Sam dressed in his shirt was another piece of gold he would hoard.

He shuddered when he recalled the leather pants Jaime

had *wanted* him to wear. He may have been soaking in his brother's joy for the holiday, but even that had its limits.

Sam remembered how much he'd loved Halloween as a kid, even after their mom died. He had so many wonderful memories of trick-or-treating with Jaime and watching spooky movies together. Tonight, seeing all the trick-or-treaters in their costumes running along ahead of their parents made Sam yearn for something he'd scarcely let himself imagine.

A little one of his own, bouncing with energy as they walked down the sidewalk, squealing at the spooky decorations in people's yards. Maybe another perched up on the shoulders of the tall, broad, gentle man at his side.

The clarity of that vision hurt his eyes.

When the door *snicked* shut behind Jaime and Finn, Sam stood in the living room, listening to the warm crackle of the fire and watching the shadows dance along the wall, lit only by the low-burning lanterns and fairy lights strung along the floor and banister.

He felt more than he heard Silas come up behind him, standing close enough for the heat radiating off his chest to warm Sam's back.

"What do you want, Sammy? Whatever it is, I'll give it to you," Silas whispered, grasping his shoulders and turning him so they were facing each other.

Sam saw everything he'd ever wanted right there already, glowing in Silas' eyes. "I want tonight to last forever. I don't want it to be over yet," Sam whispered back, tucking a strand of loose hair behind Silas' ear.

He pressed his cheek into Sam's palm. "Then it doesn't have to be. Come on," he said, taking Sam by the hand.

He half expected Silas to pull him up the stairs to bed; he would have followed easily. He was surprised when instead, Silas guided him to the open space in front of the fireplace and reached for his phone.

Tapping the screen a few times, he tossed the device onto the sofa just as the first few notes of a song began to play through the wireless speaker perched on the coffee table.

It was immediately familiar, one of those old melodies that'd been in so many movies and television shows over the years that Sam couldn't pinpoint when he'd first heard it. The music started slow, and he imagined dashing gentlemen in tuxedos finding their lovely matching dance partners and pulling them to the ballroom floor, settling into each other's arms before they began to sway in time with the music.

Sam could feel his heartbeat in his ears.

A blush sat high on Silas' cheeks. "I think of you every time I hear this song. Please dance with me, Sammy?" Silas asked, holding out his hand.

Sam would have climbed a ladder to the moon, carved out a piece of glowing rock, and brought it all the way back down for Silas, had he asked.

Sam took his hand. "Ok," he whispered, not trusting his voice with more words than that.

He only had a moment to be self-conscious, a fraction of a second to wonder what to do with his feet before Silas tugged him close with an arm around his waist, guiding Sam's hand up and over his shoulder while he cradled the other in his giant palm.

Then Silas moved, and Sam couldn't think about anything anymore except the way he knew, deep in his bones, that they were always meant to do this. They had been molded for this exact moment, their bodies fitting together so perfectly it couldn't have been an accident.

Sam had never believed in coincidences, and the way they held each other as they swayed to the soaring music was fate.

Silas spun and twirled Sam, who grinned at how brightly this moment shined. Together, they danced in circles in front of the fire, laughter filling the air when Sam stood on his tiptoes to twirl Silas under his arm, and he had to duck and crouch to squeeze through.

The sheen in Silas' eyes told Sam he hadn't chosen this song on a whim; by the end, they'd stopped spinning, catching their breath and swaying together while Silas seemed to be silently begging along with the singer that they stay together forever.

They held each other close as the music faded out, leaving only the sound of the crackling fire and wind whistling down the chimney.

Words didn't fit in this moment, with Silas bent low to rest their foreheads together, but when Sam looked up, he found a question waiting in his eyes.

"I still don't want tonight to end," Sam answered hoarsely.

Silas nodded, gathered Sam in his arms, and kissed him.

It was searing.

Sam opened his mouth immediately, yielding everything he was and had ever been to this man who'd so very patiently tempted his heart out of the cage of his ribs and held it tenderly.

It would never fit back inside Sam's chest now, nor would it find a home with anyone else. Silas was the keeper of his heart, the hunter who'd coaxed his broken and weary soul into the world and shown him what it meant to be alive.

"Take me to bed, Silas," Sam breathed before fisting his sweatshirt and pulling him back into the kiss.

He'd told himself one more day. One more good fucking day.

The memories of making love with Silas would probably haunt him forever, but at least they'd be good ones.

Pulling and pushing and stumbling over each other, they somehow made it up the stairs and into their bedroom, where Silas laid Sam out like he was the most precious gift.

He quickly shifted back into his human form, tucking the ears and claws away for now, and peeled Sam's clothes off like he was opening a present with wrapping that was too beautiful to tear, kissing every inch of exposed skin as he went.

It wasn't until Sam was fully naked, watching Silas shuck off his own clothes far more hastily than he'd done with Sam's, that he realized they'd never been fully bare before each other.

The thought made Sam almost shy when Silas crawled up the bed to hover above him, his massive cock hard and hanging heavily between them. "Tell me what you want, Sammy," he repeated, the same words he'd spoken downstairs a few minutes or hours or lifetimes ago. "Tell me what you want, and I'll give it to you."

Sam cupped his face between both hands, pulling him down so their bodies were flush. "All of it, Silas. I want to be full. I want to feel whole. Give me everything."

Silas moaned, his voice hitching as he took Sam's mouth back in a messy kiss, rutting their cocks together. "Yes. Always, yes."

Despite Sam's request, Silas took his time, hands dancing along Sam's shoulders and chest, tweaking at his nipples until Sam whimpered and arched into his touch. He continued lower to his stomach, kissing along the soft pouch under his belly button before firmly grabbing at Sam's thighs to angle one up and around his shoulder.

All the while, Silas pressed reverent words into Sam's skin. "Beautiful... beautiful. I should have taken more time to taste, to memorize, I should have..." he trailed off, and Sammy didn't hear the rest before Silas bit into the soft flesh of his thigh, causing him to cry out from the pleasure-pain.

It hadn't been hard enough to break the skin, but Sam would have a mark—like Silas intentionally left a piece of himself behind.

He soothed the area with his tongue before taking hold of Sam's cock and lapping at the head, tasting the precum leaking from his reddened tip. He didn't linger, though, hastened by Sam's demanding tugs in his hair and pleas to hurry.

The way they were exploring each other tonight felt wholly different from the way Silas had taken Sam apart the last time. This was frantic and bittersweet in a way that had tears threatening to fall, like they were rushing to consume as much of each other as they could before the clock struck midnight.

The lube was within reach, and apparently, Silas wasn't in the mood to tease anymore because he quickly slicked up a finger and massaged around Sam's opening, slowly sinking inside.

Sam shivered at the sensation, adjusting quickly, and he was flying by the time Silas had three fingers scissoring inside him, curling as he opened Sam more hastily than he'd done a few days ago.

"Silas, Silas I'm ready. I need you. I—*humph*—I want your cock inside of me."

Sam wasn't as stretched as he should have been to take him, thick and long as he was, but he wanted it to hurt a little at first. He craved the strain of taking Silas into his body; he wanted to feel it tomorrow so he'd know for sure this hadn't been a dream.

A reminder that he'd been whole, even for a short time.

Silas gave him one last kiss that was mostly tongue and sat back on his heels, the feral look in his eyes equally desperate. "Condom?" he asked, wild-eyed and wrecked.

Sam shook his head. "No. Like this. Fill me up."

Silas nodded, slicking up his cock with a few pumps before wiping his fingers off on the sheets. He stuffed a pillow beneath the small of Sam's back and took hold of his legs, wrapping them around his waist so his ass was propped in Silas' lap.

He leveraged one hand on Sam's hip and notched the broad head of his cock against Sam's hole with the other.

Before he pushed in, he leaned over and pressed his forehead into Sam's. "Stay with me, Sammy. Don't look away."

"I'm right here," Sam said, grabbing onto Silas' shoulders.

Silas surged in.

Sam's mouth dropped open, his breath whooshing out in a gasp that Silas breathed in. He didn't close his eyes, though, not even when he winced from the stretch that was well on the side of too much.

He would never look away.

"I'm hurting you," Silas said, his voice broken. Their mouths were so close Sam felt the words more than he heard them.

Silas began to pull out, but Sam locked his ankles tight around Silas' back, digging his nails into his shoulders. "Don't. I'm fine—just give me a minute."

Silas coaxed him into another wet kiss, hands gingerly holding Sam's face still, thumb caressing his cheek.

It didn't take Sam long to adjust; soon, he was circling his hips and whining into Silas' mouth. "More. More, Silas."

Silas huffed and pressed in further. It took Sam's breath away again, but the stretch was no longer painful—it was *right*.

Sam threw his head back and moaned, relishing in Silas' slow thrusts as deep as he could go.

Silas braced his weight on one forearm and took hold of Sam's waist with his other hand, holding him down for Silas to take.

And he took.

In deep, slinging thrusts, Silas pistoned in and out of

Sam, sweat dripping off him. "You feel so good, Sammy," he said, but it almost sounded like he was about to cry.

Overcome with whatever emotion it was that poured out of them both, Sam clawed at him, gripping handfuls of his ass and pulling him down, stuffing his fat cock inside over and over and over.

He couldn't get enough. It would never be too much. He would never be too full—not of Silas. Not of this.

Sam's own cock jerked with each thrust, bouncing off his belly. Silas nailed his prostate every few thrusts, driving breathy *uh, uh, uh's* out of him.

It was all-consuming; the sensation of Silas moving in him was more than Sam had ever known—had ever thought possible. He'd have fingerprints bruised into his waist and thighs from where Silas held him firm.

He wished he could have them tattooed. The bite mark, too.

What Silas did to him was more than sex—it was owning. He dropped his weight right on top of Sam, holding him down, and tangled his fingers into Sam's hair, angling his head to the side so he could nip and suck along his neck.

"You're everything... everything," Silas mumbled before biting into Sam's neck, his shoulder, his pec.

Marking him. More reminders that they'd done this— that Silas had wanted him enough to leave a trace.

More gold to hoard.

Sam carded his fingers through Silas' hair, holding him close.

He wanted this to last forever. His cock ached to be

touched, the friction of their bodies just shy of enough to get him off, but he didn't reach for it. He wanted Silas to stay in him always.

Silas shoved an arm beneath Sam's shoulders, cradling him close when his thrusts became more erratic. He was almost there. "Let me keep you, Sammy. Please let me keep you," he begged.

Sam held on tight and had no words except for Silas' name, over and over.

Silas came on a broken shout, trembling above Sam while he shoved his cock inside as far as he could go.

Unable to take it any longer, Sam fit a hand between them and brought himself off seconds after, only needing a few pumps until he spilled warm between them.

Sam clung to Silas for long minutes, well after the cum drying on his belly became uncomfortable. If he never let go, Silas couldn't pull out and leave him empty and incomplete again.

Of course, he did eventually pull out, and Sam shuddered at the loss.

Silas didn't get up this time, though, not even to clean them off. He fished for his discarded sweatshirt, quickly swiping at the sticky cum on their stomachs before nearly tackling Sam back into bed, bundling them under the covers, and wrapping himself around Sam.

Sam relished the sensation of being squashed by Silas.

Rubbing his nose back and forth through the soft hair on Silas' chest for long minutes, Sam finally spoke into the quiet. "That was..." he trailed off, unable to find the words.

"Yeah. It was," Silas whispered back, not needing him to.

His arms tightened around Sam, and he took a deep, sure breath, like he'd finally come to a decision. "You can let go with me, Sammy. I love how strong and confident and independent you are. It's sexy as fuck. But here, with me... you can be soft."

Cupping the back of Sam's neck possessively, Silas continued, "I'll be whatever you need me to be, for as long as you need me to be it. So, just... *stay?* Please. Whatever secrets you're keeping, whatever you're holding back, it doesn't matter. I choose you. Every day."

Sam's tears tracked down his nose, landing softly on Silas' chest. He pulled back just enough to look at him fully. "You can't know that, though. You can't promise me that. You don't know everything."

"I *can*," Silas growled. He rolled so that Sam was on his back, staring up at him. "I can promise you that because you're *mine*. You've always been mine. And I've always been yours. I don't care about the rest."

Sam began shaking his head. "What are you saying?" he whispered.

Silas searched his face. "I have waited for most of my life to find you again. I have scented every breeze and ocean current and grocery store aisle and gas station and bookstore —for *you*. Don't you understand? You are my mate, Sammy."

Sam could only blink, mouth slightly parted in awe.

Mate.

He was Silas' mate. Silas was *his* mate.

Yes.

Sam felt like he'd been staring at the same scattering of stars across the night sky his whole life, never finding a rhyme or reason to any of them, only for Silas to come along and turn him around, pointing to the constellations just over his shoulder.

Magic had been there all along; he just hadn't been looking properly.

Sam had accepted that he could never be Silas' everything. He'd accepted that, if he should stay, their time together was finite—and Silas would still be worth it.

Now, though... "Why didn't you tell me this before? Why keep this from me?" Sam asked hoarsely.

Silas' brow pinched, his eyes pleading. "Because... because I want you to choose me, too. I want you to want to be with me. And because I love you. I love you so much, and I couldn't bear it if you thought the only reason I wanted you was because of some bond neither of us chose—because I *do* choose you. And I can't breathe at the thought of letting you go. I *won't* let you go. I know you're going to try and leave. I've seen it on your face all week—"

"Silas—" Sam said, trying to get his attention, but he pressed on.

"—but I truly don't think I can let you. Just give me a chance. Choose *me*. Tell me what you need from me, and I'll give it to you every day. I knew I wanted you the instant I heard you barging into my house to go toe-to-toe with a stranger, a *shifter* for fucks's sake, all to rescue someone you love. I need you like air. More. These past five months have been torture without you. Do you want to know why there was a path for Riley to follow back to your apartment? Because I was there every day. Every fucking day, Sammy. I can't let you go. I won't. So don't ask me to. *Please—*"

"Silas," Sam interrupted again, raising his voice a notch and cupping a hand to his cheek.

Silas stopped this time, out of breath, and looked at Sam like the entire universe hung in the balance of what he would say next.

"Silas. My Silas."

It was time.

He'd planned to wait until morning—wanting to cherish one more night in Silas' arms—but he couldn't put it off any longer.

Silas deserved the truth.

As terrified as he looked that Sam would leave, Sam was equally terrified that in a few moments, Silas would be the one asking him to.

Lightly pushing against Silas' chest so he could sit up, Sam swung his legs out of bed.

Silas stayed frozen, watching as he walked over to his ever-shrinking pile of things, the rest having already dispersed and found a home throughout the house.

He pulled a folded-up piece of paper from the pocket of his unwashed jeans and carried it back over to the bed. Worrying at the corner of the note, Sam found Silas' eyes.

Committed to memory the love he saw there.

Love. Yes. Silas had called him that from the very start.

"You deserve so much better than me," Sam said, amazed he even had a voice at all. "But I will give you all of me, anyway. I choose you, Silas. And if you still want me after you've read this, I will choose you every single day for the rest of my life."

He passed Silas the note and flipped on the bedside lamp so he could read.

"What is this, Sammy?" Silas asked, sitting up.

"It's everything. Everything you've deserved to know from the very beginning."

THERE ARE NO COINCIDENCES

SAM

SIX MONTHS, FOUR DAYS, AND FIFTEEN HOURS AGO

Ping

> *Ping*
>
> *Ping*

The repeated notifications jolted Sam from his fitful dreams. Rolling over in bed, he checked his phone to see it was barely five o'clock in the morning—he'd only been asleep for a few hours, at most.

Fearing it was Jaime texting after another one of his nightmares, Sam rubbed the sleep from his eyes and breathed a sigh of relief when he saw it was only one of the Google alerts he'd set up.

His momentary relief turned to dread, however, when he realized what that meant.

Sam's hands began to shake as he pulled up one of the

alerts, and his body tensed, muscles locking up until he couldn't really feel anything anymore as he read the headline it directed him to:

Eye witness in gripping Monroe murder trial uncovered: Jaime Lamont saw everything!
By: Derek Koven

Sam threw himself out of bed and began pacing the apartment, fumbling with his phone to dial the number he'd sworn he would never call again.

Derek picked up on the fifth ring. "I knew you'd call," he answered sleepily.

"You're a piece of *shit*," Sam snarled in answer, anger and fear making his voice crack. "You said you wouldn't publish it, you spineless fuck!"

Derek exhaled a tired sigh, like Sam was a toddler throwing a tantrum. "We got a tip-off on who the unidentified witness was yesterday. The story was already a go. I just got ahead of it. You should thank me; I left out the part where the police thought your brother was the one who did it for a while."

Sam tore his fingers through his hair, pulling at the ends. "I don't give a fuck about your excuses. You published it— that's a forfeit of our agreement. Give me my money back, or I'll report you to the police for blackmail."

Derek chuckled. "No, you won't, because then you'd

have to tell them how I found out. You'd have to tell your brother you got tipsy, fucked a guy in a bathroom, and then cried about how hard it was to take care of him all the time after he saw someone nearly get ripped in half."

Sam covered his mouth and squeezed his eyes shut, not sure if the sound he was holding back was a scream or a sob.

"Look," Derek continued, "I'm sorry about the way everything had to happen. The trial's in a few weeks anyway. This couldn't have gone on any longer after that. It was going to come out anyway. Let it go."

Once he was sure he wouldn't start crying, Sam took a breath and said, "Go walk off a cliff and make the world a better place, Derek," and hung up.

Then, he cried.

Deep, chest-wrenching sobs Sam hadn't even known he was capable of spilled out, months worth of dread and anxiety and shame. All the words of support and under-standing and love he hadn't been able to share with Jaime, all the little secrets he'd kept and lies he'd told—everything he'd shoved down and suppressed forced its way out of his chest.

After a few minutes, he collected himself enough to call Detective Sutton to ask what they planned to do to protect Jaime, only for her to sleepily feed him some bullshit about making sure a patrol vehicle would be in the area.

"He lives in the middle of nowhere, Alaska, for fuck's sake! Monroe is a half-hour's drive from Jaime's cabin. What the fuck do you mean, a patrol vehicle will be *in the area?*" he'd snapped back.

She didn't deserve his venom, but Sam was too much of a coward to give it to the person who did.

Detective Sutton sighed. "We'll make sure someone is parked out there for the next couple of days, how's that?"

Sam pulled his lips back in a near snarl. "Would it take more manpower to make sure he stays alive or to investigate his murder once he's killed? Let's not forget the whole reason this is a problem in the first place is because you haven't even caught everyone involved in the first one. Do you really want a second on your hands?"

"Jesus Christ, Sam, I'm not implying—"

"THEN WHAT CAN WE DO TO MAKE SURE HE STAYS SAFE?" he yelled over her.

She was quiet for a few heartbeats. "There's a security firm that operates out of Silver Rapids. They take clients that travel through the area, set up local security systems, that sort of thing. It would be expensive as hell, and we don't have the budget, but if you have the money and they're available, I can coordinate with them to provide around-the-clock body protection until the trial."

Sam didn't even have to think about it. "What's their number?"

It wasn't until she'd given him the contact information for the security firm and they hung up that Sam fully processed what she'd said.

It would be expensive as hell.

Of course, it would be.

Scratching a hand across the stubble he'd let grow out, Sam went to pull up the financial stats on his most recent audio.

It'd been a while since he'd shared anything, and all the audios he'd put out in the last few months had been noticeably lackluster. He'd been losing a few subscribers here and there instead of gaining like he needed to make back what he'd paid for Derek's silence. Besides, what he brought in barely covered his rent and the money he sent Jaime to help with his expenses.

Before he could flip to the app, though, a text from Derek came through. Tensing, Sam debated deleting it outright without opening it, but the old fear won out.

What if he was threatening to share even more information, and Sam was caught off guard?

FUCKFACE

For what it's worth, I really am sorry. If you're in a bind, give this number a call. Just be careful.

Just be careful? What the fuck did that mean?

Sam looked up the number Derek had forwarded along with the message, but couldn't find any information.

Sitting down on the edge of his bed, he quickly ran through his options. He could try and ask for a loan, but that would take too long and require him to provide too much financial information which could lead to questions about the money transfers to Derek.

He could ask Jaime to come stay with him until the trial so he could keep an eye on him, but really, Sam wouldn't be much use in a dangerous situation, and he couldn't face being around Jaime that much without telling him the truth.

He could depend on Monroe PD's finest to keep an eye on things, but Sam trusted them about as far as he could throw them.

With his thoughts spinning and cluttered, Sam felt backed into a corner.

If you're in a bind, give this number a call.

He should delete that text and never think about it again. He should treat any suggestion coming from Derek like it was radioactive waste. He should come clean to Jaime, beg for his forgiveness, and ask for the police's help to keep him safe.

He should have done a lot of things.

Instead, Sam called the number.

CHAPTER 16
SILAS

Silas stared down at the neatly folded paper, heart galloping in his chest.

Reaching out, he took Sammy's hand and pulled him closer. "Sit with me while I read it."

Sammy let Silas tuck him back into bed with his legs thrown over Silas' lap, but he immediately buried his face in the crook of Silas' underarm rather than look at him while he read.

His heart ached that Sammy actually thought whatever was in his note would be enough for Silas to reject him.

Never, his wolf snarled.

Never.

Looking down, Silas' hands shook as he unfolded the paper and began to read.

Silas,

    I love you.

    I have a lot of things to share but that feels most important. I love you, and I'm sorry I have to tell you this way. I'm afraid if I try to say it out loud I'll chicken out before I'm done, and you deserve to know everything.

He pressed a kiss to Sammy's temple and wiped at the tears already forming.

    Ok. Now, the hard part.

    I'm the reason Jaime's name was leaked to the media last spring.

Silas blinked, surprised. Of all the secrets he'd speculated Sammy was keeping, that wasn't one of them.

    I met a man named Derek in a bar two months after Jaime was attacked in Vera's house. I don't normally go to bars, and I hardly ever drink because I'm afraid I'll become a fuck-up alcoholic like my father, so the few I had hit me harder than I'd expected.

    I was lonely and very scared that Jaime

would never get better, that he needed serious help that I couldn't give after what he'd gone through, and I needed someone to talk to and feel close to. Those aren't excuses, just... context, I think.

Derek and I hooked up, and then he let me talk, and I'm deeply ashamed that I accidentally let slip that my brother was the one who'd seen the murder.

I chose the wrong person to confide in, and I've regretted that every single day since. The next day, Derek asked me for money and threatened to publish Jaime's name when I refused. I had no idea he worked for the local news station.

Silas forced himself to unclench his hand where he'd partially crumpled the letter.

Sammy had been scared and alone and needed someone, and *Derek* had taken advantage of that. When Silas found him, and he *would* find him...

His wolf's answering growl rumbled low in his chest.

He pulled Sammy even closer and rubbed his cheek into his hair before continuing.

I ended up paying him every bit of my savings over the course of the year to keep quiet.

But then, last spring, I woke up and saw the articles with Jaime's name all over the internet, and I knew he'd published anyway after he realized I had nothing left.

The police had told us to be careful because they thought there were more people involved in the murder than the one they'd arrested, but when Jaime's name was leaked, they weren't going to offer him any protection beyond a cop car parked in his driveway.

I was scared and ashamed and didn't know what to do. The detective gave me your security firm's contact information, but I didn't have the money to pay for it.

I had already called Derek and demanded he give me my money back since he'd broken our agreement, but he refused. After we hung up, though, he texted me the phone number of someone I could call if I needed quick money.

A horrible, sinking pit settled in Silas' stomach; he was so afraid he already knew where this was going. He soothed a hand up and down Sammy's back and read on.

Please understand, I don't regret that I met you, Silas. Meeting you has been the best thing that's ever happened to me. In the five months we spent apart, I'd lie awake at night and imagine all the things I should've done differently, all the ways I could've been a better brother or friend, but I've always been grateful we met.

Even still, I do wish I could go back and just come clean to Jaime right then. I wish I would've admitted what I'd done, explained why I'd ignored him for the better part of a year, and begged for his forgiveness.

I wish I hadn't called the number Derek gave me.

But I did. I called Cain and borrowed every bit of what I paid for Jaime's security in exchange for a favor, any favor, that he could call in at any time. I didn't realize who he was, what he'd done, and how involved he was in all of this until we were on our way to help Jaime and Finn at the safe house. By then, it was too late. I couldn't go back, and I didn't want to drag you or Jaime or anyone further in with me.

Sammy had been so upset after their phone call with Jaime and Finn. Silas had assumed it was his way of processing the shock, fear, and adrenaline they'd experienced waiting for Jaime to call back, but in retrospect, he could see that was when everything changed.

His own words came back to him. *I'd do anything to keep him out of our lives.*

Oh, Sammy.

I lied to Jaime—there has never been a stalker. The only danger in being close to me is becoming trapped in one of Cain's twisted games. But it's the lie I told you, Silas, that I don't want you, that haunts me the most.

I do want you. You are good and strong and whole. You're the funniest person I know and the only one who's ever made me feel safe to be myself. You're who I've been waiting for, without knowing I was waiting for anyone. I know you'll be an amazing alpha. You're the glue that holds all of us together, Silas. Me most of all. You deserve so much more than what I've put you through.

I've saved all the money from my insurance claim, security deposit, and work these past months. Double what I borrowed. The night we returned from your parents' house, I sent Cain a message offering it all in exchange for leaving you and your family alone. Forever. I don't know if he'll agree, but it's the least I can do for involving him in your life again. And if you'd like me to leave you alone forever, too, I will.

I'm so sorry, Silas. For lying, and keeping the truth from you for so long. I never meant for any of this to happen. I'll understand if you need time to think or if you'd like for me to leave. Honestly, I still don't know if I should have already. But I choose you, and that means I trust you to make that decision for yourself.

If you decide you'd like me to stay, I promise to love you as much as it's possible to love someone every single day for the rest of my life. You are the keeper of my heart, and there will never be a secret between us again.

Always yours,
Sammy

Silas delicately refolded the letter and reached over Sammy to lay it on the nightstand.

Both of their hearts pounded in the quiet. Pulling Sammy up so that he straddled Silas' lap, he cradled his face in both hands. "When did you write that?"

Sammy looked down, avoiding Silas' gaze. "Two days ago."

Two days.

Silas fingered a stray bit of hair at Sammy's nape, curling from his sweat. "Why didn't you give it to me then?"

Sammy's shoulders curved inward. "Because I wanted one more day with you. With all of you. One more day where you wanted me before you knew."

Silas lightly curved his hand around Sammy's neck, gently possessive, and tipped his chin up with his thumb. "So you weren't planning to leave me?"

Sammy shook his head, eyes finally meeting his. His voice was raw and pleading when he said, "I *can't*. Maybe I should have. You were right, I thought about it in the beginning. I thought about leaving and never telling you the truth. But I just can't, Silas. I—"

Sammy's swallow rolled along Silas' palm. He continued, "I love you. I love you, and I need you, and I can't go back to missing you. I can't go another day without hearing you laugh. I don't deserve to stay, and if you want me to go, I'll respect that. Even... even now that I know I'm your, um, your mate."

Silas gently shifted him from his lap and slid off the bed.

Wordlessly, he pulled Sammy forward so he sat on the edge and knelt before him, the position making it so he looked up at Sammy ever so slightly. Silas lost himself for a moment in his eyes, so deep and open he could dive forever and never mine all the emeralds they held.

They had so much to discuss: Sammy's money, Cain's involvement from the very beginning, Derek's last name and home address... Except, out of all the things he'd shared, all he'd confessed, there were only two things that truly mattered.

Two things that shone in Sammy's eyes so brightly.

I love you.

I want you.

"You should put something warm on," Sammy whispered, filling the quiet and tracing along the goosebumps that had formed on Silas' arms. "It's snowing out. You'll freeze."

Silas blinked, just now noticing the snow falling outside through the window over Sammy's shoulder.

A wet chuckle bubbled out of him, and the outline of Sammy momentarily blurred through his tears. "Stay. Stay with me forever, Sammy."

Silas dropped hasty, tear-soaked kisses all over Sammy's hands, his shoulders, and his face. "Stay with me and help me be the best alpha I can be because I'm not whole—not without you. Stay with me so I can tell you I love you every day because you deserve to hear it every day. Stay with me to build a family, if that's something you want. Stay with me to build a pack. Stay with me so I can take care of you and let you be soft because you deserve that every day, too," he continued.

They were both fully crying now.

Silas beamed through his tears, canines on full display. He'd never been good at hiding them from Sammy.

He'd never needed to hide them from Sammy.

Not once.

Grasping his mate by the shoulders, Silas finished, "Stay with me so that we fight our battles together. I need your claws and teeth on my side. Please stay with me, Sammy."

Sammy ran a shaky hand under his nose to clear it, only to

end up streaking snot across his cheek instead. Silas grabbed a tissue from the nightstand and gently wiped it away.

"Are you sure you want me? Did you read all of it? Do you know what I've d-done—" Sammy stuttered through hitched breaths.

"Shh," Silas soothed.

He guided Sammy forward so his cheek rested against Silas' chest and rubbed his back. "I read all of it. I know that you were lonely and dealing with an incredibly stressful situation while providing care for your hurting brother. I know you sought solace in a companion, that you were looking to trust someone, to lighten the heavy burden from your shoulders because you were carrying too much. I know he used that against you, blackmailed you, and emotionally manipulated you for months before selling you out to my uncle."

Emotion swelled in Silas' chest. "I know you did your best to deal with all of that on your own. I know you chose to protect your brother at a steep personal cost, and I know you put my well-being above your own over and over. Which won't happen again, but we can talk about that later."

Sammy was shaking. "It's not—that's not—you're making me look better than I really w-was. I shouldn't have d-done any of that."

Silas shushed him again, gently rocking back and forth. "I know you made mistakes, but we all do. I'm framing what happened to you in the way someone who loves you would. You've been far too unkind to yourself, love. It's not healthy to be so harsh. I wonder if talking to someone, a professional, would help you."

Sam pulled back, wiping at his face with the used tissue. "I'll think about it."

Silas smiled. "Good."

Sammy peered up at him through wet lashes, his eyes even greener from crying. "So... you want me to stay."

"I want you to stay."

"Even though I'm just another way for your uncle to mess up your life?"

Silas' face hardened. "Come here," he said, tugging Sammy off the bed so he was straddling Silas' lap again. "You are *mine*. My Sammy. My love. My mate. And I am yours. Nothing else matters."

"But—"

"No," Silas cut in, kissing the words from Sammy's lips. "None of that. Not tonight. We can talk about everything else in the morning. Let me just—let me show you you're mine. Can I?"

There was so much relief and trust and love shining in Sammy's eyes it nearly broke Silas to see it; he'd really thought he would be turned away. "Ok. Yes, show me how to be yours."

Sammy's hands began running all over Silas' back, frantically pulling on his arms to get closer, like he'd finally let go of the fear anchoring him down and keeping him from embracing Silas fully.

Nipping and sucking at every inch of skin he could reach, Sammy consumed Silas like he wanted to crawl inside him.

Silas grew hard again at the attention, rallying even

though they'd just had sex not even an hour ago. He growled, finding Sammy's lips in a brain-scrambling kiss.

It wasn't until Sammy ran his hands through Silas' hair, fingers catching on his wolfy ears, that he realized he'd partially shifted at some point in their conversation.

Our mate.

Want to be with him.

He's ours.

Make him ours.

Sammy gently massaged the base of his ears, and Silas melted, whining as he pulled away to catch his breath.

Fucking hell, that felt good.

"Sssammy—Sammy. I need to shift back. You've gotta quit that, or I won't be able to," Silas said, words slurring through his elongated canines.

"No," Sammy said, gripping his shoulders. "I want all of you. Like this. Show me how."

Drunk on Sammy, on everything they'd shared tonight, the part of Silas' brain that thought beyond *take mate now make him ours, knot him and bite him and keep him forever* hadn't caught up with his mouth yet. "You want to take my knot, love? You want my cock like this?" he asked, the low timbre of the alpha coming through.

He grasped Sammy by the hips and spun him around so he was on his knees, facing the bed.

"Shit," Sammy swore, reaching back to grip Silas' thigh. "Yes. Yes. So much, yes. Fuck me like this. I need it. *Please,* Alpha."

Silas' brain went completely offline, the alpha in full

control now, and words began pouring from him unbidden, falling onto Sammy's shoulders and neck between biting kisses. "You are mine. I won't ever let you go. I'll hunt you down if you try to leave me again. But you won't, will you?"

Sammy huffed. "No, I won't. Now *show* me," he said, petulant and trying to grind his ass back into Silas' cock.

Silas pushed him forward, so Sammy was braced against the side of the bed, his hands tangling in the sheets. "So greedy. I've already fucked you once tonight, and you're desperate for it again. You need it, don't you? You need my cock stuffing you deep. No one else can fill you the way I can. Say it." He smacked Sammy's ass for emphasis. "Say you're my mate, and my cock is the only one you'll ever need again."

"Silas, *please*," Sammy begged, reaching between his legs to jerk himself fully hard.

Silas smacked one of his cheeks again, nearly drooling at the way it jiggled. "Not until you say it."

Sammy whined. "I need your cock. I need you to fill me up. I'm yours, and you're mine. All mine. Now fucking show me—*Oh!*"

His words were cut off in a high-pitched moan as Silas pushed two fingers inside him at once, remembering at the very last minute to shift his claws away first.

He twisted and probed, stuffing the cum that'd trickled out from their first round back inside. Silas stalked every one of Sammy's hitched breaths, every facial expression, looking for any hint of discomfort or that it was too much.

Gauging his brows were pinched in pleasure and not

pain, Silas stood just long enough to grab the discarded bottle of lube off the bed, slick his fingers back up, and push three in at once.

Sammy jerked and moaned when Silas massaged over his sensitive prostate, precum leaking from the tip of his cock.

Silas gripped Sammy's lightly freckled hip with his free hand to keep him still and added a fourth finger, tucking his pinky in just enough to stretch Sammy's rim in preparation for his knot while he scissored and wiggled the others around inside.

Sammy was a mess.

Completely uninhibited, he pushed off the bed, sat back on his heels, and rode Silas' hand like it was the best fuck of his life.

The bond between them was a roaring blaze, a beacon lit on the mountaintop for all to see—bright and eternally fed. It would never go out. Sammy would never leave; Silas would claim him tonight and keep him always.

Blinking, some of Silas' humanity returned with the thought.

He pulled his fingers out, wiping them on the duvet, and turned Sammy just enough so they could look at each other. Panting, he said, "Sammy, love. We should talk about this first. I'm sorry, I shouldn't have started before you were sure."

Sammy stared up at him in a lust-induced daze before his gaze sharpened, eyes fierce and blazing. "I want you, Silas. I choose you, I choose this. I'm sure," he said, cupping Silas' face.

Silas nuzzled into the caress. "We can't go back. If I take you right now, I'll knot you, and if I knot you, I'll bite you. We'll be tied together forever. You'll always feel me with you. You can't leave after that. I wouldn't survive it. We can wait, Sammy. Wait until you're sure, until you're ready—"

Sammy turned his body further around to face Silas, his fingers digging into the hair at his nape. "Stop. I stayed away because I genuinely believed you were better off without me, not because I wasn't sure about you. I have wanted you since the day we met. I wanted you when you asked me if I knew what a fucking moose was. Driving away from you that day felt *wrong*, and every day apart was like half of me was missing. This bond between us isn't one-sided, Silas. It would be easier to chop off my own arm than leave you again."

Sammy tucked the strands of hair that had come loose from Silas' half-back bun behind his ears and continued, "If you want to stop, we'll stop. I'll wait as long as you need until you're sure of me. But I love you. I want you, always. I'm not strong enough to keep away from you for another moment. That's not going to be different in the morning, or tomorrow, or a year or lifetime from now."

Silas leaned down to kiss Sammy before pressing their foreheads together and cupping his shoulders. "I want to do this with you. My wolf is clawing up my throat to make you mine. It's just... There's nothing more sacred I can share with you than sealing our bond. There are mating ceremonies, sure, but this is the important part. This is what ties two fated people to each other forever. I've never been with anyone like this," he gestured to his partially shifted body. "I just want to know you're sure and that I haven't pressured you into it. That you know what it means—for us both."

Sammy took Silas' face between his hands. Tenderly, he kissed his forehead, one cheek, then the other. He kissed the tip of Silas' nose, nuzzling him there with his own, before delicately kissing his lips. It was chaste, probably the tamest kiss they'd ever shared.

And it would've brought Silas to his knees had he not already been there.

"I never thought I'd get married," Sammy said quietly. "Never thought I'd find someone I loved enough to commit my life to—but then I met you. I would marry you right now if you asked. I would make you mine in every way I understand and every way that's new to me. I'll take you as my mate right now or in ten years. As long as I'm with you, I'll be happy."

Silas kissed him, and that gravitational pull settled, solidifying with a resounding *click* that felt final—absolute. He pulled back just enough to speak. "I love you. Will you be my mate, Sammy?"

Sammy's smile was blinding. "Yes," he breathed.

Unwinding Sammy's arms from their fierce hold around his neck, Silas turned him so he was facing the bed again and pulled down several pillows to tuck under their knees.

"I think this angle will make it easier to take me," Silas rumbled into his ear, dropping soft kisses along Sammy's shoulder blades, his heart rate speeding up again.

Partially shifted, he really was a lot. Too much. Sammy would need to be open for him.

Sammy nodded, almost bashful at Silas' fussing, a blush

creeping up the back of his neck. "I want to be full of you, Silas," he murmured.

Silas licked up his nape with the flat of his tongue in response, savoring his scent as he followed the blush into the soft stubble by his ear.

Toasted marshmallows and crackling embers.

Silas tasted himself, too. He tasted his own scent mixed in from their lovemaking and days of sharing space and a bed.

Together, they tasted like *home*.

Their cocks had flagged while they'd paused to talk, but Silas didn't regret the interlude. He had more control over himself now; the alpha was still there, still ready to take what was his, but it didn't feel like a frantic fuck spinning out of control the way he'd felt a few days ago when Sammy had called him Alpha. Silas had been seconds away from knotting him right then and there.

"You'll tell me if I hurt you," Silas commanded roughly.

"I'm stretched from the first time," Sammy responded, rocking into Silas.

Silas reached around to stroke his erection back, palming his hip again. "Still. If I hurt you, tell me. We'll take a break and try again some other time. There's no rush, love. I want this to be good for us both," Silas said.

Sammy turned and lifted his face, so Silas led him into a filthy kiss that was mostly tongue.

Then Sammy grabbed the lube and smacked Silas in the chest with it. Smirking, he said, "Come on, *Alpha*. I think I can handle it. Get yourself ready and show me what you've got."

Silas growled, nipping and tugging on Sammy's earlobe. "Careful what you ask for, brat."

He did as he was told and slicked up his cock before tunneling three wet fingers back inside Sammy for good measure, savoring his surprised gasp and the noise he made when Silas *tap-tap-tapped* along his prostate.

"Fucking hell, I'm ready," Sammy said, digging his hand back into Silas' thigh.

Silas pulled his fingers out, watching as Sammy's stretched hole gaped in his absence, slick and begging to be filled again.

He pushed on the small of Sammy's back, coaxing his ass out with the other hand. "Look at how open you are for me, how filthy your hole is from the last time I was inside of you."

Sammy exaggerated the curve of his spine even more and pushed, flexing his hole. A bit of Silas' cum slipped out. "Alpha, *please*. Fill me up again," he crooned.

Mate is empty.

Mate wants to be full.

Knot him. Make him ours!

Silas cursed—so much for keeping his wits about him.

Knocking Sammy's legs wider, Silas shuffled forward so his knees bracketed either side of Sammy's, rutting his cock through the cleft in his cheeks before resting it there.

His chest rose and fell in great heaving breaths at the sight, and he grabbed hold of Sammy's hips to keep steady. In his partial shift, his hands were so large they nearly overlapped when he stretched his fingers to pull Sammy's cheeks apart.

From this angle, the leaking head of his cock reached up

to the dimples that framed his lower back. Silas pressed his thumbs into them, imagining himself tunneling all the way in there, snug inside his mate.

"Alright, love. Since you asked so nicely, I'll give you what you want. I'll stuff my knot nice and deep and make it so you feel me for days," he slurred through his teeth.

Silas guided Sammy so his back was flush with his chest. Gently, he wrapped one hand around his throat—not to constrict, but to hold. He wanted to feel the sounds Sammy made when he opened for him.

Sammy whimpered at the touch.

Fitting his lube-slick cock right up to Sammy's hole, Silas said, "Give me that noise you made the first time I put my cock in you. It's mine," and pushed the head inside.

Sammy made the punched-out gasp Silas craved. He swallowed the sound, high from it.

"*Shit*, Silas. I don't think it's going to fit," Sammy said roughly, clawing at Silas' hip.

Unable to hold back his own groan, he released Sammy's throat and pulled back just enough to watch his cock sink in a little more.

The initial stretch was easier this time, with Sammy still loose from their first round, but there was so much more of him left.

"Do you want to stop?" he asked, breathing like a freight train.

Sammy's nails dug in more. "Don't you fucking dare," he snarled.

Silas chuckled. "Then we'll take our time, work you open

nice and slow until your hole swallows my cock like the needy brat you are."

Silas was mesmerized by the way the tight ring of muscle clenched and gave way, clutching the head of his cock as he made a few shallow pumps. "That's it, love, open up for me," he said, pushing in deeper. "Fuck, you're still so tight, even after you've already taken me once tonight. Your needy little hole is sucking me right back in."

Sammy huffed and reached forward to fist the sheets.

He couldn't tear his eyes away from where they were joined. Sammy's ass was presented perfectly for him to take; he wanted to savor the sight.

Mine. All mine.

Silas slapped one of Sammy's cheeks. "All for me, yeah? No one else gets to see you stretched so wide."

Sammy keened and rocked backward, taking more of Silas. "No one else. I want your cum. Come on, Si. I want to feel you so deep. Plug me up. Give me everything."

Being inside Sammy was overwhelming; Silas felt more alive than ever before. Spurred on, he thrust forward in one long, slow push and fully seated himself.

They cried out together.

"Alright, love?" Silas asked through panting breaths, afraid he'd gone too far, too soon.

"M'fine," Sammy slurred. "S'deep... s'good, Si. So good." Sammy's chest expanded in a heavy breath, and he swayed his hips from side to side, pressing back even more.

"I can feel you—here," he continued, one hand releasing his white-knuckled grip on the bed sheets and cupping his lower belly. "Feels like you're all the way in here."

"*Fuck*," Silas swore. He reached one arm around and fit his hand atop Sammy's, pressing it into that soft pouch. He crossed his other arm around Sammy's chest and shoulders, seating his ass further into the cradle of Silas' hips.

He scooted his knees forward even more, and Sammy used the hand that wasn't pressed to his belly to frantically scramble for purchase on Silas' thigh, fitting them together so tight.

Silas pulled out and drove in again, hard, using his grip on Sammy's upper body to push down as he thrust up. "There? Can you feel me right there?" he asked, pressing harder on Sammy's lower belly at the same time he bottomed out.

Sammy made a small, choked-off sob. "Yeah."

"Good?" Silas asked, grunting with another deep pump into his mate.

"Yeah," Sammy repeated. "S'good. Don't—*hnnf*—don't stop!"

Setting a steady pace, Silas drove up into Sammy in short, brutal thrusts, holding him close as he made space inside his tight hole, cock lodged deeper than he'd ever been inside anyone else.

"D'you like it, mate? Feeling me so far inside you—*ah, fuck*—your tummy bulges?"

"*Uh-huh*," Sammy choked out. "I like it, I like it—it."

Silas would be worried he was hurting Sammy if not for the constant litany of husky sighs, moans, and jumbled pleas for more.

Still, they probably wouldn't be able to fuck like this every day.

Every other day, his wolf growled, preening at doing such a good job of reducing his brat of a mate to a puddle of pleasure.

With his orgasm bearing down on him, Silas released his hold on Sammy and planted one hand on the small of his back, tipping him forward against the mattress. He gripped Sammy's hips and powered into him, feeling his cock start to swell at the base, catching on Sammy's rim.

"*Oh, oh, oh!* Silas! It's—*hnngh*—I'm so close!" Sammy shouted, using one hand to brace against the mattress and the other to furiously stroke his cock.

Silas couldn't pull his knot out anymore; his eyes rolled back from the pleasure of locking into Sammy's warm hole. He leaned over, grinding and rocking as much as he could.

Sammy shuddered and screamed beneath him, his orgasm painting their sheets, clenching with every pulse.

Silas' teeth ached. "*Fuck,* that's it, love. I can feel you coming on my cock—milking my knot. I'm gonna bite you now—I'm gonna—*fuck!*"

Silas roared through his release, feeling like he'd just opened the valve on a firehose inside Sammy. Hips kicking, Silas turned his head and bit into Sammy's neck, anchoring them together.

Tying their souls forever.

Fleeting sensations and feelings and memories that weren't Silas' flooded his mind.

The sound of his own laughter. A large, warm hand pressed against his back and around his throat. Floating weightlessly up the stairs, carried by a pair of strong, sturdy arms. A love burning so intense it brought tears to his eyes.

The crackle and pop of a fireplace while he spun, spun, spun around their living room, smiling so wide his face hurt...

He was seeing himself, seeing *them*, through Sammy's eyes.

The wave of realization swelled and broke. Silas wrapped his arms around Sammy's middle, holding him close while they shuddered together from the profound intensity of their joining.

They were more connected now than they'd ever been, and with sharp clarity, he knew their bond would remain even after they left this earth together.

Together.

Mine.

Ours.

Mate. Mate. Mate.

Sammy was his; in this lifetime and in every other.

Finally releasing his bite, Silas rested heavily against Sammy's back, panting, until he had enough strength to lift them together onto the bed.

Careful to hold Sammy's hips close so his knot wouldn't tug uncomfortably, Silas shuffled them up the bed, snuggling into warm flannel sheets and the scent of *them*.

"I love you, Silas," Sammy whispered, holding tight to the arms still wrapped around him.

The rumbling purr in Silas' chest surged to life, and he didn't care at all that one of his arms was already falling asleep. "I love you so much, Sammy. You're mine. And I'm yours. Always."

"Always," Sammy repeated.

The shimmery, bubbly feeling that had accompanied

Sammy's thoughts when Silas first bit into him washed over him again, like a final settling of the bond.

Silas listened to the soft sound of his mate's breathing grow deeper, steadier, until he was certain he was asleep.

Silas followed quickly behind, and for the first night in weeks, he wasn't afraid that Sammy would be gone when he woke up.

CHAPTER 17
SAM

Dim, grey morning light fell across the mussed duvet, weak through the still-falling snow and the hushed protection of their bedroom.

Tucked in beneath the covers and sprawled out practically underneath Silas, with only his nose poking out from the sheets to breathe, Sam thought if there were ever a moment he would choose to freeze time and live in forever, it would be this one.

Except he needed to shower, because they'd fallen asleep last night before Silas could even comfortably pull out, and when his knot had finally softened, Sam was covered in... them.

Silas shifted, making sleepy little growly noises and snuffling his nose into Sam's hair, pulling him further into his arms.

At least he seemed content with the way they smelled.

The usual weight squatting on Sam's chest whenever he woke up was missing, replaced with a contented peace so light he could have floated away had Silas not anchored him down.

His first thought upon waking had shifted throughout the past few weeks.

I have to leave.

I have to tell Silas and leave.

I have to tell Silas and he'll make me leave.

I have to tell Silas and beg him to let me stay.

I have to tell Silas.

I have to stay.

This morning, his first thought was *I get to stay.*

With the clarity of hindsight, Sam knew deep down that was what he'd always wanted, he'd just been too afraid to even wish it at the start.

He turned his head and placed kisses all along the giant arm wrapped around him.

"Good morning," Silas grumbled in Sam's ear.

God, his deep morning voice should be illegal. He could convince Sam to join a cult with that voice.

Or go *running.*

Smiling to himself, Sam yawned. "Morning, you Giant Oaf. I thought I told you not to squish me while we slept."

Silas chuckled and rolled so he was fully on top of Sam, bracing his weight on his knees and elbows. "Don't even try and pretend you're not basking in it, love. You can't lie when you're asleep; you've wiggled back underneath me three times already this morning."

Sam wrapped his arms around Silas' neck. "And don't you pretend like you didn't love every minute of it either," Sam said, lifting his chin.

Silas' grin was all teeth and trouble. "I won't."

Just as Sam was gauging whether or not he was too sore for a repeat of last night, because really, that knot was *not* for the faint of heart, Silas rolled off him. "Come on, love. We need to get the fire and breakfast going or I'll start taking bites out of you. *Again*," he finished with a smug half-smile.

Sam sighed. "Shower first?"

Silas' eyes flicked up and down Sam's naked body, predatory. "Alright. It's time you pay for all that teasing you've done, anyway."

Sam pushed Silas back down, straddling him.

Slinking down his body, nuzzling at every place he'd discovered that made Silas quake in pleasure, Sam finally peered back up at him just as his mouth hovered over his cock, filling in where it lay between his legs.

"And it's time you invest in some real goddamn shampoo and conditioner," Sam purred, before he bit at Silas' thigh and bolted for the bathroom, his shrieking laughter ringing out as Silas sprung up and chased behind, shockingly light on his feet for a man of his size.

Sam happily spent most of their shower on his knees, and they'd just finished rinsing the soap from each other's skin when the hot water ran cold.

~

THE SNOW STOPPED FALLING midway through making breakfast.

Together, they fumbled their way through chocolate chip pancakes—*obviously*—scrambled eggs, and bacon. Sam wouldn't ever stop being amazed by how much food Silas consumed.

"I bet your parents' grocery bill was cut in half when you left for the military," Sam quipped while he flipped his third pancake. He'd messed up the first two but was finally getting the hang of it now.

"Probably more," Silas answered, chewing on a piece of bacon. "Finn was living with us almost full-time by that point. Mom and Dad used to joke they'd come home and find us eating the firewood if they weren't careful."

Sam smiled. "They are lovely people. I'm glad Finn had somewhere good to be. From what Jaime's mentioned, his mom sounds like a total bitch."

Silas rumbled in agreement, pulling the *second* tray of cooked bacon from the oven. "She can rot in hell for all I care."

They were comfortably quiet for a few minutes while Sam finished making the rest of the pancakes and Silas scrambled their eggs. Elbow to elbow at the stove, Sam savored how wonderful it felt to do something mundane with Silas, and not be afraid it was all about to end.

As they sat down at the small kitchen table, plates piled high, Silas asked, "What was your mom like?"

Sam looked up, surprised by the question. Several of his usual deflections were on the tip of his tongue.

I don't really remember.

She was nice.

Of course, she loved us but those last few months were hard.

"She was a lot like your mom," he answered instead, unable to look away from Silas' warm gaze. "The way they smile, maybe? It caught me off guard when we first got to your house. I'd forgotten the way she'd smile at Jaime and me, and when I met your mom..." he nodded. "She looks at you the way our mom looked at us."

A wave of warm comfort seeped through Sam, and he knew deep in his bones it came from Silas. From their bond; new, but strong. "I feel that," he whispered.

Silas reached across the table, taking his hand. "Is that alright?"

Sam nodded quickly. "Yes. Thank you."

Silas released him and picked up his fork, tucking into his eggs. "Tell me more about her."

Buoyed by Silas' steady encouragement, Sam found words and memories and stories he'd long since buried. Between bites of pancakes that were good, but not as good as Finn's, Sam yapped away about all the things he remembered of her.

How she'd loved to take them both on errands, chatting with them like they were little adults while they sat in the grocery cart and walked alongside her, how she'd involve them in picking out all the ingredients they'd need to make chocolate chip cookies or brownies or whatever other sweet treat she'd planned for the week.

Sam talked about watching movies with her, and how she'd use a different voice for each character when she read to them before bed, inspiring Sam to make up his own voices and characters and skits.

Sam felt worn out after he finished, in a relaxed, pleasant way. He'd not realized how much he'd needed to talk about his mom with someone. Being so open with Silas felt like absolution.

"Thank you for letting me talk about her," Sam said a little while later, while they loaded the dishwasher after breakfast.

Silas smiled. "She deserves to be remembered."

"I wish you could've met her. She would've loved you; you would've made her laugh."

A bittersweet feeling spread through Sam at the image of introducing Silas to her. What would she have made of both her sons ending up with suspiciously large and hunky men?

He decided she would've adored it.

A peculiar look came over Silas' face, and he paused what he was doing to turn toward Sam. "You probably don't remember... It was so long ago, but I think I have met her."

Sam cocked his head, confused. "What?"

Silas smiled at him; the smile that had felt familiar all those months ago, even though they'd only just met. "It was the same day my parents left the pack. We'd driven to Anchorage that morning so Dad could make plans for us to leave. Mom stayed at the library with me. I don't remember very much at all, just that it was a fun day in the big human city. When we went inside, I smelled you."

Sam was lost. "You smelled me? How old were we? How did you know it was me?"

Silas shook his head. "I was six when my parents left the

pack. So you were five, maybe? I think I caught your scent first but wasn't sure what it was, and then I found you. I remember we read books together. You said you wanted to learn to fly. But then my dad came back—he'd been followed by someone from the pack—and your mom came over, and you all left."

Sam blinked several times, rapidly. "I don't remember that."

Silas took his hand. "I didn't remember either—not until I met you again. I think your scent triggered the memory, and your voice."

Sam cocked his head again. "You said you smelled me in the library? Like, did I stink?"

Silas blushed, rubbing the back of his neck. "Uh, no." He cleared his throat. "You've always smelled like, um, marshmallows. Toasted marshmallows and fire. When we met at my house that first time, well *second* time, I knew I'd met you before, and I knew who you were to me. I knew you were my mate," he finished quietly.

Sam thought back on that first time he met Silas; the first time he *remembered* meeting Silas. He was so caught up in his fear and shame, and yet... "Your smile was familiar," he whispered.

Silas squeezed his hand. "I'm sorry I kept it from you and didn't tell you sooner."

Sam shook his head. "I understand, and I'll also understand if you're upset over what I kept from you until last night."

"Sammy—"

"No, please," Sam cut in gently. He swallowed and tried

to send his own comforting assurance down the bond the way Silas had done for him. "I know everything we shared last night was real, but I shouldn't have waited so long to tell you. I shouldn't have kept the truth from you."

Sam looked away, unable to make eye contact as he explained. "At first, I couldn't imagine sharing my deepest regret, the worst thing I've ever done, with anyone. And then I didn't want to share it with you because I couldn't bear the thought of your rejection. And then I knew I *had* to share it with you, even if it meant losing you, because I love you too much to have kept it from you any longer."

Silas listened, patiently waiting while Sam finished.

Then he tugged on his hand, pulling him close. "I'm glad you told me. I'm not upset at you for waiting, as much as I wish..." Silas cupped Sam's shoulders. "I wish you'd never had to bear all of that on your own. I wish *Derek* had been a better man."

Silas' eyes darkened, and he gritted his teeth together, nostrils flaring. "And I want to find him and make him regret what he did to you. I want to make him regret it very much."

Sam shook his head. "I haven't spoken to him since the day Jaime and Finn were attacked at the safe house. I blocked him. I don't want to give him space in my life ever again, Silas. I don't want him to take up space in yours, either. In ours. Especially not now that we're here, together."

Silas' eyes darted back and forth between his before he slowly nodded. "I'll try."

Sam cocked an eyebrow.

"I won't intentionally seek him out," Silas amended.

"But if I happen to run into him at the grocery store..." he rumbled.

Sam stood on his tiptoes and pecked the underside of his jaw.

Silas softened. "I also wish you hadn't felt trapped and out of options when Jaime was in danger, and I do wish you hadn't kept the truth about my uncle all to yourself. Like you said, though," a small smile appeared on Silas' lips, "I don't regret that we met."

The purr Sam loved so much rumbled to life in Silas' chest, and he was wrapped in a fierce hug.

Speaking into Sam's hair, Silas said, "I promise, you will not shoulder your burdens alone again. We have each other now. You're my mate; that doesn't just mean the sex is fantastic."

Sam rolled his eyes and made to step away, batting at Silas' chest. "I don't recall saying it was *fantastic*," he sniffed.

Silas' grin was feral. "That's because you were too busy screaming on my knot, brat."

Sam tried to scowl, but melted into Silas' stolen kiss instead.

Coming up for air, Silas knocked their foreheads together. "You are never alone with your troubles, Sammy, and I am never alone with mine. Not anymore."

Sam had to blink away his tears. "I don't deserve you."

"Yes you do, and I'll remind you often."

"I love you," Sam whispered, gripping tight to Silas' shoulders.

Silas' purr grew louder. "Also, you're not giving my uncle a dime of the money you've worked hard for."

"I would rather give him every bit of it over owing him, Silas."

Silas' face hardened. "You owe him nothing. You're mine. You're *ours*. Jaime and Finn and Sheppard's, too. You're pack. We'll protect you, just as much as you've protected us."

Something slithering beneath Sam's skin told him he still didn't deserve that.

Turning to continue wiping down the counters, Sam said, "I wrote a letter for Jaime, too. I'd like to go over there sometime today to talk with him if the roads aren't too bad. It's time."

"Hey," Silas said, knocking their shoulders together. "Jaime loves you. I love you. You've never had to earn that. He may be upset, but you'll work through it together."

Sam hoped he was right.

A FEW HOURS LATER, Silas and Sam stood on Jaime and Finn's front porch, stomping the snow from their boots while Silas pounded on the door.

Sam was jittery with nerves, anxiously patting his pocket for Jaime's note.

His fears for this conversation were different after opening up to Silas. He was boosted by his understanding and love, but Sam's wrongs toward Jaime went deeper; his lies were more numerous.

Finn answered, throwing open the door and looking

slightly annoyed. "What could possibly be so important you went out in this—oh."

The annoyance turned to stunned silence, and then a slow grin split his face. "Well goddamn *finally*. Fucking hell, do you know how hard it was to keep my nose to myself around you two? Come here."

Sam thought Finn was talking to Silas, but instead, he stepped up and wrapped Sam in a big bear hug. "Congratulations, I'm so happy for you two," he said, setting Sam back down.

"Thank you," Sam said when he could breathe again, and was sure he wouldn't get teary in front of Finn.

Once was quite enough.

Finn winked at him, like he could tell Sam was trying not to be emotional, then pulled Silas into an embrace.

Sam stepped inside to give them a moment.

Jaime came down the stairs just as Sam finished taking off his boots. "Hey," he said, yawning.

It was well after noon, had Jaime just gotten up? Maybe he was getting sick?

"You good?" Sam asked.

For some reason, Jaime blushed. "Uh, yeah, all good. Just tired from Halloween yesterday. Big day, you know."

Sam eyed him for a moment, taking off his coat. "If you're not feeling well, we can come back—"

"HOLY SHIT!" Jaime exclaimed. "I mean, oh my God."

Sam dropped his coat, looking around. "What? What's wrong?"

Then, Jaime was hugging him. "I'm so happy for you!"

Sam relaxed into the hug. "Um, thank you? How did you know?"

Jaime pulled back and waved Sam into the living room. "Well," he cleared his throat. "I can see the, uh, you know," Jaime gestured to Sam's neck, "bite."

Sam slapped his hand over the still-tender area. It hadn't bled or bruised the way a normal wound from an animal would've, but the mark was easily identifiable. He'd caught Silas smugly staring at it all morning.

Sam's gaze fell to the similar scar on Jaime's neck. Fucking hell, he did not want to swap matching tattoo stories. "Uh, yeah. Can we never talk about that part?"

Jaime nodded emphatically. "Deal."

Sam sighed, sitting on the sofa. "Good. But, yeah. Silas and I are... together. Mates?"

Sometimes he still thought someone would cart him away for saying this shit out loud.

Jaime beamed. "I'm so glad."

Just then, Finn popped his head in through the front door, dropping an armful of clothes and two cell phones. "We're going for a run, be back in a bit."

"Sounds good," they called together.

Sam chuckled when he saw the two giant wolves tear into the woods together through the window.

"So, why did it take you two so long to sort things out?" Jaime asked. "I mean I don't want details but like, since you're mates, how did you manage to stay away so long?"

Sam patted at the note in his pocket. "Well, that's partly what I'm here to talk to you about."

Jaime cocked his head to the side. "Oh?"

He wouldn't find a better opening than this.

Pulling the folded-up paper from his jean pocket he handed it to Jaime with shaking hands, the same way he'd done with Silas last night.

It felt like he was ripping his heart out of his chest and handing it over instead, all over again. "Yeah. There are things I kept from him, and you. Things I lied about. I've explained it all in there so that I know I've remembered everything."

Jaime's brow knit, and he flipped open the note and began to read.

Last night, Silas had anchored Sam during this part, holding him close, but now, watching Jaime read the letter, he felt like he'd fly apart. He wiped his palms along the tops of his thighs, staring at the floor.

Sam didn't want to see the moment Jaime's expression changed from confusion to anger.

This letter was shorter, having much the same information as Silas' without all the love declarations. It probably took Jaime only a minute or two to read, but it felt like a lifetime.

When he was done, he set the letter on the arm of the chair. "Oh, Sam..."

Sam was still looking at the ground. Thickly, he said, "I'm sorry. I'm so, so sorry. Please understand Jaime, it's not that I didn't want to be there for you, or that you were a burden, or that I resented you, I just..." he glanced up and saw tears in Jaime's eyes. "You were so broken, and I couldn't make it better. I wasn't enough, and I didn't know how to handle that. You needed help. *I* needed help. I failed you.

I'm sorry."

Sam was fully crying now. "And then I pushed you away after because... because how could I comfort you, how could I tell you it would all be alright when it could have all gone wrong because of me? When it *did* all go wrong because of me? Even afterward, at the safe house... I still couldn't admit it. I was so ashamed. And I couldn't drag you into my issues with Cain, not when you'd just crawled out of the darkness with Finn. You were happy for the first time in so long. I couldn't do it—"

For the second time that day, Sam's words were cut short by Jaime throwing his arms around his shoulders. "Oh, Sammy. It's ok. It's ok."

Sam wrapped his arms tight around Jaime in return and held on, sobbing. They were the same deep, chest-wrenching sobs he'd let out the day Derek had published Jaime's name, except this time they felt like the final purge before forgiveness.

Scraping the rot out of a wound so it could finally heal.

"I'm sorry I lied, I'm sorry I fucked up, I'm sorry I wasn't enough. I'm sorry. I'm sorry," Sam repeated over and over.

Jaime was crying too. "I'm sorry, too. I was so caught up in my own shit, I didn't see something was wrong with you, too. I should've known..."

Sam pulled back, shaking his head. "No. It's not your fault, Jaime. Don't do that."

Jaime wiped at his tears with a tissue and passed the box to Sam. "I forgive you. I don't remember much from those early days after it happened, except for you. I remember you were there. I remember you swept into that interrogation room and pulled me out like fucking Batman. I know that couldn't have been easy. You're always so strong. You're the strongest person I know. But we all need help sometimes, even you."

Sam shook his head, laughing. "I'm not strong at all. I just hide it."

Jaime peered at him. "That's absolutely not true. I want to give you the contact info for the agency where I found my therapist. I really think you should reach out. You don't have to share everything with everyone, but you need to be able to talk to *some* people."

He nodded. "I know. Silas suggested the same."

Jaime smiled. "You told him all this?"

Sam nodded. "Last night, after you left. I thought he'd ask me to leave after I shared everything. I thought you might, too," he finished softly.

Jaime pushed at Sam's shoulder and winced like the move had hurt him. "I love you. You're my brother. You're my best friend. That's what I've missed most, Sammy. I'm a big boy. All grown up. I've never really thanked you for everything you gave up to try and give me a normal childhood, mostly because I don't know how to do that while also telling you that you shouldn't have had to. But I don't need you to be my parent anymore. I don't need you to protect me. I just want my friend."

Sam wiped his eyes, grumbling, "I'm your big brother. I'll always protect you."

Jaime smiled. "And I'm *your* brother. I'll protect you, too. And I know Silas will."

Sam softened more at that. "He does," he whispered.

"He's good to you?" Jaime asked quietly.

Sam nodded, feeling the blush creep up the back of his neck. "Yeah."

Jaime smirked. "Good. How did he take it when you told him all of this?"

The blush spread further into Sam's cheeks. "He told me he loves me and asked me to stay. And then he asked me to be his mate."

Jaime's smirk turned into a wicked grin. "And then you drank a cup of hot tea together before falling asleep watching Wheel of Fortune?"

Sam shot him a warning glare. "We said we wouldn't talk about that part."

Jaime cackled, tipping back onto the sofa. His gleeful smile settled into a contented happiness that made Sam choke up a little to see. "It didn't all go wrong, you know."

"Hmm?"

Jaime turned to him. "What you said about it all going wrong because of you. It really didn't. I've told Finn—if I had to, I would do it all again to be here, with him. With *them*. Wouldn't you?"

Sam blinked and smiled. "I've never believed in coincidences... and yes," he nodded, "I would."

They sunk back into Jaime's giant sofa together, side by side, sharing a moment of easy quiet. "Can I ask you something?" Sam whispered.

Jaime turned his head where it rested on the cushion. "Of course."

"Do you remember Mom?"

A few heartbeats passed. "I remember her laugh," Jaime said quietly. "You have it, you know."

Sam whipped his head toward him. "I laugh like her?"

Jaime nodded. "Sometimes I'm glad I remember less from when it all happened, when she got sick, and when dad checked out. I know that's selfish, but it's easier to just remember the good. Walking to the bus together every day, going on adventures to the gas station for snacks. Those are the memories I wanted to keep, I think. And her laugh—I hear it every time you do. Which I hope will be more often, now."

Sam was crying again.

Fucking hell, it was like he'd spent the last twelve hours weeping out years of pent-up emotions. "Thank you for telling me that."

Jaime smiled. "Come on. Let's make hot chocolate before they get back."

Sam scooted forward to heave himself out of the giant couch. It pained him to admit it, but Finn was right—the thing was a monster.

Jaime winced as he stood, and Sam saw a scratch on his arm peeking out of his long sleeve. "Are you alright? Did something happen?" Sam asked, pointing toward the wound.

It was Jaime's turn to blush, and he tugged on his sleeve. "I'm fine. Very, very fine. Finn and I, uh, took a walk last night in the woods and I tripped, that's all."

Sam raised a brow, following him into the kitchen. "You took a *walk*? Last night after you left? In the dark?"

"Mhmm."

"Before or after it started dumping snow?" Sam asked flatly.

"It wasn't a long walk," Jaime said, shoving his face so far into a cupboard he'd need spelunking gear to climb out.

Sam narrowed his eyes. "Jaime, you can tell me if Finn hurt you. I'm not afraid to run him over with my car."

"Ouch. I feel like you skipped your way to that solution with a little too much pep in your step, brother of mine," Finn said from the kitchen doorway.

Sam jumped and quickly turned to see Finn holding back a smug grin and Silas standing behind him, beaming, ruffling the snow out of his hair before pulling it back. "*God*, make some noise when you walk," Sam grouched, glaring at Finn.

"No one's hitting anyone with their car," Jaime said with an exasperated sigh. "Finn didn't hurt me. I promise. Not... well. Finn has never done anything I didn't enthusiastically want him to do."

Sam narrowed his eyes further at Finn. "So you *did* give him those scratches?"

"Love, I don't think you want to pull on that thread," Silas said.

"I would never hurt Jaime," Finn said, smirking and walking over to help Jaime with the hot chocolate. "And I'm not upset you threatened to run me over. I'm very happy Jaime has a brother who would do that for him."

"Then what happened?" Sam asked.

Silas wrapped an arm around his shoulders. "I'll fill you in later if you really want to know."

"How do you know what they're talking about?" Sam accused.

Silas snorted. "I found Jaime's Halloween costume in the woods out on our run just now."

Jaime palmed his face and elbowed Finn.

Sam stared, confused, for one heartbeat longer before turning bright red. "You're right. I don't want to know. The car thing still stands, though," he said, pointing a finger at Finn.

Finn only grinned. "I'm so glad we're all one big happy family."

CHAPTER 18
SILAS

Sipping hot chocolate while tucked in next to Sammy on Jaime's man-eating couch, Silas was struck with the memory of sitting in this very spot six months ago, hearing Sammy's voice through the phone for the first time.

The first time in a very long while, anyway.

His wolf had perked up, even then. *Pay attention,* it'd whispered.

Silas turned and smacked a kiss to Sammy's cheek—because he could. "How's your hot chocolate?"

Sammy took a huge gulp. "Mmmhmm," he hummed before taking another.

Silas laughed.

Setting the mug on the coffee table and wiping at his upper lip, Sammy asked, "What's *in* that?"

Finn smiled. "It's French hot chocolate. Way thicker than the packet version."

"S'wonderful," Jaime mumbled from Sammy's other side, sipping from his own cup.

Silas hadn't had time to ask how their conversation had gone, but he felt the lack of tension in Sammy. He saw the way his shoulders were more relaxed and noted the easy way he laughed.

Jaime seemed lighter somehow, too. Like they'd both stopped walking on eggshells around the other.

Silas hoped that was true; he hoped they could finally rebuild the friendship that'd been jumbled up in the last couple of years, now that the rubble had been cleared.

Finn had yanked him in for a tight hug when they'd first arrived, clapping him on the back. "I'm so happy for you, Si," he'd said.

"Thank you, Finny," he'd mumbled back, always grateful for the joy they'd shared over the years in each other's accomplishments and life events.

Then Silas had motioned for Finn to follow, suggesting they go on a run and let the boys talk. Finn had looked at him curiously and seemed loath to leave Jaime, even more than usual, but Silas had explained that they'd need some privacy.

Shifting quickly, they'd loped into the woods side by side, easily falling into step next to each other to run the loop around the house on the snow-covered trail Finn had worn into the ground.

While on their run, Silas used that still new, indefinable way they could sense each other's thoughts and feelings to give him the gist of what Sammy had shared.

He'd stumbled upon Jaime's Halloween costume by accident.

The snow had dulled the scent, so he hadn't realized what he'd stepped on until he was right on top of it. Once he *had* smelled the garment, he'd stepped back quickly, huffing at Finn, who'd merely scooped the pants up in his jaws and kept on trotting, pointedly not communicating with Silas through the bond anymore.

Silas had moved on quickly, too. It wasn't his place, and he really didn't want to imagine further. But from what he could tell, he and Sammy weren't the only ones who'd had an eventful Halloween night.

Finished with their hot chocolate, Silas and Sammy were just putting their coats and boots back on to head home when Silas' phone rang, Sheppard's name popping up on the caller ID.

"Hey Shep," he answered.

"The doctor's here at the safe house to see Riley," he'd responded, getting right to the point, per usual. "You should, uh, you should get over here."

Silas looked over at Sammy. "Sure, Sammy and I are just leaving Finn and Jaime's. We can head right over."

Sheppard blew out a sigh. "Finn's there with you?"

"Yes, why?"

There was a pause before Sheppard lowered his voice. "He should probably come too. With Jaime. Just... make sure you come in with him."

"Ok? Is there something wrong? Is the doctor giving you trouble?" Silas asked.

The three of them turned his way, honing in on his conversation.

"No, not at all. He seems like a nice guy. I'll explain

when you get here. Or maybe I won't have to. Just... get over here," Sheppard said.

"Alright," Silas answered warily before he hung up.

"What was that?" Finn asked.

"The doctor's finally here. Sheppard says we should all go meet him. Something seems weird, though, and he wouldn't explain," Silas said.

"He probably just doesn't want us to fight with Riley and Buck again," Jaime said, grimacing.

"Yeah, that's probably it," Silas said to reassure himself and the others. "C'mon, let's get over there before it gets dark."

~

THE SAFE HOUSE Riley and Buck were using was located in Silver Rapids, on the outskirts of the small town opposite where Jaime's cabin lay.

Pulling into the drive, Silas turned to Sammy. "I have a weird feeling about this. Sheppard sounded funny on the phone. Stay close to me for a bit, yeah?"

Sammy looked like he was about to argue, but his brows softened. "I can handle myself, Oaf. But yes, I'll stay close."

Silas kissed the back of his hand. "Thank you."

Stepping out of the truck, they sidled in next to Finn and Jaime as they made their way to the front door.

Before they went inside, however, Sheppard slipped out to greet them, shutting the door behind him. "Wait a second," he said, holding up his hands like he was already trying to calm them down.

"What the hell is going on?" Silas asked.

Sheppard shuffled nervously. "It's nothing bad, I swear. He seems like a nice guy. Really nice. I just... I could be wrong. I don't think I am, but I could be. Uh..."

Silas had never seen Sheppard acting so strangely before. It set his teeth on edge, and he reached over to bunch his hand in the back of Sammy's coat, ready to pull him away.

"What are you trying to say, Shep?" Finn asked.

Sheppard opened his mouth to respond, but before he could, a man Silas had never seen before stepped outside and began speaking. "He's worn out for now, I think we should let him rest. I can find somewhere to stay overnight and come back in the morning. Oh, hello," he said, turning to the four of them.

Silas could immediately sense he was a wolf shifter—an alpha. He had big, broad shoulders and dark blonde hair that was greying at the temples. Silas estimated him to be in his early fifties, maybe a few years younger than his parents.

His face was weathered from the elements, but his blue eyes were bright and youthful and kind when they fell upon the four of them standing together in front of the house. He smiled, looking a bit nervous at their attention.

"Sorry that it took me so long to arrive. I set off as soon as I got your message but had to ground the plane halfway here to let a storm move through. I'm Will, the doctor."

Silence followed, broken only by Jaime whispering, "Oh my God," as he took Finn's hand.

The rest of them stood there, gaping.

They were nearly identical. Or they would be if Finn

were twenty years older. Their scents were similar as well—too similar to be a coincidence.

Without a shadow of a doubt, Silas knew that this man was Finn's father.

～

"So... Uh, I can update you inside?" Will said, clearly uncomfortable from their staring. He made to turn back around but halted in his tracks when his eyes finally stopped scanning them as a group and focused on one person.

Finn.

He blinked several times, opening and closing his mouth like words kept getting lost before he could form them. "Uh... are you... do I know you?"

Finn was staring, too. Silas saw the confusion, then realization, then... *something,* on his face. Anger? Embarrassment?

"No, you don't," he said gruffly.

"We should go inside," Sheppard said, opening the door for them all.

Finn gripped Jaime's hand and led him in first, rushing past where the doctor stood, still staring like he'd seen a ghost.

Sammy leaned in close. "Is that..."

"Yeah. I think so, yeah," Silas whispered while the others shuffled in after Finn and Jaime.

"Did he ever know who his dad was?" Sammy whispered.

Silas shook his head. "No. He was never in the picture."

They filed in last, and Silas grabbed Sammy by the hand and made a bee-line for where Finn was leaning up against the opposite wall. Every one of his instincts was screaming to keep his pack close.

Jaime's arm was pressed up to Finn's on one side, and Silas tucked in on the other, sandwiching him between them. He pulled Sammy close as well. They probably looked ridiculous that way, but Silas wouldn't let his brother face this conversation alone.

The doctor stood on the other side of the room, with Sheppard and Buck seated on the couch between them.

"Where's Riley?" Sammy asked, looking around.

"He's asleep. Meeting with the doctor wore him out," Buck answered, looking back and forth between them all. "Do you two know each other? The resemblance is uncanny," he said, focusing on Finn and then Will.

Finn stayed silent. Silas leaned into him even more.

"I... I don't—I don't have a family. I don't have siblings," Will said like he was trying to make sense of Finn; passing him off as some long-lost cousin or something.

Buck raised his eyebrows at that but didn't push further.

Finn's face hadn't shifted from the frozen, stony glare he'd donned when they entered the house. Silas had seen that expression before; most often, when he'd been forced to stay at his mom's growing up.

"It doesn't fucking matter," Finn growled. "What's wrong with Riley?"

Will blinked; he was clearly still processing the situation but gathered himself quickly. "He was kicked out of a pack, violently. That kind of break from a family or support structure is very stressful, and in extreme cases can damage our immune system. I suspect he's been dealing with high levels of stress and anxiety for years, and probably malnutrition as well. It's more than likely why he's healing at such a slow rate for a shifter."

"But I thought shifters always healed faster than humans?" Jaime asked.

The doctor nodded his head. "Usually, yes. But we aren't entirely paranormal creatures; we're humans, too. A mix of both. And the literature on the impacts of long-term stress and anxiety on human bodies is extensive."

"So you're... human and wolf shifter?" Sammy asked, cocking his head.

"As far as I can tell, that's the best way to think about it," the doctor answered. "From a medical perspective, anyway. There can be cultural differences, and those exist even between packs."

Will ran a hand through his hair in a gesture Silas had seen Finn make a thousand times. It was fucking bizarre.

"It's not an exact science," the doctor continued with a sigh. "There's still so much that's unknown about the magic of paranormal beings, and the interplay of also being human. It's not a guarantee that a human medicine or remedy will fix a shifter illness, but it's a good place to start."

"Are shifter illnesses very common?" Buck asked, glancing over his shoulder toward the room Silas assumed Riley was sleeping in.

"Not common, no. Some of the old northern packs have records dating back decades, even centuries, though. There are documented cases of wolf shifters dying of infections and human illnesses, particularly in correlation with periods of pack wars and social structure upheaval."

"What about other kinds of shifters?" Buck asked.

The doctor shook his head. "I don't have access to documentation to answer that with any authority or confidence, but I suspect it depends on the types of shifters we're discussing. What stresses out a wolf shifter—removal from a pack setting or family, for example—may not impact say a bear shifter as significantly, as bears naturally spend extended periods in isolation."

Silas was fascinated. He was hesitant to trust this man; both because he was a stranger, and because of the situation with Finn, but there were so many questions he wanted to ask.

Like why he, Finn, and Sheppard had suddenly started hearing each other's thoughts a few weeks ago, for one.

"So are you saying you can't help Riley?" Sammy asked.

"I'm saying there's not a shot or a pill I can give him, but I think rest will do wonders. Community, too, if possible. There's no given duration for how long this will last for him, but in the interim, his wounds should be cleaned and treated the way you would a human's. I'll do some reading this evening to see if there's anything else I can find, and come back tomorrow."

"I'm going to go check on him," Buck said roughly, standing.

"Actually, could I talk to him? Just for a minute," Sammy said, stepping forward.

Buck eyed him, then nodded. "Sure. If he's awake, I don't see why not."

"I'll come with you," Silas said.

Sammy squeezed his hand. "I really won't be long, I just want to ask him something about the wreck that never made sense to me. You should stay," he said, shifting his eyes to Finn, who was doing his best to not look at the doctor slowly making his way over.

Jaime was standing nearly in front of him like a guard dog.

Silas squeezed his hand back and sent a wave of gratitude down their bond. Sammy may pretend to be standoffish toward Finn, but he cared for him deeply. "Ok. Thank you."

Sammy disappeared around the corner just as the doctor spoke. "Uh, what's your name?" he asked Finn, cringing.

Finn gaped at him, incredulous. "You don't even know my name?" he asked.

Protect.

Protect.

Silas wanted to tear into the doctor for putting that hurt in Finn's voice. Jaime looked ready to hit him.

Will took a step back, the question startling him. "Look, I —I'm not blind. My sense of smell works just fine, I'm not denying the...resemblance. But I don't have—I mean no one's ever—"

"Margaret Winters. That ring any bells?" Finn snarled.

It took a few seconds, and then all the color drained from Will's face. "*Maggie?* But she—I was only in town for a few days. She never said, she never called me. She never told me she was *pregnant*," he said, whispering the last word and looking alarmingly pallid.

GO! PROTECT!

Silas stepped closer to his friend, ready to shove the doctor out the door at one wrong word.

Finn's voice was accusatory. "She said you left. That you weren't ready to be a father and left her. She said she never heard from you again."

Will was shaking his head rapidly, and held his hands out in supplication, eyes darting between the three of them. "Look, um—"

"*Finn*," Jaime snarled. "His name is Finn."

"Finn," the doctor continued, "I know you have no reason to believe me, but I don't know why she would tell you that. I *never* knew about you. I never knew I had a—a son."

PROTECTPROTECTPROTECT.

He choked on the last word, and Finn looked so much like that lost, lonely boy sitting in the back of the classroom on Silas' first day of human school, his instincts roared at him to *do something,* to go, *keep safe, go! Go now!*

Jaime, still hovering nearly between the two shifters and glaring daggers at the doctor, said, "I think it's time to call it a night." He turned to look up at Finn. Softer, he continued, "We can pick up this conversation in the morning?"

Finn nodded, dazed.

The sound of a truck starting nearby and speeding off pulled Silas' focus away from Finn and the doctor.

Something was wrong.

As the others shuffled toward the door, he realized—it was too quiet.

He couldn't hear Sammy anymore.

GOGOGOGOGOGO.

Silas had kept one ear tuned in on the muffled, low tones of Sammy's conversation with Riley in the other room, but he'd been distracted by the doctor's claims that he didn't know Finn existed. When had they gone quiet?

"Sammy?" Silas called, voice raised. He was across the room in three strides.

"What's wrong?" Jaime asked.

"SAMMY!" Silas shouted, throwing open the door and finding the bedroom empty.

GOGOGOGOGO!

"Riley?" Buck called, hot on his heels, peering in over his shoulder.

But there was nothing to see.

Riley and Sammy were gone.

"Where the fuck are they?" Jaime yelled, turning to Buck.

The curtains gently blowing in the cold breeze were the only answer, the open window the only sign anyone had been there at all.

Fire roared through Silas' veins—panic and fear so acute he couldn't think or feel beyond *FINDMATEFIND-MATEFINDMATE*.

He turned, catching Buck by the throat and pinning him to the wall, claws digging in. "Where did they go?" he snarled.

"I don't—I don't know—" Buck gasped, pulling at Silas' hand.

"You've been the only one around that little shit for days. *WHERE DID HE TAKE MY MATE?*" Silas roared. The alpha was fully in control now.

Buck choked on the words forced out of him at Silas' command. "I—don't—*know*."

A pair of strong arms wrapped around him and yanked him back, pulling him away from Buck. "Calm down!" Sheppard hollered, tightening his hold when Silas struggled against the vise grip he'd locked him in.

Then Finn was in front of him, partially shifted and teeth bared, fisting his sweatshirt in both hands.

GET AHOLD OF YOURSELF, he shot down the link the three of them shared. "Calm down and breathe," he said out loud.

Silas took two deep breaths. "Sammy's gone, Finny—Sammy's not here. I have to go find him—how do I find him?" he asked, his broken voice his own again.

He struggled free of Sheppard's grip, needing outside, needing to track the scent, to catch up, to *go*.

Finn palmed the back of his head, pulling him down to his height. "Get yourself together, Si. They can't have gone very far. You know how to find him; you've done it before, remember? At his apartment? Focus," he snarled.

The doctor came running back inside the house, also partially shifted. Silas hadn't realized he'd left. "My rental's gone. Their scent cuts off where it was parked. Riley must have stolen it."

Blood *whooshed* in Silas' ears.

"We have to do something!" Jaime yelled, driving his panic even higher.

"Where?" Finn asked, giving Silas' shoulders a firm shake. "*Focus!* Where is he, Silas?"

Silas squeezed his eyes shut, steadying his breathing.

He hadn't had to think about it before—he'd just acted.

One breath.

Go! GO!

Where?

Two breaths.

GOGOGOGOGO.

TELL ME WHERE YOU STUPID DOG!

Three breaths.

YOU KNOW WHERE! NOW GO!

CHAPTER 19
SAM

Sam woke to the sound of snow-packed gravel crunching under tires.

The vehicle came to an abrupt stop, throwing him forward against the seatbelt. His head pounded in protest.

Had he fallen asleep on the way home? Reaching up to cradle the ache in his temple, he turned to ask Silas what'd happened, only to find a considerably smaller person sitting in the driver's seat instead.

Riley.

Sam was startled, his memories rushing back.

He'd stepped into Riley's room to ask him a question. His explanation of the wreck had never sat right with Sam, and after his conversation with Jaime, he'd remembered something else that'd bothered him, too.

Riley had been awake, standing next to the window, thrown open in the cold. "What are you doing?" Sam had asked after closing the door behind him. "Aren't you meant to be resting? Shut the window. Standing in the cold can't be good for your scratches."

Riley had turned to regard Sam, before looking down at the wounds on his arms. He'd looked harder than Sam remembered; still small, yes, but not slight and trembling. His eyes were clearer than they'd ever been.

The reserved, doe-eyed man had disappeared; for the first time since Riley had arrived, Sam realized he was looking at a wolf.

"Your brother cares about you very much. He was ready to fight me over nearly killing you at your apartment," Riley had said.

Sam had stepped back, caught off-guard. "Jaime has always been all-in for the people he loves." Trying to take control of the conversation, he'd asked, "Who's 'us', Riley? Back at Silas' house, you said Cain would let 'us' go. Who were you talking about?"

Riley's eyes had sharpened. "The doctor said I'm not healing because of the pain and stress of being separated from my pack—from my family. I think you can relate to that. I think you and your brother would do anything to protect each other."

Alarm bells had begun to ring in Sam's mind. His eyebrows had narrowed, confused. "I know you're not the one who wrecked the car. I know you're taking the fall for someone. Why?"

The alarm bells rang louder at the apology in Riley's eyes. "I really am sorry about this," he'd said.

All Sam remembered after that was a hard *thud* and pressure in his head.

Then, nothing.

Focusing back on where Riley sat in the unfamiliar vehicle, Sam asked, "What's happening? Why are you doing this?"

He peered around the dark outside and patted his pockets for his phone, hoping to find an identifiable landmark so he could call Silas.

His pockets were empty, and the sun had already set. There was nothing but dark, snowy taiga all around, wind-blown snow drifts dancing in the headlight beams. The pounding in his head intensified.

Riley turned in the driver's seat to face him. "Your phone is in the yard, back at the safe house. And please don't try to run. I don't want you to be hurt."

Fuck that.

Sam fumbled with the seatbelt release and threw open the door. He jumped down into the snow, stumbling a few steps while his head spun.

Riley was out and around the vehicle before Sam could take more than a few strides. He caught him by the wrist, pulling him upright so he wouldn't tip over into the snow. "I said don't run. We're in the middle of nowhere. You'd freeze in minutes."

He draped a heavy coat over the one Sam already had on. It was huge—fitting almost like a poncho, and tailored for a man much bigger than him as it fell nearly to his knees.

Where had Riley found the coat? Whose vehicle was

that? Sam accepted it though, automatically slipping his arms in to shield against the bitter wind.

A boost of energy shot through him. Not his own, but borrowed.

The bond.

The message that came with the energy bolstered him even more.

I'm coming.

I'm coming.

"Where are we?" Sam asked aloud, voice cracking in desperation.

If he could figure out where he was, maybe he could communicate his location back to Silas, and then Silas would come, and Sam wouldn't be lost anymore.

"Don't you recognize it?" a cold, familiar voice spoke from behind him.

Sam whipped around, cursing as the quick movement throbbed along his temple. The surge of energy he'd felt moments ago drained out of him, replaced by crippling dread.

Cain stood before him, partially shifted, with several others hovering close behind.

Next to him though, was a boy.

He looked like Riley; similarly slight, except he had a shock of bright blonde hair on his head, and he couldn't have been older than thirteen or fourteen.

A couple of your neighbors saw someone run off into the trees immediately after the wreck. They all described him as a young, thin male. Possibly a teenager, with light blonde hair.

Oh.

"Jack, are you alright?" Riley called out from beside Sam. He sounded exactly the way Sam had moments ago—desperate.

I think you and your brother would do anything to protect each other.

Oh, no.

He didn't fight Riley's iron grip on his wrist as he pulled them closer to the group.

"Riley, I'm sorry," the boy said shakily, stepping forward.

Cain put a hand on his shoulder. "*Wait.*"

The grating sound of the alpha command stopped the boy in his tracks, a shudder passing through him, but he spoke over it. "It was an accident, Riley. I was just trying to help, so we could leave, like you said. I didn't mean to hurt anyone. I didn't know you'd get kicked out. I'm sorry," he finished, voice trembling.

The fear in the boy's eyes broke Sam's heart.

"I was right," Sam said softly, voice filled with sadness. "You weren't driving the car. He was."

Sam had wondered why Riley would've been so careless as to leave behind a cell phone, and how he'd even managed to wreck in the first place.

But someone as young as Jack?

Sam pictured the boy, scared and indecisive, hovering on Sam's porch—shuffling around, trying to work up the courage to come inside, or maybe trying to fight Cain's order and leave, before he returned to his vehicle, only to become overwhelmed and lose control.

Had he also been ordered to kidnap Sam and take him back to Cain? Had that part of Riley's story been real?

It didn't matter. In the end, Jack was just another one of Cain's pawns.

Riley's gaze was wild, feral. Sam had felt that way once—backed into a corner with no one to lash out at except the one person reaching his hand out to help.

"It's ok, Jack. It's alright," Riley said before he turned to Cain. "It's done," he snarled. "I brought you someone who can show you where they live. Our debt is paid. Let us leave."

Again, Sam was shocked to see another layer of the wolf pulled back. How had they all fallen so easily for the sickly, weak, bland facade?

"It's not done until I can see the house," Cain replied coldly.

Realization shuddered through Sam when he finally noticed the storage shed just over Cain's shoulder—the same one they'd left their vehicles in when they'd snowmobiled to Cal and Meera's.

"No," Sam said, shaking his head back and forth, fighting Riley's grip again. "No, I won't do it."

Cain gripped the boy's shoulder tighter. "Yes, you will. I'm calling in my favor, Sam. Bring me to where they live, and you, Riley, and Jack here can leave unharmed."

Riley yanked Sam's wrist so he spun to look at him, much harder and stronger than Sam would have guessed him capable of on looks alone. "Show them," he snarled.

"But—I have money," Sam choked out, looking at Cain. "I told you, It's all yours. Let us leave, and it's yours."

"I don't care about your money. Show me where my brother lives," Cain growled, enunciating every word.

Sam was frozen.

He couldn't do it—not this. Not *them*. Not now that he had everything he'd ever wanted.

Silas.

Jaime.

Finn and Sheppard and peace and joy every time he heard them laugh. It was real—it was *his*.

Cal's quiet office flashed through his mind; all those books and photographs and memories. The way Silas' mom had smiled at him when they'd arrived. Curling up on the sofa with Silas while Jaime and Finn dozed nearby; Cal and Meera puttering around in the kitchen behind them.

It was a home. A family. A pack.

His pack.

He'd never deserved them, but they'd welcomed him anyway. Cal had stopped him from spiraling—from running. He'd shown Sam that choosing Silas meant trusting he'd be chosen in return.

Sam had kissed Silas for the first time in that house. He'd lain with him and dared to dream of a future where they could be together in that house.

If he told Cain where Silas' parents lived, if he was responsible for ruining the safety and happiness they'd built, he would never forgive himself.

No.

No, I won't.

Home!

Silas, please hear me, I'm at your parents' home!

Find me!

Sam flung the thoughts out, hoping Silas would hear and

understand. He looked at the boy, and then back at Riley, the pleading fear in his eyes shattering Sam's heart.

"I *can't*..." he said, his own plea.

Two brothers who would do anything to protect the ones they loved.

Two brothers Cain had manipulated and maneuvered until they were at odds; unwilling antagonists in each other's lives.

Two brothers at an impasse, neither willing to help the other because the stakes were too high, the cost too steep.

Cain passed the boy behind him to be guarded by one of the other shifters and strode forward, grabbing Sam by his nape. "You will show me where they live," he growled. "*Walk.*"

The command shoved Sam into the trees lining the valley.

"*Take me to Cal and Meera's house.*"

Sam's feet marched forward—completely out of his control—headed directly for the storybook cabin.

He blindly stumbled down the snow-covered terrain, desperately trying to angle his steps away, to turn them so he wouldn't lead Cain right to their front door, but it was useless.

Sam walked, bringing them closer, and closer, and closer to the house that was hidden unless you knew where to look.

"I can't see anything," he said once the light of the moon was completely shadowed by the trees all around. Tripping over a low-lying shrub, he stumbled and caught himself. "I can't see where I'm going."

"Fucking useless humans," Cain growled, tilting his chin

at one of the men behind him, who produced a flashlight. Shoving it into Sam's hand, Cain barked, "Now, take me to Cal and Meera's."

Even with the torch, Sam understood why Silas had made him wear a helmet while they'd snowmobiled this path the first time. The foliage and trees studding the plain meant he couldn't move in a straight line, and the fresh snow covering the ground made it so he couldn't tell where to step to avoid twisting an ankle on a rock or fallen tree limb.

Home.

I'm at your parents' home.

Please find me!

Sam screamed the words down the bond, trying and failing to fight the alpha order.

"I—I still don't know where I'm going," he said a few minutes later, stopping to catch his breath after trudging up a slight incline. The coats were keeping him plenty warm, but snow caked his boots and his feet had become heavy. "I'm lost. I didn't pay attention when we came the first time. I won't be able to find it in the dark."

That wasn't true. Sam knew exactly where he should go.

He felt the call of the house just up ahead like it was a part of him. Almost as though he was a lonely, wandering planet that had entered the sun's orbit, that shimmery ripple of magic drew him in, beckoning him home.

The house wanted to be found.

"Liar," Cain snarled. "I know we're close, I can smell the magic."

He shoved Sam to the ground, his knees cushioned slightly by the snow. Cain's voice took on the timbre of the alpha again, and kneeling there, Sam wondered how Silas could ever think they were the same.

Silas' alpha command was a shot of adrenaline up Sam's spine—lightning bright, it was a call to stand tall together, to show his strength.

Cain's demand was dominance; it ripped submission from him, a hand on the back of his head forcing him to grovel.

The only person Sam would ever grovel for would die before he asked him to.

"*Tell me where!*" Cain ordered.

I'm sorry, I'm sorry, I'm sorry, Sam thought, trying and failing to fight the words bubbling up his throat, to push down the directions on the tip of his tongue.

He opened his mouth, voice hoarse. "I—won't—"

"*Show me!*" Cain roared down at him, raising a hand as if to hit him.

"You're nearly there," a calm, female voice answered. "It's just ahead of you, through those trees."

Shocked, Sam was released from the heavy weight of the order all at once.

Coughing and choking, he looked over his shoulder to see Meera, appearing almost regal as she stepped out of the shadows alongside Cal, both of them partially shifted and poised to fight.

Cain sneered at her in acknowledgment, scanning the forest over Sam's head, eyes darting back and forth until they settled, focused.

He'd found the house.

"*Do it,*" Cain said over his shoulder.

Two of the shifters standing behind him broke away from the group, headed for the structure just visible through the trees.

Riley had lingered behind everyone else during their trek, following warily, eyes always on Jack. With their bargain complete, he shot forward and grabbed his brother's hand. "Come on."

Cain watched with disinterest as they shifted and ran, disappearing together into the night in the opposite direction of the house.

Sam tried to scramble to his feet, but Cain shoved him back down into the snow.

Cal snarled, shaking the ground beneath Sam's feet. "Let him go," he commanded.

Cain sneered again. "Hello, Brother."

"*Let. Him. Go,*" he repeated.

A howl cut through the night. Another joined it, and another. Sam whipped his head in the direction of the song. Were there two of them? Three? More?

Even though the howls sounded distant, the remaining two shifters behind Cain began to pace restlessly, peering around.

Silas.

Silas is coming.

Sam would recognize his voice anywhere, in any form.

Cain released Sam, and he scurried backward, tripping as he stood and ran toward Meera. She wrapped an arm around his shoulders. "Are you alright?"

Sam nodded rapidly. "You didn't have to do that. You didn't have to tell him. I didn't want to, I tried not to—"

"Shh," she said, pulling him close. "You're more important, Sammy. It's alright. Everything will be alright."

Cal stepped forward, blocking them both from Cain. "Why are you here? Why do all of this?"

Cain bared his teeth. "I let you leave. You broke our bargain, sneaked away in the night like a coward, and hid from me for years. *And I still let you go.*"

His yellow eyes flashed. "I would have continued to let you all live out your weak, pathetic lives in peace if your alpha son hadn't stepped out of line. If he hadn't made his own pack—his own territory. It's a fucking insult!"

"You're the coward. No one would follow you if you didn't force them into it. Do you want to see pathetic? Look in the fucking mirror," Meera shot back, her arm tightening around Sam. "Leaving was the best choice we could've made."

Cain's face twisted into a feral snarl. "And you tore apart everything when you did! Do you have any idea of the damage you caused when you ran? The instability you created? Everyone *left*. The old den is gone. There's barely anything remaining of Salt Creek, all because you were selfish and put yourself above the pack."

"Not once in your life have you ever put someone above your own interests," Cal roared. Again, Sam felt it shake the ground he stood on. "People left because you're a power-hungry, controlling monster. Giving my family peace and safety was the only decision I could have made and still lived with myself."

A wild gleam appeared in Cain's eyes; they looked almost orange, now. He gestured behind the three of them. "I hope it was worth it. I told you, brother. I always collect what's owed to me."

They all turned together.

The glow in Cain's gaze had merely been a reflection—the source lighting up the night around them. It didn't make sense to Sam at first; he blinked, not understanding what could be so bright all the way out here. When the smell of smoke hit his nose, he realized what he was seeing.

Meera let out a broken sob.

"No!" Sam cried, stumbling toward the house. "No!"

But it was too late.

Cal and Meera's house, Silas' childhood home where Sam had spent a handful of his happiest days, was a blazing inferno.

CHAPTER 20
SILAS

The metronome of Silas' giant paws hitting the snow-covered ground tied him to the present.

Thud

This way.

Thud

To Mate.

Thud

To Sammy.

His steps weren't alone, though.

The steady beat of three others joined him; their gait kept pace with him as they flew up the valley pass. He could feel them flanking him on either side, as well as through their shared pack bond.

The connection was clearer and stronger than it'd ever been.

A third link had also joined Finn and Sheppard in his

mind; quieter and more muffled than the other two, but there.

Will.

He thundered along next to Finn on Silas' right, while Sheppard joined him on the left. Later, Silas would have space to consider how much it meant that the doctor had dropped everything to join them in finding Sammy. Later, he'd be able to fully appreciate how much Finn loved him, that he'd leave his mate amid their panic, trusting Buck to keep a watchful eye.

He still couldn't describe exactly how he knew where Sammy was, just that he knew he needed to get to his parents' house *now*.

Right now.

Silas hadn't been able to push the truck any faster than a crawl once they got halfway up the mountain road, tires churning in the snow, so they'd taken it as far as he could stand before they'd shifted.

Four legs would carry them faster.

Instead of following the road, they'd cut up and over the pass into the valley that cradled his childhood home so they'd end up approaching from the opposite direction.

Thud

Go!

Thud

To Mate!

Thud

GO!

Fear rushed down the mate bond.

Hear me! Find me! Home! Accompanied it; Sammy's desperation tasted like a greasy penny in his mouth.

Silas hated that he wasn't there already, hated that he didn't know what was happening, and yet he craved the messages—allowed them to flood his veins, pushing him faster and faster at the reminder that Sammy was awake and aware enough to call for him.

He released a piercing howl. *I'm coming for you*, he cried, flying up the pass. Alongside him, the others joined in unison. Together, their song was a warning. A battle cry.

The alpha's mate had been stolen, and blood would spill for it.

Silas scented the smoke before he saw it. His bones grew heavy with dread when a faint orange glow appeared on the horizon, lighting the way to Sammy.

GOGOGOGOGO.

He couldn't think about what that orange haze meant. Couldn't imagine the worst, couldn't let the fear slow him down. He just needed to keep going.

To Sammy.

To Sammy.

To Sammy.

They tore into the trees that sheltered his parents' cabin, a place that had always been filled with peace, safety, and love. Terror gripped his heart in a vise when the fire came into view, and he whined at the sight of his childhood home up in flames, stark against the snow-laden ground.

Had his parents escaped?

Were they trapped inside?

Was Sammy trapped with them?

Silas' feet faltered at the thought of arriving too late; imagining nearly everyone he loved clawing and scraping at those flaming walls, unable to get out because he hadn't been there to protect them.

Memories of his dad teaching him how to split logs right there on the porch flashed through his mind.

The lullabies his mom had sung to him after he'd woken from a bad dream filled his ears, drowning out the roaring fire.

He remembered one early spring morning not long after they'd moved in, he and Finn had plopped on the living room floor to watch cartoons. Silas was startled when Finn spontaneously shifted into a lanky four-legged wolf pup for the first time, finally comfortable enough in his own skin to let the wolf take over. He'd also shifted, and they'd tore through the house together, growling and yipping, until his mom shooed them out the door where they splashed in the river for the rest of the morning.

Silas thought of Sammy—soft and warm underneath him, smelling of dark chocolate and coal fire while the wind *whooshed* down the chimney, and how they'd fallen asleep in each other's arms afterward.

His heart stuttered as those joyful memories blazed and smoldered, disintegrating in a heaping pile along with the rubble.

But through the smoke choking him, he caught a hint of something else. Something that beckoned him forward—a call that was even more important and precious than the memories he watched burn.

Toasted marshmallows.

Family.

Pack.

They were alive. His family was alive, and they needed him.

Bolstered, Silas led the four of them around the house, their tight formation cleaved apart by the roaring fire, splitting into pairs as they closed in.

What did they look like, emerging from the flames on either side like hounds out of hell?

His heart soared when he finally, *finally,* caught sight of Sammy, standing tall and whole. His parents were there too. The bright glow of the cabin lit up the anger and grief written on all three of their faces.

Each of them was an irreplaceable tether in his soul, and finding them alive and unharmed was a balm to his senses.

Matematematate.

Yes, we found Sammy.

Silas sprinted for them, but his momentary relief bled into sheer panic when he realized who was behind them.

Fully in his wolf form, Cain stood large, ready to pounce on three of the people Silas loved most in this world.

Except they were still facing the fire. Too shocked to turn around, they remained unaware of the horror behind them.

Cain is here! Someone shut down the bond.

Cain!

Cain!

Cain!

Like a warning siren, his uncle's name bounced around in Silas' head, focusing him, sharpening his panic into anger, alive and hungry. His senses honed in on one singular task—ensure Cain could never hurt the ones he loved ever again.

Protect mate.

Protect pack.

Protectprotectprotectprotect.

There were other shifters with the encroaching alpha, but at the sight of the Silver Rapids pack they ran, tail tucked between their legs.

Pathetic.

They were nearly there when Cain leaped.

Silas' heart dropped out of his ribs. Like it was happening in slow motion, Cain's jaws opened, aimed right at his dad's exposed and vulnerable throat. In one last desperate move, unaware his pack had fled and left him unguarded, Cain made to rip apart Silas' whole world.

His rage could have rent the ground beneath his feet.

With a roar, he let go of all restraint and lunged, his powerful hind legs propelling him forward, cutting off the attack.

Go for his throat!

GOGOGOGO!

PROTECTPROTECTPROTECT!

Silas had feared his uncle his whole life.

He'd built him up to be the larger-than-life villain who could take away everything Silas loved with one swipe of his paw. He'd eked out his corner of safety and happiness in Silver Rapids, despite the looming threat of discovery and retaliation, living his life constantly vigilant of who and what his uncle could take from him.

And yet, with the four of them bearing down on Cain,

Silas realized for the first time how much stronger he was than his wretched uncle. Not only in size or physical ability —but in all the ways that mattered more.

Cain's strength came from threats, bribes, and coercion, whereas Silas' came from love, trust, and loyalty. In the end, it'd left Cain alone and defenseless, while Silas had brothers he'd fight and die alongside.

Go for the throat!

Flank him, cut off his retreat.

Pin him down.

Now! Do it now!

Silas listened.

The voices weren't that of his friends, but of his pack. The four of them weren't speaking to each other—their wolves were.

He trusted it, trusted them, and slipped deeper into his wild subconscious than he'd ever been before.

His thoughts became bits and fragments of feelings, sharp and present and *now*. Alongside his pack, Silas cut Cain down with a coordinated ease that felt like a trick.

If he'd had other shifters standing with him it would have been harder—they may not have all made it through alive. Alone though, Silas' initial bite was devastating.

Blocking the attack meant for his father, Silas latched on, jaws shredding flesh, tendon, and muscle as he ripped out Cain's throat.

The sound would've been horrible to human ears.

Now, though, the heavy *splat* of blood gushing out sang through Silas' veins. Still, his uncle would have healed from the wound if they'd stepped away, shown mercy, and given him a reprieve.

They didn't.

Not now, with their wolves in control and Silas' childhood home burning behind him, the bitter taste of terror from finding his mate stolen still fresh in his blood.

PROTECT!

PROTECT!

PROTECT!

Cain lashed out with teeth and claws as the other three closed in, flanking him, pinning him down for Silas' death blow. The hot tang of blood flooded his mouth when he closed his jaws around the Salt Creek Alpha's neck a second time.

Then, there was only pulling.

Twisting.

Tearing.

A wet *squelch*, and Cain's head was no longer attached to his body.

No final words.

No regretful pauses.

Only swift, efficient death, in the wake of a lifetime of destruction.

Silas flung the decapitated head into the burning remnants of his childhood home, so those yellow eyes could never take from him again.

He wasn't sure how long he stood panting over his uncle's lifeless body, still deep in his wolf's mind, watching—waiting to make sure he wouldn't rise again.

"Silas, it's alright. It will be alright," a gentle voice said,

sounding very far away. He had to protect it. Had to protect them. He snarled down at the blood-soaked snow.

Protect family.

Protect pack.

Protect mate.

"*Silas,*" someone else said, their voice similarly muffled. "*Son, come away from there. He's dead—it's done. I'm so sorry you had to do that.*"

That voice was also his to protect.

Protect.

Protect.

Protect.

"*I know,*" a third voice said, closer, the sound becoming clearer the more they spoke. "I understand. You protected us, but now it's time to come back."

He whined. That voice was the most important one to protect.

"Silas," it said. *He* said. "Silas, look at me."

His wolf obeyed, finally lifting his eyes from the red all around.

The boy with the pretty fox-colored hair returned his gaze.

The man who smelled like toasted marshmallows and crackling embers.

His mate, who loved him.

Sammy.

Holding out a hand, Sammy approached. "There you are," he said again. "You were so brave. You got here so quickly. You protected us."

Silas sniffed the air. Whose coat was he wearing? His wolf grumbled that his mate smelled like another.

Silas bumped his forehead into Sammy's outstretched palm. "Thank you," Sammy whispered. "Thank you for finding me."

I'll always find you, he thought, wishing he could speak the words aloud.

His wolf grumbled again.

Blinking, Silas realized his wolf was waiting for something. Waiting for him.

Thank you, he thought. *Thank you for finding him. Thank you for protecting us. I'm good now. We're good now.*

The alpha retreated with a huff, and Silas' mind was fully his again.

Grumpy dog, he thought fondly.

Shifting hurt like it hadn't since he was a teenager growing faster than his parents could buy shoes, but after a moment he found himself back on two legs, staring down at his very human bare feet.

Sammy threw his arms around him. "*Silas,*" he whispered, over and over.

Silas wrapped Sammy up in return, squeezing him tight and breathing in his scent.

Sammy. Our Sammy, his wolf rumbled.

Yes, Silas thought back. *Our Sammy.*

"I'll always find you," Silas breathed, because he couldn't say it before, and Sammy needed to know. "No matter what, I'll always come for you."

"I know," Sammy said, taking Silas' face in his hands and pulling him down to kiss him.

A smudge of red appeared on Sammy's cheek where Silas held him. He was probably covered in blood.

And he was naked in the snow.

"You've got to be freezing," Sammy said, also taking stock of his lack of protection from the cold. "Here, take this." He removed the stranger's coat and draped it around Silas, quickly rubbing his hands up and down his arms to warm them. It fell to his mid-thigh—not ideal, but at least he wasn't totally naked in front of his whole family.

His wolf preened at his mate's fussing.

The garment was surprisingly warm and easy to put on. It smelled like the doctor; Sammy must have taken it from the car Riley had stolen.

The preening turned to grumbling at the mention of the thief.

"Are you ok?" Silas asked, voice rough as he cataloged every inch of Sammy that he could see for scrapes or bruises. There was a small cut along his temple. "Did Cain hurt you? Did Riley?" Silas asked, rage still simmering beneath his skin, ready to boil over.

"I'm fine," Sammy assured, "really."

The cold was beginning to hurt Silas' toes, so he'd need to shift back quickly. Frostbite would heal, but it was annoying as fuck.

Peering over Sammy's shoulder, the rest of their group had turned away, probably to offer them privacy. Sheppard, Finn, and Will, still in wolf form, sat like sentries on either side of his parents, guarding their mourning.

His mom had a hand on Finn's giant shoulder,

comforting him while he watched the last of their home burn, whining softly.

Staring up at the dying flames, the surge of anger and adrenaline that'd fueled their sprint up the mountain and dominance over Cain poured out of Silas all at once. Leaning heavily into one another, he and Sammy slowly walked over to the group.

Cain was dead. Silas had killed him.

Would he feel guilty about that soon? *Should* he feel guilty about that?

Silas looked toward his father, his back to Silas with his arms wrapped around his mother. Their bodies shook with tears.

Did he mourn his dead brother? Was he angry with Silas for what he'd done? Should he have shown mercy? Should he have let his uncle go?

His dad turned as they approached, and Silas hesitated a step, waiting, but then he was pulled into one of those giant bear hugs—the ones that could fix anything.

"I'm so sorry, son. I'm so sorry you were the one who had to do that."

Silas buried his face in his dad's shoulder. "I'm sorry. Should I have let him go? I didn't think, I just—"

"You protected our family," his father said roughly, cutting in.

He pulled back, and took Silas' face between his hands, his expression fierce. "You protected your pack. Don't apologize for that. Whatever comes next, we'll face it together."

Silas wiped at his tears. "Ok."

He pulled Silas into another hug. "I love you, son. And I'm so proud of the alpha you've become."

Devastating relief melted Silas' bones. When the hug ended and he stepped back, Sammy's sturdy grip was the only thing holding him up.

Cain was dead. He could never hurt anyone Silas loved ever again.

It was done.

"Are you alright, Sammy?" his dad asked, turning toward him.

Sammy nodded quickly, his arm still wrapped around Silas. "Yes. Thank you. I—I'm sorry. I didn't want to bring him here. I tried not to."

Silas bunched his fingers in Sammy's coat, imagining him alone with Cain, wandering through the woods.

"It's ok, Sammy," Meera said. "We've never fully understood the magic surrounding our home, but I don't think you would have found us if you weren't meant to, even with the order."

Silas' father beckoned Sammy forward and wrapped him in another hug. "I'm glad you found us. I'm glad we arrived when we did," he said, finally letting Sammy go. "We're built to withstand my brother's wrath, but you aren't. I'd let him burn down a hundred of our homes before he hurt you."

Sammy wiped at his face and leaned back into Silas.

The home he'd grown up in, the one that'd made him feel protected and loved, was a skeleton of itself.

The fire must have burned hot to start, but without fuel, it was dying quickly. All but the strongest structural elements had collapsed inward.

"It's only a house. We can build another one," his mother said, voice tear-soaked, but strong.

But we can't rebuild each other, he thought, looking over to Finn and Sheppard.

Of course, it'd never actually been the house that'd kept him safe and made him feel loved. It had always been his family. His pack.

They were who he'd protected tonight. They were what mattered most.

Silas stepped away from the group to take the coat off without tearing it, and shifted back into his wolf form, unable to stand the cold any longer. He tossed it to Will, who bobbed his head in thanks.

The sound of approaching snowmobiles cut through the quiet, and soon Jaime, Buck, and the DA appeared through the trees. They must have collected him on their way out here.

Whipping off his helmet, Jaime ran for Sammy and wrapped him up tight. "Sam, are you ok? What happened?" He released his brother and peered around, noticing the dead wolf. "Who is that?"

Finn stepped forward and butted his head into Jaime's shoulder, rumbling deeply as he rubbed his cheek along the top of his head.

"I'm alright," Sammy replied, "but Cain... he burned down the house. He was going to attack Cal. Silas and everybody got here just in time, and..." Sammy gestured at the decapitated carcass.

Gabe stepped up to Sheppard, who was still in his wolf form. "I can't believe you lost Riley, *and* you're making me deal with another headless animal that's actually a person," he said, sighing deeply.

Somehow, Sheppard managed to look contrite.

"I'm calling fire emergency response out here. The house is gone, but someone needs to make sure the fire doesn't spread," Gabe said, stepping away.

"Is Cain really dead?" Jaime asked quietly.

Silas huffed, pushing his head into Sammy.

"Yes. Really, really dead. His head's in there," Sammy pointed at the charred remains of the house. "An improvement," he sniffed.

"And what about Riley?" Buck asked, finally speaking up. He'd been scouring the area when they arrived, probably looking for signs of him.

Silas snarled. *For his sake, I hope very far away.*

Finn growled with him.

Sammy scratched at Silas' ears, soothing him. "He ran off. Cain was already here when we arrived. I was passed out for most of the drive here and had just woken up. I think he hit me on the head with something," he said, rubbing his temple.

Silas whined and licked a long wet kiss up Sammy's cheek. A ghost of a smile appeared on his face, even though he wiped at it with his coat sleeve.

"Cain had a boy with him," Sammy continued. "A young teenager, maybe? He looked like Riley's brother. I think he was the one who really wrecked into my apartment. And I'm pretty sure Riley would've taken any one of us who knew where your parents lived if given the chance. I was just his best opportunity."

"Why, though?" Jaime asked.

Silas grumbled in agreement with the question.

Sammy shook his head. "I'm not sure, but I think part of what Riley said was true. I think he only did what he did to get them both away from Cain. Truthfully, I can't say I would've done anything differently."

Jaime's eyes softened.

Buck rumbled. "Which way did they run?"

Sammy pointed off in the opposite direction of the house.

Buck nodded in thanks and turned to Sheppard. "Can I speak with you when we get back to the house?"

Sheppard raised an eyebrow and nodded.

"We should go," his dad said, turning away from the fire. "It's too cold to stay out any longer. Fire emergency response will make sure it stays contained."

Those who couldn't run on four legs loaded up on the snowmobiles.

Silas took one last look at what remained of his childhood home, whining softly. He turned away, finding Sammy watching, waiting until he was ready to leave.

Silas butted his giant head into his shoulder, nudging him onto the snowmobile, and they left. A pack of wolves guarding their journey home.

Back to Silver Rapids.

CHAPTER 21
SILAS

The whole group piled into Silas and Sammy's living room.

"Will you two stay for a few minutes? Not long," Silas said to Finn and Jaime on their way inside. "I just need you all under one roof for a little bit, if that's ok."

Finn clapped him on the shoulder, forever understanding. "Of course."

They'd collected their clothes and vehicles from the safe house in Silver Rapids before Gabe excused himself, citing his need to communicate with the fire responders and figure out what to do about Cain's death and Riley's disappearance.

Buck left shortly after as well, following a brief, hushed conversation with Sheppard.

The rest settled into the sofa and haphazardly arranged kitchen chairs with heavy sighs.

"We'll say goodnight," his mom said, dropping a kiss on

top of his head, and then Finn's. She squeezed Jaime and Sammy's shoulders on her way by. "Tomorrow, we can talk through what happens next."

"You're welcome to stay in the safe house here in town for as long as you need," Sheppard offered.

"Thank you," his dad responded. "We'll probably take you up on that once we've had a chance to rest and plan." They disappeared up the stairs and into the guest room, shutting the door softly behind them.

"I should go, too," Will said gruffly, eyes lingering on Finn before flicking away. "I'll uh... stay in town for a few days, if that's alright."

Silas looked at Finn, and then the doctor. "You're welcome here as long as you'd like to stay. Thank you for coming with us tonight. It means a lot."

The doctor bowed his head. "I'm glad I was here in time to help. I'm glad... yeah," he said, eyes darting back to Finn and then away again. "If you don't mind me asking," he continued, "have you three always been able to link minds the way you did tonight?"

Silas looked at Finn, again. He wouldn't engage further if it made him uncomfortable, but Finn nodded his agreement.

"No," Silas answered. "It started very recently. Within the last month."

Will's eyebrows creased in thought. "What were the circumstances?"

"Um..." Silas said, peering at Sammy. He'd never actually fully explained this. "Sammy and I hadn't accepted the mate bond yet, but I was aware of it. Sammy was in a dangerous situation, and I just... knew. I knew I had to find him. The way I knew tonight."

Sammy took his hand. "That's why you called me," he said.

Silas nodded.

"And that's when the telepathy started?" Will asked.

"Shortly after," Silas answered. "Finn called me and said he could sense I was stressed, and when all three of us arrived at the hospital our shared thoughts became clearer. It's happened on and off since then."

"Hmm..." the doctor said, lost in thought. "Maybe some kind of survival mechanism induced by stress and proximity. There are old records of mind speaking in a few of the northern packs, but if others are still capable of it in recent times, they've kept it to themselves. I'll do some reading."

He stood to leave, but Silas stopped him. "Before you go, could you take a look at Sammy's head? Riley hit him and knocked him out," Silas growled.

The doctor nodded. "Of course. Want to step into the other room, Sam?"

Sammy nodded and squeezed Silas' shoulder, leading the doctor into the kitchen. Jaime trailed after them, clearly not ready for Sammy to leave his sight just yet.

Alone with Finn and Sheppard in the quiet, Silas whispered, "I don't know how to do this. I don't know how to be a good alpha. Silver Rapids doesn't need one; things have been working just fine the way they are. Most of the people who live here couldn't give two shits about me."

Finn sighed. "Now, that's not true. Nearly half the town stopped by to say hello last night for Halloween. I think I heard you introduce Sam as *your, uh, Sammy* about thirty times."

Silas snorted at Finn's attempt to mock his voice. "We weren't subtle, were we?"

Sheppard gave him a look. "Not even a little."

Silas smiled. "Still. That doesn't mean people need someone running around town shouting about being the *alpha of Silver Rapids*."

Finn rolled his eyes. "You've literally never done that. And if you start getting weird about it, I'll tell you. Cain may be gone," he continued, "but that doesn't mean people don't need someone watching out for them, and keeping an eye on things. Especially around here. Who knows what trouble could crop up."

Silas shifted in his seat, unsure what to do with his hands. "But you'll do it with me, right? I mean, you'll be my..." he trailed off.

"Pack?" Finn finished for him.

Silas nodded.

Finn smiled at him. "Of course, we'll be with you, and so will Sammy and Jaime."

Silas nodded again, not sure he had the words after their tumultuous day. "Thank you, Finny."

"Finn's right," Sheppard said gruffly. "We're yours, and you're ours. And you don't have to ingratiate yourself with every resident in the area to have a positive influence on this community. You'll learn, and we'll learn with you."

Sammy and Jaime walked back in from the kitchen, Will following behind.

"I'm fine," Sammy said in answer to Silas' concerned look. "Just need some rest."

Silas and his wolf relaxed at that. "Thank you, Will," he said.

He'd feared that acknowledging and becoming an alpha would turn him into something he wasn't. And he *had* changed, he just hadn't anticipated it would be for good.

Silas had worried that he'd never measure up, that he'd never be everything he needed to be for his pack—but he'd also never considered that he would grow and become what he needed to be *because* of them.

He wasn't an alpha without a pack, and there was no pack without Finn grouching about Silas nosing around the food prep, Sheppard's quiet drawl, or Jaime cackling in triumph at beating everyone in a board game.

He wasn't an alpha without his match. His equal. His mate.

He wasn't an alpha without Sammy.

They would rebuild, because they had each other to rebuild for.

Everyone stood to leave, Sheppard patting him on the back before he quietly excused himself. Before they could go, though, Will stopped Finn and Jaime on their way out the door. "Um, Finn. Could I talk with you for a minute?"

Finn gave him a long look. "We can talk here," he gestured to the living room, clearly not ready to be alone with the doctor.

Jaime took his hand.

"If you'd like, I mean, if it's alright, I'd like to see you again. Maybe have lunch. I haven't spoken with Maggie in, well. Over thirty years. But I'd like to," Will said, stumbling a bit over his words.

Finn heaved a sigh. "I haven't spoken to my mother in about ten of those years. She wasn't great to grow up with. I tried to be home as little as possible—Silas' parents were the ones who really raised me. Good luck, but I won't be involved in that conversation."

Deep sadness crossed Will's face. "I'm very sorry. I'll... respect that. I'd still like to see you again, though?"

Finn looked apprehensive, like he wasn't certain how serious the doctor was about the offer. "Sure. Lunch could be good," he replied. "Come by the security office and we can plan something."

Will nodded. "I will."

Would he honor that promise? Silas wasn't sure; he may wake up tomorrow completely overwhelmed by it all and leave. Only time would tell.

Jaime had a similarly apprehensive look on his face, but he held his tongue.

"Right," Finn said. "Let's call it a night."

AFTER EVERYONE ELSE HAD GONE, Silas and Sammy flicked off all the lights, and quietly tread upstairs.

Once in the safety of their bedroom, with the warm glow of the bedside lamp casting deep shadows across Sammy's face, all of the night's emotions came pouring out.

"*Sammy*," Silas said, before wrapping him up in a fierce embrace.

"Are you alright?" Sammy asked, speaking softly into Silas' chest. "After... Cain."

Silas tucked his face into Sammy's hair. "I don't know. I think so? Or I will be?"

Sammy nodded, squeezing tighter.

They held each other like that for long minutes, speaking volumes without saying anything. How had Silas survived before now without Sammy's comforting scent and strong arms holding him tight?

Never again.

They would always have each other to cling to when the winds of life became too strong to weather alone.

Without speaking, they undressed and stepped into a hot shower together. Exhaustion blanketed heavily over them both—Sammy could barely keep his eyes open, but they gently washed each other before drying off and tucking into their soft flannel sheets.

Silas cradled him close while they lay together in the dark, soaking each other up. He gently scratched his claws through Sammy's soft beard. "I was so afraid, Sammy," he whispered, thinking back on those agonizing moments when Sammy had been taken. "I was so afraid I'd lost you."

Sammy wiggled closer, lightly dancing his fingers through Silas' chest hair. "I was scared, too. I was scared I'd wasted so much of our time telling myself I couldn't have you when we could've been together."

Silas nuzzled his face into the crook of Sammy's neck, mouthing at their mating mark. Not to arouse—they were both far too tired, and there were no magical walls to spare his parents—but just to remind them both it was there.

"I would have waited forever for you. I don't regret a second of the time it took us to get here," Silas said, purring in the quiet.

Sammy kissed him, before tucking back into his chest.

Just as Silas was about to doze off, Sammy whispered, "Silas?"

"Hmm?"

"When we, uh, *mated*," Sammy smiled like he still found the word new and remarkable, "you mentioned something about a ceremony. What are those?"

Silas pulled back a little to look at his face. "Oh. Well, they're not very common anymore. They used to be more popular when one mate would leave their pack to join the other's. They were sort of like a wedding, but it was more of a formal declaration of being mates to smooth over any territorial issues of pack jumping. The actual mating would happen after."

"Oh," Sammy said, avoiding his eyes.

Silas tipped up his chin. "Sammy? Was there a particular reason you wanted to know about mating ceremonies?"

He huffed and scowled at Silas. It would have been scarier if he wasn't clinging on with every limb available. "I just thought, you know... I mean if they're supposed to happen before the mating than it's fine. We don't have to have one. Goodnight."

Sammy tried to roll over, but Silas held him down, shifting his body on top so he couldn't turn away. Silas was doing his very best to be serious and not grin like a lunatic. "Love, are you trying to ask me to have a mating ceremony with you? Do you want to declare our love for all to hear?"

Sammy's scowl turned into a pout. "I mean, maybe. I guess if you wanted one it might be nice."

"Was that a proposal?" Silas quietly teased, still not letting Sammy wiggle away. "I never thought the day would come."

Brows softening, Sammy traced a finger along Silas' jaw, over his lips, and up his nose. "Yes," he whispered. "I do want to declare you as mine. Will you do that with me, Silas?"

Silas had thought he'd experienced the peak of joy running through the valley of his childhood home with Sammy in tow. Then, he'd thought it was when Sammy had said '*I love you*' for the first time. Then he'd thought the peak of his joy was holding Sammy in his arms while he quaked in pleasure, screaming his orgasm on Silas' knot.

But now, this was the new height of his happiness.

They were already bound together forever, and yet his prickly mate still wanted to proudly declare their bond in front of those who mattered most.

Silas kissed him, pressing his answer onto Sammy's lips. "Yes. Let's do it. Let's get *mated*."

PART FOUR
FULL

CHAPTER 22

SAM

They shared their wish for a mating ceremony with Silas' parents the next morning over breakfast.

Through hugs and tears, Meera and Cal explained the only formalities that made up a mating ceremony were for the couple to join hands before their pack and state their claim beneath the light of the moon. Some packs planned days-long celebrations around the event, and some only held mating ceremonies on full moons, or special nights of significance throughout the calendar year.

Wide-eyed, Silas and Sam looked at each other—neither of them wanted something so formal. A simple ceremony with their family as witnesses would be more than enough.

"We also have something we'd like to discuss with you both," Cal said, taking Meera's hand.

"Oh?" Silas asked.

She nodded. "We've been thinking about our future for a

few years now. It's not sustainable for us to live so far from a community for very much longer."

Silas' brows creased. "You aren't *old*, Mom."

She smirked. "Thank you. No, we aren't old. But our grocery runs are a chore and a half, and as we age, it won't be good for us to be so isolated. We've been considering a move into Silver Rapids for a while now."

"But... What about the house?" Sam asked.

Cal's smile was sad. "We were going to give it to you two."

"*What?*" Silas asked.

Sam was stunned.

"Things are different now," Meera continued before he could process. "But we'd still like to discuss some options with you. Quite a bit of that land is ours; you could build on it if you'd like. We could live here, or some other place in Silver Rapids. We'd still be close, it just wouldn't be a mission and a half to buy milk and eggs."

Silas took a deep breath. "I don't know what to say." He looked at Sam. "I mean... Thank you. That's more than a gift, that's—thank you. We need to talk it over together, though."

They nodded. "Of course, there's a lot to sort out first, and no rush. Think about it."

Still stunned by their conversation over breakfast, Sam called Jaime later that day. He was over the moon when Sam shared that they wanted a ceremony, and immediately went into planning mode for outfits, decorations, and food preparations.

Sam reeled him in right away, panicking a little at all of his ideas.

Honestly, he'd be happy walking out into the yard with Silas that night in their jeans and sweatshirts. The more Jaime talked about having Silas fitted for a suit, though, the more he warmed to some of his suggestions.

Some of them. Sam was almost certain the reindeer-pulled sleigh he'd mentioned had been a joke.

Jaime and Finn offered up their cabin to host, as their backyard sat right on Loon Lake. With the moon shining high over the frozen water, it would make a beautiful place to hold the ceremony.

Plus, Finn had insisted on preparing a meal for afterward, and cooking would be easiest in his own kitchen.

That was how Sam found himself staring into Jaime's bedroom mirror, two weeks after he'd sort of proposed to Silas, anxiously smoothing down the lapels of his suit jacket and fidgeting with his tie.

Why in the hell had he agreed to dress up again?

The image of a dress shirt straining across Silas' chest came to mind, buttons threatening to pop. Oh yes, that was why.

Under his suit, he had on a white button-down shirt tucked into slacks that matched his jacket, and he'd meticulously trimmed the edges of his beard. They'd purchased actual shampoo and conditioner, thank God, so his hair was back to normal.

Silas was getting dressed in the guest room, Finn was downstairs finishing the food preparations, and Sheppard, Gabe, Cal, and Meera were gathered in the living room, waiting in the warm house before they started the ceremony.

"Alright, are you ready?" Jaime asked, stepping out of the bathroom and quickly running a comb through his hair.

"You look great all cleaned up," Sam said, grinning. Jaime wasn't wearing a tie, but he had tucked a shirt into a nice pair of dark slacks with a sport coat over top.

"I'm supposed to say that to you," Jaime said. "And you do. Navy looks good on you."

Sam felt the blush on the back of his neck. "The tie works?"

It was a pinkish-salmon color—a gift from Lana. She couldn't arrange travel in time for the ceremony, and frankly, he wasn't at all prepared to explain why it wouldn't be a normal wedding or why everyone was so growly with each other, but he'd felt loved opening the gift and card she'd sent.

"Totally works," Jaime answered. "And, uh, it should go with this." He picked up a small, square box sitting on top of his dresser and handed it to Sam.

Opening it, he was stunned to find a beautiful, classic silver watch inside.

"It's nothing fancy," Jaime said, smoothing down his shirt. "But I got it engraved."

Sam gently removed the watch from the gift box and flipped it over.

For Sammy, the best brother, and my best friend.

"Thank you, Jaime," he said, the words blurring through his tears. "This is—I will cherish this. Thank you. You didn't have to."

Jaime reached out to help fasten it. "I wanted to. You are, you know. The best brother. You deserve to be happy."

Sam turned the watch this way and that on his wrist, admiring it, before he yanked Jaime into a fierce hug. "I love you. Thank you for all of this."

Jaime patted him on the back and released him, smoothing down Sam's mussed tie and lapels. "I love you, too. And I love planning this stuff, you know that."

"FOOD WILL BE READY IN HALF AN HOUR!" Finn hollered up the stairs.

Jaime grinned. "He kept saying how happy he was that you guys decided to do this so I'd have something fun to plan, but really, he was just as excited to make all the food," he whispered conspiratorially.

Sam laughed.

"Ok, I'll go down and get everyone outside," Jaime said, heading for the door. "Don't you two take too long or Finn will get grumpy about overcooked chicken."

Sam took one more look in the mirror after Jaime left, checking he hadn't nicked himself trimming his beard, and stepped out.

The living room was quiet as he descended the stairs, Jaime having efficiently ushered everyone outside already. Silas' profile was silhouetted where he faced the fire.

Sam took a minute to stare—because he could.

Silas was also wearing a navy suit and a matching salmon pink tie, but his button-up shirt was the same dark blue as his suit, providing a beautiful contrast to Sam's outfit. He had all of his hair neatly pulled back around his wolfy ears—which he kept out around Sam nearly all the time now—highlighting the sharp angle of his jaw.

Yeah. Absolutely worth all of the hectic planning.

"Hi," Sam said quietly, interrupting Silas' silent reverie.

A grin stretched Silas' face as he turned to greet him. "Hello, love," he rumbled, striding over and devouring him with his eyes. "You look amazing. Wow."

Sam blushed again. "So do you," he mumbled, reaching for Silas' tie to pull him down into a wet kiss.

Groaning, Silas' hands wrapped around Sam's back before falling to grip his ass, hiking him up so he could deepen their kiss.

"Like, really good," Sam said, breaking away and running his hands down Silas' tucked-in shirt. The buttons strained just the way he'd hoped.

"Do we have to go out there? Can't we just get on with the after part?" Silas asked, still eyeing Sam up and down.

Silas' parents had stayed with them for a week while they sorted things out and made a plan, before moving into the safe house Sheppard had offered.

Since then, they'd had sex nearly every day, exploring each other and covering most of the structurally sound surfaces of their home, but Sam had wanted to wait until after their mating ceremony to take Silas' knot again. Both so he wouldn't be sore for tonight, and to make it feel special.

Sam gave him a look. "We're not doing that in my brother's house."

Silas nipped at his ear. "Spoilsport. Then let's get out there, yeah? I can hear teeth chattering from here."

Sam nodded, suddenly nervous. Not about claiming Silas forever; that felt as easy as breathing. He was nervous about being so exposed in front of everyone, though.

But when Silas took his hand and led him out the back kitchen door, there was no room for Sam to be nervous anymore.

Jaime had worked actual magic with the decorations.

Plain cedar and fir garland draped around a simple wooden arch framing the view of the moon hanging low over the lake. Warm twinkle lights wrapped around the supporting posts, and lanterns were nestled into the snow creating a short walkway from the kitchen door to the open arch.

Their family, their pack, stood in pairs on either side of the path, each sharing a plush, warm blanket wrapped around their shoulders and holding a lit candle.

It was understated and cozy and perfect.

It was *them*.

Sam blinked, taking it all in. He found where Jaime stood up ahead, and Sam wasn't sure he'd ever smiled so wide in his life.

He couldn't wipe the grin from his face as he and Silas walked hand-in-hand to stand beneath the decorated arch, bathed in moonlight and the warm glow of the twinkle lights.

Silas' dad cleared his throat. "Who stands before this pack?"

A hush fell across the lake, as if nature itself leaned in to witness the magic invoked through Cal's words.

"I do," Silas answered, strong and sure as he gently squeezed both of Sam's hands in his. "Silas Granger, Alpha of the Silver Rapids pack."

"And I do," Sam echoed, squeezing back. "Sam Lamont."

"Declare your claim," Meera called.

They'd practiced this part; Sam hadn't wanted to fully write individual vows, but they had come up with some words together.

In unison, Silas and Sam said, "By moonlight, I declare you as my mate. You are mine, and I am yours. I shall never seek another, for you are the keeper of my heart."

Silas' joy rang through the bond clear as a bell. He leaned down, pressing their foreheads together, and whispered words meant only for Sam. "I promise to always keep you warm and to carry your burdens alongside you. I will never leave you alone."

Sam framed Silas' face between his hands. "I love you. I will always stand with you."

Silas took Sam up in a fierce kiss, spinning him around before setting him back on his feet. A blush crept up the back of Sam's neck when he realized their family was cheering.

"Let's eat!" Finn shouted out.

Silas peered down at Sam, eyes gleaming. "Mmm... let's."

~

THE FOOD WAS DELICIOUS.

Finn had roasted several trays of small chicken-looking things he called *Cornish hens,* plus more side dishes than Sam could count. He scooped small spoonfuls of each, not wanting to be too full for *later,* but Finn never missed when it came to food.

He'd gorge on leftovers tomorrow.

Sam burst out laughing when Silas sat down at the table next to him with one plate full of sides, and the other stacked with four of the small chickens.

"Laugh all you like, love. This is fuel for later," Silas said, winking at him.

Cal and Meera joined them with their own plates, so Sam shoved a forkful of fancy potatoes in his mouth to stop his retort about finally knowing where all that food went.

Several hours, and a piece of cake he'd wished was three times bigger later, Sam leaned heavily against Silas on the comfortable couch, feet tucked up underneath him.

Sheppard and Gabe had excused themselves after the meal, and Jaime and Finn were padding around in the kitchen, cleaning up. Joining them in the living room, Cal and Meera sat by the fire.

"How are you settling into the safe house?" Silas asked.

Meera nodded. "It's an adjustment. We're still processing everything we lost, but I think we'll be happy with the move once we find somewhere to make our own."

Silas looked at Sam. They'd discussed Cal and Meera's offer thoroughly. Sam couldn't deny that he adored the idea of building a home with Silas; starting a life together, especially somewhere as beautiful as the valley Silas had spent his childhood in, sounded like a dream come true.

Silas had asked if it would interfere with his work, to have potentially intermittent WiFi access in their home.

He'd explained that he'd needed a break for a long time, and that space would be good for him. He wanted to assess his professional goals moving forward.

"You know I want you to be happy, yeah? You don't have

to stop your audio stuff because we're together," Silas had said. "And I still want to listen to that with you, by the way."

Sam had nodded, quickly becoming side-tracked by their initial conversation at the prospect of listening to himself get off thinking about Silas, *with* Silas. "I know. This was a long time coming, though. I wanted a break before everything happened with Derek. I'd been saving so I could take time off and build a portfolio for some other work; I've been thinking about trying audiobook narration. I'm not saying I'll quit, just that I want to figure out my options."

Silas had also been excited about the prospect of building something new together, so when he raised his eyebrows at Sam at Meera's statement, Sam nodded.

"We've thought a lot about your offer," Silas said to his parents. "And if it's still something you're interested in, we'd love to talk through giving you our Silver Rapids house and building out where the old house used to be. Or any other options you have in mind."

Cal and Meera smiled warmly. "That's wonderful. Let's talk logistics soon," Cal said.

Not long after, Silas and Sam hugged their goodbyes, thanking Jaime and Finn for the beautiful ceremony.

"It was perfect," Sam said to Jaime. "Just what we wanted."

Jaime gave him a knowing smile. "I'm so glad. Now go on, we'll see you later."

Sam looked forward to it.

~

THEY BARELY MADE it through the front door before Silas pinned Sam against the wall and kissed him until he couldn't breathe.

"Gonna give you my knot tonight, Sammy. Gonna make you scream on it," Silas moaned into his neck. "Maybe I'll stay inside you until I'm hard again, hmm? And then fuck you a second time? You'll be soaked in my cum. I'll use you like a sleeve, make your hole gape on my cock."

Clawing at Silas' lapels, Sam pulled at the straining buttons he'd stared at all night. "Fucking do it then," he snarled, desperate for the feel of his bare skin.

Like he weighed no more than an armful of split kindling, Silas grabbed Sam by the thighs, lifted him, and carried him upstairs.

So fucking hot.

Sam wrapped his legs around Silas' waist and clung on while he sucked at the tendons on his thick neck.

Once in their bedroom, Silas pressed Sam back up against the wall and stole his breath with another kiss. Loosening his tie, Sam groaned when Silas dug one claw-tipped hand into his hair and tugged, angling his neck for easier access to nip love bites along his jawline and throat.

"Let me undress you," Silas begged, speaking into his ear. "Let me see what's mine."

"Me too," Sam said, voice husky with emotion. "I want to see you."

Slowly, Silas lowered Sam's legs to the ground. He braced his palms against the wall when Silas took a step back, unsure if he could stand without his big body holding him up.

Silas had always held him up.

Despite their hot and heavy start and the want clawing up Sam's spine, the quiet way Silas looked at him now felt so very tender. Like this was yet another way for them to discover each other, another layer of intimacy peeled back to uncover the beating heart of *them*.

Unhurried, Silas reached out and finished removing Sam's tie first. Sam mirrored the movement; the sound of fabric slipping against itself as he pulled the tie from Silas' collar was loud in the hushed protection of their bedroom.

Wordlessly, Silas used both hands to slide Sam's jacket off his shoulders, dropping it to the floor. Sam did the same for him, lingering over the broad planes of his chest, heaving with each breath and soft touch.

Sam's buttoned shirt was next, and then Silas'. And so it went, each of them toeing off their shoes and reaching for each other's buckles until their pants *clinked* as they dropped to the floor, followed by the quiet slide of their underwear.

Standing bare before one another, Silas' eyes danced up and down Sam's body, taking all of him in. "Beautiful," he breathed.

The floor creaked as they stepped away from their discarded clothes, and Silas drew Sam in close until they were a long line of heat against each other.

Sam hummed, breath whooshing out when he felt Silas hardening against his stomach. He pressed kisses all across his chest, the hair tickling his nose.

Tipping his head back, he found Silas' warm gaze. "I love you," he breathed.

Silas' eyes crinkled at the corners. "And I love you."

He bent down to press his lips against Sam's, soft and gentle, before deepening the kiss, lighting them on fire. Silas coaxed him open with his tongue, diving in while he took Sam by the shoulders and guided him down until he was reclined on their bed.

Reaching for the bedside table, Silas grabbed the lube and tossed it on the bed before laying next to Sam, angled so that he hovered over him, hard cock jutting into Sam's hip and his weight braced on one elbow. "Let's get you opened up, yeah? Make you ready for me? Spread your legs, love."

Sam did as Silas instructed, almost shy. None of this was their first time together, but still, it felt sacred.

Silas trailed his hand down Sam's stomach, teasing kisses all over his collarbone and chest. Swiping up the lube bottle, he slicked up his free hand and took hold of Sam's cock, lazily pumping him.

"Tell me how that feels," Silas said, nibbling on Sam's ear.

Sam threw his head back, mouth dropping open as he enjoyed the tortuously slow pull, followed by a teasing swipe of Silas' thumb along his cockhead. "Good," he said, unable to think of more descriptive words. "Feelssgood."

Silas chuckled.

A shock of cold lube against his hole made Sam twitch and let out a quiet, "*Ah!*" but Silas immediately soothed it with the warm pad of his finger, running languid circles over him until it slipped in without resistance.

"So fucking easy, love," Silas said, voice rough. "Like butter. Look at how hungry you are for me—any part of me."

He pulled his finger out and inserted two, crooking them just right.

"*Silas*," Sam panted, grabbing hold of his forearm and thrusting his hips up to try and push his fingers deeper. "I need you. I really do. Don't tease me."

Growling, Silas pushed three fingers in, and then four, not giving him time to adjust in between. "Yeah? You want it hard? You want it rough?"

Sam's breath hitched. "I—I want my alpha to fuck me. Don't hold back. I want it to feel too big. I want to know you're dripping out of me for days. I want you to keep your cum inside me with your cock and then put more in after that—*oh!*"

Silas pressed firmly on Sam's prostate, cutting off his words and causing his hips to jerk. "Fucking hell, Sammy," he snarled, pulling his fingers out and kneeling between Sam's spread thighs.

Slicking up his cock, Silas gave himself a few hard jerks before leaning over Sam and pulling a leg over his hip. "Tell me what you want again. Let me hear you."

Silas breached him, hot and too big and perfect, just as he begged for more. "*Oh my God,*" Sam moaned. "I want—I want you to fuck me hard. Fuck me hard."

Silas tunneled deep on the first push before he pulled out, nearly all the way, and thrust back in. Bracing his hands on either side of Sam's shoulders, he hovered over him. "Who do you want to fuck you hard? Who?"

Another rough thrust had Sam quaking. "You. *You,*" he sobbed.

Kneeling again, Silas hooked both of Sam's legs over his

elbows and leaned back down, folding him up like a parcel. "That's not what you said," Silas panted, pounding into Sam. "Who do you want, Sammy? Say it."

Blearily, Sam caught on. "My alpha," he got out between gasps, "I want my alpha to put his cum inside me." Throwing his arms around Silas' neck, Sam melted into the pressed position, eyes rolling back as Silas fucked into him at the perfect angle.

"That's right," Silas growled. "You want *me* to fuck you, mate." Silas bit at the mating mark on his neck, hips pounding him into the mattress.

Silas' knot swelled rapidly while he rocked them together, quicker than it had the first time. Sam cried out at the thick, heavy press inside him, needing the pressure to feel whole. He'd missed this—how had he gone so long without Silas filling him so completely?

Legs shaking, he was nearly over the edge. He tried to squeeze a hand between their bodies to jerk himself off, so close to coming, but Silas batted him away. "*Mine,*" he snarled, lifting enough to take hold of Sam's cock, working him in rough pulls.

Oh, fuck yes, that was it.

All folded up underneath Silas, with his knot a deep, pleasurable ache pressed up against Sam's prostate and his hand wrapped around Sam's cock, he was making sounds he'd never made before. "Coming. I'm coming, Si—" he croaked. "*Ah!*"

Sam curled inward with the force of his orgasm, eyes squeezed shut, fingers and toes flexing from the strength of each kick of his hips. His cum caught in the hot slide of their bellies, and he groaned at the sight of Silas dipping his hand in the sticky mess before sucking his fingers clean.

The taste of Sam was his undoing. Silas came with a shout, rutting into him and dropping all of his weight down so Sam was thoroughly squished.

Sam basked in the hazy pleasure, feeling Silas' cock twitch now and then when his hole clenched around the knot.

Silas released Sam's legs, large hands unfolding his body so he lay flat. Then, they rolled so that Sam was on top. Scooting further up the bed, Silas sat up, his back braced against the headboard with Sam straddling his lap.

Perched the way he was, knotted, with most of his weight on Silas' thighs because his legs were still unsteady, Sam was just a smidgeon taller.

He smiled, fingers playing with the hair that had fallen around Silas' face, body loose and cum-drunk. "You like it when I call you Alpha," he teased.

Silas' eyes flashed, grinding his knot up into Sam until they both gasped. "I like it when you do a lot of things," he replied, voice a low rumble.

Sam had thought his dirty talk had been just that—talk. Surely, Silas couldn't go again after taking Sam apart so thoroughly, could he?

As if he'd read the question in Sam's eyes, Silas planted his feet on the mattress behind Sam, supporting his back, and grasped his hips. "Grab the headboard, love," he ordered.

Blinking rapidly, Sam did as he was told.

His mouth fell open on a pleasured cry when Silas lifted

him up and off his knot, which had shrunk some, now only a slight swell at the base of his cock, before plunking him back down onto it.

"*Oh, shit!*" Sam wailed.

"Good, Sammy?" Silas asked, panting from the effort of lifting him off his cock and dropping him back down over, and over, and over. Cum and lube from their first round had indeed slipped out, easing the way.

"*Uh-huh,*" he answered, unable to say anything else.

His hands scrambled along the headboard, trying to help lift himself, trying to participate, but the pace Silas set was brutal. He threw his head back and braced his hands on Silas' knees instead, giving in to the near-too-much pleasure of taking Silas' knot, over and over.

Sam was a complete mess. He let Silas use him like a cock sleeve, just the way he'd said he would, moaning and cursing and crying out.

The orgasm Silas worked out of him with a hand on his cock and his knot pressed up against his prostate again shook his whole body. He didn't come very much; only a few small spurts trickling out, but he screamed through it, clawing at Silas' chest from the devastating pleasure.

Exhausted and overstimulated, he collapsed, completely limp in Silas' arms while he finished inside Sam, clinging to him and breathing like a bull. His cock slipped out soon after, the knot having never fully inflated the second time.

Everything was hazy for a while.

Vaguely, Sam was aware of Silas carrying him into the shower, grumbling good-naturedly about his prickly mate not wanting to wake up *itchy* in the morning. He chugged the glass of water Silas handed him after he was clean and dry, wrapped in a warm towel.

Silas found one of his old t-shirts for Sam to wear, even though he had his own pajamas now.

When Silas tucked them both back into bed, with only the soft light of the moon shining in, Sam was struck with how similar, and yet so very different, it was to the first night Silas brought him home.

"Thank you for taking care of me, that first night. I didn't know how much I needed that until I met you," he whispered in the dark.

"Always, Sammy."

So much had changed since then.

Sam could barely fathom that he'd once considered himself ok with all of his secrets and fears keeping him from Silas—keeping him from his family, from being *alive*.

He'd allowed himself to be ruled from afar, silenced, manipulated like a pawn in someone else's game. Yet, all Sam had needed to win was to trust the people who loved him—to let Silas in.

Cain was dead. He could never hurt any of them ever again. Whatever they faced next, they'd do it together, just as Sam had vowed.

"I love that you call me Sammy, you know," he said.

Silas nuzzled into his hair. "I know." He shifted, adjusting so that Sam was tucked right up against him. "I'm excited to build a house with you. I'm excited for whatever life brings, because of you."

Sam nuzzled into Silas' chest. "You're my home. I'd follow you anywhere, Silas."

"And you're mine," Silas answered, kissing his forehead. "Always."

Sammy's heart may not be his own anymore, but there was no one else he'd rather give it to than Silas.

His love. His mate.

EPILOGUE
SILAS

SOMETIME LATER

Stuck inside a stuffy conference room in Anchorage, Silas and Finn were three hours deep into pitching a security system to developers of a new sporting goods store in town.

Silas had heard this spiel a thousand times and could recite it in his sleep.

In fact, he'd already given it once today. However, their client, Brandon—*or was it Brian?*—had asked Finn to go over the proposal again.

And again.

They were meant to be on their way home by now, and with every minute that ticked by, Silas grew more and more agitated.

One of his socks had slipped ever so slightly down his heel, he could smell the egg-salad sandwich Brett had eaten for lunch from across the room, and if he asked Finn to *"go over how all this works"* one more time, Silas would start banging his head against the table.

Just as Brayden, or Brenden, or whatever the fuck his name was, asked Finn to run through the pricing estimates again, Silas' phone buzzed in his pocket three times in quick succession.

Bzzz, Bzzz, Bzzz

Casually, he pulled it out under the table to peek at the back-to-back notifications. His heart skipped a little when he saw they were incoming messages from Sammy.

He knew Silas would be in this meeting. Sammy had kindly listened to him whine all week about having to wake up early to drive to Anchorage today. He also would've called if it were an emergency, so the likelihood that Sammy's messages were important was low.

Still, Silas had already become bored enough to covertly read the label on the mini water bottles Bradley had handed them when they'd arrived—twice. He'd certainly read whatever Sammy was chattering about while Finn explained their pricing summaries *again*.

Phone still hidden under the table, Silas unlocked it with a swipe, opened their messages, and choked.

Coughing like he'd just swallowed a fly, Silas bumped the underside of the conference table with his knee, shaking it. Leaning into the crook of his arm to stifle his coughs, he hurriedly locked his phone screen.

"Sorry," he croaked to Finn, whose brow was creased in worry. "Just... swallowed wrong. Excuse me, I'll step out."

"Of course, the restroom's down the hall on your left,"

probably Brian said, before turning back to Finn. "So, what's your timeline for installation?"

Silas quietly shut the door behind him and paced down the hall until he couldn't hear the sound of Finn's repeated explanations anymore.

His coughing had subsided, but there was no way in hell he could stay in that room for another minute with what Sammy had just sent him burning a hole in his pocket.

Slipping into the one-room, single-occupancy bathroom, Silas flipped the lock and strode over to the sink, setting his phone down before he splashed cool water on his face.

As if that would help.

Casting a furtive glance around, like the office staff were crowded in there with him and peering over his shoulder, Silas opened Sammy's message again.

He didn't know where to look first.

Sammy had sent Silas a mirror selfie.

Except instead of the usual pose where he'd stand and face his reflection, he was kneeling on their bed, back to the full-length mirror mounted on their bedroom door. His face was turned to the side, coyly looking over his shoulder with those *fuck me* eyes that drove Silas crazy, and he'd angled the phone over his shoulder to take the picture.

That pose alone was enough to make Silas hard, the bulge in his pants growing alarmingly fast.

God, his mate was hot. He wanted to tip Sammy forward on the bed so his ass was in the air, and show him exactly what those *fuck me* eyes earned him.

But Sammy wasn't just kneeling on the bed.

Silas followed the bare, lightly freckled planes of his

back, muscles flexed from twisting for the photo, all the way down to where a hot pink jockstrap framed his thick, perky ass like a fucking work of art. Silas zoomed in, breathing heavily as he focused on the way Sammy's cheeks were pushed out and tilted just enough to highlight his slick, pink hole, stretched around the dildo Sammy was riding.

Fucking hell.

With the photo, he'd sent a six-minute-long voice note, along with the message:

> **SAMMY LOVE**
>
> I miss you, Alpha. Will you listen to me get ready for you while you're at work?

Fucking. Hell.

That brat. That beautiful, naughty, perfect brat.

Not long after their mating ceremony, Silas and Sammy listened to one of his audios together for the first time.

He'd come embarrassingly fast.

Like, real-life Sammy had barely wrapped his lips around Silas' cock before he'd blown his load all over his face to the soundtrack of audio-Sammy whimpering that he wanted to fit all of his alpha's cock in his mouth.

They didn't do that very often, but when they were in the mood Silas loved to play one while they fucked. Sammy seemed to enjoy it too—it was almost like a chance to act out his fantasies.

Listening to one Sammy gasp into the sheets while he took Silas' knot was everything, but hearing *two* of his mate? It completely overwhelmed his senses in the best way possible.

His wolf preened and strutted around in his mind every time audio-Sammy begged for his alpha's cock, knowing he'd been thinking about Silas, pining for him just as Silas had in return.

Sometimes it made his heart ache, knowing they'd wanted each other from afar for so long, but what he'd said to Sammy was true—he'd have waited forever and didn't regret a second of the time it took for them to find their way home to each other.

Silas debated whether or not he should listen to the audio message Sammy had sent.

Finn had just started re-explaining the pricing estimates, and if Brad agreed to hire them for the installation, the paperwork would take at least ten minutes to talk through. If Sammy had sent the voice note now, that meant he *wanted* Silas to listen to it before he drove home, right?

Silas shoved his hands into his pockets, hoping he'd find what he was searching for—*yes*.

He pulled out his keys, the case holding his wireless earbuds securely attached so he wouldn't keep losing them. Hoping Brady had at least six minutes worth of questions left in him—*sorry, Finny*—Silas turned on the tap to muffle the noise, put in his earbuds, and hit play.

"Hi," Sammy began softly, almost like he was whispering right into Silas' ear. His husky voice and low chuckle shot straight to his cock, already hard and pressed uncomfortably against his zipper.

"Are you listening to this while you're at work?" he teased, voice breathy and so, so fuckable. *"Were you in a meeting when you saw my picture? Maybe you should find*

somewhere more private. As fun as it would be to spread myself open for you on a big conference table, I don't want anyone else to see that beautiful bulge in your pants. Because you are hard, aren't you? I know you are. Better go hide somewhere and keep quiet, so no one hears you fisting your giant cock while you listen to me ride this dildo and scream your name."

Fuck. Silas palmed his cock through his slacks and slowly worked his fly open, careful not to catch his raging erection in the zipper. He dropped his pants and underwear just enough for his cock to swing free, a bead of precum already forming.

He pulled up the photo Sammy had sent, zooming in just enough so he filled the screen, propped it up against the mirror over the sink, and took himself in hand, pumping so his cockhead was fully exposed.

"I miss you, Alpha," Sammy went on, pouting.

There was rustling in the background, like limbs sliding against bed sheets, occasionally punctuated by those soft mewling noises and wet gasps Sammy made that drove Silas' inner predator mad; that made him want to *hunt* and *take.*

He imagined Sammy opening himself up too fast—he was never patient enough to fully prep the way he should before demanding to be fucked.

Silas braced his other hand against the wall, leaning over the sink as he jerked himself at a steady pace.

"I woke up this morning so horny, so needy—but you'd already left. I'm empty without you here to fill me up. I don't want to be empty," Sammy whined, voice hitching when a wet, rhythmic *schlick* sound started up in the background.

Was he jerking himself off, too? Or was he lubing up that dildo he'd sat on before taking the picture?

Silas matched the pace of his own hard pumps to the sound, eyes gobbling up the photo of Sammy, but that quickly became too much.

Quietly cursing to himself, he released his cock so he wouldn't come too soon, and fondled his balls instead, breathing through the pleasure racing up his spine.

"I need a fat cock in me right now. Please Alpha, will you hurry home? I'm so empty. I can't wait. I'm sorry. I'll just get started before you get here, ok? I'll sit on my dildo and get all stretched out for you, so when you come home you'll be able to put yours in right away. Will you do that? Will you hurry home so you can fill your mate the second you walk in the door? I need—need—ah!"

Sammy sobbed, and Silas imagined him dropping his weight down onto the dildo, his slick hole stretching around the girth while he let gravity seat it deep inside.

Silas squeezed at the base of his cock, staving off his orgasm again. He pressed his lips together to muffle his heavy breaths, hoping the sound of the running tap was enough to mask what he was doing.

"I—I just sat down on it, Alpha. Oh, it feels good. S'good, Si. I'm sorry I couldn't wait—wait—wait." Sammy's words were accompanied by the steady sounds of him riding the dildo; his rhythmic *uh, uh, uh's* each time he lifted and dropped back down, along with the wet *schlick* of the cock pumping in and out of him were fucking filthy.

Silas began pumping himself again to the rhythm, knowing he wouldn't be able to hold off a third time.

"*I need—you. Need you. Please come home. Please hurry, Oh, fuck!*" Sammy's voice began to shake as he bounced on the dildo.

He worked himself roughly, trembling, twisting his hand and occasionally sliding his thumb over his cockhead just the way he liked, his breath fogging the mirror as pleasure raced up his spine.

He shifted his stance wider, cock throbbing as he prepared to shoot into the sink, staring at the photo of Sammy and imagining it was his ass Silas tunneled into.

"*It's not as big as you are, Alpha,*" Sammy said through hitched breaths. "*It won't go deep enough. S'not enough. I want your cock inside me—me.*"

Another shaky breath as the sounds of Sammy riding the dildo sped up. Silas imagined he was jerking his cock now, too. "*Shit. I want to feel you come in my tummy. I want you to press on it when you knot me. I want to keep it inside. I'm so close, Silas. Come home. Come—come—I'm coming!*"

Silas hurtled over the edge to the sounds of Sammy's orgasm, toes curling in his shoes as he clapped a hand over his mouth, balls pulling up tight and painting ropes of cum into the sink basin.

Chest heaving, he listened to the soft moans Sammy made while he came down from the release, followed by more shuffling. He imagined him lifting up and off the dildo, letting it slip out while his gaping hole clenched, searching for Silas' knot.

Sammy's voice was suddenly very close, like he'd leaned right into the microphone. "*This one was just for you, Alpha.*

I'll be waiting," he breathed, chuckling again as the recording cut out.

Oh, that little brat would pay.

Silas hastily cleaned himself up and tucked his cock back into his pants.

He wiped down the sink with hot, soapy water, washed his hands, and checked his reflection to make sure he didn't look too much like he'd just jerked one out in the office bathroom before he unlocked the door and stepped out.

No one was in the hall, thank God, and when he quietly made his way to the conference room, he could still hear Finn and Brandon talking about contracts.

Thinking twice before going back inside right away—Finn would never let him live it down—Silas kept walking past the conference room toward a side door that led outside.

Stepping out into the freezing wind, he blew out a heavy breath, letting the cold air out his scent for a minute.

Pulling out his phone, Silas tapped out a reply to Sammy.

SILAS

You'll pay for that, brat. You'd better be ready for me when I get home.

SAMMY LOVE

I'm waiting 

~

THEIR NEWLY BUILT cabin sat nestled into the same cluster

of trees Silas had grown up in, warmly lit with smoke cheerily dancing from the chimney.

They'd moved in last fall, and with snow thick on the ground, he parked his truck in the warming shed, shoved his clothes into a satchel he looped around his neck, shifted, and ran the last leg home.

Familiar sounds of the forest all around greeted him; the distant echo of shifting river ice, the rustling of nearby wildlife, and the way the trees whispered *welcome* every time he and Sammy came home.

Home. We're home, his wolf sighed.

When he reached the porch, Silas didn't even put his clothes back on.

He scented Sammy waiting inside, so he shifted back to two legs, dropped his bag by the door, and tracked the crackle and pop of Sammy's arousal into the living room where he stood, naked and ready.

Mate is here. Mate wants us.

Matematemate.

Yes, we're home with our Sammy.

They didn't exchange words.

Sammy cocked one eyebrow at Silas, flooding the bond with the want pulsing through his veins, and that was all the go-ahead Silas needed.

Everything after that was a blur of wet kisses and sizzling touches and the most delicious sounds Silas could draw out of him.

Sammy had already prepped—just like he'd said he would—so Silas laid him down with rough hands on the rug in front of the fireplace, quickly slicking up his cock.

He knelt between Sammy's legs, wrapped one around his hip, and pushed into him, hard, eyes locked together so he could watch Sammy react to the sensation of taking him inside.

"That feel good?" Silas asked, already out of breath from slinging his hips into Sammy.

"*Uh-huh*," Sammy said.

Silas bared his teeth. "Have I already fucked all the naughty words out of you, mate? You had plenty to say earlier."

Sammy only cursed, back arching and tweaking his own nipples while Silas continued to pound into him, face slack with pleasure and pouting.

Taking hold of one of Sammy's hands, Silas laid it over his soft, lightly freckled stomach, just below his navel, and pressed down hard. "Feel that? Feel me moving inside of you? That's what you fucking do to me."

Sammy cried out. "*Fuck!*" he yelled, wrapping his other leg around Silas' waist and drawing him closer, deeper. "Mine. Your cock is mine."

"That's right it fucking is, mate. It's yours. I belong to you," Silas said, voice low and rumbling, jarred by each of his heavy thrusts into Sammy.

"Deeper. I want you deeper," Sammy wailed, pressing against his stomach even more.

Silas pulled out and flipped him over. "You want it deeper? Want it on your belly, brat? Yeah? Here you go."

Silas slapped his oversized cock against Sammy's ass, once, twice, watching it jiggle.

Pushing on his lower back to keep him lying flat, Silas

used his other hand to thumb one cheek to the side, opening Sammy up just enough to sink into him again with a heavy thrust.

"Oh my God, Silas," Sammy said, grunting, face turned to the side and hands searching over his head for something to hold on to.

Silas draped his body over him and took hold of his hands, barely bracing his weight on his knees. Sammy always came the hardest when he was helpless underneath him.

With Sammy's legs tucked together, Silas' cock would feel massive. "It'll feel even bigger this way. That's what you wanted, right? To feel me in your fucking throat?"

Sammy gasped something Silas couldn't understand, words jumbled around with each of his thrusts.

He picked up his pace again, driving into Sammy so hard he was jolted forward. Silas pressed more of his torso down onto him to hold him still, completely surrounding him, head bent to suck on their mating mark while he rocked them together.

"I can feel it in my stomach," Sammy croaked, fingers tangling with Silas' and clinging on. "Just—keep—*yes!* There! Oh God, Silas, it's too big. It really is too big," he sobbed, crying real tears.

Silas had learned early on—that didn't mean stop.

Sammy kicked up his heels between Silas' legs, toes curling as he ground his cock down into the rug while Silas pegged his prostate over and over. He screamed through his orgasm when Silas shoved his knot inside one final time, roaring his own release soon after.

Long minutes later, he grasped Sammy's hips and rolled

so they were spooned together. Still panting and sweaty, he danced kisses along Sammy's shoulders and up the nape of his neck, rocking his hips ever so slightly where they were locked, making him squirm.

"Sensitive," Sammy mumbled, reaching back to grip Silas' hip.

Silas chuckled. "Well, mate. Do you still feel empty?"

Sammy huffed, shimmying his hips further onto Silas' knot. "Tease me and you'll get one of those every time you leave the house."

Silas grinned, pressing his teeth into Sammy's neck. "I don't think that's quite the threat you think it is."

"Hmmm," Sammy mumbled, linking his fingers through Silas'. "How was the meeting?"

"He made Finn talk his ear off first, but he signed, so I suppose it was worth the trip. How was your day?"

Sammy yawned. "Good. I got the audiobook samples sent off, we'll see if their agent is interested."

Silas adored seeing Sammy work.

Sometimes he'd stay up well after Silas fell asleep, and he'd wake in the middle of the night to find Sammy still in the makeshift recording booth he'd built in one of their spare rooms. His mate didn't have an off switch when he worked on something he enjoyed, so Silas had to make sure he ate and slept regularly when he was sucked into a project.

"That's wonderful news, love. I'm sure they'll love it. Speaking of loving something..." Silas nibbled at Sammy's earlobe. "Thank you for my message earlier."

An adorable blush crept up Sammy's neck. "Did you like it?"

Silas growled. "That picture nearly gave me a heart attack. I had to excuse myself to the restroom when I saw it, where I came all over the sink listening to you."

Sammy turned as much of his upper body as he could to look at Silas, eyes full of mirth and faux disbelief. "You did not."

Silas kissed him. "I did, you brat, and I fucking loved it."

"Please tell me you at least cleaned up after yourself."

Silas laughed, causing Sammy to gasp and squirm some more. "Yes, I left it better than I found it."

Sammy looked so quietly pleased with himself that Silas had to squeeze him in a tight embrace, just because.

~

The rest of their evening was quiet and uneventful.

The blustery wind rattled the windows and whistled down the chimney just like it had in his childhood home, but the sound was a little different now—the same melody, in a different key.

Maybe that was because of the time that'd passed, or because they'd used updated building materials, or maybe because someone else's magic blanketed their home, knitting protections into their walls and foundation.

Silas let the bittersweet sound wash over him, relishing it as he sat in front of the fire.

It reminded him of rebuilding, and quiet nights holding his mate, and the cacophony of so many feet, new and old, padding around the hardwood floors when they'd host pack dinners.

"You should be in bed by now," Sammy said quietly, several hours after they'd cleaned up the mess they'd made of the carpet. He was leaning on the door frame that led into the kitchen. "You were up early."

Silas stood and stretched. "You're right. Come with me?"

Sammy nodded, his smile warm and open. Silas thought back to a time when he'd scaled walls just to see that smile.

He never took for granted that it was given so freely, now.

"Let's go to bed, you giant oaf," Sammy said, pulling Silas up the stairs.

Silas had stopped counting the moments he'd thought he'd reached the peak of happiness. It was a silly thing to do when he woke up next to Sammy every day.

Even through life's hardships, they'd laughed, and cried, and mourned together. They'd cheered each other on, held each other up, and learned each other's strengths and weaknesses.

Sammy's love for Silas was as fierce and fortifying as the wind; mountains bowed to it. Sometimes it still took his breath away to feel it ringing down the bond.

The love Silas felt for Sammy in return was steadfast; as enduring and powerful as a river. Calm and unwavering most days, an unstoppable force of nature on others.

Together, they could face anything.

Silas let Sammy, the man who smelled like toasted marshmallows and crackling embers, lead him upstairs.

He let his mate lead him home.

ACKNOWLEDGMENTS

Thank you so much for reading Sam and Silas' story. It sounds cliché, but Sam was a tough nut to crack. He kept his secrets from me for a while. However, once I finally had a grasp on who he was, he became the easiest character I've ever written. To those who are prickly (but secretly so soft), those who struggle with not feeling good enough, or those who would rather hide than disappoint the people you love, I hope Sam's journey can be as meaningful for you as it was for me. Overall, I was in a much healthier place writing this book than *Under the Lupine Moon*. Still, Silas was a much needed healing character to dive into. He deserves so much love and friendship.

First, so many thank-you's to my alpha reader, critique and brainstorm partner, and dearest friend, Emory Winters. You helped me figure Sam and Silas out, and your feedback is always invaluable. Your support makes those early stages of writing so fun, and this book would not be the same without you! Thank you for always being a steady presence when I have a meltdown in your DMs, and for making me cackle like a hyena.

To my lovely beta readers, A.L. Davidson, Logan Sage Adams, and Thea Verdone, and my sensitivity reader

K.M.D. Oca, your feedback truly makes this story so much better. It's an honor to call so many talented authors and artists friends. Thank you for reading (and re-reading!), and for your time and knowledge in helping me make this book the best it can be, and for being my friend.

One tiny little snippet of this story may or may not be based on true events. I will never confirm or deny which part —let the rumors fly. (Do I know a werewolf in real life?! I wish.) But my friends and fellow authors in the Rainbow Quill have heard the real story, and for all your support and laughter, thank you. I'll never be able to articulate how much you all mean to me, and I'm so grateful for the community I have found in you all.

Finally, to all the readers who've packed their bags and come back to Silver Rapids with me, I shout the biggest thank you. Your enduring support and love for this world and the characters in it mean more to me than I can express. I hope you've enjoyed Silas and Sam's book, and seeing Jaime and Finn again.

There's more story left to be told. With the addition of several new characters, who can say where the world of Silver Rapids will go next? I mean, I can, obviously. But I do like to tease. I'll see you back here, soon!

ABOUT THE AUTHOR

A. Knightley lives in the wilds of the Midwest with her dog. She loves to write paranormal romance stories with heaping doses of spice and happily ever afters. She can't wait to share what's happening next in Silver Rapids, and beyond. To stay up to date with what she's working on next, you can connect on Instagram @author.aknightley.

ALSO BY A. KNIGHTLEY

THE SILVER RAPIDS SERIES

Under the Lupine Moon, Book 1

By the Blood Moon, Bonus Story

Below the Hunter Moon, Book 2